A DEBT OF
WAR

Jerry,

Thank you for taking a look at this. I hope you enjoy the story, and hope you and your family are well.

Best wishes to you always!

[signature]

A Novel by
MICHAEL RINGERING

A DEBT OF WAR
Copyright © 2021 Michael Ringering

FIRST EDITION SOFTCOVER
ISBN: 1622534794
ISBN-13: 978-1-62253-479-1

Primary/Chief Editor: Robb Grindstaff
Contributing Editor: Anne Storer
Cover Artist: L1-Graphics (Alena)
Interior Designer: Lane Diamond

EVOLVED PUBLISHING™

www.EvolvedPub.com
Evolved Publishing LLC
Butler, Wisconsin, USA

Printed in Book Antiqua font.

BOOKS BY MICHAEL RINGERING

<u>NOVELS</u>
A Debt of War
Six Bits
John's Donuts [Coming 2022]

<u>SHORT STORIES</u>
A Calico Tale
A Face on a Train
The 9:15 to Grand Central
Willy the Whale

DEDICATION

For Larry Ringering, the heartbeat of our family, and Captain Jake Ringering, who passed in the line of duty. May father and son rest in peace in the loving arms of our Lord and Savior.

A Fireman's Prayer...
When I am called to duty, God wherever flames may rage,
Give me strength to save some life whatever be its age.
Help me embrace a little child before it is too late,
Or save an older person from the horror of that fate.
Enable me to be alert and hear the weakest shout,
And quickly and efficiently to put the fire out.
I want to fill my calling and give the best in me,
To guard my every neighbor and protect their property.
And if according to your will I should lose my life,
Please bless with your protecting hand my children and my wife.
~ Author Unknown

PART ONE

Chapter 1

Cody, Wyoming, November 2009

"Unto the Almighty, we commend the soul of our dear departed sister and commit her body to the ground; earth to earth, ashes to ashes, dust to dust; in sure and certain hope of the resurrection to eternal life through our Lord Jesus Christ at Whose coming in glorious majesty to judge the world."

Father Giuseppie Crocetti, reciting from the pages of a Bible once belonging to Pope Pius VIII, led the service in a last farewell. A harsh blast of Cody wind pushed snow against his face, forcing a stutter. He nodded to the family.

Paul Bacca stepped forward with spade in hand and pitched a ceremonial load of earth atop the mahogany casket.

His youngest, Abby, released a bouquet of tiger lilies and purple mums, a most cheerful contrast to the gray backdrop of winter's vicious clutch.

"May the angels lead you into paradise," Father Crocetti continued, "and the martyrs receive you at your coming and bring you into the holy city Jerusalem. May the choirs of angels receive you, and may you, with Lazarus once poor, enjoy everlasting peace."

The crowd responded, "Amen."

Paul settled his chin on the spade handle. Tears traced around his salt and pepper Vandyke. Gone was the woman who wiped his nose, patched his cuts, and supported his dreams. A woman exemplifying character, courage, and compassion, taken for eternity; a best friend and confidant, swept from the living sooner than imagined.

Abby took the death the hardest, suffering her first close passing in fourteen years of life. Her grandfather died mere months following her birth.

An apologetic groundskeeper relieved Paul of the spade.

Monica, Paul's wife of thirty years, eased into him and placed a gloved hand upon his shoulder. Her perfume tickled his nostrils with a delicate aroma of orange and jasmine. She pressed her lips to his cheek. The warmth of her breath proved a welcomed sensation. "You sure you're up for the reception?"

Paul redirected his attention to a mature, silver-barked, leafless cottonwood anchored behind his parents' gravesite. It pleased him their plot would enjoy years of protection from future summer suns.

A streak of crimson dashed across his sightline. A cardinal landed upon a single, stout branch. His mother loved all things cardinal, most notably the St. Louis baseball team. The bird ruffled its feathers, turned full frontal to show off its brilliant black, silky mask, then fluttered away.

Monica whispered her husband's name to regain his attention.

"I'm sorry. Yes. May do us good to hear memories others have of her."

Two months prior, the family learned of the brain tumor. Whether too tired, stubborn, or ready to join the one love of her life, his mother declined treatment when physicians offered minimal chances she'd celebrate her next birthday. In her mind, not worth the agony and burden of fighting on.

Paul suspected her desire to move on. She had lived a grand life, raised a fine family, and loved but one man.

Despite the sting, he suspected his parents whole again. Their reunion forced a delimited smile, as their love proved one of a kind. He spent thirty years building a prestigious publishing company and had worked with more authors than what seemed totaled the population of Cody, where his parents' farm nestled on some five hundred acres east of Yosemite National Park. He read more manuscripts than could fill the downtown Barnes & Noble of his beloved Denver yet had not recited a sequence of prose to date able to characterize the love his parents shared. Their strong faith in each other, honest living, and dedication to family had shaped the life he and his siblings enjoyed.

Paul peered over his shoulder. His brother Kim, sisters Rachel, Heather, and their families huddled close, doling out final hugs. His son, Paul Jr., an accomplished editor home from New York, eased from behind to wrap his arms around his younger sister.

Paul turned for a final glimpse of the grave before escorting his family to the first of five limousines idling nearby.

Abby gazed through the tinted glass at the headstones along the front fence line as the convoy headed toward downtown. Paul marveled at the many ways she resembled her mother — soft complexion, green eyes, the way she laughed and cried.

As the limo cleared a hedgerow where her grandparents' plots appeared, Abby jutted forward. She grabbed her father's wrist.

"A soldier," she said, pointing. "Daddy, look."

Paul turned as the limo accelerated. A grouping of evergreens cut off his view. "I don't see anyone."

"A man... I mean a soldier. I saw a soldier standing over Grandma's grave."

Monica peered around her husband's frame. "A soldier?"

"Yes. Tall, white hair, in uniform."

"You're mistaken," Paul said.

"No, Daddy, I saw him by her grave, holding a white box."

Paul grabbed his daughter's hand. "Sweetheart, I didn't see anyone in uniform. You have Grandma's gravesite mixed up."

"Didn't Grandpa fight in the war?"

"Yes, but I didn't see anyone in uniform."

Abby pushed hard against her seatback, agitated. "I know what I saw."

"Many people visit graves," Monica said.

"Well, don't blame me if Grandma spends the rest of eternity with a box buried on top of her."

Chapter 2

The driver delivered Paul and his family to beneath a valet canopy. As his brother and sisters exited their limos, a hearty breeze pushed snow sideways. Abby joined a favorite cousin. Paul leaned against his seatback and crossed his arms.

"What?" Monica asked.

Paul shook his head. "Abby doesn't exaggerate."

"Maybe a friend of your father who wanted a private moment."

"Perhaps, but, what if Abby's right, and he intended to bury something with her?"

"That's ridiculous. Who'd do such a thing without asking?"

"I suppose. Common courtesy would suggest you'd ask first."

"What do you want to do?"

"Go back and see if there's a box on top of her coffin."

"Does it really matter at this point? Anyway, I'm sure she's mistaken. You said yourself you saw no one in uniform." Monica drew her hand against his cheek. "Shall we go in?"

**

Paul received an instant, pleasing surge upon entering the hall, knowing his mother's wish had played to perfection. She insisted on a celebration, not a sob-fest. From the looks of it, he thought they'd crashed a wedding reception. Smiles and laughter warmed his heart.

An acoustic trio entertained with gentle renditions of the standards his parents so loved, reminding him of the two engaged in a deep embrace, dancing to the sounds of Sinatra, Martin, and Cole.

Paul waded through the crowd, spotting familiar faces but recalling few names. Many dressed in their Sunday best, others in jeans or overalls. No matter, guests mentioned his mother with tender remembrance and affection.

"Hello, Paul, it's good to see you," a red-haired woman said, taking hold of his forearm. "You don't remember me, but your mother and I knitted together. I'm sorry for your loss. When they made her, they broke the mold. I loved her dearly."

"Thank you. That's kind of you to say."

He turned and stumbled into another expectant guest.

"Hello, Paul. I used to deliver milk to the ranch."

"Joe Hoffert, of course. It's great to see you again. You're looking well."

"I've slowed a bit but could make a delivery in a pinch if needed. I appreciated William's faithful friendship. And your mother, well, I never knew a woman with more gumption. I'm sure you're proud of her. Don't know anyone who lived a purer life."

"We're proud of them both, and they appreciated your friendship. Dad spoke highly of you often."

"Thank you. I can't help wonder what plans you have for the ranch?"

"We haven't had time to discuss it."

"Would hate to see it sold off. It's a staple in these parts."

"Yes, sir. We'll work through this and figure out what's best."

"I'm sure you'll make the right decision in God's good time. Good luck to you, son."

Paul hastened his escape. He released a deep exhale upon plopping down in a cushioned chair next to Monica.

She slid a glass of iced tea in front of him. "Did you think this many people would show?" A lemon wedge worked loose and landed in his lap.

"No," he responded, wiping his pants. "I don't think we have near enough food."

"Kim took care of it. He found a barbecue caterer close by."

Paul managed a quick sip of tea before a tap on his shoulder interrupted. He accepted a wireless microphone and fell in behind the funeral director.

"Good afternoon. I'm Paul Bacca, the eldest of the Bacca children. Thank you for joining us. We did not expect so many and apologize we've run out of food. My brother ordered more. Hope you all enjoy Happy Meals." A wave of laughter erupted.

"We appreciate your prayers, friendship, and support. Mom and Dad loved this community and all of you." Paul paused to a respectful round of applause.

"Until the food arrives, please pass the mic around and share a story or two. I'm sure you can guess Mom and Dad didn't tell us kids everything." A second chorus of laughter ensued. Paul passed the mic to the first hand raised.

"I remember when Abigail and William..." a woman began.

Paul resettled in his chair. He stretched his legs and extended an arm around his wife's shoulders.

Near the conclusion to an amusing tale of his mother chasing an escaped Appaloosa on foot down Stampede Avenue, Monica alerted him to Abby. She worked toward them, weaving around tables at a frantic pace.

When agitated, her steps shortened and arms locked at her side. She rushed in behind her father, dropped to a knee, and whispered into his ear.

Chapter 3

Paul scanned the front entrance. Abby swore the soldier she noticed at the gravesite had settled against the doorway leading into the reception hall, looking over the crowd like a hawk searching for prey.

"He's looking for somebody," she insisted.

Paul moved around the table to achieve a better angle. Abby followed on his heels. He spotted the soldier.

"Daddy, look, the white box," she said.

"Okay, you stay here. I'll take care of this." He turned her by the shoulders.

"Why can't I go with you?"

"No, you stay here with your mother."

"I saw him first."

"Do as your father says," Monica ordered.

Abby stomped toward her mother and plopped down on an empty chair. She folded her arms in angry protest.

Paul edged along the wall. Near halfway, the man turned. Their eyes met. The soldier's posture eased, and demeanor turned eager. A broad, toothy grin erupted. Paul slowed his approach, working through his memory. He knew this face.

The man's skin appeared as leather. Thin cheeks and dark eyes sunk deep into their sockets suggested he'd entered his eighth or ninth decade of life. He wore a brown Eisenhower dress jacket and olive-green collared shirt with tie tucked between the third and fourth buttons. Two silver oak leaves affixed to shoulder straps identified his rank as a lieutenant colonel. He boasted a Distinguished Service Cross, Purple Heart, Silver Star, and Bronze Star, all dangling from the flap of the left breast pocket, below a patchwork of service achievement medals.

Paul's gaze shifted several times to the box. The soldier's right arm hung limp. *I've seen this man before.*

"Paul," the soldier said, drawing out the name as if the two had known each other for years. His smile widened. "I'd have recognized you anywhere."

"I'm sorry. Have we met?"

"Not formally. The name's Allan Jekel. I'm a friend of your parents. I'd shake your hand, but my right arm doesn't work anymore."

Paul waved in dismissal, then laughed. "It's an honor to meet you, sir. I knew I recognized your face. You've had several titles land on the *New York Times* best-sellers list."

"Back in the day," he said. "Please, call me Allan."

Paul smiled. "I'd be hard pressed addressing such a decorated veteran by first name only."

"That, too, was a lifetime ago. I've not worn this uniform in years. I'm sorry for your loss."

"I didn't see you among our guests."

"No, you didn't. I pulled in as you folks exited."

"My daughter noticed you. Why did you wait until we left?"

"I'm a stranger to all of you and wanted a moment alone with your mother. I didn't want to make a spectacle of myself."

"We'd have welcomed you."

"I appreciate that."

"I'm stunned my parents never mentioned the acquaintance. You'd think, since I'm in the publishing business, they'd at least have —"

Allan interrupted, pointing to two cushioned benches placed opposite an open-pit fireplace. "Excuse me, son, do you mind if we sit? I'm able to stand at attention only so long these days."

"No, not at all."

Paul assisted the old warrior to the bench before settling opposite. Other than the useless limb, the man appeared healthy as a horse.

Allan let the box slip onto the bench. "I've known your parents fifty years. Finest people who ever lived."

"You served with my father?"

"You could say that."

"Dad shared so little of his war experience. When we asked about it, he didn't want to talk about it. Over time, we let it go."

"William felt the war a heavy burden he needed to keep buried." Allan removed his cap. "The war proved different for your father. Different from any soldier I served with. When he came home, he left it all behind. He had to. He didn't want it clinging to his psyche for eternity. He wanted to live life without the memory of it all. I respected his desire to let it be."

"It puzzled us why he never received an invitation to a reunion, a letter from the war department, or entertained a buddy at the house," Paul said. "Sometimes, I wonder if he took part in the war at all."

"You should count your blessings that he spared you his horrors. He suffered many."

"I find it odd you seem to know me so well."

"I spoke with your parents at least once a month. What fine children they raised. You're family to me, albeit from a distance. I'm most proud of you, Paul. You've carved a good life for yourself. You've done a remarkable job leading this family and built an amazing career. Your parents glowed with pride over your accomplishments because you earned them on your own."

Paul's eyes turned wet.

"I can appreciate your emotion," Allan said. "It's a great feeling knowing how proud a man has made his family."

Paul honed on the box.

"I guess you're wondering what I have here?"

"You must consider it important. My daughter thought you intended to bury it with her grandmother."

"No, would never do something so impolite."

"That's what my wife said."

"Your mother wanted you to have this. I present it as her final request."

"Her final request?"

Allen nodded.

Paul leaned forward to accept.

"Go ahead," Allan said. "It won't open itself."

Paul's body straightened. He'd opened countless boxes and envelopes containing similar contents, though more accustomed to printer-generated text on bright white stock, not typewritten copy on dingy yellow parchment. He read the manuscript title aloud.

"A Debt of War, a Novel, by Jacqueline K. Astell." Paul flipped through a couple pages. "Wait a minute, the poet?"

"One in the same."

"I don't understand. This belonged to my mother?"

"Given to her by Astell herself."

"They were friends?"

"More than somewhat."

"Another untold secret," Paul mumbled.

"For the same reason she never mentioned me. Your mother did not want to cross into your realm for fear of influencing your decisions.

She wanted you to succeed on your own merit, in your own way. And you did."

Paul thumbed through half the stack. "Since when did Astell write novels?"

"She didn't. This was her lone attempt, and she never published it."

"Why not?"

"I'm not sure."

Paul crossed his legs. "Are you familiar with her story?"

"No, other than she lived in anonymity."

"Right. She disappeared after producing a renowned series of seasonal poems." Paul scanned the manuscript with fascination. "Why now?"

"Your mother mailed the manuscript several months ago and asked if I'd give my opinion. We discussed it two weeks ago, and...." Allan looked to the floor. "When we spoke, she mentioned little time remained. Said she'd wake at night and hear your father calling. Said it brought peace. I asked if I could visit, but she declined. She did not want anyone to see her in her condition. Before we said goodbye, I promised to hand-deliver this to you upon her death."

"Why after she passed?"

"A final gift. Thought you might want to publish it."

"I can't publish this."

"Don't worry, she owns the rights, and passed them to you. You'll find the documents in the safe behind the Rockwell in your father's den."

"They must've trusted you without reserve. No one outside my siblings knows about that safe."

"For whatever reason, they trusted me, and I them."

"Can you offer a synopsis?"

"I think it best you form your own opinion."

"Can you at least share your thoughts?"

Allan slid to the edge of the bench, absorbing the warmth of the flame. "It's the most remarkable story I've ever read. I dabbled in fiction a few times, but this outdistances by miles anything I produced."

"You think it's publishable?"

"I'd say so, but your mother wanted you to decide its fate. Said Astell worked on it for therapy, much like why Churchill laid bricks. It cleared her mind, eased her stress. Your mother described it as her favorite work of fiction. She meant this as a final, eternal connection between the two of you."

"I don't know what to say. To have an original, unpublished copy of Astell's lone novel, well... wow."

Paul glanced toward a large window. A white Bentley pulled up and parked under the valet canopy. The driver exited and assumed an attentive stance near the back-passenger door.

"My ride," Allan said.

Paul flashed a teasing grin.

"It's the one asset I've purchased with royalty money. I love old cars but can't drive. I have the best of both worlds."

Paul assisted Allan to his feet. Allan passed a business card.

"I'm in town a few days on business. Call when you finish reading. We'll talk."

"You're not from these parts?"

"No, born and raised in Alton, Illinois. I settled in Quantico, Virginia following the war."

"You've traveled a fair distance."

"I'd travel any distance for your parents. Call me when you finish. I look forward to your reaction."

"I doubt I'll have time to read this week. We have to tie up several loose ends."

"You'll find the time. I see it in your eyes. You desire to know what your mother found so intriguing, and you'll begin and won't put the damn thing down until you finish."

Allan extended his hand. Paul accepted.

"I fulfilled your mother's last request. She wanted you to read this, so I'm asking you to read it as soon as possible."

"Can't argue with a last request."

"I'm glad we met, son. You're what I expected and just as your mother described. Don't forget to call."

"I promise. I find it strange we never knew you but appreciate making your acquaintance."

"Likewise, son."

Allan grabbed for Paul's arm. Paul delivered him to his driver. Allan slipped into the back seat, leaned forward, and saluted. Paul reciprocated. He stood at near attention until car and passenger disappeared.

He returned to the ballroom with box in hand. Abby greeted him with a barrage of questions. Paul's mind swirled as to how his mother had kept such secrets all these years.

"My goodness," Monica said. "You look like you've seen a ghost."

"I think I did." He placed the box in front of her. "You're not going to believe this."

Chapter 4

From the head of his parents' dining room table, Paul sipped a glass of wine as his siblings and their families finished a roast ham and turkey breast provided by their parents' congregation.

Though drained of emotion, they enjoyed the opportunity to swap stories of the ranch and their mischievous childhood exploits. Six years had passed since they'd gathered for a meal in the same place.

With dinner complete, and the mood mellowed, the pace of Paul's reverie slowed to a crawl. He studied his siblings' faces as if new acquaintances, contemplating how each would cope with the finality of it all.

Despite twenty Baccas jammed around a rectangle suited for sixteen, the table never felt more desolate. Two empty place settings magnified the sensation. Paul did not object to his sisters' desire to honor their parents' memory, but the empty place settings drew all eyes as would a highway accident. The vision of his mother and father holding hands, as they often did during dinner, burst to the forefront of his consciousness. He wished to tell them he loved them.

A gentle nudge brought him upright. He accepted a pan of blackberry pie and passed it on to his brother's youngest son. Paul's appetite had dwindled—an oft-side effect when a topic weighed upon his mind. Colonel Jekel swirled about, but not near the degree of the manuscript.

"Why do you suppose they kept the colonel a secret?" his brother Kim asked.

"Don't know. I'm more mystified by her not mentioning her friendship with Astell."

"I've never heard of Jacqueline Astell," Kim said.

"You'd have to know how to read, honey," his wife teased, prompting snickers from her sisters-in-law.

"It's strange she didn't mention her to me," Rachel said. "Mother knew of my love for poetry and even gifted me two of Astell's poems — 'Summer Song' and 'Your Eyes.'"

Paul took another sip of wine. "For whatever reason, she wanted to keep it to herself, until now. You know Mom, she walked to the beat of her own drum."

Monica rose to collect plates. She turned to Paul and coaxed a slight smile with a warm smile of her own. "Don't stay up too late."

"What are you talking about?"

"Oh, please, go on with yourself. I'll bring some coffee later."

Paul let go a laugh, knowing well she understood the significance of the manuscript. If he enjoyed it, he'd not stop until finished. He'd lost count of the number of times she'd wander downstairs in the wee hours to find him hard at work, pouring over a potential bestseller. He overheard her mention to friends his passion for reading keyed their marriage, as she always knew where to find him, either his office downtown or office at home.

He drew a final sip of wine, then excused himself. "I'll use the den."

He collected the manuscript and proceeded down a narrow hallway under a stone archway supporting a second-level balcony. A set of French doors guarded his father's private space—hallowed ground in Paul's eyes. He'd spent hours in the room discussing life, love, and career. A place that transformed him from child to man.

He brought the doors together, turned, and inspected the room in full. It remained as his father left it the day he passed. The scent of cherry pipe tobacco and leather stirred the earliest memories of his youth.

He depressed two buttons on a control panel, propelling a Lionel train in motion affixed below the crown molding. His father loved trains—both real and model—and often treated his boys to a few hours at the station Sunday afternoons to watch the iron horses pull away. To this day, the thrill of a distant whistle brought Paul and his brother to pause.

Paul eased behind the high-back leather chair at his father's desk, tracing his fingers across its top. A letter written to a local business lay unfinished atop a dark-green blotter. His father's favorite pen lay at an angle alongside where it slipped from his fingers with the discharge of his final breath.

William lived by simple means, defined by sparse yet well-crafted furnishings. A single desk centered before a bank of windows stretching the length of the room, framing a view of majestic Hart Mountain. He'd placed two leather chairs opposite the desk, and two more facing the fireplace. A wood bench constructed of timbers salvaged from an abandoned gold mine and an end table supporting a collection of smoking pipes accounted for all else.

On the wall to his left hung the Norman Rockwell classic, *Freedom of Speech* — his father's favorite — and to the right, a canvas of a young girl feeding a fistful of grasses to a grouping of cattle in a pasture dotted with wildflowers.

"I miss you so much, Dad," he whispered.

He dropped the manuscript on the recliner and pulled the chain of a brass gooseneck lamp. His mother had stuffed both kindling and wood boxes full; he suspected she'd lit an occasional fire. Few moments brought more pleasure than the crackle of a burning log, the comfort of a good flame, and the scent of oak or hickory wafting through a room.

Paul loaded the fireplace and set the lot aflame. He added a couple oak logs for good measure, and in seconds, a wave of warm air raised the hairs on his arms. He retreated to the recliner and brought the manuscript to his chest.

Since first entering the room, he avoided eye contact with the massive portrait above the mantel. The children had gifted the oil on a Christmas Day: an image of his parents seated in a swing under a gazebo, built on an island in the center of their pond. They all agreed the work was a perfect depiction of the love they shared and a lasting image each child held dear.

Paul allowed his emotions to pour forth. All he had become proved a direct product of their guidance and love. The release provided a momentary cleansing. He wiped his eyes with a shirtsleeve, thumbed through the stack of yellowed paper, and separated the document near its midpoint. He settled into the soft leather and read aloud again the cover page of this historic document.

A Debt of War
A Novel
By Jacqueline K. Astell

He kicked off his shoes, repositioned his bifocals, and turned to page one.

PART TWO

Chapter 5

A Debt of War
A Novel
By Jacqueline K. Astell

~~~

New York, NY, July 1926

A palatable breeze from the southeast delivered the smell of sea salt and relief from sweltering humidity and a blistering summer sun. The chaotic magnificence of the New York City skyline appeared off the ship's port side, but the lad insisted on a spot on the starboard handrail.

His mother, Liesel, held tight to his shirt collar, tempering his anxiety and wonder, as the magnificent monument approached. He'd seen pictures of the woman made of copper, but never expected his first encounter to include a bid farewell.

Jakob von Rüdel covered his ears as the mighty ship gave a blast of its horn. In five days' time, he'd make port in the country of his father's birth.

The ship drifted slow and steady alongside the noble lady. Jakob marveled at her size and peppered his mother with questions, for which she had no answers. The moment cemented in his memory as he prepared for the majesty of open sea.

His father, Franz, spoke well of Germany, despite ravages of the Great War, and his accusations of evil brought upon her by those who sold her out in the conflict's final days.

"We must return," Franz often crowed, "and help rebuild her economy and industry."

Franz accepted an instructorship of divinity in Berlin. They'd occupy a farm owned by his adoptive dead father, where a flourishing cattle business provided a steady sustenance.

Jakob left few regrets and associations behind. His family's meager existence meant transporting little of material worth. He'd made few friends, as his father forbade most social contact. His mother, too, offered no protest, taking only a few sticks of furniture and the babe growing in her womb.

Soon upon arrival in Germany, the family noticed drastic changes in Franz' political and religious views, but more so in his temperament. The slightest hesitation to an order provided an excuse for Franz to take out his hatred of Jews and communists. Jakob bore the scars on his back and backside of many a leather belt as a result. His mother's cheek had become a favorite target for the back of his father's hand.

Franz once supported the democratic form of government but gravitated more toward a fanatical nationalistic theory intended to draw the working class from communistic views and toward a system strategy opposed to big business, the upper-middle class, and capitalism — a political product based on racism.

Jakob braved protracted sessions of his father's vainglorious rants against the Versailles Treaty, the need for broadened borders, the squashing of communism, and expulsion of Jews and other races hellbent on destroying the country's commerce and infrastructure. His ideals of a developed master race confused Jakob, as his religious studies painted a different expectation of each man.

Jakob first learned of Adolf Hitler during the Great Depression. With millions out of work and several of the country's major banks collapsed, Franz resigned from his instructorship for a position in Hitler's National Socialist Workers Party.

The family suffered little during the unrest, despite their father's absence. On occasions of his return, he proved unrecognizable, a rabid animal whose vile hatred for those not of pure German blood both confused and fascinated Jakob. Franz no longer resembled the man of Jakob's American youth, trading former principles for an emerging political doctrine determined to control all aspects of everyday life.

The beatings continued. Franz forced Jakob to recite Nazi doctrine and statements of allegiance so anti to his view of life. For his fourteenth birthday, Franz treated Jakob to a trip to Berlin to indoctrinate him in the ways of party politics. Jakob witnessed the handy work of the SS — many thousands strong — whom his father supported and revered. Jakob stood by as thugs harassed and pummeled Slavic, Romani, and Jewish store owners. The day of his return to the farm, the mob pulled a Jewish husband and wife from their place of business and hanged them, side by side, on a sidewalk lamp post.

Jakob returned transfigured from child to man. The brutal vision of the innocent dragged from their property, fitted with nooses, and hanged, etched permanently in his mind.

The look of pride and power on his father's face solidified Jakob's moral compass. He would never subscribe to such desires to maim and murder, as the word of God resonated more than the hypocrisy of humanity.

In the typical spirit of rebellion, Jakob countered Franz's behavior with acts of kindness toward those considered enemies of the state. He became a protector of the bullied, accepting the wrath and ridicule of boys feeding off the political firestorm of the times, further instigating violent encounters with his father. It pleased Jakob, despite the pain, that his actions drove Franz to such ill temper.

The invasion of Poland and Finland in 1939 set forth Jakob's destiny, as Hitler's desires for expansion and dominance drew the world into a conflict a mere twenty years post the "war to end all wars."

When Jakob turned nineteen, his father returned from Berlin to place him on a train shipping boys his age off to war.

In the days leading to his departure, neither spoke nor acknowledged the other. Their lone interaction came in the form of a surprise assault, in which father caught son unawares.

Chapter 6

Duren, German, April 1939

Sascha's frenzied attack upon the gate proved futile in her desire to escape the stall holding her hostage. Frantic snorts gave way to an indignant whinny, though failing to create disturbance enough to summon others to the scene.

Her master lay crumpled, cheek flush against knotted hardwood stained with a century's worth of excrement. Specks of debris held captive in a dust cloud flashed in brilliant sparkles as the mass floated by a wedge of sunlight seeping through a knothole in the barn's planked outer shell.

Sascha remained resolute in her personal war against the barrier. The seventeen-hands-high Holsteiner rammed two thousand pounds of bone and flesh against the stall door, despite the attacker having fled. A self-inflicted gash on her massive chest dripped blood, mixing in a pool rushing from the nostrils of her master's damaged nose.

With the force of a steam shovel, Sascha dropped her massive hooves atop the gate, producing a thunderous cacophony and sending timber shards and hardware ricocheting in all directions.

With foam frothing at her muzzle, she nudged her master's shoulder with the same tender touch he afforded her on their rides through the glens flanking the River Roer.

Sascha attempted again to revive his senses with a snort of breath upon his neck.

***

Jakob rolled onto his back, expelling a pain-filled groan. His lower lip felt the size of a mature peach; the bridge of his nose burned with the intensity of a blacksmith's poker. He placed a hand on Sascha's jowl to ease her concern.

In the crisp and throaty manner with which a good German spoke his native tongue, Jakob eased his best friend's fears. "*Lieber Sascha, alles in ordnung,*" he said. "All is well," he repeated in perfect English.

Blood drained into his throat, forcing a choke. He patted the end of Sascha's nose. "Not the first time, dear one."

Through a swirl in his head, he recognized this attack as the most vicious he'd received. He'd never seen his father in such a rage, though his initial refusal to join the *Hitlerjugend* rated a close second.

Jakob wiped at his nose. He arched his back to release a twinge between his shoulder blades before attempting a half-hearted sit-up. Sascha bent low and brushed her mane against the back of his hand. Jakob grabbed a clump of the silky strands and held on as she pulled him into a sitting position.

The taste of blood stirred a nauseous wave, but not enough to expel what remained undigested from mid-meal. Jakob harvested a clump of saliva, squinted while swirling the mess in his mouth, and spit. A tooth separated and ticked across the planked floor.

With knees tucked against his chest, he cupped his hands to his nose. The bone felt intact. He released a deep breath as Sascha nuzzled his neck. Another gentle push motivated Jakob to his feet. He grabbed hold of her for balance.

She stood steady as an oak as he brought a palm to his forehead, discovering another gash above his right eyebrow. He turned, wrapped his arms around his friend, and settled against her jowl. She responded, dipping at the throatlatch to rest her head on his shoulder.

"I am okay," he whispered. A fist or unknown blunt object deprived him, for the moment, of her usual sweet, piney scent.

Sascha and Jakob shared attributes one would expect of childhood best friends — trusting, understanding, loyal.

***

The unbreakable alliance had formed on a late winter afternoon when Jakob was twelve as he trekked along a narrow lane in the bitter cold under a purple sky. He often fell victim to daydreams when engaging horses or other such beasts of burden, as they drew a deep passion and fascination from within him. He longed for the day to acquire a horse of his own and schemed often how he might make it so.

On this day, he happened on a group of men harassing a massive horse half-buried in the snow. He settled against a corner fence post, his heart sinking, as they used all means to maintain her prone position.

With her each attempt to return upright, the men responded with harsher tactics. A tall, thickly built man dead-dropped his knees hard upon the horse's neck; two others spread across her girth, bobbing as corks upon the ocean. A fourth conspirator, whose dead-black eyes, scarred face, and scruffy dress intimated shallow character, planted heavy kicks against her hindquarters and belly. Jakob could no longer stomach the brutality.

The crunch of his footsteps prompted the horse's ears to perk. Jakob marveled at the animal's beauty and majesty. He had not seen eyes so radiant, so similar to the color of the harvest moon. Her winter coat glistened like mink.

An old man in a trapper hat sprang from behind a cart loaded with hay. Breath escaped Jakob's lungs in a rush when the farmer produced a bolt-action rifle and took dead aim at the animal's forehead.

"No, stop," Jakob yelled, distracting the gunman. He scampered through the snow on all fours to fall across the animal's head. He saw no outward signs of injury.

A man from behind grabbed a handful of his coat collar and tossed him into a snowdrift. The old man gasped, dropped his weapon, and rushed to Jakob's aid.

"Are you crazy, Josef?" he screamed, planting a stiff forearm into the back of the man's head as he passed. "Do you know who this is?"

The old man helped Jakob to his feet, brushing at his clothes, and returning his fur-lined cap to the top of his head. He turned to his hired man.

"Have you gone mad? Did you intend to bruise the son of Franz von Rüdel? Stupid. Stupid."

The farmhand turned a nervous eye, his face flushed.

"My nephew meant no harm. Are you hurt?"

Jakob returned to the animal, knelt near her head, and placed a hand on her magnificent jowl. "Why must you destroy her?"

The farmer retrieved his rifle. "She cannot pull the cart or plow and I cannot afford to feed an animal unable to earn its keep."

"I see no injuries."

"Front, left fetlock. Inflamed for weeks. She refuses to pull the slightest load."

"What a beautiful creature."

"Beauty does not harvest crops or deliver spoils to market."

"May I have her?"

"And your father's reaction to a broken nag exhausting his stocks of grain?"

"He spends little time at home these days and would not notice. I shall give her time to heal."

The farmer grunted. "Not a life worth saving."

The animal's breathing settled with each of Jakob's strokes on her neck. He wondered if she had experienced a loving touch in her young life. "But, a life, nonetheless. God breathed the same breath into her nostrils as into yours and mine. Are not all God's creatures worth something?"

The old man stammered, muddling over such philosophy. "You have much depth for so few years of life and living."

"I learned to read at a young age."

"Reading qualifies you as an expert on such matters?"

"It does not, but all who read can read the Bible. Because you cannot produce as others do does not make you worthless."

The old man offered no response.

"You are not worthless," Jakob whispered into the mare's ear. "I will take you home and help you heal."

"Not so fast," the farmer said. "I raised this beast from a foal. She cost me feed and lost production. I deserve compensation."

"You mean to kill her."

"I have cost in the bullet and in her disposal. No matter, if you desire her, I deserve compensation."

The man fumbled with his rifle. "My dear boy, I am a poor farmer with many mouths to feed. Whether I kill this animal now, or allow you to take her, I must buy another to work the fields."

Jakob knew well the difficult economic times and struggles of his neighbors. The farmer smelled an opportunity to exchange life for death. Regardless, and no matter the price, Jakob would not allow this animal shot.

Before he could begin negotiations, the horse expelled a thunderous bellow. A grunt later, she rolled onto her haunches. Another determined push brought her out of the snow. Jakob's eyes widened at her magnificent frame. "Does she have a name?"

"I call her Ida."

"I shall call her Sascha. A defender of mankind."

"When she becomes your property," he reminded.

Jakob brought a hand to his brow. He approached the horse, reaching well above his head to rub the bridge of her nose.

"When I finish school in the spring, I shall report to you and work your fields until I pay the debt in full. It equates to one less hand to pay and more money to invest in a new animal." Jakob extended his hand.

The farmer hesitated. Jakob's skinny frame concerned him.

"What will your father say?"

"He expects me to work for those things I desire. He provides nothing for nothing in return."

"How do I know you will come when school lets out?"

"You have my word."

The farmer grabbed hold of his beard, then instructed his nephew, "Fetch young von Rüdel a rope."

True to his word, Jakob labored through late autumn, earning sole ownership before the start of the next school period. Within days of his thirteenth birthday, he saddled Sascha for the first time.

Chapter 7

Jakob rubbed his nose and held steady against Sascha. The blood had clotted. With faculties restored, he led her through the stable to a gated entrance, where he released her into the pasture. He planted a loving tap against her rump before peeling off through a side gate onto a cobblestone path to the family's stone cottage.

Sascha leaned against the fence with an angry snort at yet another barrier between them. Jakob returned. As always, his touch calmed her. He pressed his forehead against hers.

"I find this world fractured, Sascha, and these times as evil as any I've known. I could stand to never see this place again. I wish we could travel the plains of the American West to the mountains of Colorado, and onward to the great Pacific Northwest."

Jakob kissed the tip of her nose and patted her neck. Sascha kept a keen watch until he disappeared behind the smokehouse.

Jakob paused at the heavy oak door to the dining quarters. He peeked through a rectangular pane and spotted his mother on the far side of the open floor plan instructing his sister in the ways of knitting. Near the room's center, the family's live-in maid—an aged Belgian widow—leaned over a table covered in flour, forming dough balls into loaves.

Franz sat at the head of the family's table, his back to the door, honed on flames chewing away at logs in a walk-in fireplace. He rocked on the back legs of the chair, clinging to a glass, a bottle of schnapps within reach.

Jakob studied his father's profile, his hair a darker shade of gray and cropped short at the sides to match the Führer's iconic look. His frame had thinned, but he remained an intimidating and menacing figure, thanks to scars and pockmarks from a bout with smallpox, broad shoulders, and a well-maintained, muscular torso.

Franz had long since traded family, farming, and live stocking for plotting, planning, and warmongering. The Nazi regime, the SS in particular, provided a collaborative to fuel his wanton desires for continental superiority and revenge against those who choked his people of their dignity and post-war rights.

With the invasion of France days away, Jakob knew the chance slim he'd survive it all. He closed his eyes and drew a deep breath. The click of the latch brought his father's chair to the floor.

Jakob passed through the threshold with cautious reserve, calculating how he intended to explain his love for a Jewish girl.

Jakob's sister, Kirsa, reacted to his condition first. With the swing and creak of the door, she paused mid-stitch and expelled a chilling shriek at the blood splattered about his face and shirt.

Liesel gasped. She tossed her knitting aside and sprang from her rocker to fall in behind her daughter, who had set out in pursuit, screaming her brother's name.

Franz met Kirsa and grabbed a fistful of her dress. "Liesel, take your daughter upstairs and remain until I summon you," he yelled over his daughter's wailing.

Liesel brought a hand to her mouth as Jakob wiped away blood trickling from the gash above his eye.

"Upstairs," Franz directed. "Do not make me tell you again." He flung Kirsa toward her. Liesel collected her and fled up a narrow staircase near the front entrance. The women's sobbing muted with the slam of a door.

"Tanja, search the grounds for eggs."

Without comment, the maid dropped a half-rolled loaf of bread and hurried through the front door, picking at dough affixed to her fingertips.

Jakob kept a tight grip of the windowsill, working through a dizzy spell. Franz downed what remained in his glass, then hurled it into the fireplace, sending shards ticking across the floor.

He turned with a snarl and advanced, his face beet red and eyes bloodshot. Jakob feared another blow. He crumpled against the wall in a defensive position. Any attempt to flee would mean certain and unpleasant consequence.

Franz closed in, pushing a wave of alcohol and musty wool into his son's face. He grabbed Jakob by the collar and forced him into a chair.

Jakob settled against the seatback. He focused his tired eyes on a crack snaking across the flagstone floor.

Franz moved to the fireplace, where he stopped short and settled into an attentive position. A deep breath tempered his wrath. Ever conscious of his appearance, he grabbed the bottom of his jacket and snapped it downward, erasing wrinkles formed during the tussle with his daughter.

He retrieved a gold-plated cigarette case, gifted by the Führer, from an inside pocket. Jakob held tight to the corner of the table in a state of near collapse.

Franz completed an about face. "You disgrace the Führer, the Fatherland, and my name. You have engaged in illicit behavior with a filthy Jew whore."

Jakob could not reconcile hatred for a people who'd not caused his father or family an instance of inconvenience or harm. Franz's hatred and violent rants stirred a great moral conflict within. Jakob despised any man finding pleasure in the persecution of the weak or those unable to protect themselves.

"You are alive due to our kinship... period." Franz approached Jakob with fists clenched. "Have you spent your seed between her filthy legs?"

Jakob shook his head. "We have kissed and held hands, nothing more."

Franz gritted his teeth. Spasms exploded along his jawline. "You will never see her again."

"She is but a woman, Father, nothing more."

"She is the scum of the earth."

"But a product of the Fatherland. Her mother sprang from German blood."

"Impregnated by a Jew swine, a sub-human, who tainted the purity of a Germanic woman and removed her from her people."

"Shana does not differ from you or me."

Franz sent Jakob to the floor with a vicious backhand. Jakob rolled onto his back, grasping at the point of impact. Franz straddled above and planted the heel of his boot against Jakob's chest.

"Never again equate a stinking Jew with a true Aryan," he yelled. He drove his heel into Jakob's sternum. "She exploits and steals. None but those of pure blood may call themselves loyal servants of the Fatherland. None. Say she is a filthy Jew whore."

Jakob shook his head in defiance. Franz ground his heel deeper. Jakob wailed.

"Say it."

Jakob refused.

Franz pulled the Luger from his side holster. "Say it, or so help me, I will splatter your brains and kill your horse."

Jakob contemplated taking the bullet, forcing his father to end the bitter struggle between them, his personal internal struggle with Nazi ideology and a Germany he no longer recognized.

In a blink, his conscience brought forth the image of his mother and sister. Who would take care of them? Who would save Shana, care for Sascha? For the love of them all, he succumbed and choked out the lie in a whisper, "She is a filthy Jew whore."

Franz holstered his sidearm and stomped on Jakob's mouth. Blood sprayed from his bottom lip as he rolled onto his stomach. Franz settled into a chair, lit a cigarette, and pulled in a deep drag and released. "You will soon know what it means to fight and die for the Reich. You will know the nobility of the Führer's plan and the reasons we must fight."

Jakob maneuvered onto his knees, wiping at blood trickling through a sparse smattering of stubble.

"They often place sons of ranking officials in positions of relative prominence, but you will know the fury and atrocities of war. You will know the battlefield, the front line, and the struggle to survive one moment to the next. I have arranged placement for you in the Fourth Army."

Jakob crawled back into a chair, recalling how this man had once taken great pleasure bouncing him upon his knee.

"Send me off to war if you please, Father, but I shall not kill. I will not kill in the name of aggression or what God has breathed life into."

Franz flicked his cigarette at his son's head. "You will kill or perish at the hands of your own countrymen as a traitor to the Führer. However, I shall inform General von Kluge of your intent not to engage the enemy."

"You wish me dead, Father?"

"I wish you to do your duty to preserve our destiny."

"What is our destiny, Father?"

Franz folded his arms. He leaned deep into the seat. "The Führer has dreams, as do I, to reunify Germanic nations, to purify and preserve our race. Unless we act now, unless we gather our peoples persecuted because of their Aryan heritage, millions of our children will wither on the vine and die. Do you desire to witness persecution without cause?"

"What honor comes from preserving one race by destroying another?"

"The *races* you speak of are sub-human and unfit to share our Germanic lands. Weeds must die to reap favorable crops."

"What of our own people Hitler has ordered euthanized due to sickness or disability?"

"A preeminent nation purges the weak to allow the pure and mighty to flourish. A great nation demands that nothing comes before country."

"What about what the church and Bible teach?"

Franz's patience waned. His neck glowed bright red. "Foes surround the Fatherland, determined to wipe clean our freedoms and enslave our population. We must stand and defend ourselves against all aggressors. Organized religion offers no value or substance for our future."

"What did we defend when the Führer sent troops into Austria and the Sudetenland? Or Poland, Denmark, and Norway?"

Franz slammed his fist on the table. "Ignorant fool," he yelled, spraying saliva. "You know nothing of what you speak. You will soon realize the errors of your ways, if you live long enough."

Jakob did not understand his father's Germany. He did not belong in a country where he found no political parallel and little worth, where friendship with other nineteen-year-olds proved impossible. Hitler's war machine stirred the nation into a frenzy. He wanted no part in supporting an insistence non-Aryans be ground into the earth as one would a worm. He felt it unfortunate his father found such favor within the Führer's inner circle.

"You will do what I tell you and defend the Fatherland, or I will kill you myself. Go to your room and do not return until morning."

Jakob pushed from the table with what little energy remained and shuffled toward the stairs.

"Do not concoct any plans to flee. If I hear so much as a squeak in this house, I shall put a bullet in your horse's head. If you do not do your duty, she will die all the same."

Jakob grabbed hold of a simple newel post and pulled himself up to the first tread. "Father, what you want for Germany, I desire the opposite. You wish for death and destruction. I wish for life and prosperity. You wish for chaos. I wish for calm. You wish to eliminate cultures. I wish to celebrate all created by God.

"I will go where the train takes me, and I will stand alongside my countrymen as ordered. But I state to you my solemn oath — I will follow the laws of God, not the laws of Hitler's murdering machine. I will not kill for you, your Reich, or your Führer, and will not despise any man, woman, or child because of the blood from which they sprang."

"Then you shall die a traitor's death," Franz replied.

"I would rather die the death God intends me, rather than the death he intends you."

Chapter 8

Jakob woke to a warm compress against his forehead. His eyes fluttered open to see his mother and sister flanking his bedside. Both smiled in response.

Kirsa offered a ladle of cool water. Jakob sipped it dry, flushing grit caked in his throat. Liesel ran her fingers through his sandy-blond hair, still matted with dust and flecks of hay.

A single gable window exposed a cloudless sky. A rooster heckled from afar to announce dawn's first light.

Liesel placed a hand on his shoulder. "Would you care to sit?" With her help, Jakob scooted into an upright position. He spotted a tray loaded with *brötchen*, jam, soft-boiled eggs, and sausages. The joy of the moment proved fleeting. In an instant, the comfort of warm quilts, soft pillows, the smell of homemade foods, and his mother's touch, slipped away. War awaited him in a matter of hours.

Liesel placed her hand in his. She knew what stirred his angst but had no words to comfort.

"Is he mad, Mother?" Jakob asked.

Liesel slumped. "He so obsesses over Hitler's ideals. I liken him to an adolescent who fell in with the wrong sort. I hurt when he hurts you."

Jakob pulled his mother close. She buried her head in his chest and sobbed.

"He may beat me down, but he will never change me. I will never subscribe to his ways."

She placed her hands on his cheeks and kissed his forehead. "I will pray for you and your safe return."

"What shall I do, Mother? I must defend the Fatherland, but how can I kill in the name of senseless aggression, or in the name of a regime I have no belief in or loyalty to? How can I go against the word of God? What shall I do?"

She traded a glance between her son and the nightstand where he kept his Bible. "We have but one mortal life, and I do not believe our story ends here. A good man of God must do what his heart dictates. If the mind and heart contradict one another, go with your heart. God will be with you."

Heavy steps approached from the hallway. Liesel sprang from the mattress. Kirsa raced around the foot of the bed to fall in behind her.

The bedroom door swung open with a push of Franz's boot tip. He centered under the jamb, tucking in his shirt. "Eat up, boy. You will not experience such bounty in the days ahead. We leave in two hours."

He moved into the hall before adding, "It will please you to know I have arranged for you to see your Jew pig before you board your train."

Jakob's stomach dropped. He turned to his mother. Liesel bowed her head, then turned from him in shame.

***

Though appreciative of the hearty meal, Jakob had no appetite to make the slightest dent. He packed a modest suitcase with a few meager possessions. He exited the attic, leaving the room in pristine condition.

He led his mother and sister from the great room onto a large stone slab serving as the front stoop. The morning air pushed sweet scents of pasture, livestock, and blooming foliage. The wondrous aromas, combined with a crisp spring breeze and a symphony of calls and cackles from creatures both domestic and wild, made for an eternal memory.

Jakob dropped his suitcase, turned, and collected his mother into his arms. Liesel pressed against his cheek. Jakob felt the heat of her skin and moisture from streams where tears trailed. He expelled a heavy sigh.

"Do what you must," she whispered. "Do what God places in your heart. Live for His world, not this one." She kissed his forehead. "I will pray every day."

He settled to a knee. Kirsa shook, unable to speak through her grief. "Keep watch for a full moon, dear one. When you gaze at its brilliance, think of me, because I will be thinking of you."

Jakob kissed her, patted her behind, and promised a return. He asked her to care for his beloved Sascha. He collected his suitcase and stepped from the porch, then turned to blow a kiss.

He walked the short distance to where the stone path branched off the pea-gravel surface outlining the main drive. He paused, mid-step, to pass his suitcase to his father's personal valet. Franz sat in the back of a black Mercedes convertible, fingering through a stack of papers. Jakob turned toward the pasture.

"Get along, boy," Franz said. "You have five minutes."

Jakob spotted Sascha grazing on the other side of the pasture. She nipped at alfalfa, unaware at the depth at which her life was about to change. Her ears perked at the sound of his boots on stone. She erupted with excited kicks and snorts before digging her hoofs into the soil and bolting toward him. Jakob entered the pasture with outstretched arms. Sascha eased into him with a loving bump. He hugged her neck and settled his cheek against her jowl. His heart split at the reality of the moment.

"My departure will confuse you. I wish God could allow me a momentary miracle to speak so you could understand why I must leave."

He pushed from her and placed his forehead against hers, breathing in her scent. His stomach seared at the reality of their separation.

"I will return to you, I promise."

Sascha wiggled her lips against his chin. "Wait for me. Soon, we will reunite and take to the many miles of trails yet to explore."

Jakob patted her and planted a prolonged kiss on the bridge of her nose. The blare of the car horn cued his release. He fled down the path. Sascha rumbled back and forth along the fence line.

Jakob joined his father in the back seat, closed his eyes, and listened to Sascha snort in disapproval.

"On your way, driver," Franz barked. "We must not keep my son's lover waiting."

Chapter 9

Wilkes-Barre, PA, December 22, 1941

O'Dell Denny did not own a car. When he set out this frosty morning for the Wilkes-Barre railroad station at the request of the United States Army, he did so in a 1935 Lincoln Model K convertible inherited by his bride of six weeks.

The lifelong Texan brought little to the union in the way of possessions. His collective worth included a change of clothes, two five-dollar bills stuffed in a tattered wallet, a houndstooth dress jacket won at a Houston rodeo, a grungy Stetson, a saddle, and a black Arabian mare named Bella.

Annalise cared not. While her groom lacked in assets, he excelled in character, honesty, common sense, and the desire to do right every time. She marveled at his intellect, despite his achieving a mere fourth-grade education, and the depth at which he shared ideals of life, love, and matters of the human heart.

Both received a lifesaving breath the day their paths crossed. The encounter, though brief and from afar, propagated an instant, potent attraction between them, rendering the unfortunate lot in their lives repaid in full. Annalise found favor in his dusty, rugged, cowboy ways. O'Dell was struck spellbound by the soft, pink sheen of her slender face, long auburn hair, and eyes sparkling with the brilliance of spurs in a Texas summer sun.

The auction concluded with a final smash of a gavel on a tin pan. Annalise tangled up in an anxious crowd moving one way, O'Dell in a group moving the other. He'd searched above heads and around livestock, but the woman he'd marry on the spot disappeared into the masses.

O'Dell guided the Lincoln along a well-traveled but undeveloped roadway, spying his bride out of the corner of his eye. Annalise spent the first hours gazing out the passenger side window as the winter landscape passed at a gentle pace. As if not enough, the couple would say their goodbyes on her twenty-third birthday.

Along with millions of other wives, Annalise prayed the conflict would resolve itself without aid of America's fighting men. She had told O'Dell of her hope that he would be categorized 4-F for some abnormality. To her great disappointment, he passed his physicals with flying colors.

Since exchanging vows, O'Dell grew to adore her innocence, vibrant and expansive smile, and the never-before-known contentment in her eyes. Japan's dastardly attack on Pearl aged her by decades.

O'Dell gazed into the distance of a long straightaway framed by steep walls of granite, topped with slender pines cradling clumps of snow within their branches. He reflected on the moment she shared the news of Japan's attack, how she slothed her way across the pasture with face flushed, before burying her head into his chest.

"What's happened?" O'Dell asked, accepting her into his arms. The two held each other as a frigid December wind scattered specks of snow.

"The Japanese attacked Pearl Harbor. The man on the radio said it came without warning, said Roosevelt will declare war on Japan and Germany."

The news did not surprise. O'Dell hoped the conflict with Hitler's advance across Europe would resolve without the nation lured into a second world war.

"I ain't ever stirred another man's hive on purpose and don't expect it done to me. They'll pay for this. To my dying day, and their dying breath, they'll regret this action."

"What are we going to do?"

"We gotta rise and strike, and I gotta do my duty."

"I can't stand the thought of our being apart. You're the love of my life."

"And you mine, but I can't sit back and do nothing. They're gonna need us all to whip those dirty shits."

Annalise tightened her grip around his waist. "I don't know what I'll do if I lose you."

O'Dell pulled in a deep breath, taking in the stunning views he so loved. The farm, though meager, stirred powerful emotions of what it could become.

"Nothing will keep me from getting back to you."

Annalise rolled her head across his chest. "You know what will happen? With your knowledge of veterinary medicine, they'll make you a medic, and you'll be in harm's way the moment you head overseas."

"I'm also a damn fine cook. I could work in a kitchen behind the lines, or they might make me an instructor." O'Dell smiled; Annalise did not. "You're a horrible cook."

O'Dell removed his gloves and placed his hands against her cheeks to comfort her. "What would you have me do?" She placed her hands on his and closed her eyes.

"It ain't as if I have a choice, right? I mean, if I don't sign up, they're gonna come a-calling. I promise, I'll do my duty and come home. Besides, I can't think of a greater honor than saving a man wounded in battle. Can you imagine helping a fella back to his wife and children?"

"I know you can't watch from the sidelines. That's what I adore most about you."

O'Dell placed his thumbs on the corners of her mouth and eased upward to force a faux smile. Annalise responded with a giggle before planting a soft kiss against his lips.

***

As the big city of Wilkes-Barre appeared beyond the wide expanse of the Susquehanna River, O'Dell broke from his reverie and slowed the Lincoln to a crawl. He followed directions provided on a handwritten note by an administrator at the Wellsboro Armory.

Another left and a half-mile brought the couple to the Lehigh Valley Railroad Station and a lengthy line of cars awaiting directives from a military representative. Annalise kept a vigilant gaze out the window.

"Anna, sweetheart, I know you're upset, but this ain't normal for you. There's more on your mind than you're letting on. I wish you'd talk to me. I don't want us to part this way."

"I'm sorry," she said. "I cannot move past the feeling we'll never see each other again."

"You don't have to apologize. You're nervous, I'm nervous, the whole damn world's nervous. Every person you've loved has left you, but I ain't leaving. I promise, I'll come home."

"I'm so scared."

A rap against the driver's side window jolted O'Dell out of his contemplation of turning the car around and taking a chance the Army would forgo chasing down one no-show. A tall, slender man in a uniform that appeared brand new out of the box leaned in.

With a gruff voice and snappish attitude, the soldier asked, "Army?"

O'Dell nodded.

"Your paperwork," he demanded.

Annalise dug through her purse and passed the documents.

"You're headed for the induction center at New Cumberland. Park your car and report to table 1-A inside. You'll receive further instructions once checked in."

"Do ya know where I'll be a headin' from there?"

"Camp Croft, South Carolina, or Fort Bragg, North Carolina. It doesn't matter, you'll go where you're told. Now, move it."

The man tossed the papers to O'Dell's lap and waved him forward.

O'Dell hurried through the checkpoint to an open parking space. He cut the engine and held tight to the wheel. "What a horseshit birthday."

"I hoped this day would never come," Annalise said. "I love you so much, O'Dell, and don't have words to tell you all you've become to me. My soul is leaking away."

O'Dell turned from the window. "I know ya love me. I promise, I'll write every day. No matter what happens, you're my gal forever."

He placed a palm under her chin to draw her face toward him. "I love you."

Her expression softened. O'Dell leaned in and pressed his lips to hers, absorbing her scent and taste, losing himself in the sensation of where his lips began and hers ended.

Chapter 10

Hand in hand, O'Dell and Annalise made their way toward the station at a pace slower than other families. They paused short of a covered portico to bask in the shadow of the majestic, red brick structure, with its steep rooflines, sharp-angled gables, and multiple chimneys. To the unknowing, it appeared more a holiday retreat than a portal for travel.

Annalise fell into a momentary lapse, admiring the architecture, delaying the inevitable. She enjoyed the glamour of travel by rail. The scent of hardwood floors melding with suitcase leather, smoldering coal, and gear oil, all piqued her senses of adventure. Her anticipation bestirred at the sight of a loading platform packed with anxiety-riddled travelers awaiting the conductor's cry to board. Her heart skipped at the prospect of a club car with an unmolested view of bountiful pastures and mountain ranges sure to pass along the way. This moment, however, proved far from any adventure she cared to partake.

"We should go in," O'Dell said.

She held firm against the pull of his hand. Upon release, she cupped her hands against her mouth as tears flowed.

O'Dell dropped his bag. "I wish you'd level with me."

She could not speak. He searched over the crowd, spotting many other wives attempting to conceal their emotions. Her reaction surprised him. She'd lived through much adversity and heartache, and worked hard to project a tough and energetic charisma. She'd only cried in front of him once—on their wedding day—though through a smile wider than the Rio Grande.

He didn't attempt to comfort with words. Instead, he held her, stroked her hair, and allowed her to let spill what needed spilled.

Annalise pushed from his grasp, straightened her hair, and brushed at the front of her coat. She pulled in a deep breath. "I'm so sorry. I promise, it won't happen again."

"If there's something other than my leaving on your mind, please tell me."

"No, nothing."

O'Dell didn't buy it, but let it go. He retrieved his bag and grabbed her hand.

The scene inside proved less chaotic than expected. Never had they experienced a more somber ambiance in such a public venue. Each expression exhibited identical, unspeakable shock.

Signs posted above temporary tables at the far end of the concourse beckoned Uncle Sam's recruits. O'Dell exchanged his suitcase for the draft documents. He kissed Annalise and pointed to a row of chairs where other wives sat waiting out the check-in process.

Annalise struggled through families moving toward the loading platform as if on their way to the gallows. She took a chair next to a woman wiping her tears, rocking a newborn. The two exchanged smiles.

"I'm so sorry," Annalise said. "My stomach feels knotted, too."

"I guess we're all in this together now."

"I'm Annalise."

The woman cleared her throat. "I'm Patricia. My daughter Jenny."

"It's nice to meet you both. She has the bluest eyes I've ever seen."

"Same as her daddy's."

"May I ask her age?"

"She turns one month Christmas Eve."

"Your first?"

"First and final. Doctor said I can't have another."

"I'm sorry."

"It's okay. I'm blessed to have any at all. I'm content with God's will."

"You must be suffering so, I mean, the baby, and your husband leaving."

Patricia again burst into tears.

Annalise grabbed her wrist. "Please, I didn't mean to upset you further."

"It's okay. I haven't stopped crying since hearing the news of Pearl Harbor. The moment it broke, I knew my Johnny was gone."

"I expected the same of my husband."

"My Johnny's eldest brother served on the Oklahoma. Those boys didn't have a chance."

Annalise brought a balled fist to against her chest. "Oh, my. I can't imagine."

"When he learned of the attack, he went into a rage. He doesn't even remember. He delivered the news to my sister-in-law. The most painful moment in my life."

Annalise straightened in her chair to search the line of men. Her imagination concocted scenarios her stomach could not bear. She needed to see O'Dell's face.

Chapter 11

How could I ever live through such heartbreaking news? Annalise questioned, having grown oblivious to Patricia's detail of the family's tragedy. She spotted O'Dell speaking to another volunteer. It did little to ease her anxiety.

"Annalise?"

"I'm sorry, Patricia, please forgive me. What did you say?"

"I said, as of yesterday, they still haven't found my brother-in-law's body."

"I don't know what to say. It's all so unspeakable, so unreal. I ... I don't know."

"It's a hard reality we'll all face in the coming days. I don't think we're prepared for what evil lurks at our doorstep."

"I'm sure you're right."

"My husband seems to have made a friend," Patricia said, pointing.

"Oh, that's my husband, O'Dell."

"They're carrying on as if they've known one another for years."

"I hope O'Dell's blessed enough to make good friends to help him through this."

Patricia repositioned the baby in her arms. The child cooed. Annalise grabbed hold of her finger. "I can't imagine the fear you're feeling."

"We didn't plan on Jenny. Johnny's pulled by the obligation to provide for us and the duty to avenge his brother's death. I fear Jenny will distract his focus and get him killed."

"It's my fear, too... I mean, I wouldn't want O'Dell distracted."

"Do you have children?"

"No. I also fear it'd place him in grave danger." Annalise paused and changed the subject. "Where did you and your husband meet?"

"We lived across the street from each other all our lives, attended the same schools. The only man I've ever kissed. God willing, I hope to never kiss another. Tell me your story."

"We noticed each other at a livestock auction but missed out on meeting. I fell in love the moment I spotted him. We met by chance a few months later."

Annalise crossed her legs and turned toward Patricia. "I'll tell you it was the shock of my life."

She spoke of a routine visit from old Lucian McKenna, the county vet, and spotting O'Dell step from the truck with medical bag in hand. At first, O'Dell did not seem to make the connection. When the vet introduced him to their client, he broke into a wide, mischievous grin. "It's you."

With nerves at fever pitch, O'Dell had some difficulty making conversation or performing duties in her presence. He stammered, wiping sweat from his brow, examining her stock for no particular reason, and avoided making eye contact.

The vet, a gentle, graying man who viewed O'Dell as his own, winked at Annalise as if recognizing his apprentice's smitten state. Annalise found great amusement in her future husband's boyish, nervous ways.

Annalise escorted the two from the pasture upon the vet's conclusion her stock was in good health. She peeked over her shoulder, watching O'Dell kick at the dirt, as if angry for not having the words to express what splashed about his mind. His brooding proved a waste.

Annalise had decided the moment he stepped from the truck he wouldn't leave without the two securing another meeting. To their divine providence, neither had to make the first move.

As the trio approached Lucian's truck, he said, "I've not known two people more suited for one another in all my days. I suggest you stop this silliness and get acquainted."

He turned to O'Dell. "Anna will expect you for dinner Sunday next at five. If you're late, you're fired."

Annalise's smile stretched to both ears. O'Dell removed his Stetson.

"I'll look forward to it, Mr. Denny," she said.

As the truck pulled away from the property, O'Dell rolled down the passenger side window, and with Stetson waving and chest thumping, yelled, "Miss Annalise, I'll love ya till the day I die."

"Oh, he didn't," Patricia said.

"Sure did. Caught me by surprise, but not as much as when he stepped from the truck when they first arrived. I didn't mind though, he only said what I was thinking."

"Well, we're headed to North Carolina," O'Dell said. The women pushed from their chairs.

"Honey, meet Johnny Montgomery. We're headed to the same camp."

"Mr. Montgomery," Annalise said.

"Ma'am," he replied, touching the bill of his Fedora.

"O'Dell, meet Patricia and Jenny."

"Nice to meet ya, ma'am. Looks as if you have your hands full, there. Johnny tells me you live in Mansfield."

"Lived there all our lives," she replied.

"Not too far from our patch of earth. You girls need to watch out for each other."

Annalise scrounged through her purse for a pencil and scratch paper. With addresses exchanged, and O'Dell's suggesting Johnny meet him in the last car, Annalise and Patricia traded hugs and promises to keep in touch.

Johnny and Patricia reclaimed the chairs. O'Dell and Annalise fell in behind others heading for the tracks. Neither said a word as each contemplated the thousand little things they wanted to say.

O'Dell spotted an empty bench and worked through the crowd. Annalise rolled her hands together as if cleansing — a telltale sign her nerves were in tatters.

"Please, look at me," O'Dell said.

Annalise turned with eyes streaked with thin lines of blood.

"I'm coming home. You understand what I'm saying? I'm coming home and we'll grow as old as two gulf turtles."

"Promise me you'll pay attention and not get distracted. Promise me you won't take unnecessary risks."

"I promise. I ain't going there to be a hero."

She flung her arms around his neck. O'Dell pulled her tight. The two exchanged whispers and kisses until the engineer unleashed the screech of the locomotive's steam whistle. The call to board followed.

They walked arm-in-arm toward the last car.

"O'Dell, I... I want to tell you ...."

He dropped his suitcase.

The beaten look on his face broke her concentration. Annalise closed her eyes, took hold of his hand, then brought it against her lips. "I love you. Please never forget you saved me. I had nothing until I met you."

O'Dell dragged a coat sleeve across his eyes. "We saved each other. Take care of yourself and Bella." He pulled her close and kissed her, then hopped aboard the car just as the train pulled from the platform.

Annalise followed in the train's wake to the edge of the platform, waving and blowing kisses. The engine switched tracks to a more southern route. O'Dell leaned from the car, waved his Stetson, and yelled, "Mrs. Annalise, I'll love ya till the day I die."

Tears soaked her face as she staggered toward a bench, attempting to convince her shattered conscience she'd made the right decision. She settled to her knees, begging God to bring her husband home, while seeking forgiveness for sending the love of her life off to war without knowledge of the life budding in her womb.

Chapter 12

High Wycombe, Buckinghamshire, England, August 1942

O'Dell fumbled through a collection of medical bags gathered in haste. Simultaneous to his nervous poking and prodding, he glanced through the mist-covered windshield of a surplus ambulance, searching the pre-dawn sky for any signs of the wounded plane.

The driver, an aged army vet serving in identical capacity as he did during the Great War, puffed away on a cigar, as if on the banks of a quaint, secluded pond, awaiting a bass to strike his line.

"Easy, cowboy," he said, blowing a cloud of smoke out the driver's side window. "You've checked that damn bag a dozen times. If you don't have what you need, improvise."

O'Dell cupped his mouth and blew into his palms. Months of officers lecturing on first aid and first response protocols — from tending migraines and amputations, to using proper techniques for bandaging — had come down to this moment: he, the lone conduit between life and death.

His nerves bubbled at a fever pitch, a level beyond what he recalled when settling onto the back of a pissed-off Brahma in those seconds before the gate swung open. A B-17, returning from an overnight bombing raid against a German-occupied railroad at Rouen-Sotteville, suffered multiple direct hits from anti-aircraft flak, her belly gunner chewed to pieces.

O'Dell pulled a medical combat field manual and flipped through the first pages, rereading a paragraph related to blood circulation.

"You don't need the instruction book," the driver said.

"I ain't ready for this," O'Dell replied. "I ain't ready to make life and death decisions."

"Yes, you are. You've had the best instruction in the world. Do what your gut tells you, regardless of your patient's pleas, and rely on your training. I promise, your instincts will kick in."

O'Dell returned the manual to his medical bag.

The driver pointed to the windshield. "Ain't time, anyway. Here they come."

A bright orange glow bored through the blackness, heading right for them. The ambulance shook as the plane passed overhead, its four engines grinding and sputtering, with one on the starboard side spitting a flame trail down the length of the fuselage. Rescue and fire crews took off in pursuit. The ambulance followed.

By the time they pulled alongside the plane, fire crews had dispensed the first round of foam. The crew exited through the bomb bay door, delivering the injured gunner to an adjacent field overgrown with heather and other grasses.

O'Dell rushed to a hover position. Perception did not align with reality. His muscles tensed as the injured crewman appeared like a creature from space. The boy's intestines spilled through a gaping hole in his abdomen. His right arm dangled from shredded flesh and splintered bone. The right side of his face was missing, as if sliced away by a rip saw.

As O'Dell's partner predicted, instincts prevailed. He dropped to his knees and pilfered through his medical bag. He buried a morphine syrette in the boy's thigh. His ambulance mate, with the help of a crewmember, loaded the soldier onto a litter. O'Dell pushed the needle end of a blood plasma bottle into the soldier's good arm. He inserted a pressure bulb and pumped.

The soldier's eyes flittered. O'Dell cut away additional clothing and pushed the boy's intestines back into his body cavity. He layered the area with sulfanilamide and covered the wound with a large dressing. He sealed the edges with tape as the boy released a breath—his last.

Unaware of or unwilling to accept defeat, he turned his attention to the severed arm. The driver grabbed hold of his coat collar. O'Dell swung his arm to fend off the clutch. He set to unwrap a Carlisle bandage.

"Stop, Denny," the driver barked. "He's gone."

O'Dell placed his fingers against the boy's neck. He slumped and dropped his chin to his chest. The gunner's eyes pointed lifeless toward the heavens, tears leaking from both corners. The pilot pulled the IV.

All fell silent. O'Dell settled on his hands and knees, absorbing his first taste of death. He backtracked through each step, dissecting each decision. A gust of wind brushed straw reeds against his face. "What a goddamn waste," he whispered. The boy's face burned permanently into his memory.

"One man dies, another is pushed from the womb," the driver said. "If you expect to survive tomorrow, you reconcile the death of these boys today, because it'll become as common as the sun rising and setting. More men will die than you'll ever save, and it'll have nothing to do with skill, but everything to do with the tools we've invented to kill each other." He patted O'Dell's shoulder.

"Remember, supplies you waste on a dying man, you waste for a man you might save. The dying need only a final moment of compassion and comfort."

***

Wellsboro, Pennsylvania, Soldiers & Sailors Memorial Hospital, August 1942

Annalise dug her fingers into her friend's forearm and pushed at the urging of the doctor on call. A second effort brought forth the little miracle. A slap, then a squeal, sent Annalise sinking into her pillow with a smile spread across her face.

"Well done," Margie McKenna said, patting her shoulder.

A nurse wrapped the boy in a down blanket and passed him into Annalise's waiting arms.

She looked into her baby's eyes. He searched her face before drifting off to sleep. Annalise placed a kiss against his button nose. Tears of joy, mixed with anguish, dripped from her eyes. He looked the spitting image of his father. She held her son several minutes before a nurse removed the baby to conduct a standard physical.

"He's a fine-looking lad," Margie said. "Lucian and I are so happy for you two."

Annalise agreed. "He's an absolute miracle."

"Have you decided on a name?"

"No. He'll go unnamed until O'Dell comes home. We need to decide face to face, not in letters. I do have a preference, though."

"Don't you think it's time you let O'Dell know he's a father?"

Following a lengthy nap and a manufactured dream of mother, husband, and son walking through a field of golden wheat, Annalise set pencil to paper.

17, August 1942
My Dearest O'Dell...

Chapter 13

East of Bastogne in the Ardennes Forest, December 1944

"Sergeant, you go out there, you *will* die."

The argument raged more than an hour as platoon members attempted to convince the medic to ignore the gut-wrenching moans of an unknown wounded soldier to their rear.

The consensus held steadfast; a sniper planted the soldier as a decoy in a ruse to lure an unsuspecting target for a kill shot. O'Dell held resolute to his take—a human being, not a soldier, needed his help.

He peeked through a dense layer of pine branches cut and draped for concealment, hoping to gain a bearing. They stumbled upon the cavernous foundation of a century-old barn during a chaotic retreat. Sub-zero temperatures, made razor sharp by a northerly gust, clawed at the stubble of his unshaven face. His eyes darted across the blackened horizon.

Despite the groan waning, O'Dell grew confident of the line to travel. It may prove a foolhardy proposition and a death wish, as his mates suggested, but he could not devalue his desire to save each life.

He dipped below the branches to accumulate what little medical supplies remained. The regiment, fifty men strong five days earlier, suffered a devastating blow by a swift and pitiless German onslaught pushing nine armored divisions across the Our River. The rush forced the Twenty-Eighth Infantry from its stronghold near Hosengin, Luxembourg, to their current location south and west of Bastogne, Belgium.

Days of fighting and retreating through heavy snow and plummeting temperatures cost the men in stamina and supplies. Their combined inventory included four M1s, two pistols, two flashlights, a bag full of homemade candles, a medical bag, a questionable grenade, a radio able to receive but not transmit, a knife, a pack of crackers, and a scavenged K-ration.

The loss of regiment leader, Captain James Hanraddy, proved most unsettling. A no-nonsense, bullish but likable farm boy from the panhandle of Oklahoma, Hanraddy led the men in battle from France to the Hürtgen Forest. His gruesome demise came the previous evening as the men returned from a brief scouting mission. With the hideout within sight, Hanraddy found himself in the middle of an open meadow as a German armored unit approached, cutting off his path. He sought cover in a shallow depression rather than compromise the unit's position.

With his men hunkered down, arguing as to the best countermeasure to extract their leader, the armored column lurched forward of their captain's position. As one man whispered to another that the column would move past without notice, the lead Tiger maneuvered to its left, accelerated, and rolled over the cavity where the captain lay. With Hanraddy trapped under its tracks, the Tiger completed a series of rotations and ground the captain into the frozen earth.

Despite the frantic yells of his men, the German column rushed past without searching the bombed-out remnants. As the torrent pushed forward, and the shock of Hanraddy's selfless act settled, the men conceded their position as behind enemy lines, and their highest-ranking officer a medic. Though O'Dell offered no tactical leadership experience, no man questioned his dedication to God, country, and unit.

Three days removed from his third consecutive Christmas on the battlefield, O'Dell had long since lost his fear of death. His reassignment to the Twenty-Eighth cleared division headquarters prior to the group's June landing at Normandy. Although having experienced more death and dying than any man deserved, nothing equaled what took place the days following the allied invasion of France, as the regiment thrust forward and into front line fighting.

Few could stomach what medics faced each step and second of the war. Fewer owned the fortitude to manage the emotional toll of failing to save a life more often than extending one. Death and dying became as routine as breathing.

Seeing boys in shock picking through debris for their arms, or the unimaginable task of burying corpses of children and infants slaughtered without mercy by retreating enemies, had etched for O'Dell the fine point of the value of human life.

He lost count of the times he worked to patch unspeakable wounds with scrounged supplies, under heavy duress, in the most adverse conditions, enduring enemy snipers plugging his patients with new holes as he worked to save them.

Early in his deployment, he compartmentalized the shock of mangled innards and men's screams. The faces he knew haunted him:

his brothers who pleaded for their lives so they might see their sweethearts or mothers one last time, requests for last rites, or a begged promise to send a final letter home.

It troubled his conscience when a dying man saw his face last as life ebbed from his body. Each man branded singular, each scenario a permanent memory. Those moments changed forever the convictions he held for his own safety and the promise made to Annalise to avoid taking unnecessary risks.

O'Dell collected supplies, despite an awkward silence, and every man focused on him, wondering how they might stop him, short of shooting him.

Corporal Eli Shimmel, the lone remaining original member of the platoon and only officer with extensive combat experience, settled on his haunches in a corner. He shook his head and smirked.

The son of a Jewish baker, Shimmel held a voracious appetite for killing Nazis. Nicknamed the *Iron Crosshair*, Shimmel, at the ripe old age of twenty-two, proved a skilled tactician, an expert sniper, and a man the others flocked to during times of peril. Regardless of the new pecking order created by Hanraddy's untimely death, the men would carry out their duties on Shimmel's directive.

O'Dell worked around the half-circle of men, their faces looking younger than what one would find at a high school prom. Private John Spring, Private First-Class Angelo Sperro, Private First Class Archard "Archie" Martel, Private Dan Hansel, Private Joe Polak, and Private Arthur Westwick, all his junior. He brooded over them as if younger brothers. They each fought the war hard, courageous, and with honor.

O'Dell flung the strap of his medical bag over his shoulder. He directed his attention toward the youngest member of the regiment.

"I'll take your sidearm, Spring," he said, pointing to his hip.

Spring moved for his holster.

Shimmel flashed a palm and approached. "Sergeant, I can't let you go out there."

"I understand my role, Corporal, but in this situation, I outrank ya."

"You know we're behind enemy lines. You'll compromise our position the moment you pop out of this hole. I can't let you mark us."

"I suspect you'd object to sitting out the war here. We gotta know what's out there and rejoin our division. We haven't heard anything moving since last night. Now, I'm gonna crawl fifty yards and see if I can gain a bearing. If I think he's too far off, I'll head back."

"And these men?" Shimmel pointed. "We'll have to fight our way to our rally point at Neufchateau. What happens if one of these boys needs you?"

"You know the enemy targets medics as much as they do those with four stars on their collars. No guarantee I'll last the next minute. Ain't none of us have a special pass out of this."

"Then why risk your life when you don't have to?"

"It's my duty."

"How about the regiment?"

"How do ya know it's not one of our boys out there?"

"I was last man through," Shimmel insisted.

O'Dell shook his head. "Our division scattered like mice in a cat house when those Germans busted through. Besides, I ain't never known a groan to have an accent. What if it were Spring or Polak? Would ya have me sittin' on my ass or figure out a way to get me the hell out there?"

The look on Shimmel's face told tale of the wheels spinning in his head. O'Dell knew the man was at his best when pushed into a corner.

"Okay, Sergeant," Shimmel said. "Have it your own damn way."

Chapter 14

Shimmel snapped his fingers. "Private, hand over your weapon."

Spring passed the pistol by the barrel.

"I need another clip," Shimmel ordered.

Sperro pulled one from a side pocket and tossed it.

Shimmel passed the pistol to O'Dell. "I'll lead you out. Polak, wait fifteen seconds, then fall out and fan twenty yards left. Wick, twenty yards to the right. Move with us. I stop, you stop. And keep low."

The men checked their weapons.

"Sperro, take Hansel, Martel, and Spring and fall back a hundred yards. Wick, Polak, any gunfire forward, fall back and join the others. Make sure you boys don't shoot each other. Work the signals and alerts from Utah."

Shimmel checked his gear. "You ready, Denny?"

O'Dell cracked an appreciative smile. "Thank you, Corporal."

"Don't thank me. I ain't doing this for you. I ain't getting busted because a jackass medic committed suicide. One thing, we move together and do this my way. And take off that fucking armband."

"Your way on your orders, Corporal," O'Dell said, removing the bright red cross from his sleeve, "until we find the soldier."

Shimmel's jaw clenched. He made a career of taking orders from superiors, not medics, and not from any man never having pulled a trigger.

"Let's go."

Shimmel crawled up an earthen embankment to a position at the top of a foundation wall, pushing through branches to expose the night sky. He fitted his helmet to the butt end of his rifle, eased it through the branches into the open, and rotated. Two more attempts drew no action.

He replaced the helmet and poked from the hole to achieve a visual of their surroundings. A mist settled across the landscape, though not near soupy enough to conceal movement. He figured the temperature at near zero. The hardened layer of snow posed serious concern. The air felt thick and stank of cordite and burnt timber.

"It's misty, but not near condensed enough," he said. "You guys falling back, stay tight and don't lose sight of each other. It's gonna make a hell of a noise if you start runnin' around in the snow like a bunch of apes. Move slow and follow in the tracks of the man in front of you."

Shimmel and O'Dell popped out of the den and onto their stomachs. "Which way?" Shimmel whispered.

O'Dell pointed across the corporal's nose. "See them clumps of stumps? We came through there running from them Tigers. The valley sets beyond. I think he's down there."

A groan echoed in the distance. A shiver worked up both men's spines. Their heads turned in unison toward the stumps.

"Let's go. Follow my tracks," Shimmel ordered.

He led the way, working slowly, rotating side to side with his M1 braced against his thigh. The crunch beneath their feet echoed at concerning decibels.

Navigation proved maddening. Massive trees and limbs, splintered by German 88s, littered the forest floor, forcing multiple switchbacks, and twice, a full retrace of their steps in search of a better route.

Shimmel dropped to his belly, short of the rim above the valley. O'Dell fell alongside.

Shimmel inspected his rifle. "This is just plain dumb and stupid," he mumbled.

"Bet you'd whistle another tune if it was your ass out there," O'Dell whispered.

"I ain't asked any man to risk his neck for me. You don't stick your neck out for no one in war, unless ordered."

"I'll remember you said that and try to forget the fool stunt you pulled to draw fire away from the others during our retreat."

"You have an answer for every damn thing, don't you?"

Clouds crumbled and dissolved overhead. Momentary openings projected moon glow, spawning ghostly reflections off the snow-covered landscape.

Shimmel turned slightly to catch O'Dell roll onto his back and gaze into the night sky.

"You need to keep your mind here, not on your woman," Shimmel said.

O'Dell let slip a deep sigh, cementing Shimmel's assumption. His emotional release coincided with a muffled groan to their right. O'Dell pointed.

Shimmel agreed. "Okay, let's go... nice and easy. Keep your eyes open."

On Shimmel's signal, they breached the rim, feet first. The steep embankment and craters formed by enemy shells hindered their progress, forcing awkward movements over and around a crosshatch of downed timber. Halfway down, they changed course as a painful cry broke from the darkness.

They set out on a new line, working down the slope another fifty yards. Initially, both thought they were wading through a mess of downed trees and shattered limbs. A quick burst of moonglow revealed a much different reality.

Shimmel grabbed a wad of O'Dell's coat. A slew of twisted and mangled human remains lay scattered about them. "Christ almighty, what the fuck happened here?"

Chapter 15

O'Dell slumped against a stump.

Shimmel positioned on his haunches as if readying for a pitcher's next toss. He shook his head. "I was the last man through, I'm sure of it."

O'Dell removed his helmet. He viewed the valley floor with an exhausted gaze. Bodies, frozen in time, limbs twisted in grotesque configurations, told of a horrific and desperate struggle.

The Germans pushed toward Belgium to split allied forces. News of the atrocities levied against captured American GIs spread through the ranks. Little more than a week had passed since troops learned of the massacre at Malmedy, sparking reciprocating atrocities.

"Those sons of bitches," Shimmel said. "They herded these poor bastards here and butchered 'em. Those sons of bitches."

"How the hell did we not hear this?" O'Dell questioned, running a hand over his scalp, focusing on a corpse a few feet away. The poor soul's face, frozen for eternity, depicted unspeakable horror and panic through bulging eyes and a mouth stretched open as if longing to relay the account.

O'Dell collected his helmet as another moan erupted. Shimmel dropped onto his belly in a covering position.

O'Dell sprung to action, ignoring Shimmel's warnings that the bodies may be booby-trapped. He focused on a group of corpses at the far side of the killing field piled a half-dozen high. He crept through the mess, snagging on frozen arms grabbing at his heels.

The bodies told of an onslaught from above and behind. Backs of heads blown open, torsos riddled with bullets, legs cut in half below the knees. The poor souls never had a chance.

O'Dell sifted through visions of wives, girlfriends, and mothers who'd never know the truth of their loved ones' demise.

The groan erupted to divulge an exact location.

"This way, Corporal," O'Dell said.

Shimmel strolled through the entanglement, stopping twice to inspect bodies. "I have a bad feeling about this. I think we need to leave, and I mean right now."

O'Dell pointed. "Grab those legs. We need to move these bodies."

"Did you hear what I said? This isn't a battleground."

"No shit, Corporal, it's a murder scene. Help me move this body."

"Did you look at the uniforms?"

"Goddamn it, Shimmel, grab those legs. That's an order."

"They stripped 'em of all insignias and markings."

"Would you leave markings on men you planned to murder?"

O'Dell grabbed the shoulders of the next body. As the men lifted, the victim's head detached. O'Dell let go a disgusted grunt. He redirected the head with his boot. The last body lay cut in half. O'Dell moved the legs, Shimmel the torso. The soldier underneath released a faint moan.

O'Dell slipped off the medical bag and fished through what meager supplies remained. He tossed Shimmel a flashlight and ordered an inspection of the body from head to toe. The mustard-colored beam shone weak. O'Dell tore away the soldier's field coat, identifying a single exit wound below his right breast.

Shimmel moved alongside. O'Dell applied a wad of dressing and rubbed the soldier's thigh in quick, short bursts. He popped the plastic cover to a syrette and plunged it into the boy's flesh.

"This man's gonna die," Shimmel said. "Why waste our last stick?"

"He ain't gonna die. He's in mighty poor shape and hanging on by the hairs of a bull's ass, but I see no other wounds."

"You're taking him out of here? You fucking kidding me?"

O'Dell pushed Shimmel's hand from the dressing to reinspect the wound.

"I'm gonna need your help to fold him over my shoulder."

Shimmel grabbed a wad of O'Dell's lapel. "You're out of your mind. We don't have the means to take care of a wounded man and there's no way in hell you're carrying him up the ridge over your shoulder."

"Corporal, we don't have time for this. I need you out front and without distraction. Help me get him settled."

"You're crazy. Men die. Some quick, some slow and painful. It's a damn dirty business, but that's war. This man ain't gonna make it and you're risking the lives of our men, and for what? To drag his ass back so we can all watch him die?"

O'Dell tore from Shimmel's clutch. "This man ain't gonna die. He's gonna see his mamma and sweetheart again. I'll put a bullet in my head before I abandon a breathing man on the battlefield. Now, either help me or get the hell outta my way."

Shimmel collected the medical bag. O'Dell grabbed the soldier's arms. Shimmel secured his neck and head. With a grunt, they draped the man over O'Dell's shoulder.

"There's twine in the bag. Secure his arms. I don't want him floppin' around back there."

Shimmel secured the soldier in hog-tie fashion.

"Okay, Corporal, do what you do best and find us a way outta here."

Chapter 16

Shimmel brushed O'Dell's shoulder as he moved past to take point. "If we die and ever meet again, I'm gonna punch you square in the face."

"I doubt it. I reckon we'll be in two different places."

Shimmel's eyes narrowed. "Keep up and stay alert."

Shimmel struggled to find the path from which they descended. The fog turned thick, and the moon's luminance had dimmed, tricking him into dead ends, forcing switchbacks. O'Dell's legs grew heavy and breathing labored.

Halfway along the lung-crushing ascent, Shimmel paused, burying his forearm into O'Dell's chest. A disturbance above drew his attention. He cocked his head, waited, and listened. A familiar sequence of whistles provided an audible beacon to aid their return.

With cover positioned, Shimmel relieved O'Dell of the full weight of the wounded soldier. They moved up the bank toward the intermittent signal.

Westwick greeted them at the top. Shimmel rebuffed Polak's attempt to grab the soldier's legs.

"Wick, there's a slew of dead soldiers at the bottom of the valley. Search the corpses and bring back anything you can find in ways of identification. When we return to the bunker, I'll send cover. Take no chances. You see or hear anything, head back. Don't forget to signal on your way up."

Westwick traded rifles, and in a blink, disappeared over the rim.

Flat terrain made easy their transport to the barn. Shimmel and Polak eased the man to the ground.

"Polak, help the sergeant move this man inside," Shimmel ordered.

"This ain't no man," O'Dell remarked. "He's younger than Spring."

Shimmel grunted, convinced the trip an unnecessary risk. He turned and let loose a whistle. Moments later, men exited the fog as ghosts.

Shimmel grabbed hold of Spring's coat and pointed. "You and Hansel move on my point forty yards. You'll come to a ridge above a steep valley.

Drop and cover. We found bodies at the bottom. Wick's investigating. He'll signal when he starts back up. Keep your fingers off the trigger."

"Yes, sir," Spring responded. He checked the corporal's mark and vanished into the fog, with Hansel on his heels.

"I told you two, under cover, now," Shimmel barked.

O'Dell and Polak eased their patient into the lair. Martel remained outside to cover the others' return. O'Dell went to work fighting a most disturbing stench. He tossed his last clump of clean dressing to Sperro and ordered it dampened.

O'Dell switched on a second flashlight. Stubble spotted the boy's jawline, his hair matted with mud and grime cloaking its natural color.

Sperro passed the dampened dressing, trading for the flashlight.

"Shine this on the wound," O'Dell ordered.

O'Dell cleaned the wound and doused it with sulfa powder. With Polak's help, he threaded a bandage around the soldier's torso.

"What a waste of supplies," Shimmel scoffed. He hunched over O'Dell's shoulder. "As soon as day breaks, I'm gonna find out how far the enemy pushed west. If I find an escape route, no matter how slight, we're out of here. What're your plans for this man?"

"If he can't move on his own, I'll carry him out."

"Carry him? If he can't move on his own, his ass stays behind."

"You'll have to plug me if ya think I'm leaving him behind. I ain't livin' the rest of my life knowing I abandoned one of my own."

"There're easier ways to have your name promoted in *Stars and Stripes*."

O'Dell launched his medical bag at Shimmel's head and lunged forward. Shimmel climbed on Sperro's back to get to O'Dell. Polak, a former Army boxing champ, moved in and made quick work of corralling his medic.

The scuffle ended quicker than it started when Martel poked through the pine branches.

"Corporal, the boys are returning."

Shimmel pushed off Sperro and fired a menacing glare toward O'Dell. Polak released O'Dell and patted his back. "Don't worry, Sarge, I'll help you carry him out."

"I appreciate it, Private."

"Eli has his moments, but there ain't nobody can question his dedication to this division."

"I respect that, but I ain't leavin' no man behind. He better learn to respect that about me."

"Most of us have gotten used to killing and dying," Sperro said. "What makes you so different? You sure as shit have seen more of it than any of us."

O'Dell crouched near his patient with canteen in hand. "I'm tired of the waste, tired of seeing vibrant youthful bodies turned into wads of bleeding, unrecognizable garbage. I'm sick of watching young boys, damn near children, cut down before experiencing marriage or having children of their own. I'm tired of death. Each time I save a life, I feel I've saved ten. I have to try."

O'Dell cringed as frigid water spilled into his palm. With a flick, he disbursed a trickle against the soldier's face. The boy twitched and his eyes fluttered. A second splash brought him from his unconscious state. Disoriented and confused by the men hovering above, he attempted to scoot away, but succumbed to the pain.

"Easy, cowboy," O'Dell pleaded. He placed a hand on the boy's shoulders. "You're okay."

O'Dell removed his field coat and placed it over the boy's body. Shimmel slid through the entrance, swatting his way through the camouflage. He pushed past O'Dell and aimed his rifle at the soldier's head. "You get this piece of shit Kraut outta here, or so help me God, I'll blow his fuckin' head off."

Chapter 17

O'Dell redirected the barrel of Shimmel's rifle from his patient's face. He rose, stepped into Shimmel, and demanded an explanation.

"You know who you risked the lives of these men for?" Shimmel yelled, a vein bulging on his forehead. "A goddamn Kraut."

"What're you talking about?"

Shimmel exposed a handful of trinkets. O'Dell picked through the lot before selecting an odd-shaped pewter pin the size of a nickel.

Shimmel pointed. "Seen this before?"

O'Dell brought the pinwheel-shaped relic nearer his eyes, as if a jeweler assessing a diamond's clarity.

"It's an Edelweiss flower cap badge off a German mountain infantry troop. Wick found it in the clutches of a corpse. None of our boys would have this. Those other items, well, they damn well speak for themselves."

O'Dell inspected a small, handcrafted wood cross, scribed with the name "Otto" on the backside of its center member, a tattered ID card of a German officer, and a picture of a German soldier posing with a wife or sweetheart.

O'Dell shook his head. "I don't understand. They're all dressed in standard GI issue."

"Armies have stolen uniforms since the advent of war," Shimmel said. "Two weeks back they caught Krauts posing as American MPs. This ain't nothing new. I'm telling you, those are Germans down there and this asshole's one of 'em."

"How do ya know these ain't souvenirs or plants?"

"Are you kidding me?"

O'Dell turned to his patient. The boy pitched side to side, clutching at his chest as if he could ease the misery caused by a lead projectile piercing his body at nine hundred meters per second. Their eyes met a moment before the soldier turned away, wincing.

O'Dell fixated on his face. He had an innocent, educated look about him, suggesting he held no such capacity to kill and maim, as Shimmel charged. The circumstance did not add up.

Shimmel directed Westwick and Polak to prepare to remove the soldier.

"He ain't going anywhere," O'Dell said. "If he's German, then he's my prisoner."

"I told you, once dawn breaks, I'm gonna find a way out, and we're gonna have to move quick."

"Fine. You find a way, and we'll follow — all of us."

Shimmel let go an exaggerated laugh. He altered his rifle, drawing the barrel across O'Dell's face. "What's your fuckin' problem?"

"What's yours?" O'Dell fired back, squaring his body. The men settled in as if two rams readying to butt. Hansel jutted out his chin; the others moved in.

Shimmel tossed his rifle to the ground. "My problem is I'm in the middle of a miserable war, stuck behind enemy lines, outranked by a crazy, careless medic who wants to risk lives. This ain't a goddamn game. There's a time for taking prisoners, a time to patch up the wounded, and a time to let the dying die. If we don't push the Krauts back, they're gonna cut our lines in half. We've got to find the rally point and help our boys stop this push, not risk our lives for a Kraut piece of shit who doesn't mean a thing in the grand scheme of it all. Do you think there's glory here? You think you're doing God's will or something? Well, you ain't. There's no honor in saving a murdering piece of trash."

"*Ich habe niemanden ermordet.*"

The soldier's words reverberated through a pain-filled slur, cutting short the heated debate. Each man's head turned. Shimmel pushed past O'Dell in haste.

"What did he say?" Shimmel demanded of Polak, who served as the unit's emergency interrogator.

"He said he's not a murderer."

"Not a murderer? He's a Nazi, ain't he?"

Shimmel's infuriation boiled over. He pushed through Polak to assume a position above the prisoner. The boy's eyes grew wide. Shimmel ripped off a profanity-laced tirade targeting Hitler and Germany's crimes against humanity.

The soldier pleaded, "*Ich habe niemanden ermordet, ich habe niemanden ermordet.*" He attempted to scoot from his tormentor.

Shimmel pursued as the boy pushed away, clawing at the frozen dirt. O'Dell sprung forward, having seen enough.

He pushed past the other men and grabbed for the back of Shimmel's coat collar. Shimmel shed O'Dell's grasp to deliver a solid kick to the prisoner's crotch. The ensuing groan sent the men charging. O'Dell grabbed Shimmel's waist in time to deflect a stomp intended for the boy's temple.

Shimmel pulled a gold-plated Star of David from under his shirt. "*Juden, Juden, Juden,* you piece of shit."

Chapter 18

Four men joined in to subdue Shimmel, but his insistence in proclaiming his heritage grew in crescendo. O'Dell scrambled to his feet and grabbed two fistfuls of Shimmel's coat lapels.

"You don't go near him again. You understand me?"

Shimmel locked hold of O'Dell's wrists and fought to break the grip. The two traded shoves and barbs.

Hansel pulled O'Dell clear. Spring and Polak held tight to Shimmel.

"I'm not taking orders from you. You want to shower this fucker with sympathy, go ahead. I hope they court-martial you. This asshole deserves a bullet in his brain for what his kind has done to my people."

"He deserves due process," O'Dell fired back. "If he's guilty of crimes, he'll pay for it, and I'll applaud it."

"A bullet serves as due process out here."

"You're wrong. This man has rights."

The energy and angst rippling through Shimmel's body released. His limbs fell limp as a look of bewilderment took hold. Polak and Hansel eased their grip.

The men knew but two facts regarding their fearsome corporal: his Jewish heritage and bloodthirsty hatred of Germany and the Nazis. He never spoke of family, and when talk of home and childhood erupted, he removed himself from the conversation.

"Rights?" Shimmel said, in a calm, deliberate tone. "I grew up on the outskirts of Berlin. My father owned a bakery. Mother worked for him until evening, then washed and mended neighbors' clothes until the wee hours. My three sisters and I helped father before and after school, and during breaks.

"Brownshirts harassed my father and stole his goods, as they did all the shops owned by Jews. We had little left to sell once they took or destroyed what they wanted. Father fought back by working longer hours. We hid bread in places around the streets where we lived. When he needed goods to sell, we'd scour the neighborhood collecting what we'd stashed.

"Brownshirts showed up one day with a legion of SS. They ransacked all the Jewish-owned shops and herded owners and their families into trucks. My father must have resisted. They hacked him to death with an ax. They raped my mother, one by one. Those dirty bastards inserted a shotgun between her legs and blew her to pieces."

O'Dell closed his eyes and brought a hand to his forehead. The other men stood as statues, mouths agape.

"Two days later, I'm on a train to Paris with my grandmother. We expected my grandfather to follow, but he never showed. He owned a newspaper. I'm told they grabbed him in the middle of the night and razed his shop. We'd all be dead if not for my grandmother's brother, who fled to America years before.

"The Nazis murdered my family for no reason other than their hatred of Jews, and their own ideals of a master race. You still want to discuss human rights with me? You will not find more peaceful, loving, hard-working people than my parents. They gave away more bread than they ever sold."

Shimmel stepped to O'Dell's side and pointed to the prisoner. "He's a born killer. He and his party murdered my family and stole what they worked so hard to build. They've murdered and raped millions and you want to save his life?"

O'Dell felt an immediate emotional tug-of-war, as he questioned his own reaction to such barbarity inflicted upon family members. He let go a deep sigh. "Corporal, I'm sorry what you've endured, and I won't offend you by saying I understand how you feel. I hold many matters true, no matter the circumstance, including murder. Murder is murder, don't matter the time or place. It's anti-everything good. I took this man in assuming he was one of our own. Come to find out, he's the enemy. I cannot allow his murder."

"It's not murder if we leave him or take him back where we found him. His own murdered him. Anyway, there ain't no such thing as murder in war."

"You're wrong. Rules governing war state persons taking no active part in hostilities, including members of armed forces who've laid down their arms and no longer partaking in combat due to sickness, wounds received, detention, or any other cause, shall in all circumstances be treated humanely."

"You've read the whole book, haven't you?"

"Enough to know where to draw the line."

"You think the Krauts follow rules of war? They've shot at you and that's against the Geneva Convention."

"It's the reason we must hold true. If I leave this man to die, I'm no better than a Nazi. I ain't ever gonna sink to such filth."

Shimmel shook his head. He cupped his hands to his mouth and pushed heat to ease the sting of winter on his fingers. He turned to view the rest of the men, each directing their attention elsewhere.

"What do you say, Martel? They killed your family in France, right?"

"Yes, sir. Two older sisters, three nieces, and a nephew."

"You wanna shoot this sonofabitch?"

Martel looked to his mates. "It wouldn't bother me."

"How about you, Polak?"

"I'd kill him, but not under these circumstances. If he tries to escape, I'll shoot him, and enjoy doing it, but I'm not killing an unarmed, captured man."

Shimmel turned toward O'Dell with a slow shake of his head. "You wanna save this piece of shit, save him. But the next time you give him water or stick a thermometer up his ass, remember the hundreds of our boys he's put in the ground."

O'Dell set to remind Shimmel the punishment for murder when he caught the eyes of his men reacting to the groan behind them.

After struggling to pull himself into a sitting position, his body quivering and eyes wet and heavy, the young German informed Shimmel in perfect English, "I am not a murderer. I am a traitor."

***

Paul wet his fingertips, pinched the corner of the completed page, and set it on top of a stack started on the floor. He turned to a rap on the door.

"Sweetheart?" Monica said. "I've got you some coffee."

He let go an extended stretch and yawn.

Monica pushed through the door with a small tray supporting a steaming cup, a tin of cream, and a package of ginger snaps. "How's it going?"

"Not into it too deep."

"Is it making you want to turn to the next page?"

"Oh, yes. It's intriguing, but you remember what I always say, you never know until you read 'the end.'"

"Would you care for cream?"

"No. I need thick and black."

She passed the cup. Paul took a quick sip. Monica stepped behind his chair, bent low, and planted a kiss on his head. "I'll see you in the morning."

"Goodnight, sweetheart. Thanks for the coffee."

She winked and blew a kiss. Paul stretched his legs, rubbed his eyes, and soldiered on.

Chapter 19

23 December 1944
My Dear Annalise,
Christmas is here, and my insides burn at the thought of how much time has passed since I last held you. The days are long, dark, and cold, and our resources slim, but we're hanging in there.

We got caught up in a German push and retreated and are now behind enemy lines in a burned-out barn. We've avoided the enemy so far and hope to reach our rally point soon. Corporal Shimmel took off an hour ago with three others to scout an escape route. I don't expect them back soon. There's dense fog and snow, the temperature near zero, and the terrain wooded and rough. I'm confident Shimmel will find a way out, though. I've met no one better moving troops from point to point. It's too bad he's such a pain in the ass.

Private Spring, Sperro, and Polak remained behind to keep me company. I'm lucky to associate with such fine men. I'm fond of Spring. He's a good kid. I'll remember Polak long after this mess. He says the damndest things and has a way of making the boys laugh and forget where they are. It's confounding to me what war does to your senses. The buzz of a fly or the rustle of a leaf sends me scrambling for a weapon.

I reflect often how I think I've seen and witnessed every despicable sight a man can see, only to find I'm wrong. Today proved another first. I took out on a mission to aid a soldier I heard moaning during the night. Shimmel accompanied me into a valley where we stumbled on a large group of dead soldiers, we thought Americans. We found our man and hauled him back to the bunker.

He's not American at all, but a young German. I've written and mentioned Shimmel's hatred of Germans. I know why now and will explain someday. We've not figured why he's wearing our uniform. He spoke to us in German, but later, in perfect English more American sounding than any of us. What a shock.

He's near our age and does not have the look of what one would picture in their mind of a Nazi warrior. He's the enemy, yet I don't see an enemy in him.

I'm not seeing enemies at all these days. Dead bodies draw in my mind the faces of those concerned for their fate. Last week, I came across a young German missing the entire right side of his head and face. His body lay against a stump, his arms and legs flailing about as if attempting to climb a hill. I could do nothing to help, except drop to a knee and watch his life trickle away. I could not stop considering his identity, the city of his birth, or his profession before the war. I felt sorrow and pain for him and his family, despite his taking an oath to kill me.

The tragedy of this all seems enough to pull tears, but I have none left. I'm confident I don't belong here but am needed. This side of the world sees little decency practiced these days, and I fear I'm the last with a shred of it left. We've turned into animals with one objective — survive at any cost. And they do things so uncharacteristic of themselves for the possibility they may see their children or sweetheart again. I find it a most heartbreaking reality, seeing men so desperate, they've transformed into unrecognizable creatures.

I try to maintain sanity and dignity but struggle with resentment. I find comfort knowing many boys have returned home because of me but fight envy as I send men to the rear with conditions certain to punch their ticket. I ask, 'Why not me? Why can't I go home? I've done my duty and worked as hard as any man.' I'm ashamed of these feelings.

Regardless, I patch them up and send them down the line. I know nothing more worthless than war, yet men continue to wage it, despite the horrors and pain of it all. I'm sure the enemy cries, too, don't they? Don't they also fear for their lives and the lives of their families and dream of returning home? I don't know, but I know we must stop them, and it's the right thing to do. Without this effort, who knows what'd come of the world?

I value freedom more than ever. These past years have felt like a prison term. No man deserves oppression. It's why we fight, though it pains me the price we've paid is surrendering the best years of our lives. I know I've had enough. I struggle with the loss of human life and livestock. You can't fathom the thousands upon thousands of slaughtered horses and cattle scattered about the continent. It makes a man forget God. All these beautiful horses, dragged into war by crazed men who view them as mechanical devices built in some factory.

It makes me desperate to place my hands on Bella and breathe her aroma. I miss her as I miss you. I'm sorry, my love, but I must go for now. My prisoner needs attention. I'll write again tomorrow, though the censors will eliminate most of my words.

I miss you so much. I see your face in the stars and hear your voice when the wind rustles through the trees. Please take care of yourself. Growing old with you keeps my body warm and feet moving forward. Mrs. Annalise, I'll love you till the day I die. Yours forever,

OD

***

O'Dell slipped the letter into an inside pocket. Writing home proved medicine for his soul, and an activity ritualized the day he hit boot camp. Other than a few occasions, he kept his promise to write each day.

The sight of the young German recouping his faculties stirred O'Dell's interest. The circumstance of those men in the valley kindled his imagination, but less so than the soldier's keen knowledge of the English language and admission to traitorous acts. O'Dell felt a mixing in his gut. *More here than meets the eye*, he concluded.

The German lifted his head to inspect his surroundings. He spotted Sperro tucked in a far corner, young Spring asleep against a timber at his feet. Daylight, though muted by overcast, seeped through cracks and crevices, highlighting the German's face. His eyes appeared brighter and more alert. He had cheated the death intended <u>for</u> him.

O'Dell coaxed his fatigued legs and sore ankles into action, crawling from a shallow depression stuffed with remnants of straw. The German noticed and struggled to a support position on his elbows. O'Dell proceeded forward with his medical bag. The soldier's expression eased when he honed on the faded imprint of a red cross attached to O'Dell's sleeve. O'Dell settled to a knee at his side.

"Warum würden Sie mein Leben retten wollen?"

O'Dell let slip a smile. "I'm bettin' you can do better," he said. "Guess ya don't remember speaking to us in English."

The soldier looked away. He searched his memory for the exchange. O'Dell opened the medical bag to extract his last wad of cotton. "It's okay. We won't tell anyone." He unbuttoned the boy's coat.

The German released a deep sigh and wiped his eyes. "Why did you save me?"

Chapter 20

O'Dell peeled back the dressing protecting the German's wound and inspected. He dusted with sulfa powder before re-dressing.

"Why did you do it?" the German repeated.

O'Dell grabbed a wad of his coat. "I'll start by asking you to explain this. This ain't your uniform."

The prisoner said nothing.

O'Dell released. "I guessed you for one of our own."

"Why not let your eager corporal finish the job?"

"I save lives, I don't take them—friend or foe. Besides, rules of war exist, and I aim to follow 'em. I've enough regrets. Don't need the lynching of a defenseless enemy added to the list."

"I am in your debt, though I accepted the death due me."

O'Dell brushed off the comment. He would never trust a Nazi.

The soldier let go a grating cough, summoning Sperro, Spring, and Polak from their slumber. Sperro grabbed his rifle, shuffled to the scene, and settled his crosshair on the German's temple.

"Easy," O'Dell said, "we're all good here."

Sperro released his aim.

"What's your name?" O'Dell asked.

"Jakob von Rüdel, Fourth Army Infantry," he replied.

"I'm Sergeant O'Dell Denny of the Twenty-Eighth. Private Angelo Sperro, John Spring, Joe Polak."

The young privates looked to one another, wrestling with the improbability of the encounter, struggling to rationalize an English-speaking Nazi. No one could point to the other and conclude their superiors correct in describing the enemy.

"Why did you call yourself as a traitor?" O'Dell asked.

Jakob's expression changed. He brought a hand to his wound. "An SS squad marched sixty of us into the valley."

"Those all Germans down there?"

"Yes. Accused of traitorous acts against the Reich. Before we entered the valley, they ordered us into American uniforms. Said we would have a better chance at making our destination. I knew better. Once we hit the bottom, men started running."

Polak drew near and took a knee. "What crime did you commit?"

Jakob worked his way around the dugout, looking to each man, accepting his failed and disgraced military career, and his father's probable celebration of the bullet he received in his back.

"How 'bout it?" Polak questioned.

Jakob pulled from his recesses.

"What happened?" O'Dell repeated.

"I disobeyed an order."

"What order?" Sperro asked.

"They execute you for refusing an order?" Spring interjected.

"Death by execution is a most common end to soldiers of the Reich," Jakob replied.

"What order?" Sperro demanded.

O'Dell flashed a palm. "It's okay, you don't have to answer. But, when we take ya back to headquarters, they'll interrogate the shit out of ya."

"Understood," Jakob said, resolute. "I shall tell them whatever they wish to know. It does not matter any longer. All is lost."

"I'm mighty interested in your expertise with the English language," O'Dell said. "Ain't never run across a Nazi who spoke English."

"I do not align with the Nazi party," Jakob shot back. "I am German, loyal to my country, my family, and my God, not Nazi ideology."

O'Dell shook off the comment. "I want to know the story behind your mastery of the English language, and without a hint of accent."

"I was born in the United States. My father attended university in New York, spending several years teaching English following the war. He accepted an instructorship in Berlin near my fifth birthday. I have read and studied English all my life."

"Where were you born?" Spring asked.

"Astoria, New York."

"Holy shit," Polak said. "You kidding? I'm from the Bronx."

"Practically neighbors," Jakob quipped.

"My folks came from Frankfurt. My father fought for the Kaiser in the Great War," Polak said.

"I had an uncle who served," Jakob said.

"Wow, what a coincidence," Polak said. He dropped a playful slap upon Sperro's shoulder. "Maybe they knew one another."

Sperro found little amusement in the exchange. "I'm not interested in his life story. I don't give a shit where he's from. He's a Nazi. I think we owe the men he's felled to treat him as the enemy he is. He gave us his rank and unit. Don't see a need to engage in lengthy conversation."

"Don't you find it amazing he's an American?" Polak asked.

Sperro pushed from off the ground. "He ain't no American."

"He's more American than you are, you dumb-ass dago," Polak said. "You weren't born in the States. I understand he's fighting for the wrong side, but we don't have to treat him like an animal."

"They're murdering our captured men. He doesn't deserve star treatment."

"Nobody's sayin' we give him the Bob Hope, but it's harmless to learn his history," Spring said.

"I don't want any part of it," Sperro said. "I agree with Shimmel. We don't have resource enough to take care of him."

"I didn't hear you offer to shoot him when you had the chance," Polak said.

"I ain't suggesting we kill him. I think we need to treat him how he and his kind would treat us."

"This man can't fend for himself, Angie," O'Dell said. "What d'ya suggest?"

"Leave him behind, like Shimmel suggested."

"He'll die," Spring said.

"So, he dies. You kidding me? Who knows how many of our boys this piece of shit put in the ground, and you're concerned with whether he lives or dies? Think of our boys who ain't going home? What about them?"

O'Dell lifted from his haunches. "He'll get his in the end. But ya can bet two bushels of wheat I'm gonna follow the book when it comes to prisoners of war."

"He's still a human being," Polak said.

"Then why don't the two of you rent a room," Sperro shot back.

"I'd rather share a bed with a Kraut than a fat, hairy Italian broad any day."

An animated scuffle ensued above the prisoner's position. O'Dell stepped in to separate.

Jakob lifted, and for the second time, stifled a charged exchange.

"I refused a direct order to kill a wounded American paratrooper."

The men separated. O'Dell settled to a knee. "What?"

"We engaged in a firefight. At its conclusion, officers ordered us into the fields to shoot those alive. I happened on a young American who had broken both legs. My superior ordered him shot, but I refused. I dropped my rifle. The officer pulled his weapon and shot the boy in the head and placed me under arrest."

"I don't believe it," Sperro said.

"I do not care if you believe me or not. I have killed no man. I spent the entire war firing my weapon into the ground. I do not believe in killing for an effort in conflict with my beliefs."

Jakob turned to O'Dell. "I, too, believe in life, Sergeant, whether friend or foe. I also have a conscience."

Polak reacted first to the rustling of branches overhead. Hansel slithered through the opening, gasping for breath. He spilled to the ground at O'Dell's feet.

"We ran into the whole damn German army. They're running around in all directions," he said, spitting saliva and blood. "They swamped Shimmel."

Chapter 21

"What do you mean, swamped?" O'Dell barked.

"Captured. We stumbled on a unit in total disarray. A second division came out of nowhere. Shimmel ordered us to make a break for the woods. I didn't see a way out without showing ourselves. We took off, but Shimmel ran opposite to draw their attention. He drew it all right. They jumped his ass in a blink, stripped him, and hauled him off."

"Where's Marty, Wick?"

"We lost track of each other. I'm telling ya, they're thick as mosquitoes out there. Advancing, retreating, moving sideways. I ain't seen such chaos before. At one point, we walked right past an advancing column. They didn't recognize us and kept going. I can tell you this, we're way the hell behind our enemy."

"Shit," O'Dell said, kicking at his medical bag. "And Neufchateau?"

"Didn't find a way. We'd have to trek way the hell south to avoid any trouble or fight all the way there."

"Ya hurt bad?"

"No, ran into a tree limb."

"Spring, take cover outside and stay sharp. Let me know if ya see Marty or Wick. I'll spell ya later."

"Yes, sir."

O'Dell pulled at a sleeve to expose his watch. He looked to Sperro. "We need to give them time."

"How much?"

"At least till dawn."

Shimmel provided a strategic advantage beyond O'Dell's capacity. Though complex and confounding, he held a unique talent for digging out of a hole when it counted most. He displayed the heart of a lion and an undeniable passion for the safety of his men.

"Damn it, Hansel, how the hell could ya let that happen?"

"Sorry. They cut us in half. Marty went one way, Wick the other. I hoped they'd work together to the rear and turn back. I covered and waited but never saw 'em again."

"Shit, it ain't your fault," O'Dell said. "What's the distance between us and this mess?"

"Eight, ten miles," Hansel said.

"Shimmel, that sonofabitch," O'Dell mumbled. "He rags my ass for trying to save a soldier, yet twice in the last three days he's put himself in harm's way on purpose. Speaking of getting your picture in *Stars and Stripes*. You reckon they killed him?"

"I don't know. When they grabbed him, one fella looked to run him through, but an officer barked something, and they all lowered their weapons. I guess, had they wanted to, they would've offed him right there. He didn't go without making a scene, though."

"Yeah, I bet not. I feel sorry for those poor slobs. They don't know who they're dealing with."

"Sarge," Hansel said, shaking his head, attempting to purge an inappropriate smirk. "You won't believe what he did."

"Yeah, try me."

"When they dragged him off, he broke loose, grabbed at a soldier walking in front of him and yanked his pants to the ground. The soldier stood there, bare-assed, stunned to the hilt, and Shimmel yells, 'Hey, Kraut, nice picture of your mother.'"

The men laughed.

"A Kraut popped him from behind, but two of them busted out, giving their boy the business. The last thing I saw, they dragged him into a half-track with him singing *When Johnny Comes Marching Home* at the top of his lungs. They popped him again, but it only changed his key."

"Hope they bound him because they're in a peck of trouble if they didn't."

Polak turned to O'Dell. "What now? Should we try to find Wick and Marty?"

"No. We'll give 'em some time to find their way back. You all need to rest. We'll figure it out later."

Polak helped Hansel to a far corner, where they settled against the foundation.

Sperro approached O'Dell. "You want I should take over for Spring? I'm not sleepy."

"Yeah, go ahead."

Sperro slithered up the embankment. Moments later, Spring returned, and on O'Dell's urging, settled down with the others to sleep.

O'Dell desired to close his eyes, certain his dreams would take him home. With two men fighting for their lives, and Shimmel in the clutches of the enemy, he guessed his mind would not allow such a luxury. Jakob released a grunt as he rolled over.

"How ya feeling?" O'Dell asked.

"As if I have a gaping hole in my chest."

"Does it hurt when ya breathe?"

"Yes, even when I think of breathing."

"Bullet nicked a lung. You're damn lucky it got ya on the right side."

"Lucky, right."

"You'd rather be dead?"

"A peace settled when I hit the valley. I prayed for a quick end and worked against men running to position nearer the shooters. I prepared myself to leave this mess behind. Now, I do not know. God spared me for some reason, I guess."

"I'll bet your family would appreciate knowing you're among the living."

"I do not know if I have a family. My mother sent a letter three years ago. I have not heard from her since."

"I hope ya find 'em all safe when this thing's over. Where's home?"

"Düren, Germany."

"Reckon I wouldn't know it if ya showed me on a map."

"How did you and your men land so far behind your lines?"

"Got caught in a push at Luxembourg on the edge of Hürtgen and ordered to Neufchateau. We scattered, lost contact with our group."

"Where do you call home?"

"Born in San Angelo, Texas. Traveled throughout the western states most of my youth, before settling in Pennsylvania."

"Are you a cowboy?"

"I ran cattle and plains horses. Earned extra dough at rodeos and auctions."

"A real, live cowboy," Jakob mumbled.

"Most would say I've spent more time in the saddle than on my feet."

"When I was little, my father took me to a few picture shows. I enjoyed Westerns most. Watching cowboys move herds of longhorns and mustangs under an infinite sky over miles of open land. I dreamed of becoming a cowboy. Dreamed of riding a horse from the plains to the Pacific Ocean."

The prisoner's comment caught O'Dell off guard. *How could a soldier of the Reich pine for such dreams?* His mind grew confused. The man did not figure for what he expected of a Nazi. *How could he remind me of me?*

"I have a horse," Jakob said, rolling onto his back. "Sascha. I have never known a kinder, gentler being."

"I have a black Arabian named Bella. Bought her at an auction in Colorado. Man said she did not respond to bridles. I had control of her with ten minutes' instruction. She's a sweet soul and a lifetime companion. Wouldn't trade her for all the gold in California. What breed do you own?"

O'Dell's question went unanswered. Jakob had fallen fast asleep.

O'Dell crossed his arms, stretched, and closed his eyes. *I wonder if friendship possible had we met under different circumstances?* Despite a troubled and worried mind, sleep grabbed hold, whisking O'Dell from the cold and damp burned-out barn to the lush valleys of his Allegheny homestead.

Chapter 22

Polak's incessant snoring pulled O'Dell from a deep sleep. His mind insisted the racket was a Messerschmitt crash landing on top of them.

With senses restored and the source of the disruption identified, he checked the time. Christmas Eve had arrived. The men remained asleep, though he did not understand how with Polak's snoring. Jakob stirred but did not wake.

"Hansel," O'Dell whispered. "Hansel."

Hansel's eyes flittered open. He wiped at his face, then pushed onto his knees.

"I need ya to relieve Sperro. Let me know if ya see or hear anything."

"Right," he whispered. "What time ya got?"

"Quarter past midnight. Go on now."

Hansel moved off. Within seconds, Sperro reappeared.

"Anything?"

"Nothing, other than a hell of a lot of action west of us. How long we gonna sit here, Sarge?"

"I'll give 'em until zero five thirty. If they ain't back, we'll head south and find a way to our lines. Go on, get some shuteye."

Sperro settled into the space vacated by Hansel, finding sleep within seconds.

O'Dell extracted a pencil and the last sheet of paper in his possession.

24 December 1944

My Dear Annalise,

I often wonder if you feel my presence when my dreams bring me home. Moments ago, I sat with you on the front porch swing, watching the sun dip below King's Peak. How complete I feel to hold your hand and feel your breath against my skin. How bitter I feel to wake and realize you're not at my side, but a million miles away. I don't know how or why I'm able to find sleep at all.

We received bad news today. The Germans captured Shimmel. He's not a man you can explain, but a damn fine soldier, and one I trust with my life. I'm here because he's saved me more times than I can count. His loss weighs on me. These men look to him for direction, leadership, and experience.

Now, they'll look to me. It's a damn hard thing to ask a fighting man to follow the commands of a medic. We must find a way back to our own side. Hansel found his way back. Westwick and Martel separated. We'll give them a few more hours before we head out.

I spoke to you before about our young prisoner. Turns out this fella speaks English for a good reason. He was born in New York, a town called Astoria. Can you believe it? He identified himself as Jacob Rudel. I think von Rudel, though I don't know what "von" stands for. I can tell you, he's a breathing contradiction. He's so unlike what we expect of our enemy. I made a point of calling him a Nazi, and he took great offense. It caught me by surprise. I don't know why I find it so strange. He seems a decent man, and possible friend, perhaps, in another place and time.

Maybe he's playing a game. I don't know, but feel confused as to the similarities between us, despite our coming from two different worlds with opposing ideals. He spent most of his life in Germany. Told me he'd seen Western pictures with his father as a boy, and since, has dreamed of riding the plains and running cattle. He spoke of his family and how he'd not heard from them in several years. He's uncertain he has family left. What a horrible reality to have no one. I feel a deep connection with him. Until I found you, I felt the same. I know the emptiness of having no one. Though an enemy, I pray he has a family to return to. Do you see what this madness has done? I have sympathy where sympathy should have no part.

I pray the war ends in days, rather than months or years, because the conflict rising inside my gut casts despair. I suspect some of our enemies wish to be cowboys, or settle down on a farm, marry, and have little ones to watch grow old. We're all of flesh and blood, dreams, and desires. How can we aim a weapon at one another, pull the trigger, and watch each other fall when similarities abound between us?

You'll find this hard to understand, as I did, but he suffered his wounds at the hands of his own troops. He says he refused to kill an injured American paratrooper. They marched him and several others into a valley and cut them down for treason. I've never heard of such. I've learned each life demands my best effort. I can't see myself harming another living creature, man or moth, the rest of my days. I'm afraid, my love, I've exhausted my last scrap of paper. I'll search for more once we return to our lines. I think of you by the second and count the hours until we're together. Mrs. Annalise, I'll love you till the day I die. Here's wishing you a Merry Christmas.

Yours, OD

"I stopped writing a year ago," Jakob said, surprising O'Dell. "I believe our mail service a ruse Herr Goebbels promotes so others may analyze morale, intent, and traitorous ideals. I do not believe my family received a single letter."

"It's a sad deal for a soldier not to receive letters from home. Our boys do a fine job with the mail. My wife has all but a couple, though censored to no end."

"I would find comfort knowing my mother and sister survived this mess."

"I can't imagine not hearing from my wife."

Jakob struggled but managed a roll onto his side. "Tell me about your family, your home."

O'Dell hesitated. He knew well the consequences of fraternizing with the enemy. He could not deny a feeling of mistrust but acknowledged a growing fascination for his prisoner's story. Curiosity convinced him any words shared between them would have little effect on the outcome of the war.

"Nothing out of the ordinary. I have a wife, a baby boy, and a farm in a little valley."

"Pennsylvania, correct?" Jakob interrupted.

"Right."

"I hoped one day to travel to Philadelphia. I developed a fascination for the American Revolution. I found a book on the subject in my grandmother's attic. Read it several times. I find the accomplishments of Benjamin Franklin fascinating."

O'Dell guessed Jakob knew more than he of America's fight for independence. "Never spent time there but hear tell it's an interesting place."

"Tell me about your farm."

"A place I find beyond heaven on earth. It's good for now, but I aim to add to it. Hope to have enough land to breed and train Arabians."

"Beautiful creatures, Arabians. I have a Holsteiner—Sascha. I rescued her from a farmer who intended to shoot her."

"Can't think of many things more disturbing than shooting a horse."

"Agreed. I cannot imagine life without her. Do you have siblings?"

"None I know of. Ma gave me up at birth. Never met my pa. Spent my youth in one orphanage after another. Took off at twelve to work on a ranch. The old rancher and his wife took me in."

"Seems a rough beginning."

"Ya learn to make your own way, learn to deal with alone."

"Do you find comfort in marriage?"

"Sure do. Reckon we're lucky, though she had it tough. She knew her parents before they died. Both killed in an automobile accident in Kansas City. She has an uncle living in Wellsboro. He never married and looked after her till she turned fifteen. He's the county sheriff there and a fine man. We're the same, her and I, bone for bone, and skin for skin. What about your family? You have a girl back home?"

An awkward pause ensued. Jakob's expression suggested either regret or disdain. He rubbed at a scar carved in the palm of his right hand.

"It's okay, ain't none of my business," O'Dell said.

"I do not envy you having never met your mother or spending most of your life alone," Jakob said, "but I do envy you never having met your father."

Chapter 23

"I had a girl once, Shana," Jakob said, summoning from memory the soft dimples of her cheeks, and when he drew near, how they deepened with the swelling of her smile. "I fell for her the moment I saw her."

The conversation turned public. Spring gazed wide-eyed, fighting an ever-growing confusion between his perception of a Nazi soldier and what their prisoner projected. Polak looked on with similar interest.

"One day, Sascha and I happened upon a glen. When we broke from the woods, I spotted her on the banks near a small stream with a book and pencil in hand. As we approached, she turned. I noticed she had a black eye. As I dismounted, my foot caught in the stirrup, and I hit the ground.

"She helped me to my feet, brushed off my coat, and erased my embarrassment with a wink. I cut my palm. She pulled her scarf and grabbed my hand. Her touch felt as if she had stroked me with a feather. We settled on a log near a stream. She soaked the scarf and cleaned my wound. Before we knew it, our conversation turned to life and living."

"How'd she get the shiner?" Polak asked.

"It took time, but she explained her injury," Jakob said.

"A backhand from her daddy?" Spring suggested.

Jakob shook his head.

"Who'd hit a girl?" Polak asked.

"A boy at her school," Jakob said.

"That sonofabitch wouldn't last a day in my school," Polak insisted.

"It's different here."

"What reason did he have to slug her?" Spring asked.

"You do not need a reason to accost a Jew in the Fatherland. The Reich promotes such behavior and rewards it, at least in the culture created by our great Führer. If you offer aid to any Jew, you, along with your family, can suffer unspeakable consequences, from public whippings and hangings to imprisonment or firing squads. The Nazis have established a rabid fear among the masses, a fear not seen since the days of the

Roman Empire. A fear so layered on so many fronts, control proved easy to obtain and manipulate across the populace."

"And we're supposed to believe a Kraut captured on the field of battle opposes Nazi doctrine?" Sperro said from the shadows.

Jakob turned. "And where do your people hail from?"

"Bologna, Italy," Sperro replied.

"Bologna. Capital of the Emilia-Romagna region."

"Yes. My family moved to America soon after my birth."

"Do you know Romagna's most famous son?"

Sperro did not respond. He well knew.

"Benito Amilcare Andrea Mussolini. I can assume, then, your family's loyalty to the National Fascist Party?"

"We are loyal citizens of the United States. Period."

"So, you are free to choose your political association, despite your roots."

"What's your point?"

"The point is your country of origin does not make you a loyalist to any one party, system, ideology, or faction. Every man chooses. I was born in America and raised in Germany. Not born a Nazi. Do you understand what it means to claim oneself a Nazi?"

Sperro said nothing. Jakob turned to Polak. "Do you, Private?"

"I can't even spell it."

"Nazis are made, not born. A Nazi accepts an ideology, as one accepts the ideologies of your Democratic, Republican, or Progressive parties. I have not heard you mention the expulsion of groups of peoples other than Jews considered dangerous, or the sterilization and euthanasia of individuals deemed deficient of mental faculty. You have limited views of Nazism. I support an opposite view."

"Yet, you fight on," Sperro said.

"I fight for my survival so I may attend to the long-term care of my family. I have not taken the life of a single combatant, nor will I, not in the name of a cause I do not believe in."

"So, you *are* a traitor," Sperro said.

"'I do nobody harm, I say none harm, I think none harm, but wish everybody good. If this be not enough to keep a man alive, in good faith, I long not to live...' Sir Thomas More," Jakob replied.

Sperro scratched at the side of his head, "Who?"

"Isn't he the painter?" Polak said.

"Sir Thomas More, a sixteenth-century English lawyer, philosopher, and statesman, executed by Henry the Eighth for refusing to recognize the king as head of church and state."

"What's that supposed to mean?" Sperro asked.

"I do not care what men think of me, provided I remain true to my conscience and my God. You may see me as a traitor, as do my countrymen, but I will not stray from my beliefs. I live my life for God, not mankind."

"Horseshit," Sperro said. "I don't believe a word. You're living your life for what you believe, meanwhile, your comrades butcher Jews and others, and you watch it happen."

"What have you done to eliminate the persecution of the Negro? Does there exist a more persecuted race than the Negro? Eighty years have passed since the ideologists of your nation abolished slavery, yet your government does not allow the Negro to fight alongside you. Why? As the Jew in Germany, the Negro in America suffers segregation in life, liberty, and happiness. Do *you* fight to correct such injustices?"

"Ain't got nothing to do with what you goons inflict on the Jews."

"Degrees of persecution matter little. Either a man knows freedom, or he does not. Every culture persecutes in one form or another. No race can claim innocence."

"I reckon your daddy didn't take to your Jewish girlfriend," O'Dell said.

Jakob broke from an intense stare-down with Sperro. He breathed deep and turned to O'Dell. "The day before I reported for duty, my father beat me. I had grown accustomed to his drunken outbursts, but this encounter proved different. I had not seen such rage in him.

"I met Shana two days before my departure to say goodbye. I knew we stood little chance of seeing one another again, let alone sharing our lives together. We had our moment in a room in the back of her father's shop. As I left her store, I could not help myself and kissed her on the cheek. An associate of my father witnessed it from across the street.

"I had hoped the beating ended it, but no. My father made sure the scars inflicted covered both body and soul."

"Your pop doesn't seem the father-of-the-year type," Polak jabbed.

"I left with father days later for the train station," Jakob said, his voice softening. "He mentioned I would see her before I left. I dismissed it as an attempt to further grind his heel into my wounds. I suspected something amiss when his driver turned opposite our destination. Once I gathered my bearings, dread consumed my gut. Before I could question him, we stopped near Shana's family's shop. SS officers lined the streets. A dozen empty troop trucks idled nearby. The SS swarmed each building, extracting Jews from their places of business.

"They hauled them out and separated families in the middle of the street. Soldiers pulled babies from their mothers' arms. Fathers chased in a panic, unsure of chasing wives or children. The SS punched, kicked, and beat the women and children, hauled off those unwilling to cooperate by the legs, arms, hair, anything they could grab. I have never witnessed such horror.

"They dragged Shana's mother by her hair, screaming. Shana's baby brother chased alongside. An officer sent him to the ground with a kick. The boy lay on the pavement, dazed, gasping for breath. When he attempted to stand up, the officer kicked him again. The boy fell face-first onto the pavement. The soldier took the butt of his rifle and drove into the boy's head, crushing it as if a melon. His legs kicked and jerked before falling limp. Shana's father struggled with his captor to attend his son. He launched an elbow. Another officer shot him in the head as Shana exited. She screamed and fell to her knees. A soldier grabbed her by the hair, punched her unconscious, and dragged her away."

"I can't imagine having to witness something so senseless, so evil," O'Dell said.

"Difficult to explain," Jakob continued, his words sluggish as if under a sedative. "It happened in the blink of an eye, yet it seems to have lasted an eternity. I remember my father's knuckles against the back of my neck and his hold of my collar. I guess I attempted to exit the vehicle but recall nothing other than his laughter."

Jakob replayed the multiple savage punches delivered to the side of Shana's head, and the tangled pain in his stomach at the vivid memory of her body falling limp. *How could any man allow hate to so manifest he would take pleasure in splitting the skull of a baby, or beating a defenseless girl unconscious, or deliver a bullet to the brain of a grieving father?*

"How did it all come to this?" Jakob whispered.

O'Dell's expression gave Jakob reason for pause. His enemy's eyes dripped with compassion. Had they been brothers, an embrace, if platoon-mates, a pat on the shoulder. Their status as foes allowed for one man to nod and the other accept, as would parting friends, with no words needed to cement their bond.

Jakob turned to Sperro. "Private, I do not subscribe to Nazi ideology, any more than you subscribe to Fascism. I will live the rest of my life with the guilt of sending my Shana to her grave due to a careless kiss. Character and actions alone define each man, not location of birth or the womb from which he sprung."

As the words escaped Jakob's lips, a helmet plopped through the pine branches, striking O'Dell's shin. Seconds later, Hansel slipped through the cover.

"Sarge, it's Wick and Marty."

Chapter 24

Westwick and Martel slithered into the hideout, caked in mud, and reeking of human waste. Blood dripped from Westwick's scalp. Martel rolled onto his back. A sizeable blood stain soaked through his pants at the knee.

O'Dell brought a hand over his nose. "What the hell did ya fellas get in to?"

"Kind of reminds you of home, hey, Sarge?" Polak asked.

"Horseshit doesn't smell as bad," O'Dell countered.

"It's a mess out there," Martel said. "Krauts scattered from here to hell and back. I ain't seen such chaos since Hürtgen."

"What happened?"

"Where's Hansel?" Westwick interrupted.

"I'm here, Wick."

"We figured you bought it. We tried to work toward you but hid in a ditch and waited to see what the Krauts did with Shimmel."

"You hurt?" O'Dell asked.

"We tumbled down a hillside into an abandoned latrine. I caught my knee on a stump and Wick clipped a rock. We're okay."

"Is Shimmel alive?"

"The last time we saw him, although he's a damn fool or the most fearless sonofabitch alive. He yanked down some Kraut's pants. I figured they'd kill him on the spot."

"Yeah, Hansel told us. I'd say he's one percent fool and ninety-nine percent fearless sonofabitch. What'd they do with him?"

"Loaded him in a carrier and took off north. On our way back we stumbled on a column of Tigers heading west. We entered a clearing and caught two Krauts loading supplies in a half-track and jumped 'em. We abandoned the track a half-mile south of here."

"Any direct route to Neufchateau?"

"Not the first damn one, unless you're prepared to tangle with the entire German army."

"I'd like to know where they're taking Shimmel," O'Dell said.

"I heard an officer say Linman or Lindham," Westwick said.

O'Dell turned to Jakob, "How 'bout it?"

"Limburg. Stalag 12-A. Sits southwest of Limburg midway to Deiz, eighty kilometers northwest of Frankfurt."

"What's the story?"

"A transit camp built for Russians captured on the Eastern front. They process and interrogate before distributing to other sectors, if the prisoners live long enough."

"How far ya reckon it is from here?"

"I do not know where *here* is."

The men noticed a change in O'Dell's expression. They knew the look. Jakob surmised a foolish strategy brewing. "Angie, you still have the map?"

Sperro contemplated offering a lie. O'Dell repeated the question.

"What the hell's on your mind?" Westwick asked.

"I want to see the map of this area."

"Why?" Sperro asked.

"To pinpoint our exact location."

"As it relates to Bastogne or Limburg?"

"Do you have the goddamn map or not?" O'Dell shouted.

Sperro retrieved the many-times folded relic from an inside pocket.

"Over there," O'Dell said, pointing to a slab of fieldstone. "Spread it out."

O'Dell approached with a flashlight. He aligned the map to a small compass. "Here," he said, pointing to an area northwest of Luxembourg and northeast of their rally point. He drew the limited beam of the flashlight east. Sperro pointed to Frankfurt. "How far, ya reckon?"

"A hundred and fifty kilometers seems about right," Sperro said.

"Yeah, and Bastogne is a third the distance," Hansel said.

"Right, but there's no direct route," Westwick said. "I'm telling you, the Krauts pushed all they got. It's not one or two divisions running amok."

"So, we have no way out?" Sperro asked.

"I ain't saying that, but we'd have a better chance walking into Berlin."

"So, we sit here and rot?" Polak asked.

O'Dell shook his head. "I don't think so. We sit here, we die."

"What the hell do you have in mind?" Hansel asked.

O'Dell brushed shoulders with Polak as he pushed past. Halfway across the bunker, he turned, looked to each man, and said, "I wanna go after him."

Had the Führer himself entered the hideout, O'Dell doubted he'd see a different look about his men's faces.

Following a lengthy standoff, Sperro broke the moment to express what the others were thinking. "No way. No way in hell," he said.

"Let me remind ya fellas of a few points," O'Dell started. "We ain't got ammo enough to fend off a pack of squirrels or food enough to last the next hour. We ain't got medical supplies enough, and don't tell me I wasted them on the prisoner, because we had scraps to begin with. To attempt Bastogne means breaking through lines naked, dodging mortars and bullets of our own boys with no way to communicate because we ain't got a radio. I'm tired of this shit-hole barn. I want to move out, no matter the direction."

O'Dell paused to catch his breath. "Shimmel saved my life a dozen times for sure. He's risked his life for each man in this unit multiple times. I ain't saying he's a saint, and I ain't saying he's always right. I'm saying he's risked his life for me and I'm ready to return the favor."

"You both 'bout killed each other over this prisoner," Polak reminded.

"You have brothers Joe, right?"

"Three."

"Ever fight any of 'em?"

"Sure. Plenty of times."

"Would you take a bullet for 'em?"

Polak absorbed O'Dell's point and looked away.

"We're brothers, fellas. We might argue and throw a few punches, but when it counts, we take care of each other. Shimmel needs us."

Sperro let go a sarcastic huff. "What the hell we supposed to do, walk into a prison camp and ask for our boy like it's the YMCA?"

"What's the difference if we're fighting at Neufchateau," Hansel said, "or going after Krauts at a prison camp? We still don't have the hardware."

"We may not have much, but the Krauts do," Westwick said.

"What?" Sperro asked.

"There's equipment and supplies in the half-track. I don't know what's in there, but I saw a couple tripods and several crates. I suspect we'll find ammo, small arms, food—"

"Wait," Hansel interrupted, "I don't give a shit if we find every small arm and keg of sauerkraut the Germans ever made. The fact is, six guys ain't gonna storm a POW camp and extract a prisoner."

"Right," Sperro agreed. "Who knows how many guards we'll be up against. Hell, the war might be over by the time we find the damn place."

"If we have access to arms, I say we head for Bastogne as soon as possible," Hansel said. Sperro agreed.

"You boys have a short memory," a timid voice chimed. "You're forgetting all Corporal Shimmel has done for us."

"What the hell are you talking about, Spring?" Sperro snapped. "Ain't nobody forgot what he's done or meant to this unit. But there's a time for sticking your neck out, and a time to cover your ass."

"Right," Spring said, "but *you're* rotting for sure on the outskirts of Hosingen if not for him. He didn't give a hang for his life when he took out the 20-millimeter. The Krauts had you dialed in. I think we owe him an effort. You sure as hell owe him an effort."

"Hey, up yours," Sperro barked. "I haven't asked anyone to risk their life for me."

"Me either," Hansel agreed.

"It's why we need to do this," Spring fired back.

"None of us asked, but Shimmel did it anyway," O'Dell said. "Placed his own life at risk more times than all of us combined because he gave a shit. How did you feel, Angie, when he ran into the field and blew the cannon team to hell with that bazooka?"

"I don't understand the issue," Sperro said. "He'll become a POW and sit out the rest of the war. Can't say I wouldn't mind doing the same."

"You're wrong," O'Dell said. "He won't have a prayer." He turned to Jakob. "Does he?"

Jakob thought for a moment, then said, "They took him prisoner to make an example of him. They will never allow a Jewish soldier to live to fight another day. They will do things to him one would not do to a hog, and for all to see."

Sperro fidgeted several moments. "Okay, I owe Shimmel my life. I guess it doesn't matter much. We stay here, we die. We head for our lines, we probably die. We storm a prison camp, well? What the fuck difference does it make if we die trying to reach Bastogne or save the corporal?"

"You're crazy, Angie," Martel said. "It's suicide."

"I figured I committed suicide the day I set foot in Fort Bragg."

"How 'bout it, Wick?" O'Dell asked.

"I don't know, Sarge. I guess if I'm gonna buy it, I might as well buy it trying to save one of my own."

"All bullshit," Martel said. "This has nothing to do with Shimmel, but everything to do with this push, and our boys getting the hell kicked out of them in the opposite direction."

"What if we find Shimmel before they reach the camp?" O'Dell asked.

Following several moments of silence, Martel conceded. "I think it's FUBAR, but I'll go where Hansel goes."

"How 'bout you, Polak?" O'Dell asked.

"I'll go where the rest of you go."

"How 'bout it, Hansel?"

He shook his head. "I ain't abandoning my unit. You want to take a trip to the grave trying to save him, I'll die with you."

"So, what now?" Spring asked.

"How about a plan?" Hansel suggested.

"Or a miracle," Polak added.

"Got to inventory the supplies," O'Dell said.

"No matter what we find, how do we invade a POW camp?" Hansel asked.

O'Dell's medical mind did not operate in the world of tactical strategy. Shimmel would've had a plan before they located Limburg on a map. How could he expect the men to follow when he couldn't lead?

"A hundred miles to hoof," Polak said. "We ain't done a similar stretch since boot. It's at least a two-day hike."

"Three, if you count the time hunkered in the brush," Martel added.

"We can't march the distance," Westwick said, "not in our condition."

"Who says we have to hoof it?" Spring asked. "Can't we take the half-track?"

"Great idea," Hansel scoffed. "Why don't we find us a fuckin' marching band to follow along behind. What the hell? The squeal of the track will bring every Kraut on this continent."

Jakob grunted. "You will not travel far in the track yourselves."

"Who asked you?" Martel yelled, pushing through the men to kick a clump of earth in Jakob's direction. "You keep your goddamn mouth—"

"Shut the hell up, Marty," O'Dell interrupted. He moved through the men to take a knee at Jakob's side. "What are you talking about?"

"I can drive the track and take you to the camp, but it will require at least two of you to surrender."

Chapter 25

"What a laugh," Martel said. "Surrender to you?"

"Zip it, Marty," O'Dell ordered. "You familiar with the camp?"

"Yes," Jakob said.

"What the hell do we care?" Martel said. "He ain't going with us."

"How do you know the camp?"

"I led a transport of Russian prisoners from the Eastern Front."

"When?"

"Eight months ago."

"Know it well enough to you find your way around?"

"Yes."

"Can you find a way in and out with our man?"

"I can take you there, but my presence would place you in jeopardy, as my father frequents the camp."

"Say, what the hell is this?" Martel charged. "You guys talk to this Kraut as if he's one of us."

Polak laughed. "I have news for you, brother, he is. Born in New York."

"What? Bullshit."

"It's true, Marty," Spring said. "Born in New York. Moved to Germany."

"I don't buy it."

"For Christ's sake, Marty," Polak said, "you were born in France. My family's from Bavaria. What the hell's the difference?"

"I ain't a Nazi, that's the difference. I don't give a shit if he popped out at the foot of Mount Rushmore, he's still a Nazi."

"No, he's not," Spring added.

"What the hell's the matter with you guys. He's a goddamn Nazi."

"He ain't a Nazi," O'Dell said. "The SS marched a bunch of their own into the valley for execution. He refused to shoot a downed American paratrooper."

"Bullshit," Martel said.

"He has no reason to lie," O'Dell argued. "He could have sat there and played dumb and said nothing, all the while knowing our intentions."

Spring interrupted. "At Hürtgen, a patrol captured a couple Germans, and I'll tell ya, they were damn happy to surrender. They spoke English, though not as fluent as our guy. Said the SS forced them to fight. Said they'd kill their families if they didn't."

"You're all crazy for believing this," Martel insisted.

"He had no reason to lie or speak at all," O'Dell said. "Ya have any idea the advantage he'd have on us? Could've caught us with our pants down any time he wanted. Besides, he can take us where we need to go."

"Yeah, he'll take us there and turn us over. What the hell ever gave you the notion you can trust the enemy?"

Martel grabbed O'Dell's coat sleeve. His expression softened. "Listen, they raped and slaughtered my sisters and their children, for no other reason than because they could. How can you have compassion for this asshole?"

The crimes the Nazis had piled up against humanity gnawed and clawed at O'Dell's sense of moral obligation. The horrors Martel and Shimmel suffered begged for a bullet to the prisoner's head. No one would question it. O'Dell held to faith Jakob's life was worth saving. He felt a link he could not rationalize.

He pondered the tug of war between right, wrong, and indifferent. Any courtesy offered the prisoner must feel to Martel as a bayonet rammed into his chest. O'Dell believed Jakob a decent man caught in an impossible circumstance.

"Archie, I'm sorry. I can't imagine having to live with such pain. But this man had nothing to do with those murders. His countrymen did, but he didn't. It begins and ends there. We gotta hold the individual man responsible. Hell, we've had our own troops court-martialed for raping and killing civilians. We ain't accountable for those transgressions, and he ain't accountable for what those men did to your family or Shimmel's.

"I've spent my life surviving one day at a time," O'Dell continued. "I learned to trust my own instincts, learned fast and hard to trust a man by the look in his eyes. I've looked deep into this man's eyes and see truth and decency. He has no reason to lie. I'd bet my life on it. Ya want to avenge your family's deaths, but how much killing will satisfy you? Where does it end?"

Martel turned to Hansel, a man he knew hated Nazis as much, if not more. "What do you say, Dan?"

"Marty, you missed out on this guy's story. I didn't believe it at first, but I believe he speaks the truth. We're all accountable for our own actions. Plenty of fellas back home refused to join the war because they didn't believe in it. Hell, even Charles Lindbergh spoke against our getting involved. I can't imagine every German in Germany agrees with Nazi doctrine. It's not possible. Just as it's not possible every American believes in this war."

"So, you trust him?"

"I trust his story and agree with O'Dell he had no reason to lie. He surrendered one hell of an advantage. Besides, we can kill him anytime we like, and there's not a damn thing he can do to stop us."

Martel turned to Jakob. "I'd like to see every one of you dirty bastards swing from the end of a rope. So help me God, you make one false move or put these men in harm's way, I'll kill you dead and won't think twice of it."

"I am ashamed for what happened to your family and feel your loss," Jakob said.

"You don't know my loss. My sisters, nieces, and nephews, all butchered. You don't know shit."

"And I lost the love of my life to those same men. My pain is equally real, whether you acknowledge it or not."

"You'll never convince me you desire to save an enemy combatant."

"Your sergeant saved my life. He believes your corporal is worth saving. It is important to him. Now it is important to me. I owe him a debt of war."

"Well, I sure as hell ain't surrendering to you, von Strudel," Martel mumbled as he walked away.

"I meant it in a figurative sense. My name is von Rüdel."

"Yeah, well, I said von Strudel. What the fuck you gonna do about it?"

"Knock it off, Marty," O'Dell said. "What do you mean, surrender?"

Jakob pointed to Polak. "Private, *sie sprechen Deutsch, richtig?*"

"What did he say?" O'Dell asked.

"Asked if I spoke German," Polak replied. "*Ja, aber nicht flüssig.*"

"*Genug, um zu wissen und allgemeine Fragen zu beantworten?*"

Polak smiled. "If they don't expect a long, drawn-out answer, or need me to figure a mathematical calculation."

"Anyone else speak German?" Jakob asked.

To the men's surprise, Martel raised his hand.

"What the hell, Archie? Is *der Führer* the uncle in your family no one speaks of?" Polak jeered.

"I learned from my grandmother... shit." He looked to the ground and kicked at the dirt.

Polak slapped his shoulder. "It's okay. It goes to prove a little German blood doesn't make you a Nazi."

"So, we need a plan," O'Dell said.

Jakob maneuvered into a sitting position. "Your chances of getting in exceed those getting out. We need an inventory of supplies to determine what we can carry on foot, as the camp sits northwest of the Rhine. I doubt we will find an unoccupied bridge to cross. Also, we must find three additional uniforms, four if possible, and you will have to decide which of you shall pose as prisoners."

Chapter 26

O'Dell pushed through the pine to investigate conditions. A biting wind swirled snow from all directions, reducing visibility to thirty yards. Low-hanging, blackish gray clouds churned along. They'd have to fight through another day's worth of accumulation.

"It's getting ready to dump out there, boys," he said.

Hansel joined O'Dell for a peek. "Should we wait and travel by night?"

"I don't know. What do you think?" O'Dell said, deferring to Jakob.

"I don't believe it matters. If we leave now, at least we can react to what lies ahead. We can count on checkpoints, day or night."

"Okay. Wick, you, Hansel, and Spring inventory the track. If ya find any food, send some back."

"Why don't I drive the damn thing back here?" Wick suggested.

"Too risky. Keep low and quiet. If ya see anything, get the hell back as quick as ya can. I don't aim to lose anyone else."

"Right. Spring, Hansel, on me." The men collected their gear and slithered up the embankment and out into the frozen morning.

"How ya reckon we're gonna handle those checkpoints?" O'Dell asked.

"We should pass if we have the men in the right positions. Private Polak, you serve as guard in charge. Position nearest the tailgate. Private Martel should sit opposite."

"Any strategy as far as prisoners go?" O'Dell asked.

"Sperro, for certain, and Spring, with his red hair. In the event we take fire, who would you rather see in possession of a weapon, you or—"

"Hansel," O'Dell said, interrupting. "He's by far the best weapons man. If all hell breaks loose, he's the one."

"You sit in front with me, and Private Hansel will sit in the rear."

"I have a question, von Strudel," Martel snapped. "Suppose we have to engage, what side you choosing?"

"Would you have me fire upon my countrymen when I have not fired upon yours?"

"I want to know if I should be in front or behind you."

"Enough, Marty," O'Dell said. "We ain't got time for this."

"I guess you will have to trust me, Private."

"That'll be the day."

"What if we're stopped and asked for papers? What then?" Sperro asked.

"We should not require papers," Jakob said.

"Why the hell not?"

"*Betrieb Trauer* will serve as our passport."

"What?" O'Dell asked.

"Operation Grief," Polak translated.

"A ruse to generate confusion and paranoia behind Allied lines," Jakob said. "The scheme creates false orders to disrupt communications, misdirect troop movement, and secure bridges. Hitler sent orders in October requesting Allied and British equipment, uniforms, and troops knowledgeable of American and British dialects. They trained to pose as Allied personnel."

"I heard a similar tale last month," Polak said. "A fella said they caught Germans swiping MP uniforms at a supply depot."

"American uniforms would benefit in the capturing of bridges," Jakob said.

"How do you know?" Sperro asked.

"High command tasked my father to teach the operational brigade English and British slang, proper over-the-air communications, and other organizational aspects of the U.S. Army. Insignia identification, rank structure, drill, and cultural techniques."

"Why did they pass on you for this mission?" O'Dell asked.

"They did not. I was in transit when engaged in the firefight and, well, you know the rest."

"So how does this scheme help us?"

"I can convince checkpoints of the operation and our transporting of captured prisoners. Men involved in this operation do not carry papers."

"Your boys don't send prisoners to camps, they kill 'em," Sperro pointed out.

"When we inform them of captured American medics, they will let us pass. We lack rear medical personnel."

"What a sneaky, shitty operation," Sperro said.

"In desperate times, armies undertake desperate measures. Our men take on this assignment aware of the consequences if captured. Each army carries out their own forms of espionage."

"I haven't heard of us stealing German uniforms."

"You must recognize your armed forces have strayed from the rules of war to obtain an advantage."

"All I'm saying is, I don't recall hearing us stealing uniforms or shooting prisoners of war."

"At an aid station earlier this year, my unit awoke to find two medical officers' throats slit," Jakob said. "The assailants achieved their intent, as it sent a wave of terror throughout the ranks. Articles of the Geneva Convention prohibit the killing of medical personnel, but rules of war did not stop your men."

"How do you know our guys had a hand?"

"They caught an American soldier the next night attempting to repeat."

"What'd they do to him?"

"What would you do if you caught a German slitting the throats of your medical personnel?"

Sperro let go a deep, annoyed sigh, having grown tired of walking into his enemy's points.

"I'm not sure about this," O'Dell said. "I ain't comfortable with a bunch-full of maybes. They ask a question of one of us who don't know German from Greek, and we've had it."

"Checkpoints between here and Frankfurt will know of the operation and directives of the mission, which includes those involved not speak in native tongue. We have no other choice without proper documentation."

Sperro's and Martel's attention turned toward the entrance. Hands clutching a medium-sized wooden box pushed through the pine, followed by the rest of Private Spring. He slid headfirst, coming to rest at Polak's feet. He scrambled upright to offer O'Dell the box.

"K-rations," Spring said.

"What the hell are they doing with our food?" Sperro questioned.

"We found twenty-four boxes."

The men turned to Jakob.

"Your planes often miss their drop zones. You have supplied us more than the Reich."

"And we're famished," Martel said.

"Would you have us return them? The canned meat you can have, but American cigarettes are worth their weight in gold."

Sperro grabbed the crate from Spring's hand. "I could eat a truckload of canned meat."

"What else did ya find?" O'Dell asked.

"Weapons. Ours, theirs, four boxes of potato mashers, two heavy machine guns, but no ammo, yet."

"Okay, finish up. Return as quick as ya can."

Sperro cracked open the crate with the butt of his rifle. He tossed two boxes to each man. The men ripped at the containers as children would presents on Christmas Day. Polak brought a cigarette to his lips. Martel went for chocolate bars. Sperro, cans of meat.

O'Dell's stomach churned, but not for the want of food. He approached Jakob and knelt at his side, offering a K-ration. With his men engaged in a food swap-fest, he leaned in close and said in a whisper, "Ya think I'm crazy?"

"Look what our world has become and define crazy to me."

O'Dell paused. "Yeah, I reckon you're right. Ya don't have to do this, though."

"Nor do you. You owe another man. I owe you. You repay your corporal, and I repay you. Men are made and civility achieved with such actions. I do not think this crazy."

"You're taking an awful big chance."

"No bigger chance than refusing to put a bullet in your countryman's head."

O'Dell could not grasp how a man so tied to a philosophy hell bent on the eradication and systematic expulsion of an entire people could stand on such moral principle and convince others of it. "No one would ever believe this," O'Dell said.

Jakob let slip a boyish grin. "Are you scared?"

"I guess fear can force a fella to go against conventional wisdom."

Jakob bit into a cracker. "I fear no more, nor the end. I believe our end on this earth triggers the true beginning of life."

"I feared death, but no more. My biggest fear, I guess —"

"Sarge," Westwick yelled through the pine, "heavy equipment moving all around us. If we're going, we need to go right now."

Chapter 27

"Ain't no way in hell he's gonna make this trip," Sperro said, taking the brunt of Jakob's dead weight as he worked to regain strength lost from many hours of inactivity.

"He's gotta make it. We don't make the camp without him."

"I will make it," Jakob insisted between quick gasps. "This will pass."

"Holes in chests don't pass," Sperro said.

"Joe, Marty, round up the gear and prepare to move out," O'Dell said. "Don't leave one damn thing behind. Wick, take the men outside and organize."

Jakob staggered forward and leaned against Sperro to gather his balance. He turned slow and stiff-necked.

"Wait 'til ya hit that first bump," O'Dell said.

"You get me to the track, I will get you to the camp."

"Yeah, right," Sperro said.

"I'll take him out, Angie. Take over for Wick. We'll need him on point. I'm right behind ya."

O'Dell inspected what remained of the medical supplies. He checked his pockets to ensure security of his personal items and letters home. He slipped the medical bag over his neck. "We step outside, there ain't no goin' back. You sure you want to do this thing?"

He turned to find Jakob sizing up the embankment leading out.

"We're ready up here," Sperro said, extending an arm.

O'Dell placed a hand on Jakob's shoulder. "I appreciate the chance you're taking. Ain't no one gonna believe this."

"All worth it if we meet your objective and I find my family."

"You hold up your end, I'll see to it you get home. You have my word."

O'Dell pushed, Sperro pulled. Jakob's pain-filled moan made both men cringe. Upon extraction, Jakob lay prone in the snow, wishing the bullet had clipped an area less critical to mobility. He breathed deep in the biting wind. The clean air felt a welcomed respite, despite the frigidness penetrating his body to the marrow. Sperro extended a hand. Another pain-filled tug brought Jakob upright.

"All right, boys," O'Dell said, "Wick has the point. Take it slow and keep low. We're on hand signals 'til we make the track. I'll bring up the rear. Don't forget about us. Let's go."

Westwick jumped on a line a little west of due south. Polak, Martel, and Sperro fell in behind. O'Dell slung Jakob's arm around his neck.

"I can manage," Jakob said, pulling away.

O'Dell redirected Jakob's arm. "We ain't got time to just manage."

The group slogged over the bumpy terrain and around gatherings of trees spared the ravages of mortar fire. O'Dell kept a nervous watch.

They gained a visual of the track upon exiting a tree line at the opposite end of a meadow. Westwick stalled their progress after spotting Hansel honed on a target to their right flank.

"What is it, Wick?" O'Dell whispered, having caught up.

"Hansel's on to something. Can't see what he's looking at."

A low, metal-on-metal grind pushed through the breeze, igniting the men's anxiety.

"It's a tank, or tanks," Sperro said.

"Coming or going?" O'Dell asked.

"Away from us, I think," Wick said.

"Those are not Tigers," Jakob insisted. "Engine pitch is too high."

Westwick ripped a whistle. Hansel turned and waved them forward, signaling to keep low.

"I don't give a shit their direction," Sperro said. "We need to move."

O'Dell ordered Sperro to assist Jakob. The men hustled in double time across terrain spotted with boulders. Martel dropped near Hansel to cover.

O'Dell met Spring behind the track. "How 'bout the supplies?"

"Plenty of food."

"Any left?" O'Dell said, pointing to an area littered with K-ration packages.

"Yes, sir, ten crates."

"Firearms, ammunition?"

"Two boxes of M1s with five hundred clips, a box of Lugers and rounds, four boxes of potato mashers, three boxes of Russian rifles with rounds, and two tripods with sixty belts of 250 rounds each, give or take."

"Jesus, more firepower than we've had in the last six months," Sperro observed.

"What else?" O'Dell asked.

"Blankets, binoculars, boots, a box of spades, two boxes of German rations, twelve containers of fuel, and this." Spring pointed to a case of schnapps.

"With a couple bottles missing," O'Dell said.

"We didn't drink them, Sarge, honest."

"We save these for later. You see to it we have four unopened until I say we crack 'em."

"We found uniforms, too."

"How many?"

"Five."

"Two of those belong to the men we took out," Westwick said. "We stripped them after we dragged them into the woods."

"Full of holes, huh?"

"We didn't shoot 'em."

"Joe, Marty, find yourself a uniform. Grab one for me and Jakob."

"Wait a minute," Martel said. "You give him the right uniform and you can kiss our asses goodbye."

"What the hell you talking about?"

"He can give an order at any checkpoint and have us taken out. You won't know what the hell he's saying."

"Yeah, I know," O'Dell said, turning to Jakob.

Jakob's expression mimicked the look of a doomed man whose final words had fallen deaf upon the ears of those gathered for his execution. O'Dell conceded to his gut instinct and summoned Hansel and Polak to the rear of the vehicle. He turned to Spring and ordered, "Load me up a Luger." Spring delivered.

"I won't put the life of anyone in the hands of a lying sonofabitch," O'Dell growled. "A man looks ya in the eye and gives ya insight, and ya either believe him or you don't. I've lived on the edge of truth my entire life. I know a liar when I see one. I know it in my soul, what's left of it, anyway. I say we can trust this man. Anyone who disagrees, well, I won't stand in your way." O'Dell tossed the loaded Luger to Martel.

"Go ahead, Marty, shoot him. Put a bullet in his head for what those bastards did to your family. Make him pay for it. You wanna be a goddamn hero and avenge your family, here's your chance."

Several moments passed as Martel looked to his mates. "I don't own your keen sense for the truth, Sergeant, but I'll let this play out as you wish." He tossed the Luger at O'Dell's feet.

Polak stepped forward. "Anybody else?"

O'Dell collected the weapon. "I don't have the first right to ask y'all to risk your life this way, but we're alive because Shimmel saw to it. We owe him an effort, and this man can take us there. I gave him his chance to step away from this. He declined. We're all in this together now. Let's pack up. Take the rations, M1s, grenades, ammo belts, a tripod, and the fuel, for sure. Leave the rest behind."

As they loaded the final container of fuel, Hansel honed on a ghostly mass emerging from the forest at the opposite end of the meadow. "Holy shit, holy shit," he bellowed, as pines cracked and the guttural hum of a diesel broke through the winter gust.

"He's turning, Sarge. He's turning to fire."

Chapter 28

"Move it... move it... move it." O'Dell yelled.

A flash from the tank's muzzle coincided with his plea. The men scrambled toward the track. The first shell whizzed overhead, splintering trees beyond.

"Marty, help Jakob into the cab and fire this damn thing up."

Sperro and Polak set up cover. Hansel, Spring, and Westwick stowed the remaining supplies. The tank fired again. The shell exploded a stone's throw to their rear.

The half-track burst to life, belching thick smoke. O'Dell grabbed a pair of binoculars and steadied his focus as the tank pushed from the forest.

"Oh, shit, oh, shit. Don't fire boys, it's ours." O'Dell slapped Sperro and Polak on their helmets. "Let's go."

Polak scrambled to his fee. "What the hell are they doing so far behind the lines?"

"Lost, like us," Sperro yelled.

O'Dell rushed to the passenger side and climbed in. Another shell exploded to his front right, sending clods of earth across the windshield and shrapnel pinging against the cab's front panel. He ordered Jakob to bury the accelerator.

Jakob thrust the gearshift forward. The track bucked and groaned, sending the men in back smashing against the cab wall. Another shell whistled overhead, turning trees into toothpicks. With the vehicle lurching, Jakob searched the tree line for a space to duck through. He passed a small rise to where the landscape fell forward into a valley, providing momentary cover. A shell exploded near the exact position they vacated.

O'Dell pointed to a break fifty yards forward, prompting Jakob to maneuver a wide arc to take the opening head on. A final shell exploded well to their front.

Jakob navigated a half mile through the forest, zigzagging in and around saplings and underbrush until the protective cover thinned to merge with a narrow meadow. He pointed to a road north of their position.

O'Dell ordered Jakob to stop, but to keep the engine running. They agreed each man's duty needed final definition.

"Everyone out," O'Dell ordered. "Spring, grab them German uniforms."

O'Dell stripped free of his jacket and pants. "Sperro, Spring, and Wick will pose as prisoners. Polak and Martel will sit opposite near the tailgate, Hansel in a position near the cab. If we come to a checkpoint, let Polak do the talking."

Jakob cringed as Sperro helped stuff his right arm into a German field coat one size too small. "When stopped, they will check the back," Jakob insisted. "You prisoners keep quiet, your hands behind your backs, heads down, no eye contact between yourselves, the guards in the truck, or those on the ground. Guards, keep your weapons aimed at the prisoners. If you feel a situation tensing, offer a bottle of schnapps."

O'Dell completed the exchange of uniforms. Donning German colors sent waves of traitorous angst rippling through his psyche. Jakob secured the final button of the heavy gray bloodstained jacket.

O'Dell looked to each man. "Questions, anyone?"

"*Sieht aus, als koennten Sie schiessen, Sie Scheisskerl,*" Polak said.

O'Dell discounted the smart-ass smirk on Polak's face. He turned to Jakob for translation.

"He called you a prick. Said you look good enough to shoot."

The men laughed. "Again, what happens if all hell breaks loose?" Martel asked.

"I will not fire upon my countrymen," Jakob said. "I will not fire upon any man, as I will remain unarmed. If your mission requires you to defend yourself, you do what you must do."

"Fair enough," O'Dell said. "Be damn sure to keep your emotions in check, Marty. No one fires unless fired upon. Understood?"

O'Dell stuffed a Luger between his coat and belt. "All right, take your positions."

The terrain ahead, littered with deep crevasses and exposed stone, proved a rough go, but the slope enhanced the vehicle's pace. Fog worked in concert with snowfall, limiting visibility to less than fifty feet.

"I reckon you're looking forward to getting home," O'Dell said at one point, snapping a miles-long silence.

"I see it in my mind, but not as I once had."

"Time can change everything. So, what ya gonna do? You're a man without a military and a country."

"I do not know. If my father knows of my transgressions, which he must by now, or thinks I am alive, he will use all means to hunt me down."

"Your daddy's one peach of a guy. How did ya fall so far from his tree?"

Jakob slowed the track to a crawl as the road snaked along a wooded boundary. "I knew him as a gentle, loving man, once. In his opinion, the whole of Europe accused the Fatherland of the Great War, its people victimized and manipulated by non-Aryans. His disgust turned into a hate I cannot rationalize. My mother believed he fell in with the wrong group of people at the right time."

"What options do you have?"

"Once this ends, legitimate Germans will rise from the ashes and restore our country's honor. I fear it may take a lifetime longer than mine to achieve and have conceded my future lies somewhere beyond my own border. I see myself mounting Sascha and riding as far as she can take us."

"I can't imagine having to flee my country, but a man sure could get lost in the western states."

O'Dell checked the compass. The needle confirmed their continued northwesterly route. He settled against his seatback. Visibility improved.

"I woke last evening and noticed you reading a letter," Jakob said. "I did not look on long, as I gathered it a private moment. I saw much emotion in your eyes. I no longer know the pleasure. Would you read the letter, if not too private?"

The letter proved the most private received in all O'Dell's years of service, and the one he kept on his person. He lost count the number of times he read it, the times it pushed him onward, kept his mind right, and motivations piqued to survive.

He appreciated the impact letters from home had on a man at the front lines. His memory was packed full of soldiers searching their persons for letters as their lives ebbed. He found it more common to pry a private letter out of the hands of a dead soldier than a weapon of war. A letter from home meant everything to the fighting man.

O'Dell often read his letters to men not as fortunate. Their eyes affixed as he detailed Annalise's sweet reflections and images of their homestead. This letter, however, had not known public confession.

O'Dell slid a hand into his boot. He appreciated Jakob's circumstance and acknowledged the worth if the letter provided an ounce of solace. He relocated to his lap a wallet-sized black-and-white photo of Annalise extending their son above her head. He cleared his throat. "Second of September 1942...."

My Dearest Darling,

I pray this letter finds you safe, warm, and out of harm's way. I so worry of your whereabouts, and if you'll receive this. Newsreel reports paint a most grim picture of what our boys face each day. I'm counting the seconds when our lips may touch.

I must admit, my darling, this is the most difficult letter I've written in my life, and one I hope you'll understand. I value your life beyond measure. Without you, I have nothing. Without you, I'm empty. I pray your heart forgives me for what I'm about to reveal. The truth is, my love, you're the proud father of a healthy baby boy. He arrived this morning.

I beg your forgiveness, sweetheart, for I knew of my condition the day you left for boot camp. Though I guessed it as such a few days prior to your departure, I so desired to tell you, but wanted you to concentrate and learn what you needed to learn to survive. Also, my mother's family has a history of stillbirths. If I'd told you of my pregnancy, I feared for your distraction. Had it gone poorly, I feared for your mental state. The decision not to tell felt as a noose around my neck, yet my heart convinced I made the right one.

You have a healthy, happy son awaiting his father's return. I have not yet named him and will not, until you return. He's the most amazing creature I've ever seen. He has your eyes and chin and already displays the patience I've so grown to love about your personality. I can't wait for you to hold him.

My darling, please understand my reasons to withhold this from you. You may think this a cruel and selfish betrayal, but I beg for your understanding. I'll try to send a picture in my next letter. In the meantime, please stay safe and promise you'll not take any unnecessary chances. All my love until we meet again.

Yours, Annalise

P.S. I received a letter from Patricia Friday last. Johnny Montgomery died on an island in the Pacific. My God, what will she do without him? Please, sweetheart, come home to me.

Jakob maintained a paralytic gaze forward, his heart overflowing with emotion and his mind flooded with a hundred questions.

Before he could form the words to respond, O'Dell grabbed a handful of his jacket, alerting him to an armored roadblock appearing through the fog ahead.

Chapter 29

"*Halten, halten,*" an officer yelled with pistol drawn, as a dozen German infantrymen spilled from a small barrack.

He rushed the driver's side door, flanked by soldiers covering with machine guns, and one toting a communications pack.

"Here we go," Jakob said.

O'Dell pulled his Luger.

"Easy, Sergeant. Do not give them a reason to react. Remain indifferent. You act, they react. I will do what I can to neutralize them."

Jakob exited with arms above his head. He engaged the officer before his feet hit the ground. Within seconds, his compatriots swarmed him. The conversation turned animated.

The officer pointed and shouted. O'Dell's angst piqued when the officer's attitude tempered. Jakob either identified a magic word or phrase or sold them out. *Martel might be right,* he whispered in his head.

O'Dell expected the barrel of a rifle to swing his direction. He ignored Jakob's directive and slipped the Luger from his belt. "*If you finger us, Jakob, you're a dead man.*"

A soldier stepped in front of the officer. O'Dell slipped his finger around the trigger. Moments later, to his surprise, the officer holstered his sidearm, the other soldiers dropped their weapons, and Jakob his arms.

The officer directed a handful of soldiers to the rear. The muffled interrogation leaked through the thin plating separating cab from bed. Though unable to decipher exact words, O'Dell's confidence surged as Polak responded in a calm cadence.

If the officer bought Jakob's explanations, it did not show in his eyes. O'Dell grew nervous the way he bandied between Jakob and the track. Jakob attempted to re-engage, but the officer cut off his speech with a wave of his hand.

O'Dell looked to his side mirror. The action stoked suspicion. The officer approached with Jakob on his heels. He unholstered his pistol and motioned a goon forward.

The guard, a hulk of a man with characteristics found in a sledgehammer, waved a machine gun, and motioned O'Dell out of the cab. O'Dell hesitated. Jakob motioned with a jut of his chin for O'Dell to comply.

O'Dell opened the door, intending to fire once on the ground. A rush of soldiers from the rear forced the door shut, catching the approaching guard in a swirl of activity. A soldier held two bottles of schnapps above his head; the other guards chased him as if children after a candy bar.

Pure chaos ensued as the enemy reacted to the booze. To Jakob's bewilderment, the officer turned as punch-drunk happy as his men.

A soldier dressed in winter white camouflage achieved a foothold on the step of the track's driver's side door, and with exuberant haste and a smile, flung the door open, catching O'Dell unawares. O'Dell swung the pistol toward the German. The soldier jumped from the ladder and scrambled for the rifle draped over his shoulder.

Before the German could take aim, O'Dell recognized the gaffe and released the Luger to the seat bench. He mustered a smile, and with an apologetic wave, coaxed the soldier to temper his action. The exchange did not catch the officer's attention. Jakob moved to suppress his countryman's angst.

"*Vergib ihm. Wir sind alle sehr müde und ein bisschen durcheinander,*" he said, explaining their exhaustion and jumpy mental state.

Though wary, the soldier shouldered his rifle. He brought fingers to his lips and said, "*Haben sie eine zigarette?*"

O'Dell shook his head. "*Nein,*" he responded. He knew the word *zigarette.*

"*Wir haben keine zigarette? Wir haben nur wenige uebrig,*" Jakob said. The soldier offered a sluggish salute.

With the corks pulled, the officer turned to Jakob, and with a disinterested air, motioned him forward.

Jakob climbed into the cab and cranked the engine with a tempered glance toward O'Dell. The track bucked forward against a slight slope. Jakob offered a salute and smile, but the officer paid no attention as his men broke into song and dance.

"Did he buy it?"

Jakob shrugged. "You pointing that gun did us no favors."

"What the hell did that guy expect? He's lucky I didn't blow his damn head off. Who the hell makes a careless move in such a tense moment?"

"He only wanted a cigarette."

"I didn't know... the stupid bastard."

Well beyond the checkpoint, Jakob stopped the track when yells of "Sarge, Sarge," broke above the engine in cadence with rifle butts slamming against the back of the cab.

The men climbed from the vehicle, already engaged in deep debate by the time O'Dell and Jakob joined them.

"We got trouble," Hansel said.

"Big trouble," Polak added.

"What?" O'Dell asked.

"The white rabbit grabbed the officer as we drove off. They dialed up the commo pack."

"Shit," O'Dell said.

"What happened?" Sperro asked.

"Ah, the sonofabitch caught me off guard. He opened the driver's side door on me. I pointed my Luger." O'Dell settled to his haunches. He swiped at the ground in frustration.

"What does it mean?" Spring asked.

"It means he called ahead to alert the next checkpoint," Jakob said.

"What the hell do we do now?" Martel asked.

"Damn it," O'Dell snapped.

Jakob centered on Polak. "What did they ask?"

"Types of prisoners and our destination."

"Anything more?"

"They wanted dirty books. I told him no books, but we had schnapps. I gave them two bottles. They shouldered their rifles quicker than you can blink. I could've taken all of 'em out."

"Wise move to let it be. We would not have fared as well up front."

"What now?" Spring asked.

"We have two choices," Jakob said. "Continue west or ditch the track and move out on foot."

"How far ya reckon we've gone?" Sperro asked.

"Sixty kilometers."

"Halfway," O'Dell said.

"I don't think we have a choice," Sperro said. "We use this vehicle as far as it can take us. Any chance this was the last checkpoint?"

"No," Jakob said.

"They'll be waiting for us," Spring said.

"That's why we keep moving in the track," Sperro countered.

"What do you mean?" Spring asked.

"What the hell do you mean, 'what do I mean?' We're set to storm an enemy POW camp. We need these supplies and must preserve our energy. Once we hit the river, we'll have to strap all this shit to our backs."

"Right. We take the track as far as we can. I'd rather not go traipsing blind through an unfamiliar forest," Polak said.

O'Dell agreed. "How far from the Rhine to the camp, in miles?"

"Twenty," Jakob said.

"This place gives me the creeps," Westwick said. He raked his hand through fog settled waist high.

Polak broke the huddle. "Yeah, I've been in graveyards less disturbing."

O'Dell lifted from his haunches. Near halfway to upright, a rifle shot exploded to his rear. He reacted as if a bee had buzzed his ear. The projectile pinged off the track's tailgate.

The men scattered. A second shot rang out. O'Dell managed a slight turn to move around the side of the track. The sniper's bullet hissed by his cheek, catching Westwick in the side of the head, splitting his skull in half, sending blood and brain matter splattering against O'Dell's face. Westwick crumpled to the ground without a sound. A split second later, the gates of hell, and all its fury, descended upon the men as a tidal wave.

Chapter 30

Small arms fire erupted in all directions. Martel and Hansel scattered on hands and knees east into the woods. Sperro grabbed a wad of Spring's coat, and with Polak pushing from behind, hightailed it west. On instinct, O'Dell dropped to his knees to check Westwick's condition.

Despite projectiles pinging against the track's carcass and popping in the snow at his feet, Jakob exposed himself to wrap his arm around O'Dell's neck.

"Let him go," Jakob yelled. "He's dead. We have to take cover."

Jakob dug his heels into the snow in search of leverage. Another volley littered Westwick's body with holes. Westwick did not flinch. The men slithered under the track.

Gunfire soon traded for boots rushing through snow, and an officer barking orders. Two soldiers dropped to their stomachs at the track's front. Jakob raised his hands.

A third infantryman dropped to a knee to the pair's left, stuffed the barrel of his rifle under the chassis and ordered, *"Aus, aus."*

Jakob grabbed O'Dell by the arm. They crawled into the open. Two soldiers forced them against the vehicle.

Four soldiers approached from the rear. Jakob recognized one — the white rabbit. Six additional troops converged from the front, trailing in the footsteps of an SS officer pacing through the snow as calm as a Sunday sunrise.

He approached Jakob and turned with a sinister scowl imprinted on a face blistered by flame. He motioned toward both sides of the track. All but two soldiers and his personal aid fled into the woods in pursuit of those on the run.

Jakob wondered what business an Oberführer of the Waffen SS had in these woods, so far removed from troop concentration.

"Warum haben sie auf uns geschossen?" Jakob asked, questioning why they fired upon them.

"Why did three German soldiers flee into the woods with your American prisoners?" the officer replied, in broken English.

He turned his attention to O'Dell.

"Welches jahr wurde Hitler als Kanzler?" the officer asked.

"His mission requires him to speak only English," Jakob said.

"Quiet," the officer yelled.

"Welches jahr wurde Hitler als Kanzler?" he repeated.

O'Dell recognized the word 'Hitler,' nothing more.

The officer released a sinister grin. "An American in the wrong uniform, yes?"

O'Dell breathed deep. His legs felt heavy and body bruised. He slacked against the track, still reeling from Westwick's death.

"This man saved my life. I ask you to spare him," Jakob pleaded.

"And who shall spare your life, Herr von Rüdel?"

Jakob's jaw fell agape.

"Surprised? You should not be. Your father has gone to great lengths to locate his favorite son. He desires to attend your execution in person."

"Name, function, and unit?" the officer demanded of O'Dell.

O'Dell fixated on a massive nest built into the fork of a branch of a large tree in the distance. Its construction reminded of similar roosts in the bluffs framing his farm.

The officer unleashed a backhand to O'Dell's face. "I will not ask again."

"Sergeant O'Dell Denny, medic, Twenty-Eighth Infantry, 110th Regiment."

"Sergeant Denny, I charge you with espionage and treason against the Reich and sentence you to death."

The officer stepped back, unholstered a pistol, and fired one round. The bullet pierced O'Dell just above his Adam's apple. He buckled at the knees and fell limp into the snow.

"No! No!" Jakob yelled. He dropped to his friend's side.

O'Dell grabbed at his throat, struggling for breath, with blood squirting between his fingers. Jakob stabbed at the wound as if able to stave off the inevitable. O'Dell managed a desperate rendition of his wife's name through a most horrific gurgle. Bloody air bubbles inflated upon his lips. Jakob secured O'Dell's head in his arms.

Having seen enough, the officer drove the heel of his boot square against Jakob's forehead. The blow propelled him onto his back. He lay in the snow fighting stars. Blood flowed from a cut at his scalp. He rolled onto his side, and through a blur, watched his friend's struggle ease. The officer straddled O'Dell and fired another round into his head.

Jakob jumped at the pop of the shot and dropped his head against the snow. Blood poured from O'Dell's forehead, igniting an immediate, searing heat in Jakob's chest; he felt his father's slaps against his cheeks, punches against his jaw and abdomen, and kicks to his ribs.

With each passing second, a primordial avidity for revenge struck, igniting an internal inferno to settle the score for what the war had taken from him, including an honorable man who saved his life. Something inside snapped, delivering forth a wanton craving to dispense destruction.

The officer grabbed Jakob by his coat lapels, pulled him to his feet, and slammed him against the side of the track. The blow did not register, as Jakob's newfound mania manufactured a rush of adrenaline.

"I shall look forward to informing your father of your fondness for the enemy," the officer said, ejecting spittle onto Jakob's cheek. "A great shame a man cannot hang twice."

Jakob released a menacing smirk, then hocked a clump of mucus into the officer's face. A resulting punch dropped him to the ground.

"Take him away," the officer ordered.

Jakob looked to his friend, digesting why he'd stood by him when the rules of war did not dictate such. He reflected upon O'Dell's beloved Annalise, his newborn son, who would never know his father or the truth. O'Dell's eyes directed lifelessly into the heavens.

"They will know," Jakob whispered. "They will both know."

A guard kicked at Jakob's leg. Jakob rotated and placed a hand against his outside coat pocket, tracing the outline of the Luger confiscated from O'Dell. He rose to his feet, and in a fluid motion, slipped his hand into his pocket, spun toward one captor, and uncoiled. He buried his fist, with Luger encased, into the first guard's face. The blow shattered the man's nose and sent him onto his backside. Jakob's momentum set him up to fire one round into the second guard's face before the man could react.

With his motion continuing forward, he rushed ahead, covering the officer before he managed to unholster his pistol.

"*Hände hoch. Hände hoch!*" Both officer and aide raised their hands. Jakob moved in, keeping steady aim at the bridge of the officer's nose. He clutched hold of his chest with his free hand, feeling the bite of the outburst.

"Do you know who I am?" the officer asked.

Jakob drew in a deep breath. "Remove your clothes."

"I am Oberführer Bernd von Meckel."

"I do not care. Remove your clothes."

"You will soon know my position, you swine. My brother, Ernst von Meckel, and Heinrich Himmler have enjoyed a lifelong friendship."

"I said, remove your clothes."

"You kill me, my brother will hunt you the rest of your days."

Jakob's face turned red. "I will not ask again. Strip."

The officer snapped to attention. "I shall not. You will have to kill me."

Jakob did not hesitate. He pulled the trigger. A single bullet detached a chunk of the officer's forehead. Jakob turned the gun on the aide.

"Entfernen sie seine Waffe."

The young man removed his utility belt and the belt of the officer.

"Werfen Sie es so weit wie möglich in den Wald," Jakob ordered.

The aide launched both pistols into the woods.

Jakob barked another command. The aide made quick work of removing all but the officer's undergarments. He bunched the clothes and placed them at Jakob's feet. When the young man drew upright, Jakob slammed the pistol into the side of his head, opening a deep gash, and sending the boy to the ground.

Jakob worked his way around each downed man, confiscating two pistols, a sniper rifle, and what ammunition he could carry. He bundled the take in a pile at the side of the road before returning to O'Dell's body. He emptied his pockets and boots of his personal letters, took possession of his wedding ring and dog tags. He secured the items into an inside jacket pocket.

Jakob brought his hands to his mouth, dousing his fingers with hot breath. Despite the trials brought upon by man and the circumstances dictating its improbability, the two had a chance at a friendship for the ages. He placed a hand on O'Dell's chest.

"I am sorry, I did not protect you as you protected me. I hoped someday to visit you on your Pennsylvania farm. I give you my solemn oath, I will find your—"

Chapter 31

A branch snapped to Jakob's blind side. He scrambled over O'Dell's body to the front of the vehicle and peeked under the chassis. Several figures emerged from the fog, forcing him to the opposite ditch, where he gathered the pile of confiscated supplies and fled into the woods.

The burst of energy lasted but thirty meters before his chest grew too heavy, wounds too painful, and the variety of supplies too cumbersome to carry. He hopped a large, downed tree, finding haven behind a stump measuring several times his own circumference.

He collected the sniper's rifle and checked its functionality. A pain-filled maneuver onto his stomach gained him a visual of the abandoned track. He settled the scope's crosshairs at the rear of the vehicle.

A muffled voice barked an order. Jakob tweaked the scope's range. Spring stepped into view with arms raised. Sperro and Polak followed in close quarters, with two Germans covering. The guards swung wide to pin their prisoners against the track.

Spring spotted O'Dell's body and lunged forward. A soldier grabbed him and slung him to the ground. The guard stuffed the muzzle of the machine gun in his face. Spring dropped his head and sobbed.

Jakob redirected the scope. The men gawked at the bloody mess of the man who had stitched them countless times. Though their eyes glistened, Jakob could see anger boiling—Sperro in particular. His jaw pulsated and pupils darted between Westwick, the sergeant's body, and the machine gun of the guard whose nose Jakob had broken.

Jakob pulled his eyes from the scope when the men directed their attention forward. The white rabbit, who Jakob suspected of dropping Westwick, emerged at a snail's pace. He inspected the SS officer's stripped condition.

Spring's agony rose above what little commotion nature conjured, eliciting a furious reaction from the white rabbit. He pushed the covering guard to the side to deliver a crushing kick to Spring's rib cage. Spring accepted the blow with a harrowing grunt before curling into a ball. Sperro rushed forward. Two guards descended upon him, pinning him against the vehicle. Polak did not waste the opportunity.

He dove toward the machine-gun, and in mid-roll, squeezed off one round into the head of Sperro's captor. He turned the gun on the white rabbit. Before he could pull the trigger, the sniper fell to his knees and locked Spring in a chokehold, placing the private between himself and Polak's aim. He buried the tip of a Luger in Spring's ear.

"*Waffe runter, Waffe runter,*" the German yelled, simultaneous to Polak screaming for the man to drop his weapon.

The lone soldier covering Sperro barked the same command. Sperro shouted for Polak to take the shot. Polak kept his aim square on the white rabbit's head, his finger wrapped around the trigger.

"*Ich werde ihn töten,*" the white rabbit yelled.

Jakob traded his aim between the white rabbit and the guard covering Sperro. With the situation disintegrating, he lined up the white rabbit's temple in the crosshairs, guessing Polak could take Sperro's captor if he dropped the sniper.

The white rabbit's face glowed red, deepening in contrast with each passing second. He tightened his grip around Spring's neck. Jakob would not allow a choke out. He took a deep breath and squeezed the trigger.

The white rabbit's head exploded in a red mist. Sperro kicked his captor in the crotch. Polak emptied several rounds into the guard's chest. Sperro grabbed his captor's machine gun and dropped behind the body for cover. Polak swung his weapon toward the woods. The men watched and waited.

Jakob rolled onto his back and peered into the heavens, gasping to regain his breath, fighting the remnant stench of gunpowder infiltrating his nostrils. O'Dell's desperate attempt to call out his wife's name replayed in full. "God, please forgive me," he whispered.

"Get your ass outta there with your hands up," Sperro's voice boomed.

Jakob grabbed hold of a nearby limb and coaxed his body upright. He knew they had little time to waste.

"*Hände hoch,*" Polak yelled.

Jakob emerged from the woods hauling the confiscated items.

"What the hell are you doing?" Sperro yelled. He kept his weapon aimed. Polak rushed to aid Spring. "Did you take that shot?"

Jakob dropped the bundle of goods, hopped the ditch, and pushed forward to help Polak assist Spring to his feet.

"Did you take the shot?" Sperro repeated.

"Yes," Jakob said.

"What happened to Denny?"

Jakob pointed to the officer. "He accused him of treason and shot him point-blank. I could do nothing to stop it. He knew my identity. My father sent him to arrest me."

"How did you escape?"

"They failed to search me. I had Sergeant Denny's Luger in my coat pocket."

"You killed all these men?" Polak asked.

"I did what I had to do."

"Where's Martel and Hansel?"

"I did not see which direction they fled."

Sperro turned to Polak. "Let's move out."

"And go where?"

"Anywhere but here."

Jakob patted Spring on the back. He turned from the men and stripped.

"Why are you taking off your clothes?" Sperro asked.

Jakob unbuttoned his coat, removed his shirt, boots, and pants.

"Did you hear what I said? We have to go."

Jakob turned and pointed toward the stump he had found cover. "You will need to move southwest."

"Why are you changing clothes?"

"My chances increase tenfold wearing the uniform of an Oberführer of the Waffen SS."

"Chances for what? You're going on to Limburg?"

"Of course," Jakob said.

"What? Why?"

Jakob slipped into the officer's trousers. "I intend to finish what your sergeant started."

Sperro stood dumbfounded. Polak joined at his side, his befuddlement equal.

Jakob transformed from a private to officer. He brushed the collar where blood and matter had splattered.

"You're crazy," Sperro charged.

Jakob pointed to O'Dell. "Look at your sergeant and let it burn into your conscience, then speak to me of crazy. He deserved less to die that death than any man I know. He risked his life for you, me, and countless others, and felt his corporal deserved the same. He earned my allegiance and respect, and I will not allow him to die in vain. I will locate his corporal—if alive—and extract him."

"You can't break him out yourself," Polak said.

"Then I will die trying."

Sperro shook his head. "Why? You can leave and the war's over for you, right here, right now."

"Your sergeant believed your corporal's rescue important. Now, it is important to me."

"Shimmel wanted to kill you," Sperro reminded.

Jakob did not respond.

Spring dropped to a knee near O'Dell's body, shaking with fury and grief. "You won't be alone," he said. "I'm going with you."

Polak and Sperro turned at the comment. Spring rose to face them, his expression hardened.

"Kid, you know you have little chance to survive this, right?" Polak said.

"What the fuck do I care? If I'm destined to die, I'd rather die trying to save my own than moving from stump to stump and let some lucky-shit sniper pick me off. I'm happy to die for any reason Sergeant Denny felt worthy."

"And what if I say you're not going?" Sperro said.

Spring squared up to both men. "I'd like to see you try to stop me."

Polak turned to Sperro and shrugged. "Damn, rotten kids. Can't teach 'em, can't shoot 'em."

Chapter 32

Intemperate conditions and circumstances prevented the men from executing a proper burial for their fallen brothers. Polak placed Westwick and O'Dell under a large grouping of slender pines across the ditch.

Sperro, on Jakob's suggestion, stripped the Germans of their uniforms and collected any documents. Spring settled on his haunches with hands cupped to his face, sobbing, having long since shed concern for what others thought of his reaction to dead friends.

Polak stepped in behind Spring and clutched his neck. "I know it hurts, John, and know what he meant to you, but you need to let him go because we've got a long fight ahead and need to stay sharp."

"I never told him how much he meant to me. Never told him how much I appreciated all he taught me and the example he set. I feel like I've lost a body part."

"That may be, but he'd want you to survive. You owe it to him to tell his story to your grandchildren."

Jakob kneeled near the German aide and searched his pockets, choking on guilt, as he did not intend to kill the boy. He brushed a clump of hair from the boy's face. The two could pass for twins had his eyes been a darker shade of blue.

He traded glances between the boy's pockets and lifeless gaze. Regret suffocated his senses as his mind acknowledged the contradiction of his pledge to never take the life of a man in a war he did not support or believe in. "*Gott verdammt dieser Krieg und die Männer, die ihn gestartet hat,*" he mumbled, damning the war and the rabble responsible for it.

"Hey, this guy you belted is alive," Sperro called out. "We can't take a prisoner. What the hell do we do with him?"

"Get him under cover and wrap a coat around him."

Sperro grabbed a wad of the soldier's coat collar and dragged him from the road through the ditch. The movement brought the soldier back to the conscious world. Sperro put him back to sleep with a single punch.

Polak helped Spring to his feet, then joined the others at the rear of the track to discuss next steps.

"How 'bout Danny and Martel?" Spring asked.

"I don't know, kid," Sperro said. "I didn't see them."

"We either go or prepare to fight off whoever's on the way," Polak noted.

"We just going to leave 'em behind?" Spring asked.

Sperro adjusted his helmet. "Kid, they're on the run, captured, or dead. We could set off after 'em, but in what direction? I think the last thing on their minds is working back toward us. The longer we wait, the chances grow we all die."

"Polak, take Spring. I'll sit up front. If I spot trouble, I'll smack the back of the cab. You do the same. Whatever arms we have left, load 'em all. No more leavin' our peckers hanging out."

The track fired on cue. Jakob coaxed the vehicle forward but kept watch of O'Dell's body until it faded into the darkness. He held tight to the wheel, rocking back and forth to suppress pain.

"You okay?" Sperro asked.

"Yes."

"You did the right thing, you know."

"I murdered my own countrymen."

"You murdered no one. They meant to kill Spring and drag your ass off to do the same to you. A man has a right to protect himself from friend or foe."

"And the aide?"

"Did you intend to kill him?"

Jakob shook his head.

"He intended to kill you. If you don't pull the trigger, Spring's a dead man. You saved the life of a decent kid."

Jakob conceded he could not sit idle and watch Spring die. "If the situation reversed, would you kill a countryman?"

Sperro went silent, scanning the white landscape out the passenger side window. Following a lengthy pause, he said, "I'd like to believe I'd come to the aid of any man suffering unjustly. It's why I'm fighting this fight."

"Sergeant Denny was a good man," Jakob said.

"The best. I'm honored to have fought alongside him."

"I would trade my life for his right now."

"I know you would. There's not a man here who wouldn't. But there's a reason we're alive and he's dead."

Jakob brought the vehicle to a slow, grinding lurch upon reaching a fork in the road. He veered right on a heading east. Sperro spread the map, searching for any landmark representative of their exact location.

Eight miles removed from the point of the ambush, the roadway dead-ended into a major thoroughfare, as evidenced by dirty slush rutted with jeep and tank tracks. Jakob slowed to a stop. He did not wish to venture on without a plan. He pulled back into the forest.

Sperro slid the map toward him. Jakob drew an index finger to a dot and tapped. "Our location, I believe."

"Kaisersesch," Sperro commented.

"I know this town. Visited a friend there one summer. Not too far to Limburg."

Sperro traced the map northeast. "There's a dozen towns along the route. We gonna drive right through them?"

"With all the action to our west, there may be no better time. We will run into checkpoints, at least until we reach the Rhine. We need to discuss a plan and add petrol."

On Sperro's command, Polak and Spring passed eight of the twelve containers of fuel forward. Sperro filled the machine as quick as it would drink.

"We either go in as soldiers of the Reich, or stage another prisoner transport," Jakob said.

Polak scoffed. "Sure as shit didn't work the first time. What's the chance we could explain a resupply mission?"

"You would not seek resupply from a prisoner of war camp, this one in particular. As unpleasant a place on earth as you will find. No electrical power or running water, at least not upon my last visit. The barracks would appear to your eyes as large circus tents."

"Could they have moved Shimmel to another camp?" Spring asked.

"No. He will not leave Limburg alive."

"I say we continue as you and Denny planned," Sperro said. "Spring poses as the prisoner, the rest of us guards."

Jakob agreed.

Sperro rummaged through the pile of confiscated German uniforms, mixing and matching for size. Jakob turned to Polak, holding the aide's ID to his face. "What do you think?"

"I don't know how things work in your army, but in mine, a poor bastard stuck guarding a checkpoint two hundred miles behind the fighting is as dumb as a bag of hams, sacked of rank, or both. No matter, he won't give a shit sandwich if it meets the eye test, and this does."

***

The road to Kaisersesch proved uneventful. With dusk gaining and another front dumping snow, the group moved through the town via a side road looping the main drag. They spotted soldiers along the sidewalks but drew neither their interest nor suspicion.

"Army Group B stations in Koblenz," Jakob said. "I do not know what remains of them. No matter, I expect a presence."

Sperro and Jakob swapped stories of family and post-war plans as the track rumbled through several wee hamlets—Hambuch, Zettingen, Kaifenheim, Polch, Kerben, Wolken—all quiet.

At a crossroads southeast of Koblenz, a breach in the forest revealed an unanticipated shock, forcing Jakob to stop in the middle of the intersection. Neither man needed to mention the obvious, as a dingy orange glow pluming above the southern horizon and a stiff breeze pushing a choking odor of cordite and ash told tale of a massive bombing raid.

"Holy shit," Sperro said.

"Where did they come from?"

"I'll bet it's the 447th out of Rattlesden. Sure as hell looks as if they've mangled things pretty good. I can't believe our boys have pushed this far."

Jakob let go a heavy, pain-filled sigh. "This beautiful country, ripped to shreds, its peoples obliterated, and for what?"

"I bet they're kicking the hell out of Italy as well," Sperro said. "You think they hit the camp? Would a raid help or hinder our effort?"

"Several years ago, my father dragged me to a party meeting where a young, vibrant, self-appointed demagogue wailed at the top of his lungs, '*mit der verwirrung kommt gelegenheit*' —with chaos comes opportunity."

Chapter 33

Having gathered his bearings, Jakob pleaded to avoid Koblenz common all together. He assured them he knew his way to Limburg if they maintained a westerly heading. Sperro unfolded the map and pointed to a mark made in pencil.

"See here, someone's idea of a bridge spanning the Rhine, and it's less than a thumbprint away."

"I believe the mark accurate. If so, I suspect the bridge heavily guarded. I doubt Allies have pushed this far."

"Who knows? We might be chasing the figment of someone's imagination." He turned to Jakob. "Okay, let's do this your way."

Jakob turned west. A stout breeze picked up as the track plowed through the intersection. Snow whipped sideways. A hairpin turn approached, as did a column of German personnel carriers lumbering in the opposite direction. They missed sideswiping the track by inches. Jakob evaded a tumble into a ditch.

Pasty-gray, ragged, and beaten men and boys, several clinging to the sides of the trucks with little to no winter gear or weapons, shouted obscenities and tossed objects, agitated by, or envious of, friendlies traveling opposite harm's way.

Jakob brought the track to a stop above the ditch. As the last carrier passed, a lad swinging from a handgrip tossed a glass bottle atop the hood. Both ducked as shards ticked against the windshield.

Sperro peeked over the dashboard. "Glad we didn't have a busted track. I believe those boys would've stopped and killed us."

"They seemed in foul mood."

"You think we're nearer the river or their base?"

Jakob placed the track in gear. "They have no base. Nothing but civilian recruits gathered by the SS as a last resort. No matter, no German appreciates a rear troop."

Jakob shifted into top gear as the road straightened. The upsurge proved short-lived. Two guards, both green as summer corn, stepped from a poorly built shack to the front of a draw arm with Lugers at the ready. Jakob brought the track to a stop and pulled the confiscated ID from his pocket. The younger of the two approached, the other settled in front of the grill with pistol aimed.

"*Identifizieren Sie sich! Identifizieren Sie sich,*" the guard snapped.

Jakob passed the ID.

Polak repositioned to catch what he could of the conversation.

"*Wohin gehst du?*" he questioned, paying little attention to the I.D.

"Wha'd he say?" Spring whispered.

"Wants to know where we're going."

"*Wir sind der Gefangenentransport,*" Jakob said.

"Limburg?" the guard questioned.

"*Ja.*"

"*Warum nur ein Gerangener?*"

Jakob pointed to the rear of the track. "*Wir haben einen Sani.*"

The guard turned to his comrade and ordered him to search the rear of the vehicle.

"They're coming," Polak said. He pushed Spring to the opposite bench.

The guard lurked around the corner. He took quick aim of Polak, then stretched his neck for a peek of the other passengers and stowed contents.

Polak brought one hand off his rifle. "*Ich habe ein Geschenk für Sie, Schnapps.*" He passed a bottle forward.

The guard's eyes lit up. He holstered his weapon. "*Gott segne sie, Gott segne sie,*" He planted a kiss on the faded label and disappeared around the track.

"God bless you, too," Polak quipped. "We could end this damn war today if we produced booze rather than tanks."

The young guard returned Jakob's ID as his attention drew to his mate waving the liquid prize above his head.

"*Eine Flasche Schnapps ist schwer zu bekommen, oder, Ja?*" Jakob asked, pointing out the limited supply these days.

"*Ja, ja,*" the guard agreed.

The guard stepped aside and ordered the draw arm lifted. Jakob saluted and released the clutch.

"What did he say?" Sperro asked, as Jakob slipped the track through the checkpoint.

"He wanted to know why we had the one prisoner. Said a bombing raid destroyed the camp's medical facility with many dead and injured. I told him we captured a medic."

Sperro unfolded the map. "According to this, we should be swimming in the river. I mean, we're right on top the goddamn thing."

The roadway narrowed to a single lane. Another sharp turn forced Jakob into a downshift, a stench of diesel fuel saturated the cab, forcing both men to cover their nostrils. Seconds later, the track bucked, sputtered, and stalled. They exited in haste to escape the fumes.

"Hey, something fell off thirty yards back," Polak yelled, pointing down the road.

The men stepped off the paces. "What the hell is that?" Sperro asked.

"Fuel pump," Jakob said.

"I'm guessing you don't belong to a motor club," Polak mumbled.

"Can we fix it?" Sperro asked.

"Not even if we had the tools. See there," Jakob said, pointing, "fractured right down the middle."

"Shit," Sperro snapped, swiping at the snow.

A distant hum captured Jakob's attention. He sprung to his feet.

"What?" Spring whispered, concerned by his haste.

Jakob turned an ear toward the track. Without explanation, he grabbed Spring by the coat collar and tugged. "Clear the road."

***

Jakob knew the distinctive sound of German engines and led the men to safety. Within eyeshot of the track, they hunkered behind a massive, toppled oak. A personnel carrier happened upon their lifeless vehicle. They guarded each breath to meld as one with the black of the forest. A collection of civilian recruits ransacked their vehicle under the watchful eyes of military officers.

A second carrier, packed with similar recruits, joined in, with a third transport charging past. Jakob leaned against the tree, rolling his forehead across the trunk, cursing himself for the time they wasted and valuable supplies left behind.

"What the hell do we do now?" Polak whispered.

Food, ammunition, and other weaponry passed from man to man, fire-brigade style, into the waiting carriers. The wild scramble for supplies concluded with a skeleton of a young man locating the fourth and final bottle of schnapps. The men hollered in fits of celebration, but their merriment evanesced, as a senior officer claimed the liquid for himself.

A man, with hair white as snow, cachexic about the face and limbs, attempted to open a box of K-rations. A single shot rang out. Recruits cowered, some dropped into fetal positions. Guards commenced to punching and kicking, driving the men toward the carriers as they would sheep to the slaughterhouse. Jakob turned away, having witnessed this barbaric display before.

The carriers pulled out, leaving tire tracks, footprints, someone's dead relative, and a worthless hunk of steel.

"Stay here," Jakob said. With Luger drawn, he inspected the track. The raiders accounted for all stashed items, other than Sperro's map. Jakob refolded it and scurried from the road.

"They took it all," he informed the men.

"What now?" Spring asked.

"I can smell the river," Jakob said.

"So, we head toward the prison camp on foot, no plan, and no real way to protect ourselves," Polak said.

"We're screwed no matter what direction we travel," Sperro added.

Jakob settled upon his haunches. "We need to find the river. We can assess our options there."

Jakob tracked the road until it banked off to the southwest and out of sight. Their path stalled at a ledge cleared of timber and underbrush. Water pushed rhythmically against the shoreline of the mighty Rhine.

Fighting exhaustion and a freezing burn to their extremities, they continued around a sharp bend. The level, unencumbered passage turned craggy and awkward. They pushed forward at a snail's pace, navigating over jagged rocks and natural debris. Jakob dropped and signaled the men to cover.

He identified a mammoth, manmade stone caisson rising out of the fog, and a conversation less than a stone's throw away. A dozen Germans stationed at its base, ready to protect and preserve one of the Reich's last standing spans.

Chapter 34

Jakob signaled the men to fall back, realizing they ventured too close to proceed without a plan. He prepared to fall in behind when conversation between two of his countrymen grew closer and more audible. Jakob exchanged the boulder for a massive root ball nearer the bank, loosening rocks as he moved, prompting a pause in the soldier's conversation.

Jakob held his breath, hunkering as low to the ground as his wounds would allow, as the Germans performed a brief investigation before retreating in quick step toward the caisson. Jakob moved from off the riverbank and located the other men behind a copse of thicket and small trees.

"We gotta find a way across," Sperro said.

"I do not think we can cross here," Jakob said.

"Why not?" Spring asked.

"The river splits into two channels at this location. An island sits in the middle. We would have to cross twice. It reverts to a single channel well south, too vast a distance to travel. We could redirect north and locate a crossing ahead of the split."

"We could follow this river till its end and not find another bridge intact," Polak said.

"We don't have time to search up or downstream," Sperro said, "and need to make the camp before dawn, or we lose another day. We must cross here, now. I expected the river frozen over. Thought we could walk across."

"How the hell you plan on crossing without a span?" Polak asked. "We can't swim across and we're outnumbered. We fire on them, we're dead."

"Wait," Jakob said. "The deck is in blackout."

"What, like we walk across the damn thing?" Polak asked.

"Yes."

"Right," Sperro said. "With cloud cover, fog and snow, we could move across without notice."

"And if we're stopped?" Spring asked. "I'm wearing the wrong uniform."

"Yes, but this uniform should outrank all others," Jakob said. "It might work."

"Might?" Spring said. "Easy for you to say."

"Take it easy, kid," Sperro said. "You can wear Joe's coat. I doubt they'll inspect our pants."

Each man allowed the plan a moment's fermentation.

"So, we doing this?" Sperro asked.

Spring and Jakob agreed. Polak shook his head. "I think we need to wait."

"There's no time, Joe," Sperro said. "We need to go now." He dug into a pocket for the silver-plated watch given to him by his mother prior to boot camp. He checked the time and shrugged. "Merry Christmas, boys."

***

"We can't pop out on top like a bunch of lovers," Spring whispered. "We gotta blend in."

With the bridge in view, the men quailed in a steep trench at the side of the road. Massive granite towers flanked the point of abutment, with a webbed system of steel trusses extending to support the span.

"We draw less suspicion if we come up on the far side," Jakob said.

Sperro agreed. "Spills us out on the good side of the draw arm."

Jakob did not hesitate. He led the men deep into the forest before turning east toward the shoreline.

They moved forward behind a boulder near the northern-most caisson, removed their helmets, and in unison, peeked above the natural obstacle to gauge the opposition's strength. Conversation between the Germans had lessened but impossible conditions did little to boost confidence their numbers had dwindled.

Hard-soled shoes pinged on metal rungs. "They're coming and going like ants from a hill," Spring whispered. "Are they on duty?"

"They must come underneath to take a break," Sperro said.

Two soldiers exchanged comments, drawing laughter from a third.

"Either way, they're pretty relaxed," Polak said. "They're joking about their piss freezing before it hits the river. I don't know about you, but I'd be shitting my pants knowing Russians are knocking on the door a few miles east."

"What do we do?" Spring asked.

"The more confident our movements, the less attention we draw," Jakob said. "I will take the lead. Polak, you take up the rear and keep your ears open. If stopped, I will do the talking."

Polak looked to the ground and shook his head.

"What else we gonna do, Joe?" Sperro asked. "An officer of the SS is leading the way. It's our one shot."

"I don't like the setup, not one damn bit," he protested.

"What setup? We've come this far. There's no way back to our rally point. We can't fight our way across, walk or swim across, and we can't go back. We need to use these conditions to our advantage."

Polak couldn't come up with any alternate plan, so he grabbed a chunk of Spring's collar and pulled him from his post. He took off his coat and tossed it into his lap.

"Keep your eyes forward and follow my lead," Jakob said. "Do not let your eyes stray. Remember, let me do the talking."

The men headed for the shoreline. Patches of ice covered the banks in places, though the river pushed against land unencumbered. Within moments, Jakob placed a hand on the caisson. A single lane path cut into the embankment allowed for access to the opposite side. Jakob stiffened his back and stepped into the open.

They marched in close quarters with purpose and poise, despite encountering an enemy combatant settled on his haunches against the far caisson. He cupped his hands around a small tin can leaking light flame. Though startled, he returned to his business, as if groups of men popping out of the fog occurred often.

Jakob turned the corner of the far caisson to find a handful of soldiers huddled in a tight circle, engaged in conversation, sharing a single cigarette. He passed, offering a salute, before leading the men up the ladder and onto the darkened platform. Foot traffic, though minimal, lurked enough to preserve the well-formed lumps dilated in each man's throat.

"Those Krauts let us pass," Polak whispered, his voice panicked. He rushed to grab Sperro by the shoulder. "Why didn't they salute a superior officer?"

"Shut it, Joe," Sperro ordered.

"I'm telling you we need to go back."

Sperro brushed Polak's hand from off his shoulder. "Keep moving."

The fog aided their passage, as Sperro foretold, though the uneven surface heightened the chances of a slip of the foot or trip. Footsteps passed in both directions, though bodies remained obscured. Whispers projected from all angles, spoofing their faculties into believing the enemy walked in stride alongside.

Jakob traded glances between the surface and the mass of nothingness before him. He could feel tension mounting. A gut instinct prompted a reach for his Luger. As he quickened their pace, a flash exploded forward, halting their progress as they covered their eyes.

"*Anhalten, anhalten,*" a voice boomed.

Powerful spotlights rendered them blind. A rush of footsteps approached from both directions. Rifle bolts snapped. Soldiers swarmed to gag, hood and bind Polak, Spring, and Sperro before any chance to react. Jakob attempted a peek but saw only a sea of stars.

"*Bringt ihn zu mir,*" a voice ordered.

Hands grasped Jakob's biceps and led him forward.

"Congratulations, Herr von Rüdel," a soldier said in broken English. "You have captured the American bandits and completed your mission with honor. You have brought great joy to your father. *Bringen Sie ihn weg.*"

Jakob rubbed his eyes, attempting to wipe free the large white dots exploding about. A soldier grabbed his free arm, a second slipped a canvas hood over his head. He marched several hundred steps before feeling the surface change underfoot and hearing the soft purr of an engine idling.

The soldiers bent Jakob in half then redirected him onto a soft, slick bench seat. Within seconds of the door slamming, he thrust hard against the seatback as the vehicle sped from the scene.

Chapter 35

"That sonofabitch. That dirty, rotten sonofabitch," Polak yelled.

"He couldn't have killed Sergeant Denny," Spring said, leaning against a back-corner wall, shivering, with head in hands.

"I'm gonna kill him before this war ends."

"Would you shut the hell up, Joe," Sperro said, rubbing his thigh where a German had driven the butt end of his rifle. "You want to help, figure a way outta here. Because, if you don't, we're dead men."

Polak paced about the stone and concrete cell, a dingy, windowless hole reeking of feces and vomit. He held his right shoulder where a contusion ballooned to the size of a baseball.

The docile nature by which the Germans handled their initial capture had altered significantly upon extraction off the bridge. They'd suffered brutal kicks, punches to the groin, and rifle butts to their limbs. Their captors tossed them into a personnel carrier as a farmer would sacks of feed. The officer in charge removed their hoods and relocated the prisoners to the middle of the transport for all to see and accost.

The thirty-minute commute over rugged terrain seemed to last an eternity. The Germans spit on, punched, and forced their prisoners into faux games of Russian roulette. Upon arriving at their destination, they pushed their captives out before the vehicle ground to a halt.

Covered in mucus and suffering multiple contusions, the prisoners were led deep into a bunker to a room lit by lantern. An officer ordered them stripped. A second marched them to a holding cell.

"I told you something wasn't adding up," Polak said.

"Fine, you told me. If we survive, you can hold a press conference."

"I can't believe he killed Denny," Spring repeated.

"What's not to believe, kid," Sperro said. "Shit." He slammed the meaty part of his fist against the wall.

Polak paced and mumbled how he planned to disembowel Jakob. Sperro moved to an opposite corner.

"It makes no sense," Spring said.

Polak turned. "What's not to understand? We put our trust in him and he fucked us."

"Why did he save me? Why take the shot if he planned to sell us out? He shot a countryman. They'll hang him."

"American prisoners have greater worth than one lousy Kraut. You saw what they did to the old man. The poor bastard wanted to eat, and they blew a fuckin' hole in him. They don't give a shit about their own."

Spring shook his head. "It doesn't add up. He had plenty of opportunity to turn us in and we'd have had no chance."

"All's fair in love and war, kid," Polak said. "We got sucked into playing heroes and broke the first rule of war."

"They staged that scene on the bridge for our benefit. Why didn't they remove us when we were first captured? They waited for the officer to finish his speech. It makes no sense."

"I'll tell you what makes no sense," Polak said. "Those shitheads stealing our clothes in the middle of winter. These boys best hope I don't find a weapon because I'll...."

Polak paused mid-verse as a heavy metal door creaked at the end of the darkened hallway. Four Germans appeared. An officer held tight to a set of keys. Three goons covered with machine guns.

The officer approached, his eyes dead set on Spring. He slipped a skeleton key into the lock and engaged the tumblers.

"*Dass man,*" he said, pointing to Spring.

A guard entered. He motioned for Spring to move out. Spring stepped forward.

Sperro moved in front of him. "Why not me?" he shouted. "Take me."

One guard drove the butt of his rifle into Sperro's chest. Polak lunged forward, prompting a third guard to drive him against the back wall. They led Spring away.

The officer slammed the door, set the lock, and smirked.

Sperro clutched his chest, working to regain a breath.

Polak rushed the cell entrance. "Come in here and fight me, you fuckin' coward." Polak pounded on the door. "Hang in there, kid. Hang in there." Polak slammed his head against the bars and closed his eyes.

The guards forced Spring through a narrow entrance. Within minutes of the door slamming, Spring's screams commenced.

***

"Do you recognize this man?" the officer shouted. He grabbed a wad of the prisoner's hair to redirect his attention toward the subject.

"I will ask once more. Do you recognize this man?"

The soldier squinted through bruised and swollen eyes. "Yes," he slurred.

The officer took a chair opposite, leaned against the seatback, and removed a pair of leather gloves, keeping a watchful eye as the prisoner struggled for breath.

Guards had bound his hands behind the chair with razor wire, serving as the lone anchor keeping him upright. The officer snapped a finger. A guard positioned himself behind the prisoner and snapped his head erect.

"I will enjoy seeing you and your filthy friends hanged. To what depths shall your soul sink when the last breath exits your chest and the last drop of blood drips from your Adam's apple?"

"Father, please," Jakob begged.

The elder von Rüdel leapt from his chair to deliver a backhand to the side of Jakob's face. The blow sent Jakob crashing sideways onto the floor. "You will never address me as father again."

Franz straddled his son's body. "You are not my son. Do you understand?" He ground his boot heel into Jakob's ear, sending a scream reverberating throughout the bunker.

"You have disgraced me for the last time. You will swing from a barbed wire noose in front of your countrymen."

Jakob lay motionless.

"On your feet," Franz demanded. Jakob released a moan. "Up, I said." Franz drove the toe of his boot into Jakob's calf.

Jakob stirred as the kick quaked up his spine. A heavy scent of mold and mildew pricked at his nostrils. He rolled across the frigid surface onto his side. Franz wiped his sleeves, leaned against the seatback, and crossed his legs.

Jakob's many attempts to roll onto his knees failed. His father's patience ran out. He snapped his fingers. A guard delivered Jakob into his chair by his hair. He forced his head toward the man whom his father demanded he identify, the soldier whose nose he'd broken in the ambush.

"You should have killed him when you had the chance," Franz said. "He relayed to us your association with the Americans, the good and loyal men you murdered, including Herr von Meckel. Had you killed this man, you might not be sitting here now, though I would hunt you down all the same. No soldier escapes duty, whether refusing to kill the enemy or participating in acts of treason. Even the son of the distinguished Franz von Rüdel will not escape justice."

"Mother... where's... mother?" Jakob whispered.

Franz released a menacing laugh. "You have no mother, no sister, or horse. All dead. But you shall join them very soon."

Franz waved his hand. When the cell cleared, he stood and leaned in close. "I watched men toss your little Jew pig into a ditch," he whispered.

Jakob dropped his head on the small desk. Franz leaned in and grabbed his hair.

"Dead," he repeated, smiling. "Her disgusting body rots in the ground as we speak. I made certain of her end."

Jakob's eyes welled.

"Fear not. You will soon join her. May the two of you rekindle your love in the deepest bowels of hell." Franz spat in his son's face.

"Guards." Franz paused at the cell door as men rushed to gain control of the prisoner.

"I want him cleaned, his wounds well cared for, and served exact meals as the officers. If he refuses to eat, force it down his throat. Understood?"

"*Ja großen von Rüdel,*" a guard responded.

"I want him presentable for execution." He slapped his thigh with his gloves. "My Christmas present to Herr Himmler."

Chapter 36

Jakob lost consciousness in the transfer between cells. Guards dragged him deep into a steel-reinforced bunker, where they dressed his wounds and cleaned him.

A muted crackle drew him from the abyss. He lay on his side with back pressed against a stone wall. His eyelids fluttered and limbs convulsed. The space felt warm, a delightful warmth, hinting of home. A heavy scent of hickory wafted about.

Jakob drew a hand to his face. The simple maneuver instigated immediate discomfort about his neck and jaw. His nose throbbed and eyes felt tender to the least squint. He wiped at their corners to clear crust before opening wide to appraise his quarters.

An intense luminance made difficult an initial assessment, but he soon discovered the source of the heat and bright light— a large fireplace embedded in the far wall. The cobblestone room was wider than deep and lacked electrical power. Its low ceiling exaggerated a sense of entombment.

Jakob rolled onto his back. He placed a hand against the wall supporting the concrete counter that served as his cot and grasped at notches in the stone to pull himself upright. He took a deep, pain-filled breath, waiting out a nauseous eruption brought on by a dizzy spell.

As his faculties rebooted and the room steadied, he observed a clean set of clothes, bandages wrapping his wrists, fresh dressings applied to his torso, and a patch covering the gash above his eyebrow. His skin reeked of homemade soap. They shaved his face and de-matted and scrubbed his hair to a silky finish. A plate of food rested on a crate near the door. His condition spurred recollection of his father's directive and the reason he wanted his son so well cleansed.

He placed a hand against the ear stomped upon by his father. Questions peppered his conscience, though wanting to know most how he compromised their cover.

He tumbled deep into concern for the other men until the lock popped and a skeleton of a soldier entered.

The soldier grabbed the plate of food and kicked the door closed. Another set of eyes peered through the slit but disengaged within seconds. The soldier approached with plate extended.

Jakob accepted. "*Dankeschön.*"

"*Sie haben zehn Minuten,*" the guard said, directing his focus to the plate.

Jakob informed the guard he'd not require ten minutes. He set the plate to one side. The soldier followed the movement with wanting eyes.

"*Ich bin nicht sehr hungrig, möchten Sie etwas?*" Jakob asked.

The soldier hesitated, as if considering his offer to share. "You eat all bites, or consequences," he ordered.

"Where am I?" Jakob asked.

"*Ten minute.*" The guard turned and exited.

Salted pork, carrots, potatoes, and a quarter cup of buttermilk. Jakob could not deny a desire to contradict his father's wishes and refuse the meal, but knew if he stood any chance of escaping execution, he'd need his strength. He picked over the plate with his fingers.

As warned, a guard returned, though popping the tumblers well past the ten-minute deadline. The soldier entering appeared nervous and nearer Jakob's age. He checked the hallway before stepping through, leaving the door open. He dressed in a white apron smeared with foodstuff. A Luger dangled from his waist, a most unexpected sight for a grunt.

Jakob flashed the clean surface of his plate and tossed it to the floor. The soldier waited out the plate spinning until settling top down.

"*Was willst du von mir?*" Jakob asked.

"To talk," the guard said, in a low voice, and in perfect English. His accent hinted of east coast. "Do you recognize me?"

Jakob honed on a visible scar on the soldier's chin. His face was long with skin clinging tight to the bone. His cheeks dotted with puncture marks. The wounds stirred a faint memory. "No, I do not."

"Johann Rhoden."

Jakob shook his head. The name meant nothing.

He peeked over his shoulder and whispered, "We entered primary school the same year. We studied together."

Jakob dug deep but could not place the name or the student.

The soldier displayed the back of his hands. Scars streaked perpendicular to his fingers. "Remember?"

Jakob grew frustrated at his inability to place this character in his life.

"You happened upon me as club boys attacked me with a knife and pick."

The memory burst forth and in vivid clarity, though Jakob did not connect this man with the event.

"You saved my life."

"I do not believe it," Jakob said. "It cannot be so."

"It's me, in the flesh."

"I never knew you. You left without a trace."

"Yes. My father's political affiliations created many problems for our family. Mere days after the attack, we fled for America to live with my uncle in Boston."

"Why are you here?"

"My grandfather remained behind. I received word he died and returned to attend his burial and collect family heirlooms. As the train prepared to leave, the Gestapo boarded and removed many travelers at gunpoint. They forced me into service as an interpreter."

"Where am I?"

"Limburg, Camp Twelve-A12-A."

"Limburg," Jakob whispered. "How did you learn of my arrest?"

"Your father recruited me from a camp at Ludwigsburg for a top-secret mission teaching German soldiers English. He talks ill of you and wishes you dead. I'm aware of your predicament."

"I do not know what to say. What do you want with me? Why stick your neck out to speak with me?"

"I know their plan for you. They mean to make an example of you. I could not, in good conscience, know of your presence and not thank you for saving my life. Have you defected?"

Jakob's eyes narrowed. The soldier served as an interrogator and found a useful nugget from his past to catch him in his web. He grew angry at the ease with which the soldier baited him.

"What do you want?"

"Only to help."

"I do not believe you."

"Please. I want to help you and want you to help me. I don't belong here. Do you realize what Hitler has done? We hear rumors he's murdered millions. The war will soon end, and the world will take revenge against anyone associated with these camps. I want out of here. A recent bombing raid thrust all operations into great chaos."

Jakob shook his head.

"I know what led you here. I know an American medic saved your life. You meant to help him free a man captured. I participated in each interrogation of the six brought to camp these past days."

"Six?"

"Yes. They brought in a Jew a few days ago. He's in solitary on the other side of camp. I don't know his status. Three more arrived forty-eight hours ago and two late last night. The first three refused to offer any information. They beat another to death and released another into the general prison population."

"Who did they kill?"

"A soldier named Martel. They beat him with a lead bar and hammer, but he said nothing."

"And the other man?"

"Hansel, I believe."

Jakob clenched his fists. The brutality of his countrymen overwhelmed. "What about the others?"

Johann scrambled to his feet when a door slammed shut at the end of the hallway. He drew the Luger and settled his aim on Jakob's chest.

"You must trust me," he whispered. "I shall return."

"I will not leave this camp without those men," Jakob said.

A guard entered and demanded of his comrade the reason for his delay.

"*Abholung. Abholung,*" Johann yelled.

Jakob pushed from the wall to his feet. He bent low, never taking his eyes off the gun. He picked up the tin plate and handed it to Johann. The two guards backed out of the cell. The door slammed.

Jakob sifted through the conversation, recalling the day he jumped into the fray to help the boy during the attack. His mind began spinning. He could not validate trust, but concluded he had nothing left to lose, other than his breath at the end of a barbed wire noose.

Chapter 37

By the time guards plucked Polak from the cell, they achieved satisfaction as to why their prisoners wandered so near their camp.

They beat and tortured Spring for two hours. He succumbed when they broke the index finger on his left hand in two places with a pair of pliers. They returned him to the cell unconscious and bleeding from gashes behind his ears.

"We're dead men," Sperro said.

"Not yet," Polak countered. He scraped mold from a single loaf of hard bread tossed into the cell. "They should've killed me when they had the chance. Here, you need to eat."

He passed a portion of bread to Sperro, then bit off a small chunk for himself, leaving the rest for Spring—whenever he regained consciousness. He paused in mid-chew at the familiar, high-pitched grating of the door opening at the end of the hallway. "What now?" he said.

A soldier approached toting two large canvas bags bulging at their seams. He entered the cell and dropped the sacks at Polak's feet. Polak noticed the guard's unarmed status. Despite injury and lethargy, he jumped him. He grabbed the younger man by the throat and pushed him against the wall. He cocked his elbow, intending to drive his fist through the man's face.

The soldier scraped at Polak's forearm. He had neither the strength nor angle to fend off the hold. As Polak set to unleash his fury, the soldier struggled through a choking voice, pleading, "I come on Jakob's behalf."

Polak uncoiled. He loosened his grip to allow a complement of musty and moldy air into the man's lungs.

"What did you say?"

"Jakob sent me."

"You mean the lying fuck who turned us in?"

"He did not turn you in."

"Who the hell are you?"

"Johann Rhoden. I'm an American citizen from Boston. I played baseball for Charlestown High School and earned a degree in accounting from Boston College."

Polak shook his head, not believing for a second this could happen twice in the same war. "Bullshit." He re-cocked his fist.

"Look in the bags," Johann said, pointing.

Polak kept his fist at the ready. "Ange, check those bags."

Sperro scooted across the floor. "Our clothes, German uniforms, food, water."

"Where are we?" Polak demanded.

"Limburg, Camp 12-A. I offer my help to you."

"We don't need the help you assholes offer. Look at us."

"Yes, the reason we must go. Jakob and I attended the same grade school. He saved my life years ago. I want to help him, and he wants to help you."

"You want to help? Bring him to me so I can bust his head."

"He did not turn you in. A passing troop truck picked up the soldier Jakob left alive following the ambush. He said Jakob killed three countrymen, including the SS officer who killed your Sergeant Denny. Based on his account, they calculated your movements. They set a trap at the bridge. Jakob is on the other side of camp. His father means to hang him with you and the other captured Americans."

"Is Shimmel one of them?"

"Yes."

"Is he alive?"

"To the best of my knowledge. They placed him in solitary."

"How about the others?"

"A man named Martel died of injuries sustained during an interrogation. They placed Private Hansel in general population."

Polak's fists clenched. Johann retreated, moving out of reach.

"I want no part of this. I want to go home to America. I spoke with Jakob. He'll not leave camp without you. I can help you escape."

"How do you expect us to believe you?" Polak turned and settled into a squat. Sperro worked his arms through the holes of a heavy wool sweater.

"You can trust Jakob."

Polak searched the lot for his clothes. He helped Sperro into his pants.

"What do you have to lose? If you attempt nothing, you will hang."

"What about these German uniforms?"

"For our escape. I understand your wavering, but we're prepared to risk our lives for what we believe to be right. I'm your countryman and I owe Jakob."

Polak grabbed a wad of his coat and forced him against the wall. "No countryman of mine wears a German uniform on purpose. You could've disappeared long ago had you wanted to."

Polak returned to the bag, grabbed hold of Spring's clothes, and draped them over his body. The change in temperature prompted Spring to twitch, release a faint groan, and his bladder.

"You don't understand how the Reich operates," Johann said.

"I don't give a shit. You're a Nazi."

"No, along with Jakob and millions of others, we do not believe in Hitler's quest. I returned to Germany to bury my grandfather. The Gestapo pulled me off a train to Paris, along with many others, and forced us into service. I don't enjoy free movement. I serve as an interpreter for high-ranking officials. Jakob's father forced him into service and intends to hang him for aiding you. He helped you because he felt a debt to your sergeant. You tell me what type of man holds true to such convictions. Ask yourself this—what enemy would do all Jakob has done? He killed three of his own countrymen to save you. Would you kill for him?"

"He led us to the top of the bridge and you lousy fucks have mauled us ever since. You expect me to trust you because you speak English and claim Boston as your hometown?"

Johann pointed. "Please, check the bottom of the bag,"

Polak located a lump of burlap. He pulled apart a piece of twine to reveal a loaded pistol. His eyes widened. Confusion escalated. He turned the weapon on his enemy.

"You may kill me if you wish. I'd rather die than stay here. If I don't escape this camp, they'll charge me with crimes against humanity by association."

Polak traded a quick glance between the gun and his bloodied pals. He seethed at the brutality. No prisoner deserved such treatment. He wanted revenge. He aimed the gun at Johann's forehead.

Johann did not flinch. "I will help you escape in exchange for delivering me to American officials, so I may prove my identity. Give me the gun and I'll help you."

"Are you out of your fuckin' mind? You think I'm stupid?"

"Shoot me and you'll die. Do nothing, and they'll hang you in the morning. If you come with me, you have a chance."

"Why give us the pistol then?"

"If the gesture does not serve as my bona fides, nothing will. I have placed my life into your hands."

"Joe, give him the gun," Sperro said, his voice less labored.

"He's setting us up. You know he's setting us up."

"You said you played baseball," Sperro said.

"Yes."

"Are you a fan of the Braves?"

"Since childhood."

"Who led Boston in hitting last season?"

"Tommy Holmes. He batted .309."

"Who led the Braves in hitting in 1936?"

"Buck Jordan. He batted .323. But as a Boston Bee, not a Boston Brave."

"Ever visit O'Shanty's near the ballpark?"

"Many times."

"Ever drink an ale?"

"Not personally. My father did. They serve it in hollowed-out baseball bats."

"Give him the gun, Joe," Sperro directed. "No one not from Boston would know about the bats." Sperro grabbed the potato sack and bunched it under Spring's head.

"Angie, we're walking down the same path."

"We got nothing left, Joe. Nothing but waiting until they string us up. Give him the gun. If he turns it on us, so the fuck what? I'd rather take a bullet to the head than hang."

"You have my word," Johann said.

Polak held his aim. He waited for a deviation in Johann's body language or provocative smirk to justify pulling the trigger. The determination in his eyes matched those of Sergeant Denny's when he set his mind to aid a man. Polak lowered the weapon. He turned the barrel and offered the gun. Johann accepted.

"I'll return with more food. Do nothing, say nothing. Guards will cycle through on forty-five-minute intervals. I informed one of our plans and will make sure the others leave you be. Stay against the back wall, keep your eyes down, and say nothing."

"What the hell gave you the idea I wouldn't shoot you?"

"Jakob would not go to this length for men he didn't trust."

Spring rolled onto his back. Polak rushed to his side, placing Spring's head in his lap. "Look what they did."

"More the reason we must move with haste."

Chapter 38

"Jakob, you must wake up. We have to go," Johann said.

Jakob aroused from his slumber with the help of Johann shaking his shoulders. He outstretched an arm. Johann pulled him upright.

"They expect your father at first light. He means to hang you and the Americans upon his arrival."

Jakob focused on a soldier standing guard at the door. Johann grabbed Jakob by the shoulders. "You must listen to me. Your father will arrive soon. He intends to hang you at daybreak. We have less than eight hours."

Jakob pointed to the door.

"Don't worry. That's Audric Schaal, my best friend. I have a plan to extract you and the Americans but need your help. You must get ready."

Johann exited the cell. He returned in a blink, dragging a bloated, stinking German corpse, then commenced to stripping off the uniform. "Quick, you must change. Put the American uniform on first."

Jakob did not react to the demand to undress. Johann pulled off clothing stretched by swollen limbs.

"Jakob, please, we must hurry."

Jakob fumbled with the buttons on his shirt. "What plan?"

"Here," Johann said, passing the soldier's boots, pants, and belt. He went to work peeling off the overcoat and shirt.

"Where do you mean to take me?"

"We must exit before the next guard rounds. I'll detail my plan once out of the bunker." Johann offered Jakob a rifle and utility belt.

Jakob completed the outfitting. Johann pulled a log from the fireplace, extinguishing the flame with aid of the corpse.

"This will suppress the smell." He rubbed the smoldering remnant upon Jakob's coat and pants. He grabbed a hand-full of ash and rubbed the mass into Jakob's hair and upon his face. "Here," he said, passing a helmet. "Keep this pulled low."

Johann re-dressed the corpse in Jakob's discarded prison garb. He and Audric hefted the body onto the concrete shelf. Johann rolled it forward against the wall and covered it with the blanket.

Audric checked the hallway. He motioned forward.

"Are you ready?" Johann asked.

"As I will ever be."

"Here," Johann said, passing a dog tag, folded letters, and gold wedding band into Jakob's palm.

Jakob allowed the tag to unravel. The finish, once polished to a high sheen, now stained with his friend's blood.

"Rural Route 2, Wellsboro, Pennsylvania," Jakob read. He pondered the pain O'Dell's wife would endure upon receiving news of his missing status. He slipped the tag around his neck and stowed the other objects in his back pocket.

Johann placed a hand on top his shoulder. "We must move, now."

***

Johann detailed his plan while leading Jakob beyond the bunker entrance to near a gate leading to a separate compound.

Jakob gorged himself on the night air, though the stench of burnt everything hung heavy. The temperature hovered near zero, but a high blue moon hung against an endless field of stars.

"Do you understand?"

Jakob wavered. He contemplated the reasonableness of the actions suggested and his trust of the men claiming their allegiance. His expression made clear his diffidence.

"Why would I surrender loaded weapons if I intended you harm? You could've turned the gun on me in the cell. Do you agree? You have but two friends right now. You either trust me or fulfill the death wish your father has for you, and swing when the sun rises.

"Audric will get you to each location. You must find our man. Remember, we have less than eight hours. I'll have everything ready."

Johann fled toward the main complex housing the camp's guards.

"Now we go," Audric said. He led Jakob from the secondary gate at the camp's center, leading to an area fenced off for African, French, and Italian prisoners.

They passed through a checkpoint to the indifference of several guards. Audric moved with precision, sidestepping potholes, and other obstructions as if he'd scripted the path prior. They turned a corner at a small brick hut. The first of four massive marquees were intact. They'd have to search each structure.

A guard held vigil at the entrance to the first barrack. He recognized Audric and offered a Red Cross parcel in exchange for him taking over his watch.

"I seek an American," Audric said.

The soldier promised two parcels, but Audric waved him off and passed without further comment. Jakob fell in behind. His stomach eased. For such a young buck, Audric displayed plenty of nerve and superiority. They entered the quarters unchaperoned.

The stink of nearby latrines compared little to what lurked among the prison population. The men slept back-to-back on a muck-covered floor with a mere smattering of straw for bedding. Thousands of Russian and British soldiers waited out the war in conditions unsuitable for the lowest of God's creatures. The smell of diarrhea, vomit, and body odor hung thick.

"Keep your weapon in hand," Audric instructed. "We must make this appear like a mission." He passed Jakob a small flashlight.

"Private Hansel?" Audric called out in a mocking fashion. Men groaned in disgust; others barked insults. "Private Hansel? Where are you hiding?"

Rows of men ran twelve deep, leaving a single lane in between. Jakob directed the beam from one side to the other. He illuminated the face of each man, prompting groans and salty language. He'd recognize Hansel if he saw him.

"Private Hansel, come out, come out, wherever you are. I want to play a game."

They worked each aisle. A couple men turned their heads, most kept their eyes closed, too weak to lift an arm to deflect the light. Several offered blank, unresponsive stares, having lost both mind and spirit.

"I wonder where Private Hansel is?"

"*Pejt v pizdo*," a man hollered from the back.

"I do not see him," Jakob whispered.

They moved to the second hut. Audric entered, slammed the door, and demanded to know the whereabouts of Hansel. Jakob's antennae spiked as this group of prisoners offered no response. Their silence spoke volumes.

Halfway down the last row, Jakob spotted a large man dressed in rags, lying shoeless on his stomach with head turned.

Audric moved in. "Wake up, soldier boy," he said, nudging the man's shin. The prisoner did not budge. Audric repeated the move, prompting a reaction. Jakob settled to his haunches and redirected his flashlight, exposing the prisoner's bruised and battered face. A bloody slice traced along his cheek from the back of his head to beyond the point of his chin. Jakob nodded.

"On your feet, soldier boy," Audric demanded. He pressed the toe of his boot into Hansel's thigh.

Hansel struggled to his knees. Jakob desired to assist, but worked the ruse, knowing many eyes focused upon their actions.

Prisoners spat vulgarities, angry the goons had picked this man again. Audric brought his rifle to aim as stirring ensued. The ruckus prompted additional guards to rush to the scene. Order restored in a snap.

Jakob stepped back and brought the light to Hansel's face. He dropped the beam enough for the two to make eye contact.

Audric grabbed him by the arm. "We go now," he said, pulling.

Hansel turned to Jakob before exiting. "We saved your miserable life, you lousy fuck."

Chapter 39

Audric led the men to a dead-end nook tucked behind a camp galley. He sidestepped an out-of-place wine barrel to deposit Hansel against a brick wall. Jakob moved in. Audric assumed a position in the shadows to keep watch over the grounds.

Hansel slumped against the brick, expecting his end had come. He rushed through a plea to God for forgiveness of his crimes. Jakob led him into a wedge of moonlight, breaching the eve of an adjoining rooftop. The steel-blue hue transposed their appearances from men to ghosts of men.

"Go ahead, finish it," Hansel slurred.

"I do not intend to kill you, Private, I mean to help you."

"You're a liar. We risked our lives for you. You're breathing because Denny leaves no injured man behind. You sons of bitches murdered Martel. Go ahead, shoot me. You'll be rotting in hell soon enough, along with these other maggots."

"You must trust me. I, along with several corroborators, devised a plan to extract you and the others from this camp."

Hansel's attention spiked. "What others? Who's here?"

"Spring, Polak, Sperro—"

"And Shimmel?" Hansel interrupted.

"Yes, in a holding cell on the other side of camp."

"Where's Denny?"

"They captured Sergeant Denny and I during the ambush. He was executed for wearing a German uniform. I cannot tell you the grief I feel over his loss."

"What do you mean, who shot him?"

"An SS officer charged him with treason for wearing the wrong uniform and shot him on the spot. I killed the officer and others involved in the ambush. Polak, Sperro, Spring, and I continued with O'Dell's mission to extract Shimmel. They arrested us as we tried to cross a bridge and brought us here to hang. I have friends assisting with our escape."

Hansel dropped his chin to his chest and brought a hand to against his forehead.

"I did all I could to avoid what happened," Jakob added.

"I'll bet you did. I'll bet you had no choice but to let them shoot him."

"I could not save him."

"Bullshit."

"We can debate this later. We represent your lone chance of getting out alive."

"I don't trust you. I'm not going anywhere. Shoot me."

Audric extracted a final puff from a used cigarette and flicked it to the ground. Jakob pulled his Luger and flashed it for Hansel to catch a clear visual. He tossed the weapon; Hansel caught it.

"Take aim," Jakob demanded.

Hansel traded glances between the gun and Jakob.

"I said, take aim."

Hansel centered the barrel of the gun on the bridge of Jakob's nose.

"I trust you and your group of men to the point I have delivered my sole means of defense. You have three choices. Pull the trigger and avenge the deaths of your friends, which will summon guards, and you will die. Wait until the sun rises and we can all hang together. Or exchange those prison rags for the uniforms in the barrel and help me extract the rest of the men. What say you?"

Hansel worked through Jakob's words, blinking and shaking his head, as if attempting to pull out of a dream.

"We are out of time, Private. Please, check the barrel, or end both our lives right now by pulling the trigger."

Hansel stepped back and popped the lid, exposing an American and German uniform and accessories.

"What do you need from me?"

"I have no chance of convincing your corporal of our plan. He will not believe me but will believe you. I need you to persuade him of our intent to escape."

As Hansel held his aim, Jakob moved closer to the barrel of the gun. Several moments slipped by before Hansel released a deep breath, then dropped the Luger to his side.

"Get dressed. We are running out of time."

***

Johann's attention to the simplest of details cemented Jakob's trust in the operation. Hansel's uniforms fit perfectly.

Audric detailed Shimmel's location—a bunker, he claimed, reserved for Jewish prisoners, near ground zero, where British bombers dropped their payloads in lieu of the train station at Diez.

The farther west across camp they traveled, the greater the stench. Cordite, burnt flesh, and wood commingled to assault their senses, begetting a most disturbing image of what took place. They moved through and around smoldering rubble, bodies, and parts of bodies. A malodorous scent of decomposition attached to them like a rash.

They strode through the carnage without suspicion. Two buildings from the bunker, Audric signaled the men to pause. He slipped into the shadows, returning with a seaman's bag flung over his shoulder. He passed the bag to Hansel.

They proceeded to the bunker entrance, where two civilian guards stood at attention.

"We must prepare the prisoner for execution," Audric stated.

The guards traded a glance, each expecting the other to respond. But neither spoke English.

"Wir sind hier zur Vorbereitung der Gefangenen für die Ausführung der strafe," Audric repeated.

"Nein. Nein. Herr von Rüdel gab spezifische Aufträge—niemandem ist der Eintritt erlaubt," the senior guard said, claiming orders of no admittance.

Audric detailed von Rüdel's instructions for preparing the prisoner prior to his return to camp, and consequences facing any man who dare interfere. The guards conceded. They knew well Franz von Rüdel's wrath and held no desires to push his buttons so close to the war's conclusion.

A guard lit a small lantern, unlocked the heavy, rusted door, and entered. Audric waved Jakob and Hansel forward and instructed the door shut and locked.

The men descended thirty feet down a single lane concrete stairwell, following the guard who poked about as if never having ventured into the space.

The Germans constructed the cells in such a way a man could not stand upright or stretch out. Jakob inspected each as they passed. He intended to take any man so entombed. Halfway down, he drew his flashlight into a cell to his right, identifying the root source of the intense odor. A prisoner lay crumpled in a ball, naked, with limbs twisted from the onset of rigor mortis, a Star of David carved into his back.

A faint glow spilled into the pathway at the far end of the run. Jakob pushed past the guard, eager to know Shimmel's condition.

Shimmel looked more like a piece of butchered meat pounded and prepped for the oven. He lay balled in a fetal position, naked, shivering. A single wick nub of a candle provided his lone source of light and heat.

"*Öffnen sie die zelle, jetzt*," Jakob growled. The guard inserted a key into the tumbler. Jakob opened the cell, grabbed hold of the back of the guard's collar, and flung him into the opposite-side cell door.

Hansel approached but stumbled to the ground as Audric rushed by with the butt end of his rifle angled downward. With a howl, he drove the butt into the side of the guard's head. The young boy dropped.

Audric turned to find Hansel and Jakob looking at him as if just having received the surprise of their lives. "He will not understand our actions," Audric said, before settling into a covering stance, facing the bunker entrance.

Hansel dropped the bag and rushed to the cell. Whip marks laced Shimmel's torso. His captors had etched a swastika into his back. Dried blood caked in his ears. They'd broken his nose. Jakob removed his coat, settled to a knee, and draped his body.

Shimmel's eyes fluttered with the newfound warmth. Hansel took off his helmet and bent low. Shimmel did not recognize him.

"Corporal, it's me, Private Hansel," he said.

Shimmel rolled his head. With body quivering and breath labored, he slurred in a whisper, "Go... fuck yourself... you sour Kraut... piece of shit."

Chapter 40

Despite his ghastly appearance and deplorable accommodations, Shimmel's feistiness drew a wry smile from Jakob, and a sigh of relief from Hansel. Though battered, he seemed ready for a fight. Jakob stepped from the cell to retrieve the seaman's bag.

Hansel collapsed on all fours. Shimmel's eyes opened full.

"Corporal, it's me, Dan Hansel," he said.

Shimmel inspected Hansel's face. Following a rush of intermittent blinks and twitches, he whispered, "Danny, boy."

"We're moving out, Eli." Shimmel grasped Hansel's hand and brought it to against his forehead. "You're safe now. No one will lay a hand on you again."

Jakob returned with the bag. Hansel emptied its contents. Johann had accounted for every need: food, water, medical supplies, two sets of uniforms, socks, boots, small arms, ammo, the works.

Many of Shimmel's wounds told of multiple blows. One lash cut deep enough into his side to expose rib bone. Hansel applied salve. Jakob snipped butterfly strips from multiple boxes of Red Cross bandages and patched Shimmel as best he could. The effort to clothe him took longer than expected.

They helped Shimmel into the hallway. He struggled for balance, needing the support of Hansel's massive forearm and Jakob's shoulder. As Shimmel extended his body upright, he came face to face with Jakob. He drew back with a jolt as if planting his face into a spider's web. His expression darkened.

"It's you," he said, his voice dripping with disgust. Blood trickled from his lip. Two bottom teeth displaced, producing a child-like lisp. The fragility of his current state did not temper his anger. Shimmel achieved a grip around Jakob's neck and squeezed with what little energy remained, pushing him against the cell opposite. "I'll kill you."

Hansel stepped in, forcing Shimmel's release and a pain-filled yelp.

He collected Shimmel's face in his palms. "Listen to me," Hansel begged. "Jakob wants to help us. Help you."

Shimmel shook his head.

"It's true, you must believe me. I'm here because Jakob came for me. We're all here because Denny insisted on coming after you. Angie, John, and Joe are here. Jakob can help, but you have to trust him. Trust me."

Shimmel continued his attempts to break free.

"Eli, you must believe me," Hansel said. "Look at me. Look at me."

Shimmel's body eased. "We have little time. If we don't leave right now, we're all gonna hang. Do you understand? Do you understand me?"

Shimmel's eyes darted about the room.

"I need you to answer me, Corporal."

He looked beyond Hansel's shoulder. Jakob held steady, rubbing his neck.

"We need to find the others and have little time."

"Why did Denny come for me?" Shimmel slurred. "Where is he?"

Hansel locked on Shimmel's eyes. He stood without response several moments. "He's dead, Eli. We got caught in an ambush on the way here. Denny did not want to leave you behind. We can discuss this later. Right now, we gotta go, man."

"Martel?" Shimmel asked.

Hansel shook his head.

Shimmel's eyes welled. He looked again to Jakob. "Your friends murdered my mother and father."

"I know, Corporal, but they are no friends of mine, and I will not allow them to murder you."

***

Jakob looked east as the men spilled from the bunker. A slight hint of orange hue appeared as nightfall surrendered to dawn. If they managed a successful escape, they would do so in daylight.

Audric passed a flashlight to the high school-aged civilian on watch. He ordered the lad into the bunker to assist his comrade, assuring he'd cover until they returned. The guard descended; Audric shut and locked the door as the boy disappeared into the darkness.

"We must bind your corporal's hands," Audric said, passing two leather straps to Hansel. "His condition will draw attention, but I have a plan. Walk behind him with your rifle pointed at his back."

The group worked their way across the yard at a snail's pace. The damage to Shimmel's groin forced a bow-legged waddle, his teeth grinding at the friction against his testicles.

The chosen course took them by way of a courtyard surrounded by barracks constructed for guards. At the yard's center, Russian prisoners buzzed in packs, constructing a poor man's gallows from splintered timbers recouped from the bombings. Five crossbeams, lashed in place with rope, extended perpendicular from a beam running the length of a raised platform.

Two Russians uncoiled a spool of razor wire, and a third snipped portions double in length to a full-size man.

With the gate separating his comrades' lodgings from the main prison yard now in sight, Audric expected unfettered passage, despite a co-conspirator having informed him of an officer replacing a low-level grunt in anticipation of Franz von Rüdel's return.

"Open the gate," Audric barked. The officer turned and gazed upon him with condescension, annoyed a slug of the Wehrmacht dare spew such authority.

The officer directed his flashlight upon Shimmel. "Why have you bound this man?"

"Arrested for drunkenness and brawling. Now, let us pass."

The weathered veteran obliged, though an icy gaze told of his skepticism. Audric escorted the group through.

Upon securing the gate, the officer entered an adjacent one-man shack and picked up a phone.

"Audric, he is calling us in," Jakob said.

"Of course. Now the *real* game begins." Audric turned a corner, moved through another open courtyard, and pointed to his left without a word or deviation of his stride.

A black Mercedes sat parked in front of the camp commandant's residence. A guard, a mountain of a man with ox-like shoulders, stood at attention at the back passenger-side door. Commandants directing transitory camps did not drive vehicles of such luxury; this, Jakob knew. He also knew the physical characteristics his father preferred in soldiers he placed in support positions.

By the time they reached the bunker housing the others, a man could spy a bird in flight against the sky. Three guards held vigil at the door. Audric made a beeline for a particular guard standing alone and well left of the entrance, puffing on a cigarette. He placed an arm around him. The soldier responded as if their coming had been foretold. He approached his counterparts and dismissed them from duty.

"Erik Gerok," Audric introduced. "He will aid in our escape, however, he does not speak English."

"How many more?" Jakob asked.

"Enough to do the job," Audric said.

"I don't give a shit if it involves a hundred more," Hansel said, "open this fuckin' door and let's get our boys."

Chapter 41

The door's seal popped. Hansel pushed by, antsy to reunite with pals he figured dead. He entered an awkward jog along the narrow hallway, expecting to find the men in similar physical condition as Shimmel. He stopped short of the cell and released a sigh, happy to see them all on their feet. "Dammit, it's good to see you boys," he said, before entering.

"We guessed you dead for sure," Polak said, as the two embraced.

"Not hardly. Goes to show you their incompetence around here."

Shimmel waddled in to join his men, eyes welling and emotions running high.

Jakob approached with Audric and Erik trailing. Johann exited the cell to join them.

"Is it true you killed the man who killed Sergeant Denny?" Spring asked.

Jakob nodded.

"You realize you're a dead man?" Polak said.

"A price one must consider if they plan to hold true to their convictions."

"Who are those two?" Sperro asked.

"Audric Schaal and Erik Gerok. They, too, want out of this war."

A hush settled over the men as each group gawked through the cell bars, letting simmer the utter improbability and absurdity of their association and trust in each other.

"We go now, or we die," Jakob said.

"How we gonna do this?" Polak asked.

"We'll walk out the front gate," Johann said.

"That simple, huh? Can we stop by the gift shop, maybe take a group photo before we leave?"

"We send reconnaissance parties out around the clock," Johann said. "Audric leads three to four a day. The guards will not think twice of our exit. We have a vehicle waiting north of the forest."

"You left nothing to chance," Sperro said, turning to Jakob.

"Not I... Johann. But planning and executing are different affairs."

"You sure about this?" Sperro asked Johann.

"No other options. They'll soon discover Jakob's absence."

"I've had enough chitchatting," Spring said. He exited the cell first. Jakob requested Polak and Audric take the lead. He and Erik would bring up the rear.

"You know we can't run with this group," Hansel said.

"If all goes as planned, we will not have to," Jakob replied.

Audric and Polak led the way under a sky summoning the first colors of dawn. The breeze remained stiff and marrow chilling. Erik ordered the guard into the bunker, then shut and locked the door.

The front gate was less than two city blocks away. Jakob's stomach felt aflame, coupled by the sensation of a multitude of butterflies chasing about. He kept his head down, planting his steps in the impression made by Spring, counting each stride to keep his mind occupied. He could feel his father's presence.

Guards moved in small groups toward the courtyard, paying little attention to the group marching the opposite direction. Within a half block of the commandant's quarters, Jakob spotted his father's Mercedes, though no sign of his personal valet. *He must be on the move.*

Four guards, two on the ground and two on a catwalk with machine guns at the ready, noticed the group approaching, and without orders, commenced to opening the gate. One man lifted the draw arm, another slid two massive gates, exposing an unobstructed view of fifty yards of open field and thick forest beyond.

Polak desired to run. Spring's attention focused on a single cloud, its formation a striking resemblance of his mother's profile. Hansel dreamed of a decent meal and hot shower. Sperro lamented the loss of his three brothers. Shimmel contemplated shooting the guards once beyond the gate.

Audric offered a salute as he passed. A disturbance to their rear caught their attention. Jakob searched over his shoulder for the source. An inaudible shout broke the calm, and seconds later, a guard's whistle blared, unleashing a torrent of activity.

Men barked orders. A chorus of alert whistles erupted. The group continued their trek through the gate. Audric kept a consistent cadence, focusing his sight on a massive tree across the field. Polak hesitated, Spring stalled and turned, as did Hansel. Erik and Jakob rammed them, sending Spring to his knees.

A shot rang out. Jakob turned and spotted a soldier in full sprint, with a swarm of others following in pursuit.

"*Sie stoppen! Sie stoppen!*" the soldier yelled.

Another shot rang out.

"Move, move," Jakob yelled, grabbing at Spring, and pushing Polak.

Several soldiers dropped to their knees and opened fire. The guards at the gate hesitated, their confusion evident. Spring stumbled again as he attempted to stand. Splinters exploded off the wood spires, snow popped at their feet. A guard at the gate pulled his sidearm, but Audric drew first, fired once, and dropped him. Hansel drove the butt end of his rifle into the face of the second guard as he passed. Shimmel fired a single round into his head.

A guard on the catwalk opened up with a machine gun. The second guard's gun jammed. A bullet caught Audric's shoulder, sending him tumbling. He rolled and returned fire, dropping the second guard. Polak squared up and delivered a shot to the neck of the other shooter.

The group scrambled along different routes toward the forest, as a hail of bullets clipped at their heels. Shimmel fell behind the others but held his own.

Polak outran them all. He entered the forest first, took position behind a tree, and returned fire. To his amazement, most of the shooters retreated toward the center of camp. A handful remained behind to remove the dead and secure the gate.

Jakob broke from his covered position and entered the field to assist Shimmel into the forest. Polak exhausted another clip.

The men scampered through the woods. Polak remained behind, waiting, listening. Silence ensued for several agonizing minutes before the breeze delivered the purr of an engine firing up. Moments later, a single personnel carrier charged through the gate. Polak scrambled to his feet and fled.

"Trouble, boys," he said, catching up to the others massed in a shallow ravine concealed by tangled underbrush. "They dispatched a personnel carrier."

"We got bigger troubles than that," Hansel replied. He removed his helmet and threw it against a tree. "Spring didn't make it out."

Chapter 42

"Let me go after him," Hansel pleaded.

"No way," Sperro said, pulling him by the arm.

"It's my fault. I should've grabbed him when the shooting started."

"We all knew the risk. It's not your fault and you're not going back."

"I gotta find him. Why can't I go with Polak?"

"Because you won't stop at the tree line," Sperro said. He held back a clump of thorn branches so the others could pass.

"We can't leave him."

"If he's not in the field, he never made it past the gate," Sperro said.

"They grabbed him or killed him."

"We must reach the vehicle before they do," Audric said.

He led them through a rocky passage carved by centuries of runoff.

The way spilled into a glen protected by steep bluffs posing as an ancient bulwark. Pines extended along the ridge, their trunks as straight as pencils, set equidistant, as if hand planted. A rustle to the rear forced a pause in their march.

"No sign of him," Polak said. "He's not in the field or at the gate."

"They killed him," Hansel said, kicking at the snow.

"You don't know for sure," Sperro said. "It's possible they'll dump him back in the general population."

"They'll make an example of him," Hansel said.

Jakob took advantage of the interruption to direct Shimmel to a nearby stump, where he addressed the bullet wound to his shoulder. He poked and prodded; Shimmel allowed it.

"I cannot fathom your resolve," Jakob said. "Any other man could not carry on."

Shimmel winced as Jakob stuffed a wad of gauze under his coat. Losing Spring weighed heavy. "Revenge can keep a man going under the most hopeless of circumstances."

Johann urged the men forward. Jakob re-draped Shimmel's coat before extending a hand. Shimmel paused, his cognitive function lagging. "How did you become an exception to Nazi ideals?"

"I am my mother's son," he replied. "She has no enemies, nor does she propagate malice toward others, regardless of origin or social standing. She expects and demands the same from her children."

"When I was a child, I killed a bird with a slingshot," Shimmel said. "My mother picked up the bird, and, through tears, chastised me for stealing a life created by God. Now look at me. Look what I've become. Look what they make you surrender of yourself."

Jakob reached again for Shimmel's hand. Shimmel grunted as he came upright, holding tight well after regaining balance. No words exchanged or glances traded. It would be the best Shimmel could do to express his gratitude.

The group moved up a slight incline to a plateau. Gerok crouched ahead, signaling to the northeast.

"This way," Audric urged, pointing. "Gerok located the vehicle."

The men rushed toward his position. Jakob brought up the rear, moving as fast as Shimmel's skip would allow. They caught up at the edge of a shallow, manmade trench separating forest from road. A utility truck, void of its canvas bed cover, sat on the opposite side, tucked in the woods under a thick layer of branches and brush.

Gerok exited the tree line with a guarded step, took one look, then dropped to a knee. He pointed toward the ground, alerting Johann to a set of fresh tire tracks.

"*In welche richtung?*" Johann asked.

Gerok pointed west, indicating the tracks had come from the camp. He crept across the road to the truck and removed the camouflage covering. Audric followed, slipping under the vehicle to inspect the chassis. Gerok hopped into the cab and turned over the engine. He flashed a thumbs up. Johann signaled the men forward.

Polak unhitched the bed gate, allowing the others to load. Audric hopped in the passenger seat. Gerok slid in behind the wheel and pulled the vehicle from the forest onto the roadway, turning west toward freedom, two hundred kilometers away.

***

"Straight ahead," Polak yelled, pointing to a gray speck centered in the roadway. The truck decelerated, propelling the men thumping against the side.

Polak steadied his rifle atop wood slats and peeked through the scope. "It's a half-track. Five on the ground, one up top. Holy shit, holy shit, it's the kid. Those fucker's have him strapped to the grill crucifixion-style."

A volley of shots rang out. Gerok lost control of the vehicle, veering off the road and into a tree. Johann, Sperro, and Audric ejected into a snowdrift. The others crumpled against Hansel and Polak, dropping them all to the bed.

Small arms fire erupted. Bullets pierced the truck's metal shell and splintered the wood railings. Polak grabbed a fistful of Jakob's coat and scampered over the side. Hansel attempted to pull Shimmel to safety, but he lay prone, out cold. He jumped, seeking refuge behind the rear tires.

Sperro and Johann crawled to the front of the cab. Steam pouring from the engine provided temporary cover. The men formed around Jakob, who sat crouched in the ditch below the driver's side door. All fell silent.

Polak checked the clip in his rifle. He swung around the front of the truck and fired three rounds. A second hail of enemy projectiles peppered the broadside of the truck.

"What the hell, Joe?" Sperro yelled.

"They need to know we can return fire."

Jakob flipped the latch to the driver's door. Gerok spilled from the seat onto the ground. Steam poured from a gaping cavity in his chest. Jakob checked Audric's condition. He lay crumpled on the floorboard, bleeding at the scalp, his breathing erratic.

"I do not see Shimmel," Jakob said.

"Out cold," Hansel said. "Plowed headfirst into the back of the cab."

"What now?" Polak asked.

"Got to find a way to—"

"Attention, Americans," a voice boomed. "We have you surrounded. Surrender and save yourselves."

Polak peeked around the corner. Sets of twos lay on their stomachs on either side of the half-track. A fifth combatant stood behind the cab aiming a high-caliber machine gun. An officer barked from behind the passenger door.

Polak retreated. "We're not surrounded. I count six."

"You sure?" Sperro asked.

"Yeah. They positioned too far forward. There's open field on either side."

"Well, I ain't dropping my weapon. If he wants to talk, he can talk with my rifle pointed at his head," Hansel said.

"I'm tired of this shit," Polak said. "I ain't running from this one. We either save the kid or die trying."

"We want our men," the German yelled. "I will trade your man for ours."

Polak, Hansel, and Sperro looked to Jakob.

"I don't understand," Sperro said. "Why only six?"

"It makes perfect sense. My father's ego will not allow for more. He wants full credit for my death."

Chapter 43

"I say we dig in and take them from here," Polak suggested. Sperro and Hansel tucked in close behind.

"I can take out the fifty cal," Polak said. "I see the top of the guy's helmet."

"Not good enough," Sperro whispered. "You ding him, the kid buys it. He ain't worried about us. A twig snaps and Spring's head splatters."

"If we can flank 'em, we'll have a better angle," Hansel suggested.

"He fires at first threat," Sperro said. "I don't think we'd have time to reposition and line him up."

The conversation raged, each man suggesting a plan of attack. Johann climbed into the cab to check on Audric. Jakob squatted against the rear tire, his mind churning as to how he might work a solution to spare Spring's life. He could not bear another man murdered at his expense. He set his rifle in the truck bed and drew his Luger.

"Jakob, what do you see from there?" Sperro asked.

Sperro turned. "Jakob?" He scampered to the rear of the vehicle. Polak followed.

"What the hell's he up to?" Polak blurted, watching Jakob settle into a slow trek up the road with a Luger mashed against his temple.

Hansel slid into the ditch and settled his crosshairs on the first of two soldiers on the ground to the left. He drew his aim to the goon on top of the cab. The soldier did not deviate from his covered position, appearing ready to fire upon Spring at first threat.

He fixed his crosshair on Jakob's father and wiped clean a scintilla of dust from off his scope to achieve clarity of the crown of Franz's head.

"What ya got, Dan?" Sperro asked.

"Three shots. Two on the ground to the left and Herr General. I don't have an angle right, but I have a sliver of the right side of the fifty cal's face."

"I see the farthest guy right, but he'd have to show himself more for a clean shot," Polak said.

"Shit. We need better than that. Joe, ya think you can make the woods?"

"It's sparse over there. Might have a chance with Jakob keeping them busy."

Sperro crawled to the driver's side door. "Joe, line up those two to the right. I'll watch 'em. If they rotate your direction, I'll cover. Stay low."

Polak moved into position near the front of the truck. He dropped to his belly, slithered into the ditch and out the other side, inching toward a tree twenty yards away.

Sperro wedged himself under the chassis near the front axle. "What are you doing, Jakob?" he whispered.

Jakob took a position in the middle of the road. He stopped halfway between the two parties. "Release the prisoner, now," he bellowed, drawing every eye and weapon, paving the way for Polak.

"You have sixty seconds to release him, or I will put a bullet in my head."

"I want the other traitors," Franz demanded.

"No greater traitor exists than you," Jakob growled. "A traitor to your family, country, and all humanity. Forty-five seconds."

His words drew the expected effect. Franz's face flushed red with rage.

"You will not see your mother, sister, or worthless horse again. They are all dead."

"You are a liar."

"As you wish, but you have no family. Your American pals destroyed Düren last month. You have nothing. You are finished."

Jakob fought the urge to fire on his father. If he did, Spring would die. "Thirty seconds."

"You do not possess courage enough to commit suicide."

"And you will not allow me to end my life this way. I must hang to impress the rabble for which you sold your soul."

"I should kill you now," Franz said.

"You cannot and will not. Your filthy comrades would mock you. What would Herr Himmler say of your failure to avenge his dear friend's death out of view of public eye? You cannot fail him."

Franz drew his sidearm. He repositioned in front of the track and placed the barrel against Spring's temple.

"Dan, do you have the fifty cal?" Sperro blurted.

"Negative. He's hunkered."

"Shoot him, and your career dies," Jakob responded. "Release him, and opportunity for glory awaits. Twenty seconds."

"You must pay for abetting the enemy, pay for murdering your own countrymen, pay for attempting to destroy my career and legacy," Franz yelled, ejecting spittle. "You must pay."

Franz crouched low, keeping aim at Spring. He retrieved a knife from a leather sheath strapped to his shin, exposing with deliberate sloth to allow the sun's reflection against its stainless-steel blade.

"Release their man and I shall pay your price," Jakob said. "Ten seconds."

Franz pressed the knife against Spring's cheek, drawing blood with a hairline slice from ear to chin. He spat in Spring's face before cutting the rope binding his arms and legs. Spring buckled and balled up on the ground. He rolled onto his stomach, then maneuvered to his hands and knees. Franz delivered a kick into his ribcage, stealing his breath.

"You move as he moves. You stop, he dies," Franz yelled. "On your way, *das frauenzimmer*." He delivered another kick to Spring's backside.

Spring crawled a fair distance before getting upright. Jakob approached and grabbed hold to prevent his collapse.

Franz moved to behind the vehicle's passenger door and exchanged the Luger for a sniper's rifle. He settled the gun on the window frame and fired. The round popped in the snow at Spring's heel.

"Halt," Franz yelled.

"How 'bout it, Dan?" Sperro asked.

"No shot."

"Deliver the other traitors or your man dies. Twenty seconds to decide."

"Dan?"

"Don't have it."

"We go on my shot, boys," Sperro said.

Franz pulled the bolt and ducked behind the scope to prepare to fire.

Sperro set his crosshairs on the upper half of Franz' forehead. He took a deep breath then released, as a vacuum evaporated all sights and sounds about him, offering clear focus of his target. As he readied to pull the trigger, a shot rang out. Franz's head exploded.

Jakob drove Spring to the ground. Hansel cut down the fifty-cal operator as he lifted from his crouch to fire. Polak split his first target's head. He dropped the second soldier as he attempted to run. Sperro dispensed two rounds into a target on the ground to the right. The sixth and final combatant, overwhelmed by the incoming barrage, popped up in a panic and was cut in half.

"Hold your fire," Sperro barked. Remnants of their handiwork echoed throughout the surrounding pastures with a deliberate leisure. The men held steady for signs of further threat or surrender.

Sperro crawled from under the truck. A familiar eerie stillness ensued; a deafening calm all men experience in the microseconds when guns fall silent.

Shimmel lay stretched across the top of the cab, anchored against the bed fence with rifle in hand, its barrel smoking.

Jakob raced toward the half-track and fell to his knees at his father's side.

Polak and Hansel sprinted from their position to collect Spring. Johann moved Audric's body from the cab. Sperro assisted Shimmel from the bed of the truck.

"Did you take out the officer?"

"Yeah. Came to and saw him take a pop at Spring, so I lined him up before he could fire another round."

"A hell of a shot considering your condition." Sperro let go a deep sigh.

"What is it? What's the problem?"

"Nothing, you had no choice."

"I couldn't sit and watch the lousy fuck shoot the kid, right?"

"No, but that's Jakob's father. He'd been hunting him since Jakob refused to kill a downed American paratrooper."

"His father? I don't believe it. What the fuck sort of man hunts down his own son?"

"An exact opposite of the man we've found Jakob to be."

Sperro draped his arm around Shimmel and led him to in front of the half-track with the others. Johann soon followed, wiping at his eyes.

"Audric?" Sperro asked.

Johann shook his head.

"I'm sorry."

Johann nodded. He moved past the group to offer comfort to his former classmate. Shimmel followed in his footsteps.

Jakob repositioned to his haunches.

"I am sorry it came to this," Johann said.

Jakob choked out a cough. "He lived two lives. I shall remember the man who once loved his family."

Shimmel turned from the group and dropped his head. Polak placed a hand on his shoulder. "You saved two good men."

"Yeah," Shimmel replied, "but, up to this point, in my mind, I've killed Germans, not fathers."

"You'd have a tougher time had you let that bastard kill both of 'em."

Sperro helped Jakob relocate his father's body. Johann fired up the half-track's engine.

"We need to move out," Sperro suggested. "No telling what's on the way."

Hansel turned to Jakob. "No matter what happens now, you've avenged O'Dell's death."

Chapter 44

Johann proved invaluable, making quick and efficient work of distancing the group from Limburg. At a desolate crossroads northwest of Koblenz, a point dissecting once rich pastures hosting droves of cattle, he eased the track to the side of the road and cut the engine.

"Our voices will not go unheard," Sperro pleaded with Jakob. "You may end up in a prison camp, but you'll be alive."

Jakob rested on his haunches, surrounded by all but Spring, who remained stretched out in the truck's bed.

"I will not rest until I know," Jakob said, recounting his father's claim. "I have to go home."

"Understood," Sperro replied, "but what then? You're a deserter, an escaped prisoner, a traitor."

Jakob shrugged. "All worries for another time. I must find my family."

Hansel settled on a knee near Jakob's side. "You can't stay here, whether your family survived or not."

"Is it possible the Allies have driven this far west?" Jakob questioned.

"I don't know," Sperro said. "I know the First Army pushed through Liege in September. How far beyond, who knows. Is your homestead close to Liege?"

"Eighty kilometers."

"You have no food or water," Hansel said.

"A two-day march is of no concern."

"You're gonna stroll along in broad daylight, in uniform?" Hansel asked.

"I will travel the pastures. I know this country well. Many water sources exist between here and there."

"I'll see to his safety," Johann said.

"And you were going to surrender," Polak quipped.

"I promise, just as soon as I know of Jakob's safe exit."

"I will not allow you to put yourself at further risk for my sake," Jakob said.

"Unlike the risk you took for me?" Johann replied.

"A different time and place. A different set of circumstances."

"Unlike what you did for me?" Spring said, out of sight of the others.

"And me?" Sperro added.

"And us?" Hansel said, hitching a thumb in Polak's direction.

"There's nothing here for any of us," Shimmel said. "I say we move the hell on to Düren and find his family."

"You cannot venture on in the wrong direction. You, of all people," Jakob said, pointing to Shimmel. "You all need to leave or risk capture. You want a return trip to Limburg?"

"It's done," Sperro said. "We decide our next move once we reach Düren. Hell, we might already own the town."

"I will not let you do it," Jakob said.

"And who's gonna stop us?" Polak commented. "We don't need either of you to drive this track."

"You must take advantage while you can," Jakob pleaded.

"You're free to hike the countryside or ride with us. Either way, we're going to Düren," Hansel said.

"Yeah, we'll wait for you," Polak added, "maybe have a cup of coffee when you arrive."

Jakob had prepared both mind and spirit for a solitary journey, whether in the immediate future, or what remained of his life.

Shimmel grabbed him by the collar and tugged. "Come on. Let's find your family."

***

Johann kept their progress cloaked, passing through private properties, pastures, back yards, front yards, and through buildings. He doubled their drive time with multiple switchbacks and re-routes but kept them out of harm's way and out of sight. The others napped as best they could.

Evidence of allied bombing presented well outside Düren common, escalating Jakob's fears.

"We need to ditch this track," Sperro said. "I didn't come all this way to get plugged by friendly fire. Can we hoof it from here?"

"Yes," Jakob said.

"We need to scrap these uniforms," Polak said.

Sperro shook his head. "We gotta find out what's going on in town first." He slapped the top of the cab. Johann took a sharp left and obliterated a split-rail fence. He slipped the track behind an abandoned barn.

The men unloaded what supplies remained. Polak and Hansel joined Jakob on point. Sperro assisted Shimmel; Johann aided Spring.

Jakob led the group down a fencerow into the woods. His selected route would keep them under cover most of the way. The closer they moved toward the town, the greater the devastation. Bomb craters, mere feet apart, stretched beyond sight. Dead livestock littered surrounding pastures.

At the edge of town, the men slipped into the remnants of a wasted church littered with religious artifacts. A crucifix hung lopsided near a blown out stained-glass window. Sperro scaled a pile of rubble to the second story. He took one look and ordered the men to remain dressed as is. "It ain't ours yet," he said.

Jakob scaled the pile. He pushed away a clump of bricks for a wider vista. "My God," he whispered, "it cannot be."

Few buildings remained taller than a single story. To the west, the city's railroad station lay in ruins, engines and passenger cars charred and strewn about as if accessories of a child's neglected toy set.

To the east, only piles of dirt, rock, and building material. The north, an area where a concentration of church steeples once stretched to the heavens, offered an unobstructed view of the sky.

"Obliterated," Jakob mumbled.

He slid from the pile to the hole where they'd entered the building.

"Wait a minute," Hansel said. "You can't just take off running down the street."

Shimmel grabbed hold of Jakob's coat. "Right. We need to blend in. Appear as if moving from building to building, not running."

Sperro agreed. "We move on the outskirts. I'll take the lead with Jakob. What's our distance?"

"Two miles," Jakob said.

"Okay. Joe, cover our ass. Let's go."

Jakob's heart sank each city block traveled. He recognized many shop signs embedded in rubble. He knew the owners and their families. A smattering of German personnel assisted locals clearing streets and extracting the dead.

The group pressed on from one charred building to the next, many still in possession of the bodies of its owners, before spilling out into crop fields.

The bombers showed little discrimination. Craters dotted the countryside, pristine farmland defaced forever.

Anxiety topped out as craters became more plentiful the nearer Jakob drew to his homestead. Shy of two hours since entering town, he spotted the skeletal remains of a black poplar marking their property line. The massive wonder splintered near its mid-point, with branch shards strewn hundreds of feet. He dropped his rifle and sprinted down the drive, praying his mother, sister, and his dear Sascha had been spared the nightmare.

Chapter 45

In the spring and summer months, the von Rüdel estate sat invisible behind an array of dense hardwoods and thicket, creating a mystical and mysterious ambiance. A tree-lined lane harbored the hidden gem until the third of three winding turns spilled from a gap carved in a head-high hedgerow running perpendicular to the home.

The long winter months offered no such asylum. At the second turn, Jakob should have had an unencumbered view of the front parlor's chimney. When he spotted nothing but sky, he lengthened his stride. At the final turn, he pushed through the hedgerow and fell to his knees. The house lay in ruins.

He lowered his head, staring into the snow, his tears freezing upon contact. What he knew as real, transcended to memory; what he knew as normal, appeared now as unrecognizable chaos.

He struggled to his feet and turned toward the pasture. His gut ached knowing he stood little chance of finding Sascha, but his heart stoked hope. The smokehouse remained erect, though a shell of its former self.

The gate to the pasture lay on the ground, twisted wire fence line strewn about in a tangled mess. Tank and other vehicle tracks snaked from one end of the pasture to the other. A most hideous onslaught happened here, an action far surpassing any he could imagine.

The barn looked like little more than a long-forgotten burn pile, interspersed patches of black visible through winter's white blanket, with several mounds scattered in the distance. Jakob approached over ground dotted with frozen pools of ashen slurry and pieces of hardware rusted and pitted from exposure.

His heart sank. The cattle had no chance of escape. He scanned the destruction and death, praying Sascha jumped the fence. He looked off to his right at a large chestnut under which Sascha often found solace in the summer months.

He spotted a carcass near the fence line beneath the tree and approached. His legs turned to jelly upon identification. *God only knows the fear striking her as the bombs approached.* Jakob knew of Sascha's fear of thunder. She would not have known the difference.

He cleared away snow from the remains of her hindquarter. A pack of wolves had long since filled their bellies of most of her flesh. A million tiny shards of memories and moments wedged into the pin-sized hole of his mind's eye. Anguish sent his chest into spasm. *How petrified, confused, and abandoned she must have felt.*

He ran his hand over her hoof, torturing himself with sounds and images of her final moments. So deep did he slip into the memory of her, he did not register the echo of Johann's voice calling for help.

Sperro and Hansel stopped short upon seeing Jakob on his knees. "His horse?" Hansel whispered.

"Guess so."

Hansel slumped with a heavy sigh, knowing the relationship between Jakob and his horse equaled that of O'Dell and his beloved Bella. "It's no mystery why those two connected," Hansel said.

"I had no better friend," Jakob whispered, "no better companion."

Sperro turned away.

"Jakob, you need to come to the house," Hansel said.

"What?"

Hansel could not find the words. He helped Jakob to his feet.

"What happened?"

Hansel shook his head. Jakob broke from him.

"Wait," Sperro called out, joining Hansel in pursuit.

"Jakob," Hansel yelled.

Jakob blew past the smokehouse. Johann, Spring, and Shimmel huddled at the far corner of the home where a portion of foundation remained. Jakob stumbled through the rubble toward them. Johann and Shimmel met him halfway, grabbing him as he attempted to move past.

"Jakob, no," Johann demanded.

He strained to see over their heads. Shimmel prevented Jakob from hitting the ground.

The skeletal remains of a single arm, its hand stretched as if reaching for the heavens, projected from under a cobweb of charred beams.

Jakob's sobbing renewed. He dropped his forehead against Shimmel's shoulder.

"I'm sorry," Shimmel whispered.

***

The men spent an hour digging through debris to free the remains of Jakob's mother and sister. Jakob identified the bodies but could do little else to assist. He found a spot under a tree and buried his head in his hands.

Johann suggested the flower garden as the final resting place, as his mother had turned the earth in the fall, making the task less arduous. Jakob agreed, though it mattered not.

"Only their husks remain," he said. "They have traded this world for another far greater."

Polak located a spade in the smokehouse. The men took turns digging at the frozen earth, as the last bit of daylight clung to the western sky. Shimmel spread the final covering of dirt over the shallow grave.

"Goddamn war," Shimmel charged. He took the spade by the handle and slung it across the yard. "Look at the cost. Look at this shit Hitler has stolen. It's a waste. All of it."

"You wanna offer a final word, Jakob?" Sperro asked.

Jakob shook his head. "I have made my peace. They deserved better than this life, and if given an opportunity to return, they would remain where they are."

All fell silent, a peculiar moment demanding a reaction. Jakob looked toward the heavens. "Do you hear that?"

Each man held still. They looked about, waiting, listening.

"Birds," Jakob said. "They have all disappeared."

The observation proved a switch, shedding light on an otherwise obvious void.

Polak looked to the trees, searching all within view. "I never considered it, but I don't remember the last time I heard a bird."

"Amazing how war can force nature into retreat," Johann said.

Each man returned to his private thoughts of home and family.

Shimmel turned to Jakob. "I'm sorry for the pain I've added."

"Please, do not blame yourself. You provided relief to my conscience. I did not intend for my father to survive that moment. Had you not acted, I was prepared to rid humanity of him. You carried out an act of war. I intended to murder him. You saved me from myself. I am grateful."

"What now?" Hansel asked.

Jakob did not respond.

"Does he take the chance of turning himself in with me?" Johann asked.

"I don't think so," Shimmel said.

"No paperwork," Sperro said.

"Right."

"We can't prove he helped us escape," Sperro said.

"Or he thinks Hitler's an asshole," Polak said.

"Or he's from New York," Hansel added.

Johann blew a breath of warm air into his hands, then said, "He cannot stay. All who worked at the camp knew his plight. SS and Gestapo will search all corners. The officer he killed has well-placed friends."

"I understand," Jakob said.

"Then what?" Polak asked.

Jakob settled on his haunches. "I made a promise and I plan to keep it."

Shimmel settled next to him. "What promise?"

"I promised your sergeant I would return to America, find his wife, and share with her the truth surrounding his death. She deserves to know what happened. She deserves to know her husband died a hero."

"How the hell do you plan on doing that?" Sperro asked.

Jakob shrugged.

"Sure as shit won't be easy," Polak said.

Sperro dropped to a knee next to Shimmel. "How do we hide an undocumented enemy soldier in our ranks?"

"To hell with hiding him," Hansel said, "how do we find him passage to the States?"

"I don't know. We'd have to find some proof of identity," Shimmel said.

Johann approached from the opposite end of the grave and settled in front of his friend. With a droll smile, he reached for the chain draped around Jakob's neck. "Even in death, Sergeant Denny has provided for your survival."

Chapter 46

Spring stumbled upon the hatch by accident, stubbing his toe on a heavy steel loop bolted to an access door to the family's cellar. Jakob informed them of its usual stock of grain and smoked meats.

Polak and Hansel constructed a conical pyre of beams, and other combustibles collected from the ruins. Flames roared to life as the last sliver of daylight slipped below the horizon. The men slumped against trees, stumps, anything within proximity, gorging on smoked ham, venison, and an assortment of sausages.

"It's a good plan, Jakob," Polak said. "It's the perfect plan."

"I do not agree. I find it blasphemous."

"Blasphemous? Why?" Sperro asked.

Jakob shrugged. He brought a hand against his temple and rubbed. His mind wavered to comprehend concern for personal liberation versus loss of father, mother, sister, horse, home, and all possessions.

"It contradicts an existence, his contribution to humanity, his legacy," Jakob said.

"Horseshit," Hansel said. "I'll tell you this, O'Dell would have none of this. He'd want you out of here and insist you take his tags to ensure safe passage."

"Damn right he would," Polak said.

"If you don't do this, you may never find a way out," Johann added. "They'll hunt you the rest of your days."

Jakob rubbed O'Dell's dog tag with his thumb.

"It's a means to an end, that's it," Shimmel said. "No one's saying you become Denny, you simply borrow his identify, if need be, until you reach the States. It's momentary."

Jakob continued stroking the tag. He placed the letters and picture on a stump by his side. "And if they find out?"

"Who? The Army?" Polak said, laughing. "Tell them you're General Patton if you want. They couldn't figure out the difference between a can of Spam and a can of corn right now."

"No one will know the difference," Sperro said. "The longer this mess goes on, the easier it will become."

"I'm all for this," Spring said, "but what if we connect with our outfit? What do we tell them about Sergeant Denny?"

"We tell them nothing," Polak suggested.

"You mean lie?"

"No, we tell them we don't know. We scattered, suffered capture, and escaped the prison camp with the help of Johann."

"And his wife receives a missing in action telegram," Jakob said.

"Which means it leaves her and the boy clinging to an expectation he'll walk through the front door someday," Spring added.

"Listen, all we're doing is buying a little time here. That's all," Shimmel said. "It's a sleight-of-hand trick, an illusion, for a moment."

"Right," Sperro said. "You claim his identity as a last resort. You use a different name in the meantime, and we'll vouch for you. It's not as if you stick out. Nobody's gonna give a shit."

"Why? Why take on such a risk?"

"Taking risks? You're asking us?" Hansel said. "That's a laugh."

"We owe *you* now," Polak said.

"You've no options left," Johann said. "If you stay, you die. They'll catch up to you."

Spared time and time again, Jakob could not move past the sense his life held a greater purpose. He stowed the letters and picture in an inside pocket and placed the chain around his neck, working the tag under his clothing.

"So, what shall we call you?" Sperro asked.

"You tell me."

"John Jones," Hansel offered. "Must be a thousand of 'em over here."

Shimmel finished off a chunk of venison. "I say we find sleep, and at first light, move on and find our lines."

***

Morning broke against a cloudless sky. Shimmel spotted Jakob standing alone in a wedge of sunlight near the flower garden, arms folded, head bowed. He approached.

"They have felt as acquaintances to me the past few years, not family," Jakob said. "I do not understand the feeling."

"Time has a way of robbing a man of his kinship. If you're out here long enough, it's as natural as how one's appearance changes."

"It sickens me, brings tremendous guilt."

"Yes, but seeing your love for them, well, I've no doubt they lived each minute knowing just how much, and suspect they loved you the same."

Jakob turned again to the grave. "Where do you start when you lose everything?"

"You wake each morning and breathe and do what I couldn't. Kick revenge to the curb before it eats you alive, and live the life intended for you."

"I blame my father. He did this. How do I let him go?"

"By living the life he refused. He's given you a blueprint of how not to live. I found satisfaction splitting his head until I learned his identity. He might have deserved it. Revenge against the nameless, in war, draws little emotion. But knowing the circumstances now, I'll carry this millstone around my neck the rest of my life."

"I told you, I do not hold you responsible."

"I understand. It's why I'm prepared to do for you whatever I can to make sure you have an opportunity at a life. I owe Denny that much."

"Hey, we need to move out," Sperro called out.

"You ready?"

"A few more minutes, perhaps," Jakob said.

"Take your time."

A healthy debate ensued as to the best method of transportation. Hansel and Polak sided with the status quo. At least the track would provide protection. Shimmel and Sperro argued for travel on foot.

"Taking the track is too dangerous, too loud," Shimmel offered. "Besides, I think we're close."

"What do we do about the uniforms?" Spring asked.

"I say keep 'em on," Sperro said.

The men packed up enough leftover meat to last a week. Sperro pulled out O'Dell's compass and turned east.

The group paused in the middle of the pasture and waited, as Jakob veered from them to pay farewell to his best friend. He stood above Sascha's remains. The moment branded in everyone's memories, a common link bonding them forever.

"He only thinks he's alone," Polak said.

Chapter 47

"How far to Aachen?" Shimmel asked.

"Less than five miles," Jakob said.

"I know for a fact our boys pushed through in October," Hansel said.

The men wandered into an extensive field dotted with pines and boulders. They huddled to debate options. Spring spotted a farmhouse and barn tucked in the woods at the bottom of the valley.

"What do you think?" Sperro asked.

"Don't know, but we'll have to hoof it across that open field."

"We wander out there and it's open season," Polak said.

"If we make the farmhouse, we can wait out the day and move on after dark," Sperro said.

"What makes you think we can walk in and make ourselves at home?" Polak asked.

"Look... the chimney," Shimmel said. "No smoke. You're telling me there's no need for a fire in this weather? No wood cut, either. The farmhouse is empty."

"We should keep moving north," Spring suggested.

"There's a German transfer center north of here," Johann said. "It doubles as a fuel depot."

"I say we ditch these uniforms and take our chances," Sperro said.

The men rid themselves of the German gear. Johann abstained, convinced he fared better in the proper colors.

"Okay, we go object to object in twos," Shimmel ordered. "Don't advance until the man in front of you moves. We go on a three count. Watch for signals. Anything goes wrong, find what cover you can. I'll bring up the rear."

"You up for this, Eli?" Sperro asked.

"Let's find out."

"Hey, boys, nobody's a hero, got it?" Polak said. He grabbed Jakob by the collar and moved in front of Shimmel.

"Joe," Jakob said, tapping his shoulder.

"How d'ya know my name?" Polak joked.

"I want to give you this." Jakob pulled Annalise's letter from an inside pocket, opened the envelope, and passed the picture of her and the baby. "I will keep his letters, but, if I do not make it, you need to deliver this to her and tell her the truth of what happened here."

"The boy will know the truth. You can count on it. This war won't kill me."

Sperro surveyed the field as he would a chessboard with the farmhouse the opposing queen. He counted trees and compared boulders, identifying the largest among them and their proximity to the straight line he intended to travel. "Okay, boys, here we go," he said, popping Johann on the shoulder.

The two scampered to the first tree, dropped, counted three, then moved on. Hansel and Spring followed. The others moved out on count, their steps working in unison as planned.

Sperro and Johann cut left toward a pair of pines. They decided upon a large rock formation forty yards away as their next best cover option. Sperro sucked in a deep breath and made his break with Johann.

A single shot clipped the lip of Sperro's helmet, jettisoning it off before it reached his head. He scrambled forward and hit the ground behind the rock formation. A hail of gunfire erupted. Each man scrambled for his own haven, returning blind fire to their rear and left flank.

Caught behind a thin pine, Jakob made a break for a boulder forward of Sperro's position. Bullets whizzed about, popping in the snow at his heels.

"Down, Jakob," Sperro yelled.

Jakob scrambled on all fours. A single bullet cratered the back of his helmet, propelling him face-first against the rock.

"Jakob!"

Sperro returned fire. Shimmel set to make a break to assist. A massive round exploded thirty yards beyond.

"It's a Tiger," Johann yelled.

A tremendous crack erupted at the bottom of the valley. Shimmel turned as the barn disintegrated. Three American Shermans broke free as if bulls from a stockade. Shells exploded on the hillside overlooking the field. The Tiger redirected its fire. The Shermans spread their formation, advancing at top speed, firing at will. Bazooka and small arms fire traded as a slew of GIs advanced under cover of the Shermans, firing into the hillside.

As the battle raged, Polak scrambled to aid Jakob. Shimmel barked orders for each man to move toward his position. The Shermans fired in tandem, turning the hillside into a ball of flame. A direct hit on the Tiger took out its right-side track.

Polak spotted two medics trailing the GI advance. "Medic... medic," he yelled.

The men broke from their ranks to join Polak at the rock. They dropped and rolled Jakob's body. A single trail of blood leaked from the back of his skull. The bullet missed doing extensive damage, instead, trenching a path to near his ear. The medics placed him on a stretcher and took off across the field toward the farmhouse.

"Hey, wait," Polak yelled. "Where are you taking him?"

A new volley of gunfire flared from the hillside. Polak returned fire. Sperro, Spring, and Shimmel made their way to a large boulder. Johann pulled Hansel along to join them. Polak emptied two more clips.

The men returned fire until American forces started up the hill in pursuit. They fell against the rock, heaving for oxygen.

A group of GIs splintered from the main force to advance on their location. "Drop your weapons," a first sergeant ordered. Johann raised his arms.

"Identify," he demanded.

Shimmel needed aid of the rock to pull upright. "Corporal Eli Shimmel, Twenty-Eighth Division, 110th Infantry, sir," he said. "I have with me privates John Spring, Dan Hansel, Joe Polak, Angelo Sperro, and an American-born German prisoner."

"You have proof?" He centered his aim on Shimmel's chest.

"Only dog tags, sir. We were captured before Christmas and sent to a POW camp in Limburg. We escaped with the aid of this man," he said, pointing to Johann.

"What about the wounded man?"

"Don't know him, sir. We picked him up a mile or so from here. Denny, I think. Don't know for sure. Didn't have a lot of time for chit-chat."

"We've captured plenty of Germans with fake tags and uniforms. What makes you different?"

Shimmel had pegged the man the moment he laid eyes upon him, thanks to a memorable scar above his right eye. "Because you might remember me, sir," Shimmel said. "At least I hope so. We shipped out on the same transport prior to Normandy. You took me for a fifty-spot in a poker game the night before the invasion."

The sergeant dropped his aim and stepped forward. "Yeah, I remember you."

"What the hell's going on around here?" Polak asked.

"We've waited three days for those Krauts to make a move. We heard the Tiger but couldn't see it until you fellas came along. You saved some lives today."

"Where did they take the wounded man?" Shimmel asked.

"He's long gone by now," the sergeant said. "There's a field hospital five miles to the rear. Had to move it back because of the push."

"Bastogne?" Sperro said.

"Yeah. Germans broke through our lines and surrounded the 101st. Our boys are holding on by a thread. With the hillside cleared, we're moving out. And this man?" the corporal said, pointing to Johann.

"A German soldier, but an American citizen. He says he has proof of citizenship on his person. He organized our escape from a camp in Limburg and is the lone reason we're alive."

"What's your name? Where's home?"

"Johann Rhoden, Boston, Massachusetts."

"Okay, boys, take him to HQ. No loafing."

Johann turned to Sperro. "I told you I'd surrender."

Polak extended his hand. "Thank you. I hope I see you down the road."

"Come to Boston, we'll catch a game."

Each man stepped up and offered a handshake. They found it difficult to watch Johann led away under guard.

"What'll happen to him?" Spring asked.

"He'll undergo interrogation. If he's telling the truth, they'll process him out. He's not the first American citizen captured in a German uniform. It's a goddamn epidemic. Hundreds captured linked to identical circumstances." He pointed to Spring. "You seem in bad shape."

"He needs medical attention, sir," Shimmel said.

"I'm fine, Corporal," Spring replied.

"You can't go on," Sperro said. "You have a broken —"

"I can go anywhere you can," Spring interrupted.

"We'll have a medic evaluate your wounds. Rumor has it the Germans are running thin on fuel and ammo. We stop this shit-show now, we all go home."

The soldier turned to his aide, "See if you can scrounge up some hot chow and a medic."

Two soldiers escorted the men down the hill toward the farmhouse.

"Boy, we sure fucked this up," Sperro whispered to Shimmel. "I had this turning out altogether different. I think Jakob's had it."

"Only if his luck changes," Shimmel replied.

"Think we'll ever see him again?" Polak asked.

"I don't know," Shimmel said, "but when he wakes up, I hope he remembers whose dog tags he has around his neck."

***

Cody, Wyoming, November 2009

Paul placed the manuscript on the floor, then basked in the euphoria of a prolonged stretch of his limbs. The clock on the mantel matched exactly the 2 a.m. position of his watch. He crawled out of the recliner and grabbed his coffee cup, knowing Monica had likely brewed a new pot, just in case.

Upon entering the hallway, he noticed a wedge of soft amber pushing from the kitchen. Voices exchanged in near whispers. "What in the world are you all doing up?" Paul said as he entered, trading a glance between his siblings and Monica.

"Just couldn't sleep," his brother Kim said.

"How are you doing?" his sister Rachel asked.

"Past the halfway point," Paul replied.

"And?" his sister Heather asked.

"Well, it's two in the morning and I'm looking for more coffee."

"That means he likes it," Monica said, laughing.

"Yes, so far, but have no idea why a story like this resonated with mom. She hated war and everything to do with it. Just doesn't add up why she waited until she passed before sharing it."

Kim pushed from the table, grabbed the coffeepot, and topped off everyone's cup.

"Thank you," Paul said, taking a seat near Monica.

"We were all just talking, and everyone agrees this Colonel Jekel seems to be someone other than he projects," Rachel said.

"Why do you say that?" Paul asked.

Rachel added a splash of cream to her cup, then stirred. "For all the years I was in this house, I never heard Mom or Dad speak of him, let alone, talk with him on the phone. How do we know for sure his story of knowing them is true? It's like he appeared out of thin air."

"Well, I know the man's legit from a literary standpoint," Paul said. "Just Google his name. He's published several award-winning books and is a well-known tactical expert. I don't think he's the question. It's the association."

"You really think he served with Dad?" Kim asked.

"At this point, I can only take him for his word. I will admit, though, when I asked him that very question, he said, 'You could say that.' He didn't admit to it outright."

Heather shook her head. "Something's not right about all of this."

The room fell silent as all splashed the circumstance about their minds.

Paul took several sips of coffee, then requested another top off. "Well, guess I'd better get back at it if I plan on beating that old cranky rooster to sunup," he said, pushing from the table. He offered Monica a peck on the cheek.

"How far along are you?" Kim asked.

"A little over halfway in."

"The way you read, that poor rooster doesn't have a chance," Heather joked.

Paul laughed, then waved. "See you all in the morning."

Chapter 48

Le Havre, France, February 1945

"Sergeant, can you hear me? Sergeant Denny?"

Jakob's eyes fluttered open.

"No reason for alarm. You suffered a massive concussion. You're a lucky man. A couple millimeters more and your brains splatter with the wind. Can you hear me?"

"Yes," Jakob mumbled.

"We're taking you to surgery to clean and patch your chest wound."

Jakob did not respond.

"Sergeant Denny, do you understand what I said? I need to know you understand."

"I... understand."

"Hang in there, son."

"Where... am I?"

"Le Havre, France, on a medical ship. Here we go. This won't take long."

***

"Sir? You need to wake up," the soft voice twanged. "I have medicine."

Jakob opened his eyes. His chest felt as if an auger had pushed clean through.

"The doctor says you'll be up and at it in no time, if you're a good boy."

Jakob managed a quick scan of the woman hovering. Dark brown hair framed a long face, her skin cloud white, as bright as her dress, and a hat striped with red piping. She looked tired and aged well beyond her years, but eager to lend comfort and care.

"Any nausea?"

"Yes," Jakob replied.

"This will help." She pressed a white, oblong pill to his lips. He accepted along with a sip of water.

"There you go. I'll bring chicken broth later. No solids for a few days."

"Where am I?"

"On a hospital ship off the coast of Le Havre in northern France."

Jakob looked about the cramped quarters. Men lay in steel frame cots on both flanks. Thick steel chains suspended the wounded in cots above. The scent of alcohol, disinfectant, and iodine hung heavy. Intense lighting made it difficult to focus.

"You suffered a severe concussion and slipped into a coma. You gave us quite a scare. Your friend visited several times. When they brought you out of surgery, a nurse caught him under your bunk. I guess he wanted to be here when you woke."

Jakob pushed from the mattress. "What friend?"

"Hold on there," she said. "You need to rest. I don't know his name, but I've not seen him in a few days."

Jakob fell against the mattress, puzzled by the claim.

"Now, Sergeant Denny, if you need anything, let me know. You don't move from this bed. Do I make myself clear?"

"Oh, I'm not Sergeant...." Jakob caught himself. He shook his head to clear cobwebs.

"You're not what?"

"I meant to say, I do not wish for food at the moment."

"Good, because you can't have anything of substance. I'm Charlotte. You stay in this bed, understood?"

"Yes, ma'am."

"Ma'am?" the woman said, surprised. "I'm no older than you, soldier."

"My apologies."

"I'll check on you later." She patted his hand and winked.

Jakob felt a hard object against his ring finger. Someone had slipped O'Dell's wedding ring on him. He grabbed hold of the dog tag. *Sergeant Denny, they think I'm Sergeant Denny.* He grew nervous as guilt erupted. "I have to end this," he whispered. *What will this do to her?*

Though his mind plowed through potential candidates who might pose as his friend, his body gobbled up the delightful doughiness of his pillow. His eyes grew heavy. A deep sleep came without effort or objection.

***

"Another delightful cup of scalding water?" Jakob asked.

"It's chicken broth, and you're lucky to have this," Charlotte said.

"I have sipped water from a tank track that tasted more like chicken."

"You're funny. Maybe in a few days you can have something more substantial. We must get your bowels moving first."

Jakob sipped the soup and cringed. A doctor stood at the end of his bunk, his face hidden by the bed above. He pulled a chart and thumbed through its contents.

Charlotte passed a pill and small paper cup full of water. "I'll check on you later. Please eat, then rest."

She grabbed a tray of pills and bandages and proceeded to the next row of bunks. As she cleared, the doctor approached and positioned on his haunches.

"Hey, Jakob, you okay?" he said in a whisper, smiling.

Jakob did not recognize the man at first. Black hair, a thick, black mustache, and dark-rimmed glasses confused his senses. Then it hit. "Corporal, what in God's name are you doing here?"

"Keep it down," Shimmel said, looking about with a nervous eye. "I ain't Corporal Shimmel. I'm Colonel Bass Rankin, MC."

"What?"

"I'm a doctor. At least until you're off this ship."

"How did you find me?"

"They sent me here to recover from my wounds. I didn't want to ship out until I can get you off this ship, so I stole the uniform."

"What?"

Shimmel chuckled, pointing to the nameplate. "This jackass went ashore and ended up in the can for getting plastered and screwing some Frenchman's wife. I dyed my hair and mustache with shoe polish, and no one's the wiser."

"Are you going home?"

"No, heading back to the fighting soon. Need to find the boys, make sure they're okay. How are you feeling?"

"Worse than I did the day you found me. And the others?"

"Fine. They took Spring off the line by force. Not sure where he is."

"I hope they send him home."

"You concentrate on yourself. We need to move you off this ship, and fast."

"I find this entire charade despicable."

"Listen, you're Sergeant O'Dell Denny right now, whether you like it or not. You understand me? You play this out to the end. I'll find you a way off and on your way to the States. I promise."

"How can I continue to live this lie?"

"You do what I tell you."

"Then what?"

Shimmel's eyes darted from one side of the ship to the other. "I don't know, but I'll come up with a plan."

"Your men will find out I have no experience as a medic."

"Neither do half the medics in the Army. Hell, I met a guy who sold tires door-to-door before the war. Keep your eyes and ears open, and your mouth shut. I'll find you a way off this boat and back to the States if it kills me."

"Why do this?"

"You know why. You're alive because of Denny. I'm alive because of you. It's called the debt of war."

"And what about his wife?"

"One problem at a time. You need to rest and build your strength because you're gonna need it."

"This is crazy."

"No, I'll tell ya what's crazy. Requesting a last cigarette in front of a firing squad."

Chapter 49

Jakob woke when a tray bounced off the floor. As he rolled across his pillow to locate the action, an officer approached. He did not recognize the uniform or insignia but grew nervous at his confident stride and authoritative appearance — tall, broad-shouldered, impeccable dress.

"Sergeant Denny?" he asked in a deep, commanding voice.

Jakob hesitated. He wiped away crust deposited in the corners of his eyes.

"Sergeant Denny?" the man repeated.

Jakob's body temperature spiked. Confirming meant committing, duping the United States government, the United States Army, and the family of a dead American soldier.

"Yes, sir?"

"You're Sergeant O'Dell Denny?"

"Yes, sir."

"I'm Lieutenant Colonel Robert Kasten, MIS. You feeling better today?"

"Yes, sir. Thank you."

"Glad to hear it. You've had a rough couple of weeks. How long did you go without treatment for your chest wound?"

"Not long, sir."

"You had an infection. Another couple of days and you might not have made it. But a good infantryman always finds a way, right?" he said, smirking.

Jakob's adrenaline pulsed. This was not one man checking on the welfare of another. An interrogation had commenced, with no room for error.

"I am a medic, sir, and had the situation under control."

"Right, my mistake. Where you from, Denny?"

"Pennsylvania."

"Whereabouts?"

"Wellsboro."

"And your unit?"

"Twenty-Eighth Infantry, 110th Regiment."

"How did you find your way to Europe?"

"The Japanese found it for me, sir."

The officer smiled. "I mean, how did you end up in this campaign?"

"Landed in France on D-Day."

"How did you and your men find yourselves so far behind enemy lines?"

"Got caught in a major German push near Luxembourg at the edge of the Hürtgen Forest. They ordered our unit to Bastogne. Our division split in two and ended up southwest of our rally point. A German division overran and captured us and took us to a POW camp in Limburg."

"I see. How did you manage your escape?"

"An American-born German interrogator assisted us, in exchange for helping him surrender to the proper authorities."

"I see. Interesting story."

"No story, sir."

"I ask these questions because a field medic stated at one point, upon you regaining consciousness, you identified yourself as John Jones. Your tags say otherwise. Can you explain?"

"A nickname, sir. The men considered me an average Joe, so they gave me an average name. Few men knew my real name."

"I think it fair to warn you, once the doctor in charge releases you, you'll undergo further debriefings. Your military file will arrive any day. You know, standard procedure. We've captured hundreds of Germans posing as American servicemen. I hope the United States Army can corroborate your identity and the events as you've described."

"I understand, sir," Jakob said.

"I give each man the benefit of the doubt. I view a man innocent until proven guilty. But God help him if he's guilty."

"As it should be."

"I do have some good news. If all turns out, your wounds mandate a trip home. I instructed the ship's chaplain to dispatch a letter to your wife to let her know of your condition. A nurse found a letter from home on your person."

Kasten leaned in to focus on Jakob's reaction.

Jakob played the role to perfection. He smiled. "Thank you, sir. My wife will be pleased and relieved. I hope to write her soon."

"What's going on here?" Shimmel said as he raced toward the bunk. "What's the meaning of this?"

"Asking this man a few questions," Kasten said.

"This man has not yet recovered from surgery. I do not want him disturbed. Understood?"

"Yes, sir."

"You do your work in your office, not in mine."

"Yes, sir." Kasten shot Jakob a glance before exiting.

Jakob's jaw dropped. He had not met a more intimidating figure than Shimmel.

Shimmel smirked. "Not bad, huh?"

"You are out of your mind," Jakob whispered.

"You can have all sorts of fun in the Army if you pay attention to detail. Have you been up and about yet?"

"Yes, late last night."

"All your parts working?"

"Not to perfection, but good enough."

"Good, because we go tomorrow."

"Where?"

"A liberty ship due for overhaul steams for New York City with a load of wounded, former POWs, and those who've earned their points. It's your ticket home. I need to move you before those intelligence boys grab you. They're incessant and have caught several Germans trying to escape to the States."

Jakob ran a hand through his hair. "What am I to do, alone, in America?"

"The same as the millions before you who came in search of a new beginning, and the millions more who'll follow seeking the same."

"Good evening, gentlemen," Charlotte said. She toted a tray loaded with various medicines and syringes.

"I'll check on you tomorrow, soldier," Shimmel said. He pardoned himself, brushing against her breasts as he passed.

"My, my, he's a strange one," Charlotte said. "Don't know if he's assigned to the ship or passing time on his way home. Do you know him?"

"No."

"I feel like I've seen him somewhere before. Oh, well." She drove a syringe into the buttocks of the soldier above.

"I've a surprise for you," she said. She handed Jakob a pill and a glass of water.

"Will this allow me to leave?"

"No," she said, "I meant this." She passed an envelope. "It's a letter from home. Don't know how it found you, but I'm happy it did."

Jakob accepted the letter and laid it on his chest.

"I see, you're the private type. Well, I'm not one to pry. I'll leave you be."

Jakob brought the letter to the end of his nose. A debate touched off between his ears. His stomach turned somersaults at the thought of Annalise not knowing the truth. He tapped the letter against his chest. He glanced at its front. Postmark stamps cluttered the top right. A single, handwritten phrase in pencil above the logo at the top left read Annalise and Son.

Delicate curves and feathery arcs suggested soft hands and a loving touch. Jakob rolled onto his good side and propped the letter against a jar filled with cotton.

He reached for the envelope several times but withdrew. By the soft glow of a cabin light, he dwelled on Annalise going about her chores to prepare both home and farm for O'Dell's return.

"What a despicable act," he mumbled.

"Hey, Jakob, I brought you a treat," Shimmel called out.

Jakob turned with a snap, instigating a searing barb in his rib cage.

Shimmel searched over his shoulder to ensure privacy, then passed a folded cloth napkin. "I carved up a piece of meat. Go on, take it."

Jakob accepted. He hid the napkin under his pillow.

Shimmel shrunk to a position on the edge of the bed. "Aren't ya gonna eat it?"

"Later."

"Not hungry?"

"Not at the moment."

Shimmel spied the letter. "What's it say?"

"I did not read it. I do not feel it my place to read the private words of a wife to her husband. I want to turn myself in. I cannot go through with this."

Shimmel grabbed a wad of Jakob's gown. "You can't confess. You confess and you'll face a firing squad or hang. Do you understand me? They won't give a shit you don't fancy Hitler or helped us escape, because we can't prove a damn thing."

"I understand, but I will not destroy the sergeant's legacy or play a part in further ruining his wife's life to save my own skin."

"Horseshit. Listen, six men alive know the truth of what happened. You're the one who can find her in the most reasonable amount of time. Do you know what it'd mean to O'Dell, knowing his family knew the truth and the level to which he rose in this war? You lived his death, we didn't. What it'd mean to him, his wife, and their son to know the truth? He saved your ass, and you made a promise. I'm giving you a chance to make good."

Jakob released a deep sigh.

"You chew on that awhile. I'll see you in the morning." Shimmel patted his shoulder.

Jakob rolled his head across the pillow to bring in focus the upper left side of the envelope. *Annalise and son.*

He struggled to a sitting position and opened the envelope.

> *7 November 1944*
> *My Dearest O'Dell,*
> *Several weeks have passed since your last correspondence. I hope God continues watching over you, and you're warm and safe. I find these times between letters most difficult. I know no greater loneliness than riding home from the post office empty-handed. It troubles me to the point I usually take along old letters in case I do not receive a new one. Though I've memorized each one, it brings me great joy reading your comforting words.*
>
> *I find myself these days struggling to define love, because what I feel for you goes deeper. I believe in love, then a love beyond love, a level of love not meant for us to define or understand, but to enjoy and cherish as I cherish you. Bella has become my shadow. It's baffling how she imitates your character in so many ways–her mannerisms, gentle nature, patience. It's as if she knows the void in our lives and tries her best to fill it.*
>
> *I think she knows the little man in my arms. I placed him on her back, and she held steady as an oak. She knows he belongs to you, I'm certain of it.*
>
> *She's developed a peculiarity of turning standoffish toward other men, including rearing up at Lucian and Uncle Bill.*
>
> *As for your son, he's as precious as a gemstone and growing like a weed. His appetite would make you proud. I believe he'll run before he walks. We'll spend Thanksgiving with Uncle Bill, Margie, and Lucian.*
>
> *The county re-elected Uncle Bill. I don't see him ever retiring. It's funny, I know him better now than I did growing up. He's a kind and fair man, and how he fawns over your son. It's as if he's rediscovered his own childhood.*
>
> *Honestly, I don't know what I'd have done these last months without him. I miss you beyond words, sweetheart, so I won't try*

to explain. I count the minutes until our life begins again. Stay warm and safe.
All our love,
Annalise and Son

Jakob weighed each concern and consequence of the predicament, concluding Shimmel's assessment correct. All angles, pathways, and conceivable solutions led down the same trail. *I, alone, know the absolute truth.*

Chapter 50

Shimmel blew through the hatchway toward the recovery ward, intending to reveal his exit plan to Jakob in full. His progress stalled as Charlotte grabbed his arm, diverting his advance to behind the first set of bunk beds.

She passed a chart into his hands. "Be quiet," she whispered. "Open this, pretend you're reading. I know who you are. I saw you last week. The shoe polish fooled me at first, but I'm wise to your game. You have any idea the penalty for impersonating a medical doctor, let alone an officer?"

"My uncle is a doctor," Shimmel said.

"What does your uncle have to do with anything?" She pounded his chest. "You want to get me in trouble?"

"I'm sorry, ma'am. There's more here at stake than you realize."

"Why does everyone call me ma'am when I'm younger than they are?"

"Okay, take it easy, sister. So, what now?"

"Look," she said, pointing.

Shimmel turned. "Oh shit," he whispered, looking over the top bunk. The chart slipped from his fingers. Charlotte squatted to retrieve spilled documents.

"They charged in here five minutes ago. I think it's sweet of you to want to help your friend, but you're going about this all wrong."

"What do you care?" Shimmel said.

"Because he's a sweet boy, and I sensed something fishy about this situation from the get-go."

Shimmel turned back to the action. The officer he'd encountered earlier stood alongside two others and two MPs.

"Shit," he mumbled. "That's more firepower than I expected."

The MPs assisted Jakob to his feet and ordered him into a set of prison issue. They turned him toward the bunk and bound his hands. Shimmel's stomach sunk.

"Listen, I can't explain this to you right now, but he's in trouble for all the wrong reasons. Would you be willing to back me up on this?"

"How?"

"Play dumb."

"You're crazy."

"I'm a soldier, aren't I?" Shimmel took a deep breath. "I have to help him. If you knew the truth of the matter, you'd want to help him, too."

Shimmel straightened his coat, cleared his throat, and stepped from behind the bunk. "What business do you have here?" he bellowed.

The group of men turned. An officer of equal rank met him as he approached.

"Easy, Doctor," the officer said.

"What are you doing with my patient?"

"I'm LeMaster, Army Intelligence. I've placed this man under arrest."

"On what charges?"

"Posing as an American GI."

Shimmel's voice grew more agitated. "What proof do you have?"

"We received a military flier on a Sergeant O'Dell Denny this morning, picture included. This man identified himself as Sergeant Denny and has possession of Denny's dog tags. The file and picture say otherwise."

"This man is my patient."

"Not anymore," LeMaster said. The colonel turned. "Remove this man."

Jakob glanced at Shimmel but said nothing.

"Wait a minute," Shimmel pleaded, "he requires a follow-up X-ray and further medical attention. I've not ordered his release from this ward."

"I've ordered his release, or better yet, I'm facilitating the release for Brigadier General Womack. By all means, take the matter up with him."

"You're breaching medical protocol, prisoner or not."

The MPs escorted Jakob from the ward. Shimmel followed. "I need a follow up X-ray to determine surgical success."

"I'm not concerned with surgical success. The American taxpayers have spent enough money on this man. He will be well cared for while he awaits trial. I expect his medical record complete and up-to-date as his care stands now."

"Your actions are inappropriate."

The colonel stopped and turned. "This man assumed the identity of an American soldier with intent to escape justice. Don't tell me what's appropriate and what's not."

Shimmel followed the pack of men, voicing objections, all the while keeping a mental note of each level descended and corner turned. Deep within the bowels, the group moved into a long hallway leading to a single hatch flanked by two MPs. They escorted Jakob inside. The door slammed; Shimmel slipped back around the corner.

He fled to a stock closet tucked away near the quarters he'd assumed and swapped out his current dress for a stashed set of standard issue. He returned to Rankin's bunk, retrieved a bottle of scotch, and poured a shot. After a lengthy chug, he slammed the glass on the table.

"What the hell do I do now?"

He poured another drink and leaned back. "I need help."

The scotch drained smooth, burning from lips to groin, instigating a shiver he favored. He took another swig.

"Wait a minute, those two monkeys I met," he whispered.

He wandered into a poker game days after getting back on his feet and met a seaman and orderly eager and crazy enough to do anything for a bottle of hooch and a pack of smokes. He caught the last name of one — Cooper.

Shimmel poured and sank another shot. "I gotta find a way to outrank those holding him."

He leaned into his seatback, simultaneously poking a finger through a tear along the inseam of his pants near the knee.

"A hole," he mumbled.

Shimmel's eyes darted about with excitement as two schemes collided. He plowed through the steps necessary to achieve both. He smiled. A final shot of scotch flowed smooth and easy.

***

Shimmel cracked the door of the stock closet and checked the hallway before proceeding to the ship's laundry, toting a seaman's bag stuffed full of pillows. He entered the compartment to a swell of humidity. Washing and drying apparatuses lined the right bulkhead; white coats, uniforms, gowns, and surgical scrubs hung on racks to the left. A quartet of sailors bustled about as if bees at a hive, washing, folding, ironing, and mending. One lad spotted him and called his counterparts to attention.

Shimmel returned their salutes. "At ease, men," he said. "I'm new to the ship. Wanted to see the operation." He set the laundry bag at his feet. "Where should I leave this?"

"Anywhere you please, sir. We'll take care of it."

"Thank you." He placed the bag near the stretch of garment racks.

The men returned to their duties. Shimmel inspected uniforms as if conducting a quality check. The sailors paid no attention. He turned, dug out a small pocketknife, and sliced a hole in the elbow of Rankin's dress coat.

He approached the nearest sailor. "Excuse me, son, would you have time to sew this up?" He rotated his arm to flash the hole.

"Of course, sir."

The sailor turned his back to inspect the damage before proceeding to the rear of the space. Shimmel retreated to where he placed the laundry bag below two service ensembles. He guessed the coats a perfect fit and hefty enough in rank to assist what needed done. He stuffed the garments inside the bag. The seaman returned several minutes later.

"Good as new, sir," he said, showing off his handiwork, "at least until you get a new one."

"Thank you, son."

The lad helped Shimmel on with the coat. Shimmel collected his laundry bag and headed for the exit.

"Did you change your mind, sir?"

"Forgot a couple things. I'll be back."

Shimmel returned to Rankin's quarters, removed the boot polish from his hair, shaved, and promoted himself to major general, thanks to the newfound duds.

Locating Cooper and his counterpart proved more of a challenge than expected. A two-hour search proved futile. Shimmel entered the mess hall to the smell of stale coffee, boiled cabbage, and grease. He questioned two sailors serving food, one of whom directed him to the galley.

"Looking for a man named Cooper," he said to a young man hard at work scrubbing pots. The lad pointed to a boy at the end of a prep line.

Shimmel worked his way around a sea of stainless-steel tables to the far side of the galley. "Sailor, a word, please."

The boy pulled a rag from a pocket in his apron and wiped his hands. Shimmel led him through the mess to an adjoining hallway.

"Cooper, right?"

"Yes, sir."

"Remember me?"

"I don't think so, sir."

"I met you in a card game last week."

"Oh, yes, sir, I remember now, but I didn't pull those queens from the bottom of the deck, honest. I lost money, too."

"This has nothing to do with the card game."

The boy let go a deep sigh. He looked Shimmel up and down. "Hey, I don't remember you wearing this uniform."

"Never mind. How d'you and your friend from the other night like to make a quick score—cash, smokes, scotch?"

"I'm in. I love scotch."

"What the hell's the matter with you? I've not told you what I need done?"

"I don't care, I'm in. I love scotch."

"How about your pal? He's a corpsman, right?"

"Yes. He's in, too."

"How do you know?"

"What does it pay?"

"Fifty bucks, plus product."

"He's in. I'm in. What do we have to do?"

"How old are you?"

"Old enough."

Shimmel smirked. *What a great kid.*

"First, we need you out of those clothes. Second, we need a drink. Third, we need to find your pal and see what he knows about the X-ray unit."

Chapter 51

Shimmel explained the next step posed potential consequences to career. They leaned against a bulkhead adjacent to the long hallway leading to Jakob's location.

He peeked around the corner and spotted a lone MP standing guard. The lad looked bored. Shimmel checked his watch.

"Timing's everything on this one," he whispered to Cooper. "I hope your pal made the arrangements, because we'll burn, all of us, if he didn't."

"You don't have to worry. If he said he'd take care of it, it's done. We sure look out of place all dressed up."

Shimmel released a deep breath. "Won't need these dress uniforms long if we do this right. Let's go."

Shimmel slipped around the corner. Cooper followed close behind. The MP tracked their steps.

"Afternoon, soldier," Shimmel said, saluting. "I'm here to speak to your commanding officer."

"I have orders not to let anyone pass, sir."

"What's your name, son?"

The soldier gulped. "Private Richard Foy, sir."

Shimmel snapped his fingers. "Colonel," he directed. Cooper retrieved a small notebook and pen. He scribbled the name of his dog.

"Private Fry, I don't—"

"Foy, sir," Cooper interrupted.

"My mistake. Fry, I have little time and I hope I don't have to remind you major generals don't take orders from privates. Now, open the door."

Foy snapped to attention. "Yes, sir."

The men entered. A second MP sat behind a small desk in a receiving area.

"Who's the highest-ranking officer on duty?" Shimmel demanded.

"Major Bogar, sir."

"I'm Major General Bucknell, MIS. Please tell the major I need to speak with him. I don't have all day."

The MP picked up a phone and summoned his superior.

Shimmel checked his watch.

"Bogar, I'm Major General Bucknell," Shimmel said as the officer entered the waiting area. "I'm told you're holding a prisoner extracted from the surgical ward this morning. I need two of your MPs to escort the prisoner to X-ray. We cannot complete his chart without a final picture, and as I'm sure you're aware, all prisoners have the right to a complete medical record. This will take but a few minutes."

"I'm sorry, sir. I have no authority to release the prisoner."

"I do, Major. Now, I want two MPs and the prisoner in cuffs."

"But, sir?"

"Right now."

The soldier exited through a heavy steel door.

"You never negotiate in the game of folly," Shimmel turned and whispered to Cooper. "You act the part, you become the part."

Bogar returned with Jakob and two MPs. Jakob did not react. He kept his eyes on the ground.

"Does this man speak English?"

"Yes, sir," Bogar confirmed.

"By military code, we must complete your medical file in full. Colonel Rankin will escort you to X-ray. He will take images necessary to complete said file and return you to your cell. Do you understand?"

"Yes."

"I'm sorry, I did not hear you," Shimmel said.

"Yes, I understand."

"Colonel, take your man." Shimmel turned to Bogar. "We'll have him back in fifteen minutes."

Shimmel followed the entourage down the hall to a set of stairs. A two-minute march brought the group to their destination.

"I'm sorry, sir, we cannot shoot pictures at the moment," a private relayed.

"Private, I've a prisoner who needs an X-ray. I want it completed immediately.'

"We have a situation inside, sir. They're attending a soldier who went into cardiac arrest."

"I see," Shimmel said. "Colonel, see if you can help. Private, lead the way."

Several moments later, the private returned. He picked up a wall phone near the door. "Yeah, need stretcher bearers in X-ray."

He turned to Shimmel. "The soldier passed, sir. I can take your prisoner in for prep. When the stretcher team arrives, please send them in."

"Of course," Shimmel replied.

The tech led Jakob away by the arm. An MP followed.

"You can't come in here," the tech said, planting a palm into the MPs chest. "We don't have enough lead aprons."

The tech shut the door. Within seconds, two orderlies arrived with a stretcher in tow.

"In there," Shimmel directed. He glanced at his watch, turned to the MPs, and shook his head.

Cooper led the orderlies from X-ray through the waiting area, toting a body covered in a white sheet. "Sir, I want to see this man processed as stated by protocol. I've informed the techs of the pictures needed for the prisoner."

"Fine, Colonel, carry on."

Shimmel checked his watch several times. He enhanced the charade with heavy sighs and inaudible mumbles. Confident he'd given the orderlies ample time to return to his bunk and initiate phase two of his plan, he turned to an MP and said, "Son, are you capable of getting the prisoner back to the brig on your own?"

"Yes, sir," the MP replied.

"Good. Whatever you do, don't go in there," Shimmel said, pointing, "unless you never plan on having children."

***

Shimmel stripped himself of rank. "We gotta hustle," he said. "The ship leaves in ten minutes."

"How did you come up with this plan?" Jakob mumbled. He stuffed his limbs into a standard Navy corpsman's uniform.

"I knew those MPs wouldn't check the identity of a dead man. How'd they treat you in the brig?"

"No trouble." Jakob grimaced as he forced his arms through the sleeves of a heavy wool pea coat.

A single thump erupted against his bunk door.

Cooper entered toting a combat stretcher, his friend in tow carrying several heavy blankets and a utility pouch. "Hey, what the hell?" Cooper said. "I'm gonna catch it if I don't return soon."

"Take it easy," Shimmel said, tossing his personal items in one seabag and four cartons of Lucky Strike cigarettes, two bottles of scotch, and cash in another. Cooper accepted the loot in exchange for the stretcher. He pointed for Cooper's buddy to pass the utility belt to Jakob.

"Cooper, Jackson, meet John Jones," Shimmel said. He turned to Jakob. "Our good nurse helped confiscate your belongings. Put on the tag."

Jakob opened the pouch. He draped O'Dell's tag around his neck and placed the letters and wedding ring in a pocket.

"Okay, Jackson, hop on." The sailor stretched out on the canvas carrier. Cooper covered him with blankets.

"How ya feeling, Jones?" Shimmel asked. "You able to carry one end of this stretcher?"

"I can handle it."

"Good. They're looking for a wounded man, not a corpsman."

"Okay, let's move out." Shimmel opened the hatch, peeked around both corners, and waved the men forward.

"Listen, once aboard the liberty ship, you disappear into the shadows and stay there until you reach port."

"I understand."

"I don't know how to direct you off the ship once in New York. I fear whatever process they've set up to repatriate returning soldiers may prove more difficult. You cannot allow them to detain you. They stop you, you're sunk."

The group turned a corner and shuffled down a long hallway to a set of stairs dumping into a vestibule where a main gangplank connected with the transport ship. Sailors and orderlies carried the wounded on stretchers, all merging toward a narrow exit. Men moaned, officers directed, stretcher-bearers argued who had the right of way. The echo drummed at maddening decibels.

Jakob kept his head low and eyes down. MPs stood guard, though none the wiser of his true purpose. They moved through the pack and into open air. Dense, gray-black clouds dotted the sky.

Shimmel led them down the gangplank, searching over his shoulder often for anything peculiar. Medical officers directed traffic on board. The line continued along a hallway to a compartment updated to support litters. Corpsmen scrambled about, attaching IVs to hangers and stretchers to their supports. Shimmel had counted on chaos. It aided his plan to perfection.

The men closed in on their patient. Shimmel monitored the action out of the corner of his eye, waiting for the window he needed to complete the ruse. Stretcher-bearers flooded the space. Corpsmen had little time to focus on any one man or group of men. The time grew ripe. Shimmel coordinated their movement with a simple, "Now."

Jakob turned, removed his coat, veiling Jackson's slip from off the stretcher. Jackson removed the blankets, Cooper folded and stowed the litter on a shelf above. He signaled the next stretcher-bearers to drop their patient in the open slot. Shimmel and Jackson exited, working against the grain of the oncoming rush. Cooper exited in the opposite direction.

Jakob remained behind, assisting the new patient before melding among the mass of medical personnel.

Within minutes of Jackson and Cooper disembarking, the vessel shoved off.

Chapter 52

The trip to shore took less than twenty minutes. Shimmel secured a spot on deck within view of the hold where wounded transferred to the St. Francis. Jakob remained below, heeding Shimmel's advice to assist with the injured to further blend his place among the corpsmen.

A general announcement informed all on board the ship had docked, and transfer would commence immediately. Jakob grabbed the head end of a litter supporting a young, armless soldier, contemplating the man spending the rest of his life relying on others to complete the simplest of tasks.

Twenty minutes of inching along coffin-narrow passageways gave way to fresh air and a secure environment Jakob had not known since his training days. Shimmel spotted him and rushed to his side.

"How you holding up?"

"Fine," Jakob whispered. "I cannot believe I made it this far."

"You're a long way from in the clear but have a good start."

The hold offered three times the space of the hospital ship. Bunks scaled the bulkheads with two center rows stacked three high. Jakob and his counterpart positioned their patient in a middle bunk. Jakob straightened the boy's covers and stowed what little belongings he carried. Shimmel passed the litter off to a group of seamen preparing for the next wave.

With the patient secured, Shimmel and Jakob escaped to a storage room packed with life jackets.

"I wish you could come with me," Jakob said.

"Would love to, but I need to find the boys. We still have work to do. I'll go home when it's my time."

"I understand. I would do the same thing."

"I know you would."

"I guess this is it," Jakob said.

"Guess so."

"I do not know what to say?"

"Some moments require no words, right? And we both know there's no words to describe what happened here."

The two embraced. "Find her, tell her what happened, and live life on your terms."

"I will not forget you, Corporal," Jakob said.

"Mutual." Shimmel released and extended a hand. "Go ahead, take it. You're gonna need it."

"I cannot accept your money."

"You kidding me? Did you plan to rob the First National in Manhattan?" Jakob shrugged.

"Take it." Shimmel stuffed the wad of cash into Jakob's shirt pocket. "It's not mine, anyway. I won it in a poker game."

Jakob smiled. "I do not believe you."

"It's true, but you can pay me back when we meet again."

"I hope for that day."

The men embraced a second time. "Stay safe," Jakob said.

Shimmel laughed. "You're a smart kid and will know what to do and when to do it. You'll make it."

Shimmel cracked the hatch and conducted a quick search. He stepped through the threshold and turned. "See ya around, Jones."

***

The wounded poured from the shuttle, multitudes of shattered and mangled bodies, men crippled and disfigured in both mind and spirit. Jakob worked himself into the long line. He offloaded a seabag from the shoulder of a corpsman and a duffle bag off the stomach of a soldier entombed in gauze and bandages.

He entertained thoughts of losing himself, as Shimmel suggested, but an inner guilt turned obligation drove him to want to help. He followed as a lamb would its herder, losing sense of direction and position. The line filtered into a hold smelling nothing like the space he left his armless soldier. An amalgamation of sea salt, rust, and diesel fuel unsettled his stomach.

Jakob placed the bags next to their rightful owners, then set out in search of the armless soldier. The dizzying maze of passageways convinced him of his preference for dry land, not this toxic-fumed, lung-eating environment. He passed several points twice, including a massive cargo hold. What he thought a wrong turn dumped out at the location he sought.

Personnel traded right of way entering and exiting. Jakob waited his turn near an open porthole. He drew in a deep breath of fresh air. Several ships waited in the harbor. Upon drawing in another, deeper breath, the ship's horn sounded, signaling the convoy to sea.

"I made it," he whispered, "just as Shimmel promised."

Entering the hold, he searched bunks for the armless soldier. At a point well beyond where he thought the boy had been delivered, he turned and retraced his steps. Each position supported a litter, every soldier in possession of all four limbs.

A corpsman sat on his haunches nearby, attending a new arrival.

"I am looking for a soldier I brought aboard earlier," Jakob said.

"Yeah? Well, there's five hundred to choose from, cowboy," he replied.

"He lost both arms."

"You mean the kid from Yuma?"

"I do not know his hometown."

"Yeah, we returned him to shore," the corpsman said, flicking the lead of an IV at its head to ensure a proper drip.

"Why?"

"Because he ain't gonna make it. Never should have been brought aboard in the first place."

"Do you know his name?"

The soldier lifted from his squat and turned. "Listen, Mack, there's no time to..." The look on Jakob's face stalled his words. He took a deep breath. "Jackman. Steve or Steven, I think, from Yuma, Arizona."

"How old?"

"Eighteen, maybe. There's a chance more of these boys will die before we reach home. Between you and me, the kid is better off. Can you imagine living with no arms?" The corpsman backhanded Jakob's shoulder as he passed.

"Eighteen," Jakob whispered.

"I don't recall seeing you before," the corpsman stated.

Jakob shrugged.

"What unit you with?"

"They ordered me to board and help."

"I didn't ask for your orders. I asked what unit you're with."

Jakob stammered, figuring what number to blurt out. To his great relief and fortune, an army grunt grabbed the corpsman from behind.

"We need you, now," a young private said, spinning him. He tugged him down the line to near the last set of litters.

Jakob turned and caught a disturbing image. He pulled his helmet low over his brow and turned his attention to an adjacent IV bag. He flicked the lead, aping the corpsman's action, keeping close watch of two armed soldiers working down the line from the opposite end, one with his weapon drawn.

Jakob moved toward them, mirroring their steps as they approached. They checked each injured man as they passed, paying no attention to medical personnel.

Jakob moved to within a row of their position. They scrutinized each soldier's face, comparing it to a picture taken of Jakob upon his entry into the brig. Jakob attended to the IV bag of the man in the top bunk as the soldiers moved in on the man on the bottom bunk. He worked around them, raising the crook of his arm to cover a fake cough as he passed. He paused at the next row of litters.

The soldiers turned their attention to an injured man mummified in bandages, a small slit at his mouth the sole access to any facial feature. Sparked by a sense they found their man, they began unwrapping him. The corpsman Jakob conversed with returned, berating the men as he approached. Following a brief discussion, they showed the corpsman the picture. Jakob pulled his helmet lower and pushed through oncoming traffic.

The corpsman conducted a quick search of the space before turning and pointing toward Jakob. One of the soldiers caught sight as Jakob slipped through the main hatchway. He brought a whistle to his lips, ripped off burst, then yelled, "Stop that man."

Chapter 53

"They said we might have an escaped Kraut on board. If he's unarmed, we're to place him in shackles, if armed, we shoot before he does."

Jakob overheard the exchange between crewmates armed with pistols exiting a hatch in haste. He found refuge behind a conglomeration of pipes near the ship's machine shop. The crew did not appear regular Navy. He suspected merchant officers.

He managed a slick escape of the wounded hold, exiting as a wave of stretchers entered. By the time his pursuers pushed through, he'd achieved an ample head start into the maze of passageways.

He descended into the middle deck amidships, moving toward the engine room, the vibrations underfoot serving as a beacon. To this point, his memory and internal compass worked in flawless tandem.

Jakob held his breath as the hunting party passed. They ascended a stairwell at the end of the corridor. When their footsteps dissolved, he slipped from behind the pipes.

I need a change of clothes, he whispered inside his head, checking both directions before proceeding to an intersection. A metal-on-metal grind of a hatch unsealing exploded to his rear. He shot around a corner.

Several crewmen slipped into the hallway at the far end. At the sight of drawn weapons, Jakob pushed off the bulkhead and hare-footed down the corridor.

He opened hatches as he passed, hoping to lure his pursuer's interest. He came to a set of stairs, grabbed hold of the handrails, and slid to the bottom, then switched back toward the ship's engine room and entered unnoticed.

A massive steel column offered immediate asylum. He wedged his body between it and the bulkhead. The hellish, humid atmosphere drew sweat from his pores in an instant. The smell of lubricating oil and grease hung heavy, coating the inside of his mouth and nostrils. His senses muddled to the discordant orchestration of mechanical components and parts churning, grinding, groaning. His eardrums pounded to the melodic beat of the ship's two-story pistons driving its propeller shaft; *ca-thump, ca-thump, ca-thump.* He skimmed sweat from his face and took a deep breath.

Expecting guards to arrive any moment, and believing his current cover unsatisfactory, he searched the space, seeking more favorable concealment.

An intricate network of pipes, hoses, valves, and electrical conduit ran amok in all directions, and at all angles, in a world constructed of composite irons and metals. Brass fittings and casings sparkled as stars in the night sky. Men scurried below, analyzing gauges, oiling gears and joints, pulling at levers and steel-spoke wheels, all to ensure the screws maintained a proper pace.

Jakob spotted three large steel contraptions to his rear fitted with more than a dozen pressure valves and various-sized pipes feeding an adjacent high voltage electrical panel. The farthest of the objects was located out of direct light. He checked the hatch and made a break, hopping over a guardrail and onto a catwalk. He settled among a cobweb of pipes and conduit to achieve a comfortable position and vantage point.

Two guards entered. Jakob slipped deeper into the shadows. They searched the immediate area in lackluster fashion—indicative of their amateur status—before descending the stairwell leading to the engine bay. Jakob slithered on his belly to the edge of the catwalk. The guards summoned a handful of sailors.

One guard tugged at his own shirt, appearing to describe their prey's dress. The men looked to each other and shook their heads. The guards retreated up the stairs, Jakob into the shadows. They exited without further investigation.

Jakob leaned against the bulkhead and brought a palm to his brow. With his breathing relaxed, his muscles unknotted. He felt thirsty, hungry, and eager to find a place to hide less detrimental to lung and other internal organ function. Body and mind languished in debility as the need for extended rest trumped all other desires. Before the count of ten, he drifted off to the mechanical symphony reveling about him.

***

Time vanishes in the bowels of a ship. The visual absence of dusk and dawn creates a vacuum, confusing both mind and body in short order. Jakob awoke to a small lever near his face, pumping in cadence with the engine's pistons. He pulled out of a dream of his first visual of the magnificent statue on Staten Island. He knew not if he'd slept thirty minutes or three days but hoped for the latter. The day, date, whether it was breakfast, lunch, or dinner, passed through his arousal sequence.

He slithered to the edge of the catwalk. The engine room seemed less frantic, with the ship well into its voyage and steaming at its intended pace. He counted three sailors, all young. One lad, in particular, caught his attention.

He suspected the boy equal in height and weight. Jakob noticed a standard issue blue button-down shirt draped over a bar-height chair fronting a desk. The sailor recorded readings on a stretch of various-sized gauges. Jakob counted the sailor's steps as he worked up and down the line, and the time to complete a full loop. The boy deviated from his routine once to take a sip of coffee.

Jakob timed his movement to his prey. With the sailor's back turned, he could strike without notice. He needed that blue shirt.

He slipped from behind the generator and settled upon his haunches on the first tread, waiting, watching, counting. The boy moved well to his right and disappeared for a fifteen count. Jakob descended the next tread. The sailor reappeared, collected a final reading, before depositing his clipboard on a small desk attached to the bulkhead. He grabbed a magazine and a biscuit.

"No, no, do not sit down," Jakob whispered.

The sailor planted onto the chair.

Jakob brought a hand against his face and rubbed his eyes. He settled upon his haunches, mulling a plan, something quick, unmemorable. Several schemes took shape. He vetted all before proceeding with his best option.

"All for a dirty shirt," he mumbled.

He descended the remaining steps with a confident stride. The sailor peered over his shoulder. Jakob stepped from the final tread. "Howdy," he said, and moved past with purpose.

"Can I help you?" the boy called out. He tossed the magazine onto the desk.

"Want to check a gauge," Jakob said, his voice projecting louder than intended.

"What gauge?"

"Second from the end down there."

"Don't know nothing about it," the sailor replied.

"I noticed it sticking during one of my previous tours on this ship. I had nothing better to do, so I thought I would check it to see if they fixed it."

"I've not seen you before."

Jakob extended his hand. "Jones, Yuma, Arizona."

The sailor accepted with a questioning look.

"Got assigned to this ship earlier in the war. On my way home, now. Imagine the odds of getting a ride home on the ship you served."

"Lucky you. I joined two months ago. I'm Ames, Greensboro, North Carolina."

"Nice to meet you, Ames. How old are you?"

"Nineteen, well, eighteen... almost eighteen. What about that gauge?"

"Seemed to stick once it reached 17 percent. See for yourself."

Ames returned to the desk and retrieved his clipboard. He searched the pages. "I don't recall seeing any notes on anything sticking," he said, mumbling as he moved down the line of equipment. He tapped the gauge's glass cover several times, turned, and shook his head. "There ain't nothing wrong with this...."

Jakob disappeared before Ames turned around.

He slipped off the engine room floor with three biscuits, a pair of wire-rimmed glasses, a white dog bowl cap, and the shirt. He made his way down the corridor he thought led to the supply hold, with one biscuit consumed, and the others stuffed in his pockets for later. The shirt fit as expected, the cap a bit large, but perfect for pulling low over the brow. He slipped on the glasses, betting they'd change his appearance most.

Two guards held post at the end of the passageway. Jakob approached as he did in the engine room, shoulders back, stride confident.

"Howdy," he said, drawing from his favorite Hollywood dialogue.

"Morning, sailor," one guard said, nodding.

Morning. Good to know, Jakob thought.

"You aware of the standing order, Mac?" the other guard asked.

"Standing order?"

"You know, two by two, until we reach port."

"Oh, sure. A few crewmates fell ill. We do not have the manpower for escorts. I'm heading to chow and back."

"Your funeral, pal. They've not located that Kraut yet."

Jakob tucked in the tail of his shirt. "I will keep a sharp eye out."

"We'll find him. You can bet on it. Once we hit port tomorrow, we'll have guards at all exits and portholes."

"Right," Jakob said.

"On your way, sailor."

Jakob nodded. *Tomorrow.*

Chapter 54

Ames paid little attention to his exchange with the sailor from Yuma until he discovered his biscuits and several other belongings missing. Following a thorough search, he concluded he had come face to face with the escaped Nazi.

"Wait until the folks back home hear about this," he said to a crewmate.

Shaken by the enemy's stealth, and startled at his mastery of the English language, Ames phoned the bridge.

Word of his brush with death spread throughout the ship. Guards posted at the end of the hallway, fearing they let the Nazi pass unawares, watered down their version of engaging a crewmate traveling solo to the mess.

The captain dispatched two dozen additional men. Galley and back kitchen personnel underwent grueling interviews but claimed no encounters with suspicious characters. No one recalled a sailor who looked out of place.

***

Ames's delay provided Jakob the time needed to find his way to a dry hold. He pushed through the hatchway and slammed headfirst into the chest of a sailor exiting a compact head.

"Hey, watch it, Mac," the taller man said as he pushed Jakob aside.

Jakob spun off and slipped into the head without further interaction. He emptied his bladder and bowels before consuming another half biscuit and a helping of room temperature water. He inspected his appearance, then slipped into the open bay.

The area seemed calm and organized, free of the ear-splitting, metallic pounding in the engine room. He stood near a vacated desk, spending several moments surveying his surroundings, assessing each sailor's function. A gang of six worked in perfect concert moving crates.

Two sailors checked inventory levels while four others rechecked the tie-downs on two transport trucks.

Jakob collected a clipboard full of papers and a pencil from off the desk. He moved among the boxes and crates, flipping through pages as if searching for something, all the while evaluating options for concealment. His interest honed on a back corner, where two sailors moved crates in a perfect mix of shadow and clutter. Believing his presence less conspicuous if on a mission, he approached a sailor counting crates. "Are you in charge here?"

The man shook his head. He pointed to the next aisle toward a tall, lanky fellow with slicked back hair.

"You the man in charge?"

"Not of everything," the sailor replied.

"Where do you store medical supplies?"

"Back right. Pretty thin pickings, though. A few bedpans, blankets, dressings, body bags, stretchers, gauze. We moved most supplies up top when we dropped anchor."

"I need to conduct an inventory of what remains," Jakob said.

"Help yourself."

"When do you expect to reach port?"

"Twenty-four hours, I'd say, unless we run into trouble."

"Trouble?"

"U-boats lick their chops when they spot a transport ship."

"Have you experienced a hit before?"

"Sure. If you're in the soup long enough, it happens to most. Some live to serve another day, others spend eternity as fish food."

Jakob had not considered the hazards of finding haven below the waterline. He set to formulating an alternate plan.

***

Jakob worked through multiple solutions while searching each crate for items useful to an escape. What medical supplies remained sat condensed on pallets at the end of either side of the aisle. He slipped from view, first rummaging through a crate of rations, extracting a can opener, packages of graham crackers, and chocolate bars. He plucked a canteen and filled it with tomato juice, stuffed the food items into his pockets, then the canteen into a swiped seabag.

He settled on his haunches to inspect each crate. Bedpans, body bags, a few surgical kits, blankets, gauze, bandages, surgical gowns, and casting and splint material. Nothing of significant quantity or value. He pillaged through a surgical kit, stowing a scalpel and scissors. He searched the lot a second time, churning through one idea after another.

"Wait," he whispered. He caught his breath and held it. Remnants of Shimmel's successful extraction from the X-ray bubbled forth. His chest thumped with excitement; his veins ran hot with newfound vigor.

After collecting a single body bag, he pulled his cap low and set off toward the main hatch, moving along the back bulkhead. He worked down the farthest aisle behind a long row of crates stacked mere feet from the forward bulkhead. The single-lane tunnel, doused in shadow, offered a view of the desk. He crept to the end and stopped short of a shadow line. A sailor sat at the desk, back facing, attending to paperwork.

As Jakob prepared to beeline for the exit, the sailor sprung from his chair and turned toward the hatch. Four sailors entered. Jakob retreated into the shadows.

"Seen any suspicious characters 'round here?" an armed sailor asked.

"Nope. A fella I've not seen before asked about medical supplies."

"Did he leave?"

"Nope, far back corner," he said, pointing.

The men drew their weapons and scattered. The sailor followed close behind. Jakob rushed to the end of the aisle, waited a count of ten, then peeked around the corner.

As the crew gathered in the back corner, Jakob made his break. He burst through the hatch, sending a high-pitched squeal echoing throughout the bay.

"Hey, this way," a voice yelled.

Jakob scurried down the hallway, ascended two flights of stairs before entering a jog down a long hallway toward the bow of the ship. He paused at a corner and peeked around. Three sailors exited a hatch to the left. Jakob waited out their passage down a long corridor before slipping through the same hatch.

The compact space offered a bunk bed, daybed, and three steel gray-painted lockers in the back corner. He rushed past the bunk toward the lockers. A half-wall jutted from the bulkhead opposite, concealing a single-person shower.

The first locker produced a shaving kit, and the second, barber scissors. He stripped from his clothes, flipped on the shower, and with the aid of a small mirror wired to a pipe, cut, and shaved his hair clean to the skull. He achieved an abrupt moment's reprieve as hot water doused and massaged distressed joints.

He ransacked each locker, collecting a clean shirt, socks, a pair of pants and briefs, a belt, and a pair of shoes.

He transferred the food contents from the pockets of his former pants, then secured O'Dell's personal belongings. He stepped into the shower for a peek into the mirror. It reflected a man he did not recognize.

Jakob scrubbed the scene of all visible traces of his presence. The entire operation eclipsed but thirty minutes. He pulled the drawstring of the seabag taut. The cabin door creaked open. Jakob dropped the bag as a sailor poked through.

"Sorry," he said, "have to check each bunk."

"Still looking for the escaped solider?"

"Yes, but we'll find him, unless he makes a jump for it."

"Fine," Jakob said. "We still on two-by-two?"

"Until we find him or reach port."

"Do you have time to escort me to the ship's morgue?"

"The morgue?"

"A buddy of mine passed. I want to add an unfinished letter he was writing home to his personal items."

The sailor leaned into the hallway. "Sorry, chum, need to keep looking. Anyway, you're near enough. The morgue is on the next level damn near right above your head."

"Thanks, and good luck," Jakob said.

The sailor pulled the door. Jakob leaned against the desk and let go a deep release. He draped the seabag over his shoulder, entered the hallway, then ascended a set of stairs.

Another ten paces brought him within a hatch door of his intended destination, where an aspiring artist made its identification a snap. A van Gogh it was not, as cardboard substituted for canvas, black spray paint for colorful oils, and stenciled block letters for identification.

Chapter 55

"Name?" the officer in charged barked, sending an echo across the mostly empty hangar.

"Artemus Ward," a corpsman replied.

"Rank?"

"Private."

"Serial number?"

"Three-seven-five-seven-six-eight-nine-eight."

"Port of exit?"

"Le Havre, France."

"Expired on land or ship?"

"Ship."

"Date and time of death?"

"Wednesday, 1400 hours."

The officer thanked the corpsman and recorded the time, day, and date of delivery.

"Okay, over there," he pointed, directing the bearers to deposit the white canvas bag at the end of a long row lined with similar white canvas bags. They placed the soldier's remains on the concrete floor. The parade of bearers and corpsmen lasted more than an hour.

The officer counted bags and compared the total to his paperwork. "Thirty-six on the nose," he said.

All fell silent, save the occasional groans common for a high-ceilinged, concrete and corrugated steel-paneled structure standing against sea winds. The sergeant sat at a small desk in the middle of the space, processing each soldier's deceased personnel file. He placed a phone call, which led to several in a row.

Jakob untied the laces securing his body bag, after transitioning from walking wounded to war casualty without incident. He'd played dead for near sixteen hours, as tough a physical and mental stress as humping through enemy-infested forests in pitch blackness.

The trip from ship to shore proved uneventful, though testy, as the need to remain rigid took its toll on his wounds. He'd prepared for an impromptu inspection, but it never came. Litter bearers placed him on a stretcher, and off to shore they went.

Jakob settled into a nervous fidget as the officer worked through his phone calls. Though not among the brightest speaking Americans he'd encountered, the man seemed a jovial sort, expressing pleasure the current batch of dead GIs placed him beyond the five thousand processed mark.

The man's incessant babble drove Jakob to thoughts of making a break, regardless of the consequences. During the sergeant's sixth call, he referenced a racehorse named King Shelby and twenty bucks pinned on his nose.

"Holy shit. Five hundred? On my way." The officer slammed the phone on its cradle, then exited the hangar, whistling a snappy tune.

Jakob pulled the bag below the bridge of his nose, inspected his surroundings, then kicked his way out of the canvas. He stowed the bag under the body next, and removed from his shoe O'Dell's dog tag, letters home, and wedding ring, all the while keeping careful watch of the front entrance.

Getting upright proved a challenge. Some parts responded well, others did not. He stretched and twisted his back, sending vertebrae popping from pelvis to neck as if kernels of corn under intense heat.

He moved toward an exit at the back of the hangar but paused upon reaching the officer's desk. He lifted a set of keys, a pack of chewing gum, and a pencil. The desk drawers produced a pack of Lucky Strikes, two Hershey bars, and a much-needed map of New York City. He plucked an overcoat from off the officer's chair.

"Hey, you," a voice boomed. "What are you doing in here?"

Jakob paused as he grabbed the doorknob. The officer filled the front doorway from jamb to jamb, a wad of cash in his palm.

"You're in a secure area, fella."

"Does not seem secure to me," Jakob replied.

"Oh, smart guy, eh?"

"No, sorry. I'm in the wrong building."

"We'll see how smart you are with the MPs. They'll teach you a thing or...." The officer paused mid-sentence. He noticed a gap in the row of body bags.

"Hey, what's going on here? Wait a minute, that's my coat."

Jakob shot through the exit.

"Come back here," the officer yelled over the echo of the slam of the steel door. He rushed to his desk, kicked the chair from his path, and reached for the phone.

Jakob bounced off the spare tire of a well-worn jeep parked outside. He scooted behind the wheel and searched the floorboard for the ignition button. The jeep fired on cue, rattling hangar panels to his immediate right.

He sped off down the narrow alley. A quick right delivered him onto a main thoroughfare, flanked by two of the tallest buildings he'd ever seen. The relative simplicity of a four hundred by sixty-foot ship exchanged in a blink for the mass chaos of concrete, steel, glass, and stone buildings, and brick chimneys belching smoke.

Military vehicles of all makes and models sped about. By the hundreds, men played chicken with traffic as they passed between buildings. Ships' horns blasted, train whistles echoed, truck horns blared. The harbor community bustled as if under attack.

Jakob traveled a half mile before a turn placed him between a lengthy convoy of supply trucks he suspected exiting the port. Vehicles passed along a straightaway, splitting mirror imaged buildings, each the length of fifteen ships set on end. The vista opened to the left, exposing the pier and harbor, and a mammoth train yard packed full of railcars and purring engines billowing black smoke.

The convoy turned right. Jakob followed. He drew his jeep left of center to sneak a peek beyond the lead truck. Armed guards checked credentials at a checkpoint in the distance. Within a few hundred yards, the convoy slowed to a crawl. Jakob knew dog tags would not suffice for passage, as he figured the morgue officer had called him in.

He tapped on the steering wheel, pondering the predicament, as the line of vehicles inched forward. He traded glances between the gate and his side mirror. Smoke from the train engines rose in sharp contrast to a skyline succumbing to dusk. He had but two options: hop a train or wait until dark for another way out.

He maneuvered from behind the truck in front and followed the road past a T-intersection onto a single paved lane, splitting the train yard and a jetty with gantry cranes loading materials onto barges. He parked the jeep behind a brick smokestack, equal in circumference to a ship's funnel.

He surveyed the landscape. The aggregate of manufacturing processes and mechanical components stole his breath. Never had he witnessed such industry or frenetic pace. Despite the lateness of the day, men went about their business with determined and gritted expressions, as if each task was *the* key to whipping the enemy.

Jakob exited the jeep in a stupor. "Good Lord," he whispered, absorbing the inharmonious melodies of countless machines at work and tradesmen barking directives for but a single purpose. "No army in the world could withstand this production."

He moved from behind the chimney. A gantry operator noticed Jakob exiting the jeep, making eye contact as he swung a load of steel onto a waiting barge.

Jakob paused short of the road running parallel to gaze upon the skyline of the city of his birth. The expanse appeared as a delicate oil on canvas, glowing orange and purple from the setting sun, with wisps of lingering clouds fluttering above the tallest spires of its most iconic skyscrapers. The view contradicted what he'd cemented to memory, a city untamed, compassionless, a man-eater. Vivid memories of father and mother spilled forth unfettered by time. Raw emotion bubbled deep from within but suppressed in a blink as sirens erupted from where he'd fled.

The echo sent Jakob sprinting into the rail yard like a fox from hounds, jumping tracks, dodging ground signals, squeezing between boxcars, hoping to outsmart all pursuers for the last time.

Chapter 56

"This Kraut must be dumb as a rock," said a military police officer, guarding a suspected stolen jeep.

"Yeah, so dumb, he caught a free ride halfway around the world on a military vessel using the tags of a dead soldier, made shore in New York Harbor surrounded by thousands of military personnel and civilians, and disappeared."

"Then why leave a stolen jeep out in the open?"

"Because he already figured his escape."

The MPs learned the identity of their prey after port authorities received word of the wounded GI, turned German soldier, turned medic, turned corpsman, turned corpse, from the captain of the St. Francis and shore morgue officer.

On a tip from a gantry operator, and backup having arrived within minutes of the discovery of the jeep, over a dozen military police and pier guards entered the yard with weapons drawn.

MPs collected credible evidence within minutes. One spotted a seaman's shirt draped on a ladder leading to the top of an oil tanker, another, a cap tossed between rails under a boxcar five tracks away.

Four locomotives hummed, readying for departure. Engineers received orders to stand down as personnel searched each connected car, some spanning forty deep. Guards escorted crew members to the middle of the yard to ensure no strangers among them.

Satisfied their target had not slipped into a boxcar or infiltrated the crew, the MPs released the trains.

As word of the escapee spread, authorities fielded several calls reporting strange characters and goings on. Sirens erupted across all points, spawning further confusion and paranoia among the working class.

With dusk upon them, the search expanded from the rail yard to adjacent buildings, dry docks, and parking lots designated for civilian use. Soldiers questioned each man and searched each structure.

Within an hour of their consultation with the ship's captain, Port Command received a photo of the German soldier.

"This may be the most significant manhunt since Dillinger," one MP quipped to another.

***

"Coffee?" the waitress asked.

"Yes. Cream and sugar, please," Jakob replied.

The woman smiled. She seemed a gentle sort, despite a ragged and worn appearance. He suspected she spent the first eight hours of her day at a primary job elsewhere. She scribbled out the order, coffee, egg and bacon on toast, potatoes, and a side order of peaches. She tore the sheet from a tablet and delivered it to a spike at the window separating kitchen and counter.

The dingy, twelve-stool, six-booth establishment wedged in a brick building amid the intense hustle and bustle of a mass of peoples living, working, and dying, stacked atop each other.

Jakob dispensed a stream of cream into his coffee, followed by two pinches of sugar. A patron two stools to his left finished what remained of a hamburger, perusing an evening newspaper. Jakob strained to pick out headlines, his angle sufficient to capture only the words Red Army and Berlin.

The waitress delivered Jakob's order. He tucked a napkin under his chin and took a bite of sandwich—hot, greasy, delicious. A bit of egg white separated. He brushed it from off the lapel of his black worsted wool suit coat purchased at a secondhand store four blocks from the diner. For ten dollars plus tax, he bought the three-piece number, a tie, white shirt, shoes, black-rimmed sunglasses, and a fedora. The transformation propagated confidence of blending in with the masses.

Out the diner's front window, a rush of citizens hurried along the sidewalks toward bus stops and subway centers, as Jakob contemplated his proximity to the community of his birth.

He traded a glance with a gentleman perched on the stool nearest the door. The man flashed a slanted eye, stirring a nervous tick in Jakob's stomach that he was still a fox on the run and all strangers, hounds. He wished for normal but feared he'd spend the rest of his days looking over his shoulder, evaluating all who looked his way. He bit off another wedge of sandwich. *I should have died in that valley.*

"Oh, my," the man to his left said with a hint of European accent. He stood from his stool and patted his pants and coat pockets. "I misplaced my wallet." His face turned beet red as he searched the floor and under his paper.

"I'm sorry, Miss," he said. "May I pay you later in the week?"

"I can cover it until then," she said, as if an oft-repeated response.

"I will pick up your tab, sir," Jakob volunteered. He figured the hardship on the woman if the man never showed his face again.

"I couldn't ask a stranger to pay my way."

"I will pay in exchange for your newspaper."

"I do not consider it a fair trade."

"Fair to me."

"Well, if you insist." He passed the paper. "I thank you, Mr....?"

"My pleasure," Jakob said, ignoring his probe for a name.

"Well, yes. Thank you again." The man tipped his hat and excused himself.

Jakob shifted his plates to the side and unfolded the evening edition of the *Times Herald*. His eye honed on a secondary headline: *Reds Storm Within 27 Miles of German Capital*.

"Berlin," Jakob whispered in a stupor. Though he knew the Reich could not survive a two-front war, the reality of the enemy overrunning Germany's capital proved beyond his comprehension.

Caught between the fine line of fact versus propaganda, he read on, crumbling under the weight depicting the systematic elimination of his land. Each article maintained a consistent theme: Hitler's war machine on life support, its leadership in disarray. His blood ran cold for the fate of the innocent, and hot at the cost Hitler and his henchmen paid for an attempt at continental domination, all at his peoples' expense.

First and Third Armies Ten Miles Apart Between Bonn and Coblenz.

Troops Cross the Rhine.

Yanks in Cologne.

Adolf Hitler Confesses to Inner Circle, Germany Has Lost the War.

"My God." Jakob folded the paper and tossed it aside. His emotions swelled as the air grew heavy about him.

"The price," he whispered, "and for what?" He slammed his fist on the counter. China and silverware rattled. The waitress jumped, dropping a stack of plastic cups.

"My apologies," Jakob said.

"You okay?"

"Yes, ma'am."

Jakob swiveled toward the front window. Distant sirens reminded him of his fugitive status. He requested both checks, paid, and passed a handsome tip. He thanked the woman and exited.

The night warranted an overcoat as wind gusts funneled chilled air down the street, sending paper products cartwheeling along gutters and sidewalks. Jakob turned west. He weaved through pedestrian traffic to stand under a streetlamp halfway down the block. Several initial attempts to hail a cab failed.

"We meet again."

Jakob turned.

"Did you enjoy my newspaper?" The man leaned against a lamppost, struggling to light a cigarette. He extended the pack. "Have a smoke?"

"No, thank you."

"I say, old man, you'll need to travel the next block to secure a taxi. It's more likely a taxi will run you down rather than stop in the middle of the street."

A line of cabs parked beyond the canopy of a modest hotel two blocks up the street.

The man winked and lifted his hat from off his head in exaggerated fashion, as if signaling. "Well, safe travels to you."

Jakob did not reply. The man worked himself into a throng of pedestrians and disappeared around a corner.

As Jakob stepped into the street, a pedestrian grabbed a wad of his jacket and pulled. A cabbie whipped around the corner and slammed on his brakes. He rolled down the passenger window. "Hop in, Mac."

Jakob leaned in. "How did you know I needed a taxi?"

"Saw you hailing from down the block."

Jakob slipped into the back seat, sliding across a bench splattered with stains and strips of industrial tape.

"Where to?"

"Pennsylvania."

"You know you're in New York, right?"

"Yes," Jakob replied.

"Any luggage?"

"No."

"Hmm, rarely see travelers without luggage."

Jakob shrugged.

"You'd find it cheaper taking the bus or train. Anyway, I ain't supposed to cross the New York State line, but might consider, if ...."

"How much to take me as far into Pennsylvania as you can go?"

"Fifteen bucks, without tip."

"Do you know the distance to Wellsboro, Pennsylvania, from the state line?"

"Never heard of the place." The cabbie flicked a cigarette into the street, then lit another.

Jakob stewed. *They will check mass transit stations first,* he thought. He sifted through his stash of cash. With tip, he'd have less than twenty dollars to his name. He knew the risk of public transportation too great, considering his fatigued state. *A perfect recipe for a silly mistake,* he thought. He survived many years in the most deplorable conditions without money. He could afford to splurge in the name of safe passage.

"Okay. I will pay."

The cabbie pulled a lengthy drag from his cigarette. A thick billow of smoke slipped out the side window. "You got it, Mac."

Chapter 57

"Hey, chum, wake up."

The cabbie adjusted the rearview mirror. Jakob had wedged himself in the corner against the door, face planted flush to the window. He succumbed to exhaustion well before the driver fled through the newly constructed Lincoln Tunnel.

"Hey, let's go. I need to head back to the city."

Jakob's eyes fluttered. He peeled his face from off the window and worked through a quick bout of bafflement.

"Where are we? Do you have the time?" He felt as if he'd dozed less than the duration of a single blink.

"Stroudsburg, Pennsylvania. Eleven thirty."

"Why this place?"

"Can't take you any further."

Jakob dug into his pocket, flipped through his cash, and passed fare and tip.

The driver pointed down the street. "There's a hotel on the corner, a pub across the way, a bus station a block over, and a train station two blocks south."

Jakob exited. "Thank you for the ride."

The driver tipped his cap and gave two quick blasts of his horn.

The local hotel sign flashed vacancies in bright red and blue, sending streaks of color into the street. The notion tempted—feather bed, down pillow, quilt, and a week's worth of quarantine—but Jakob knew better.

He accepted the high degree of public paranoia if the story hit the headlines, and equal embarrassment levied against the military for allowing a German to outsmart them. He needed a map, needed to know his location and distance to his destination.

He entered the pub to a volley of smoke. Cigars and pipes prevailed over cigarettes, suggesting a more sophisticated clientele, but not proving it. Dark floors and paneling, and insufficient lighting provided the perfect environment for concealment, if one so desired.

A corner jukebox wailed an upbeat Glenn Miller tune. Couples stumbled out of rhythm, slumped against one another on a makeshift dance floor. Rummies slobbered on themselves. Men laughed. Women giggled. Jakob found the gaiety extraordinary, unsettling, considering the state of current world affairs. Three unoccupied stools at the bar beckoned. He settled in the middle position. Patrons probed him but for a moment.

"What's your pleasure?" the barkeep growled.

"Beer," Jakob replied.

"What kind?"

"Any. Not partial to one over another."

The barkeep grabbed a glass mug and poured a draft from a center tap. He slid the brew across the bar top. Jakob had never seen beer lighter than his hair.

He drew a hand to catch the barkeep's attention. "Would you have a map of Pennsylvania?"

"A map?" The man scratched at his thick, sweaty sideburns. He rummaged under the counter and returned with a wrinkled relic. "All I got. It's from '43."

"May I buy it?"

"It's yours. I have no use for it."

Jakob flattened the map in front of him. He took a sip of beer and winced. "At least we produce a decent ale," he whispered. He took a second gulp; it fared no better.

He located Wellsboro. The destination lay well north and west. "A good 160 miles," he whispered. He plotted his course, cementing to memory the towns he must pass along the way.

A man squeezed between Jakob and another patron to occupy the stool to his immediate left. Jakob turned and offered a dip of his chin. He refolded the map along its proper edges, then slipped it into an inside pocket. He pushed the beer aside, as he could not tolerate the aftertaste.

A second, rotund man commandeered the stool to his right. A hard object pressed against his left ribcage, redirecting his attention.

The man to his left, pencil thin with gold wire-rim glasses, looked the part of a mathematics instructor or accountant, otherwise unremarkable, save a discolored pupil in his left eye. He concealed the gun in his overcoat.

"Planning a trip, Herr von Rüdel?" the man to his right asked.

Jakob froze. His temperature spiked.

"Or shall I call you Herr Denny? What name have you chosen today?"

The man flashed a pleased-as-punch grin. His body aped his face — round and blubbery, too blubbery for the times of rationing. The two dressed exact from the neck down.

"Please, don't let us interrupt. Finish your beer."

"I would rather not," Jakob replied. "What do you want?"

"You should reconsider. You never know when it shall be your last."

"Thank you, no. It does not suit me."

"As you wish." The man's hands presented small and meaty, his fingers stunted. He grabbed the mug and chugged the remains. "It's a sin to waste things in times such as ours, no?" He wiped his mouth with his coat sleeve.

"Who are you?"

The man released a sarcastic grin. "At least allow me the courtesy to buy your drink," he said. He deposited several coins on the bar. "Too bad your last beer was so disappointing."

Jakob hoped to goad the man into making a scene, recalling a captured American pilot's pet name for Hermann Göring. "What do you want with me, fat fuck?"

The man's eyes narrowed; his jaw clenched. Jakob winced as the barrel of the gun pushed deep into his rib cage.

"You will pay for your insolence. You will pay."

"Pay who?"

"Your Reich. I am taking you home."

"I am home, Fatty."

"I warn you, our mission is to bring you back alive, no matter your physical appearance. I will instruct you only once. You will follow me out of this bar to the back door. You will keep your hands inside your coat pockets. If you deviate from my path an inch, my colleague can render you unconscious upon my command. He has many tools at his disposal. Do you understand?"

Jakob did not respond.

"I said, do you understand me?"

"I understand."

"You will not speak to or acknowledge anyone. Understand?"

"I understand."

"We go now." The men pushed from the bar. Fatty took the lead.

The trio weaved through the crowd toward a narrow, darkened hallway. Fatty checked the alley before descending a set of stairs to a waiting car.

He opened the rear passenger side door, then grabbed Jakob by the collar and forced him against the building.

"The war is lost, and our fight over, but it rages on against traitors of the Reich. I will hunt your filth all the days of my life. Did you think you could commit treason and murder and escape justice?"

"I committed no such offenses. I did mankind a favor."

The man launched a backhand against the side of Jakob's head.

"You swine." He grabbed Jakob by the lapels of his jacket. "You will die dangling from a noose on German soil. The Gestapo will make it so."

"Gestapo?"

"We are among U.S. servicemen on their own ships, we work in Navy yards, on docks, we own secondhand clothing stores, we sit in diners and offer newspapers, we drive taxicabs. We search for those who failed in their duties."

Jakob's eyes widened.

"Oh, yes. You blew your cover the moment you stepped on the transport." Fatty snapped his fingers. The mathematician passed a black-and-white photo.

"A souvenir. We have several copies. I commend you on your escape from Limburg and France, ingenious and an impressive use of friends and enemies. You can escape the United States government but will not escape the Gestapo. You will die for the murder of your father and Herr von Meckel."

"How shall you escape the murder of innocent millions, Fatty?"

The man grabbed Jakob by the throat. "You will not speak to me again with such disrespect." He drove Jakob's head against the wall. Jakob crumpled to the cobblestone below.

"I expected more respect from the son of Franz von Rüdel."

Jakob lay on his side, cupping the back of his head.

"Lift him," the agent ordered.

The mathematician pulled Jakob to his feet.

"I will transport you underground to the Fatherland for execution."

"Kill me now, if you prefer," Jakob mumbled.

"Much too easy. You do not deserve a painless death, and I will not lose the bounty on your head. Now, inside."

The mathematician stepped forward and exposed the Luger. Fatty lumbered his way to the driver's side, forced his bloated body behind the wheel, and started the car. Jakob pushed off the wall. Blood laced his fingertips.

He crouched low and slipped into the car's back seat. He turned toward the door before readying to slide across the bench. The mathematician had wandered too close to the doorframe. Jakob pounced.

He grabbed the door handle and pulled with all reserve, catching the mathematician's forearm in the jamb. The agent let go a harrowing scream as the bone snapped. The gun fell into Jakob's lap.

Fatty made a move for an inside coat pocket. Jakob palmed the Luger and fired twice. Fatty's head exploded, sending matter splattering against the front windshield. Jakob slid across the bench and out the opposite door. He turned in time to see the mathematician disappear around a corner.

Jakob kicked the back door closed and dragged the agent from behind the wheel. He slid into the front seat and fled the scene, wiping away red and white mush from off the windshield with a leftover newspaper.

Several random turns later dumped him onto a well-traveled road and a northerly route. His shock grew at the depth at which the Nazi party sought revenge, and the several characters working in perfect tandem to deliver him unawares. The ease and freedom with which the network operated offered more than a humble wake-up call to this new game of cat and mouse.

No friends, no acquaintances. Every corner checked, each noise investigated, Jakob thought. *At least until you disappear for good.*

Chapter 58

A plop, gurgle, and swell of ripples outward toward the lake's banks completed the digestion of the stolen sedan.

Jakob stood on the shoreline, shivering, shrouded among a network of pine branches clinging to their cones, hoping not to have to re-enter the frigid waters to retrieve loose parts or stowed items.

Traveling throughout the night, with the fuel needle clinging to "E," he happened on a quaint country lane leading to a rusted gate protecting an expansive pasture and lake surrounded by cattle, just south of Wellsboro–the perfect spot to ditch the vehicle.

Upon navigating the sedan through the pasture to a point fifty yards from a natural ramp, he rolled down the window, gunned the engine, and drove the vehicle in. The car floated to near center of the lake before dipping forward and going down. He escaped through the driver's side window, reaching shore in time to catch a sunburst off the back bumper as the sedan disappeared into the murky depths.

Cattle bawled and crows screamed as Jakob waited for the lake's surface to return to its original sheet-of-glass-like state. With the last ripples breaking against the bank, he conceded the pond had swallowed the vehicle and all loose contents in full.

To his good fortune, Fatty stocked the car as if expecting to travel a great distance. He uncovered several useful items, including a toolkit, a black leather suitcase filled with clothes, a fur-lined trench coat, multiple canteens of water and packages of crackers, tins of canned meats, a Luger, three loaded clips, and a large hunting knife.

By pure accident, he stumbled upon a stash of four thousand in cash bound in stacks of Benjamin Franklins stuffed in a crevice above the wheel well. The sight of it, emblazoned with the face of his favorite American hero, stole his breath, as the take would support his meager existence for years. He rummaged through the suitcase and plucked an oversized shirt and pair of pants, then made a quick exchange of his wet wardrobe.

With the sun suspended against a cobalt sky speckled with creamy clouds loitering about, Jakob wiggled into the trench coat, located a felled branch, then retraced his way back to the main road leading to Wellsboro.

***

The days had long passed since Jakob could hike twenty miles under ten hours—routine training in the Hitler Youth—and a task he found easier than most. Current physical and mental deficiencies would allow a fourteen-hour pace.

He worked parallel to the road through brush, over fence lines, and through pastures packed with livestock. Save an incident with a bull, and a subsequent sprint across a pasture, the journey proved no more exciting than placing one foot in front of the other. Late into the night, he found cover and rest in an abandoned corn crib.

Morning broke to smeared, steel blue-gray clouds churning and rolling. Jakob trudged on. Snow drifted about as rural erections traded for structures more common to a thriving municipality. He paused to consult the map.

"It's Wellsboro. It has to be."

He continued along in a shallow ditch. A flatbed truck stacked with hay bales passed. The driver slowed to a stop. Jakob caught up and peeked inside.

"Happy to give you a lift to town, son," an old man said.

"Wellsboro?"

"Yes, sir."

Jakob stalled, taking a quick peek up the road. He wanted no help, but his legs had had it. His head felt light, and the snow had intensified in both pace and density.

"It's okay, son," the man said. "It's no trouble. I'm driving right through it."

Jakob turned to him. Kind features delivered a speck of solace he'd happened by on chance. An unintended twitch of the man's neck drew the eye, though its persistence nagged. The farmer wore a straw cowboy hat and overalls bearing stains of his craft, his eyes shone bright and experienced, his skin tanned. Jakob liked his face, liked his look; he seemed a trustworthy sort, but so did the man who surrendered the newspaper. He'd slipped the Luger in a side pocket of the suitcase. Easy access, if need be.

Conceding to exhaustion, he popped the latch and climbed in. An English pointer vacated the co-pilot's seat. The truck smelled of feed and tobacco.

"There's plenty of room for you here, Gracie," the man said. He patted the seat near his thigh. The dog folded in half next to him.

"Thank you," Jakob said. "I appreciate the ride." He patted the dog's head.

"Glad to do it." The old man placed the truck in gear to a smattering of grinds and groans. Jakob leaned against the seatback. His legs tingled as the vibration massaged his lower back and hamstrings.

"You from around these parts?"

"No, sir," Jakob replied. "From up New York state way."

"Home from the war?"

"Yes, sir." Jakob kept his head turned, watching the earth coast by at twenty miles an hour.

"Where did you serve?"

"Europe."

"Nasty business, those Nazis and Japs. I believe Hitler has seen his last days. Our boys close in each hour. They took Cologne and will cross the Rhine soon. I read yesterday we bombed Tokyo. Such death and devastation. I figured the Great War would've taught us all a lesson."

"As did I," Jakob said.

"Where ya headed?"

The dog forced her nose under Jakob's arm. He rubbed at her ears. "Nowhere in particular. I enjoy this part of the country. Thought I might start over here."

"No place on earth better for my money."

"Are you from these parts?" Jakob asked.

"Born and raised."

"So, you know most folks?"

"Most, though the community has thinned. Many of our boys won't return."

"I guess you would know of anyone hiring?"

"Could be. What type of work you interested in?"

"Not too picky at the moment. At least until I settle."

"Have you farmed or worked with animals?"

"Yes, sir. I grew up on a farm. My family raised horses and cattle. We ran fifteen hundred head of beef and several hundred milk cows."

"Raised?"

Jakob turned toward the window. "I have no farm or family left."

"I may have an interest in taking you on. I'm the county vet. Can't pay much but can provide room and board. My Margie's the best cook in these parts and we have an extra bedroom."

"At the moment, room and board trumps money."

"What's your name, son?"

"Tucker, Ep Tucker," Jakob replied, having spotted the name branded on a box crate exiting the pub.

The old man smiled. "Well, let's give 'er a try, Ep." He extended a hand. "Lucian McKenna, Tioga County veterinarian. Pleasure to meet you."

Chapter 59

"This room belonged to our youngest son," Lucian's wife, Margie, said with a smile.

Still reeling from shaking the hand of the man whose name he'd recited in Annalise's letter, Jakob did not respond as he stood in the doorway gazing at the small room stuffed with a single bed, candle stand, desk, and rocking chair.

"Mr. Tucker? Are you okay?" Margie asked.

"Yes, ma'am. Forgive my lethargy. I assume your son a casualty of the war?"

"Oh, no," Lucian said, "he died at nine. Doctor doesn't know the cause. Happened so fast. He broke out in a fever one night. Two days later, he died."

"I am sorry for your loss."

"We've a surviving son and daughter. Our daughter lives in Northumberland. She has six children and visits often. My youngest son lives in Los Angeles. He's an engineer with North American Aviation."

"A most worthwhile endeavor. I thank you for the room, Mrs. McKenna, but I would be just as comfortable in the barn."

"Nonsense," she said, with bright blue eyes matching the robin's egg shade painted along the hallway. She wore her hair in a tight bun. Unhitched, the brown with gray streaks mass would fall well below a thin waist accustomed to a thousand-and-one bends a day.

She patted his arm. "There's no reason for you not to use it. Besides, it's our duty to take care of those we can, and you look as if you could use a comfortable bed and home-cooked meal."

Jakob smiled. "Yes, ma'am."

"Make yourself at home, Mr. Tucker. If you need anything, let me know. We eat at first light and again around five-thirty. And please, call me Margie."

"Yes, ma'am."

Lucian patted his shoulder. "You look as if you've not slept for days. Take all the time you need. We'll start whenever you feel up to it. You'll find a bathroom across the hall. Firewood down the hallway and out the back door."

"I cannot thank you both enough," Jakob said.

Margie smiled, winked, and said, "It's us who should thank you for your service and for protecting our freedoms."

***

Either hearty laughter from the kitchen or a peaceful call of a whippoorwill perched outside his bedroom window surprised Jakob awake. He'd not known either disruption in years and was unsure which roused him first. He wiped away sleep and stretched his limbs.

Bright orange flames gnawed at a stack of logs in the fireplace. A soft quilt laid draped across his body, neither of his own doing. He suspected Margie saw to his comfort.

Light seeped in around the edges of drawn curtains, though offered little hint of the time of day. Jakob felt as good as he had in months. His bladder and bowels cramped, but the mattress's comfort and the agreeable warmth of the room challenged his desire to rise.

Footsteps drew his attention toward the door. He maneuvered upright upon a soft wrap against the molding.

"Mr. Tucker?" Margie called. Her soft voice reminded of his mother's. A moment's confusion struck, but quickly dissipated as he settled back into the depths of the lie dumped on this unsuspecting family.

"Ma'am?" he replied.

"May I come in?"

"Yes, of course."

She opened the door, her smile radiant. "Good morning."

"Morning."

"My word, I've not known anyone so dead to the world."

"Have I slept long?"

"Well, you fell asleep Wednesday, it's now Friday morning."

Jakob's eyes widened. "I had no idea. Please, forgive me."

"No need to apologize. I hope you don't mind, but I came in Thursday morning and brought you a quilt. Lucian tended your fire. I'm glad we didn't disturb you."

"I have not slept so deep in years."

"Good. I'll bet you're starving and in need of the bathroom. Come along to breakfast when you feel up to it."

Jakob settled into his pillow. He brought his hands against his face, resuming his befuddlement upon his hearing the name McKenna. The realization he stumbled upon the couple directly linked to O'Dell's wife damn near stopped his heart.

Killer, thief, and liar, he thought.

He floundered in his own detestation before trading the comforts of the bed for the small bathroom across the hall. He washed his face and emptied his systems. Though stiff, his joints functioned minus most of the pain that had plagued him in recent weeks.

Intermittent laughter, commingling with a radio advertisement plugging a corn planter, directed him toward the kitchen. Lucian and a man in uniform sat at a small, rectangular table covered in red-and-white checkered cloth, sipping coffee, smoking pipes.

"It's true, Margie, the dead do rise from the grave," Lucian said. He turned with a smile and peered over bifocals having seen better days. He pulled the chair next to him. "Come, sit down, my boy."

"Thank you."

A five-point star pinned above the pocket of a stained khaki shirt identified the stranger as a local law enforcement agent. Sleeves rolled to the elbows exposed taut, thickly pelted forearms.

"Ep, meet my dear friend, William Tobias Perry, sheriff in these parts." The man stood and extended a hand the size of a manhole cover.

Jakob pushed from the table. He stalled halfway up. *County sheriff*, he thought. *Annalise's uncle*. His change of expression did not go unnoticed as he reached for the man's hand. "Ep Tucker," he said. "Pleasure to meet you, sir."

"Pleasure's mine, son."

Margie reached over Jakob's shoulder and placed a cup of coffee in front of him. "Care for cream or sugar?"

Jakob fell against the seatback. *It cannot be*. His stomach tumbled. A throng of butterflies released.

"Mr. Tucker?" Margie repeated.

Jakob jumped. "Yes, ma'am," he said.

"Cream or sugar?"

"Both, please."

"Is this the first time you've met a sheriff?" Lucian asked, pointing the slit end of his pipe toward his friend.

"No, of course not. Still a bit dizzy, I guess." Jakob poured a stream of cream.

"I've slept hard before, but good Lord," Lucian said.

"I have not slept well in a long time, but look forward to getting to work," Jakob said.

"Well, guess we never discussed your wages, did we?"

Jakob took a sip of coffee—fresh and real—the best he'd tasted in years. "Wages? I believe you said room and board."

"I meant your salary."

"Yes, sir. I know. I believe room and board fair compensation."

Margie turned from two eggs sizzling in a cast iron pan. "Mr. Tucker, you're not serious. All working men deserve a fair wage."

"I find immense value in good food and a warm bed. Besides, I have no need of money at the present."

"He's a keeper if you ask me, Loosh," William said.

"Nonsense, Bill," Margie said, "Lucian, you can't allow him to work for free."

"How about a nominal token to start with?" Lucian suggested.

Jakob smiled. "Unnecessary."

Lucian scratched the side of his head. "I don't understand?"

"I have enough money. I will let you know if I run short. You do not know I can handle the job. I most desire finding peace, a soft bed, and a little food."

"I take a man at his word and expect you'll tell me if you run short."

Jakob added a touch of sugar to his coffee. "Yes, you have my word."

"I can set you up as a deputy," William joked. "Couldn't pay if I wanted but have a nice cot in the courthouse."

Jakob laughed. "Thank you all the same, but I think I found the best set-up in the state."

"Well, wait till you taste Margie's lamb chops. You'll want to pay her."

Lucian laughed. Margie blushed.

"Where did you serve, son?" William asked.

"Europe."

"Where about?"

Silence filled the room, save the *puff, puff* of Lucian drawing on his pipe.

"I understand, son," William said. "I know what's going on over there. A conversation for another day, perhaps." William pushed from the table and placed a kiss on Margie's cheek.

"Thanks for breakfast. Fantastic, as usual."

"You're welcome. See you this evening."

He grabbed a Stetson off a rack near the door. "Nice to meet you, Mr. Tucker. See you later, Loosh."

"You as well," Jakob said.

"See you, Billum, and stop kissing my wife." He drew from his pipe and offered a wink in Jakob's direction.

Margie set a plate full of eggs, bacon, and biscuits and gravy to Jakob's left. It smelled of home. Jakob moved the plate of food to his center. "Known the sheriff long?" he asked.

"Billum and I grew up together."

"Does he come by often?"

"Eats breakfast and dinner with us most days. He has no family, other than a niece who lives north of here. Ma cooks and the county pays. It's no burden. His appetite equals that of a bear, maybe an elephant, but I think we'll keep him."

Jakob laughed. "Seems a smart man."

"Yes, I've found great pleasure over the years with people who take him for some uneducated oaf and find out otherwise. I'd put him up against anyone. He has a keen common sense, quick mind, a near photographic memory, and as good and honest a heart as you'll find."

"Well, I guess it is time for me to start earning my keep. I do not know how many hours I can go, at least in the beginning."

"You're welcome to take more days if you like," Lucian said.

"No, I am eager to get to work."

"We'll start you out slow. Do what you can. Anyway, you'll spend the first few weeks observing."

"I have no work clothes."

"No problem. We'll stop by Hammer's on the way out of town. They have all the work clothes you'll need."

"What is on the schedule for today?"

"Four stops, nothing significant. Maintenance, mostly. There's a heifer 'bout to pop in the northwest corner of the county. I've saved that one for last. It's Billum's niece, Annalise Denny."

Chapter 60

Wellsboro's town square, located but a few miles north of the McKenna Farm, featured more than a dozen local businesses surrounding the county courthouse and its memorial clock tower stretching high into the Pennsylvania sky.

Hammer's anchored the first corner, adjacent to the local bakery, where the smell of freshly baked bread and pastries watered passing mouths.

With the aid of a friendly sales assistant, Jakob collected all work clothes and accessories necessary to assist the good doctor in his daily routines. He'd never owned or worn a pair of overalls. They felt strange, but he appreciated the rationale of their design and intended function.

He purchased a black felt cowboy hat with a thin, white ribbon for a hatband. He posed in front of a floor-to-ceiling mirror, losing himself in the memories of the Westerns he so loved.

Lucian stood behind, gazing like a proud father.

"I've never owned a real cowboy hat," Jakob said.

"It suits you well."

"It's more than a hat," Jakob mumbled. He searched Lucian's eyes in the mirror. "Do you know where I might purchase a horse?"

"Sure. The county co-op is just up the street on the backside of the square. A good friend of mine owns the place. He buys and sells horses as a side business. You can take him for his word. He's always more interested in finding responsible owners than making profit."

Nothing pleased Jakob more than the smell of feed, hay, manure, and leather — the essence of all he defined as good and normal. He stood in the middle of the store and breathed deep the stewpot of aromas.

"Joe, meet my new hand, Ep Tucker," Lucian said.

"Please to meet you, son," he said, with a wide, mirthful smile stretching ear to ear.

"Pleasure is mine," Jakob replied, finding a bit of humor in the man's lopsided grin and bushy eyebrows.

"We need a good horse, saddle, and tack," Lucian said.

"I see. What ya looking for, son? What purpose?"

"A horse I can ride to explore the area. A good companion."

"You vouch for him, Loosh?"

"I do. He'll take care of it. I'd bet the bank on it."

"That's good enough for me. Let me show you what I got."

Joe led the men down a hallway to a tack room. New and used equipment hung from angle irons, a Western saddle draped over a homemade sawhorse. Jakob threw a leg over. Its comfort made purchase an easy decision.

"This way," Joe said. He directed the men through a back door leading to a dry lot. Several breeds milled around bales of fresh hay spread along an opposite fence line. Jakob stepped forward. Ears perked and heads turned, but the beasts remained focused on their feed.

Jakob moved to the center of the arena, then turned his back on the herd. Many of the horses looked up to investigate, but quickly returned their noses to the bales.

One horse, after collecting a mouthful of hay, broke from the pack. The brown and white spotted beauty moved forward. Jakob felt the thud of her hooves and moved a half step in the opposite direction. The horse continued a cautious approach. As she moved forward, Jakob moved away, taking smaller steps with each thud, before coming to a standstill.

The horse came to within inches of the back of his neck, blowing, sniffing, brushing her whiskers against his hair. Jakob turned to face her. She ran her nose from his head to his shiny new boots. He placed a hand on her jowl and blew a gentle breath into her nostrils. Her ears perked as she leaned forward and touched her nose to his, then eased her head onto his shoulder.

"I'll be damned," Joe said.

Lucian shook his head and laughed. "You ever seen a horse pick a man before?"

"Only once," he replied.

Jakob ran his hands over the animal's powerful jowls. She stood seventeen hands with a patch of white extending to the tip of her nose, eyes well-proportioned and expressive, a long, muscular neck, and broad, barreled chest streaked with a delta of thick veins. Feathering originated above each fetlock. She equaled in elegance and mass to a Percheron or Clydesdale.

Jakob planted a kiss on her nose. "How did you come by a drum horse?"

"Belonged to a fella from England," Joe said. "He died not long after coming to the States. His wife needed the money."

"What a beauty." Jakob returned to near Lucian. The horse followed close behind.

"Are you familiar with the breed?" Lucian asked.

Jakob nodded. "The Queen of England and other royalty used these animals to carry kettledrums during events of pageantry. How much?"

Joe rubbed his chin. "Well, I picked her up for thirty and have five months of grain and hay in her. She's up to date on all her maintenance."

"Seventy for her, the saddle, and tack," Jakob said.

"I think you're a little high. I'd do sixty."

"Done," Jakob said, extending a hand to seal the deal.

"We'll stop by later and pick her up," Lucian said.

"No need. Buck can load her and take her out to your place, no problem."

"You will need payment for transport," Jakob said. The horse brushed against his back and resettled her head on his shoulder.

"No. Glad to do it, son. I'm thrilled she picked you. By the way, her name is Maisy."

"Thank you." Jakob turned and patted the horse's nose. "I shall name you after my mother and call you Liesel."

***

Lucian pointed to a heifer's teat. "Seen this before?"

Jakob dropped to his haunches, knowing the school bell had rung. "Yes. Rose udder."

"We call it mastitis. The old bacterial invasion of the teat canal."

"What caused this?"

"Who knows? Either host, pathogen, or contaminant. I'm betting contaminant."

"How do *you* treat it?"

"Disinfect the udders and administer an oral aspirin solution. Should clean up nice within a week. There's a bucket in the truck. You'll find a bright blue bottle of disinfectant in the utility box. Fill the bucket with water and meet me back here. You'll find the well behind the barn. I'm gonna speak with Jud to see if we can locate the source."

Their second house call exposed Jakob to an ornery billy with a lacerated neck, thanks to a barbed wire fence and greener pasture beyond. Jakob held the goat's horns as Lucian stitched the wound.

"You have a special way," Jakob said, as he steered the truck down a narrow country lane toward their third call.

"From my mother, I guess, though Dad demanded our respect for all living creatures. Mom, well, she believed all things living had a purpose and should live as nature intended."

"My mother had similar beliefs. She is my proof God made man in his own image."

"What a lovely sentiment," Lucian said. "You'll want to take the next road to the right. The Sitton farm sits beyond about a mile." Lucian ignited his pipe. The scent of rose and spice filled the cab. "What happened to your family?"

Jakob turned to view a pond playing host to a swarm of mallards. Answering meant lying, and he could no longer stomach the thought. The McKennas didn't deserve such betrayal.

Lucian let the question ride. "This road," he pointed.

Among his many skills, Lucian proved a more-than-competent farrier. Jakob had trimmed and shoed many hooves, but not attached to beasts weighing more than a ton. Lucian taught him proper angles and positions as the Belgian pull team stood at near attention. Jakob worked the last horse. They completed the job in less than an hour. The owner paid in butter and eggs.

"Is that customary for these parts?"

"No, though more so since the war. He needs the team to keep his business going."

"I bet you tell people to pay later and never collect."

Lucian smiled. He climbed into the passenger seat. "It all works out. Folks 'round here settle their debts. They may not always pay in cash or coin, but always settle. A hug, a pie, or showing up to harvest hay. It doesn't matter. You live to serve, not to be served."

Jakob eased the truck around a sharp curve. "Next farm on the left," Lucian said. "If Anna baked an apple pie, you're in for a treat."

Chapter 61

The cabin home sat nestled as O'Dell described. Jakob could have approached with eyes closed and forged a mental replica. A pleasant concord prevailed between the many wondrous natural features and manmade structures built of humble, natural material.

He stepped from the truck into several inches of snow. The scene depicted what he'd seen in many a picture postcard—a board-and-batten structure, flaked of its whitewash from years of weather, a stone chimney belching smoke into a gray-lit sky, frost clinging to corners of windows. Pines stretched beyond the roofline, their branches cupping clumps of fresh snow. A multi-colored stone wall stretched perpendicular to the entrance, separating property from county road. Simple perfection.

The moment lingered, but Jakob soon felt the crush of his reality, a dead friend's dream. A nervous urge attacked, similar to the fits of abnormal contraction suffered in the moments leading to battle. This felt worse. His knowledge of O'Dell's fate and escape using his friend's name felt more sinister than taking a man's life.

Lucian stepped onto the front porch and knocked. Jakob leaned against the truck's front grill with arms folded. The door opened upon a second rap. Lucian stepped forward to accept the woman into his arms. Her head settled on his shoulder.

Their hug lasted beyond vendor and client, as Lucian held her as a father would his daughter. He stepped back and delivered a kiss on her cheek.

Jakob's arms fell limp to his side, his mouth slipped open. Her beauty projected as simple as a drop of rain, or a single leaf splattered with the brilliance of fall colors. He suspected she did not view herself as such and would suffer a humility-laden flushing if complimented.

Lucian motioned Jakob toward the porch. He settled into a noticeable gawk. The woman cocked her head as if questioning his sanity.

"Ep, over here," Lucian motioned.

"Ep Tucker, meet Mrs. Annalise Denny. Annalise, my assistant."

Jakob removed his hat and stepped onto the porch with the grace of a three-legged goat.

"Pleasure to meet you, Mr. Tucker."

Jakob smiled and nodded, but could say nothing more than, "Ma'am."

Annalise pushed the screen door to its full extension. "Please, come in."

Jakob kicked his boots free of snow and followed Lucian into the home's front parlor. The small gathering area allowed for two rocking chairs, a smoking table between them, and a church pew-like bench on a far wall, all angled in front of a stacked stone fireplace. A bright flame crackled away. The distinct and pleasant aroma of balsam fir stoked a desire to draw a deep sniff.

Lucian settled in a rocker, pulled out his pipe, and helped himself to a tin of tobacco. He tamped down the makings and struck a match on his heel. A cloud of blue smoke released to the ceiling.

"And how's our young lady doing today?" he asked.

Annalise settled on the pew. She motioned Jakob toward the second rocker. "I was headed to the barn when you knocked. She's getting close, I think. Not moving about much."

"I want to see her before she goes down. Need to make sure the calf's in the proper position."

Jakob looked about the room. Its aesthetics equaled in elegance to what he expected of O'Dell, with most items constructed by hand, including a bookcase carved from a massive tree trunk.

"And how's our little man?"

"Growing like corn," Annalise replied. "He's asleep right now. Had an upset stomach last night but is feeling better today."

An oil painting of O'Dell in full military dress hung centered on a back wall. A small wood table below supported a single, half-burnt candle.

Lucian peeked over the edge of his glasses. "Any word?"

Annalise shook her head, a pensive expression showing the delicate features of her face. "No, nothing."

"He's alive," Lucian said. "At least we can thank God for that."

"Yes. When I received the news, I fell to my knees. I never expected he'd meet his son. I don't know the extent of his injuries. The Army does not communicate well. It's a wonder they're able to run a war at all."

Jakob could stand no more. He lifted from the rocker to a position in front of O'Dell's painting. A lump the size of a concrete block bulged in his throat. The O'Dell he knew did not size up to the man depicted by the artist; face full, healthy, alive with color, eyes wide and vibrant, glowing with anticipation of life beyond conflict, and a country-mile wide smile, unscathed by the rigors of war. Jakob wished for the power to switch places.

"My husband, O'Dell," Annalise said.

Jakob turned.

"He's a medic. I don't know how any of them survived. I read where enemies target them. They say if you kill the medics, you kill the injured soldiers. What a despicable tragedy if humankind has sunk so low."

"Yes, indeed," Jakob said. He received those exact orders during training.

"Well, let's check in with our girl," Lucian said.

Annalise led them down a hallway encased in whitewashed shiplap, made narrow by a set of stairs ascending to the left. She paused in the kitchen to set a coffeepot on the stove.

A mudroom was positioned off the back corner. Annalise pulled a heavy coat from a hook and an oil lamp off a counter adjacent to a well pump. The back door led to a covered porch constructed of fieldstone and barked timbers.

Lucian followed down a short run of granite steps toward the barn. Jakob soaked in the vista before him, as snow ticked against his face.

White pines and sugar maples swayed with the breeze. O'Dell had not exaggerated his description. "Beyond heaven on earth," Jakob whispered. The air ushered a sense of peace and space, a refined clarity squashing the worries of all other matters.

Pasture stretched several acres into the distance, flanked by magnificent promontories congested with multiple species of hard and soft woods indigenous to the state. *Heaven on earth.*

He followed Lucian's tracks toward the barn, a two-story, board-and-batten beauty, founded in fieldstone. Dormant veins of ivy clung to the siding, fanned in all directions, awaiting a stretch of warmer weather to ignite revival. A fence extended off a back corner into the woods, securing countless laying hens.

Beyond a pebble-filled creek, several head of beef and milk cows shared hay bales to the right, horses munched on bales to the left. O'Dell's Bella stood out as a green leaf on a bed of rose pedals, a perfect specimen combining grace, athleticism, and power. He held no doubt she'd equal riding on the wings of an eagle.

He entered the barn through a side Dutch door. Lucian removed his coat, rolled up his sleeves, and drenched an arm with lubricant.

"Ep, see the rope halter?" Lucian pointed. "Place it on Mom, then secure a lead rope and tie her off to that beam. She's not going to appreciate this."

Lucian entered the cow's vagina up to his elbow. "The calf's alive," he said.

Jakob had witnessed hundreds of births but never attempted manipulation.

"She reacted to my touch when I pinched a hoof," Lucian said.

He pushed deeper. "Head's deviated to the left." He grunted and plunged in nearly to his shoulder. "I got the nose. Now I'll get a hold of her jaw and pull her head down into the pelvis where it belongs. There... perfect. Mother Nature will do the rest. When Mom's ready, this calf will slip out like stool from a goose."

Jakob removed the rope.

"I'll get some coffee," Annalise announced.

Jakob stepped back as she passed. Her hair, soft as spun silk, brushed against the top of his hand as she exited.

"She's a fine woman," Lucian said, cleansing his arm.

Jakob jerked to attention.

The cow let go a bellow. Lucian patted her head. "Hang in there, Momma. You're doing fine."

"I find her of strong will and determination," Jakob said.

"Yes. She'll spit this one out, no problem. It's a bad day when you find a dead calf inside."

"No, I meant Mrs. Denny," Jakob corrected.

"Oh, yes, a fine, fine woman. She's built this farm mostly on her own, though I'm not sure what happened to her hired hand."

Lucian ducked under a ladder leading to a door at the back corner of the barn. He peeked in. "That's odd. It's cleaned out."

"What?"

"The room she built for her hired hand. It's empty. If that boy quit, there'll be hell to pay. I'm the one who recommended she take him on." Lucian returned to check on the cow's condition. Jakob assisted him into his coat.

"Don't know about you, but I could use a coffee," Lucian said.

Annalise had placed two cups on a small wood table built for two, poured them full of coffee, before heading upstairs to collect her son.

"Ahh," Lucian said, pointing Jakob to a chair opposite, "you won't find a better cup. She grinds and mixes her own beans." He took a whiff, then lit his pipe.

The two sat silent, sipping at their cups, before footsteps in the hallway captured their attention. Annalise entered with her son in her arms.

"There he is," Lucian said with outstretched arms. Annalise released the boy into his grasp. The child straddled his knee and Lucian kissed his forehead. The boy smiled.

"How's my boy this fine day?" Lucian pressed another kiss against the crown of his head.

"Be careful, I don't want you sick, too."

"There's nothing this lad can give me any worse than what can come from sticking my arm up a cow's south end."

The moment hit Jakob hard. His chest felt as if ripping in half. He released a faux yawn, a manufactured excuse to wipe his eyes.

"Where's Leroy?" Lucian asked.

Annalise shot an embarrassing glance toward Jakob.

"I am happy to leave the room, if you like," he said.

"No, that won't not necessary."

Lucian straightened. "What the heck happened?"

"He liquored up a couple days ago. Came into the house and got a bit too friendly. Tried to kiss and touch me. I told him to leave."

"That son-of-a-goat. Why didn't you tell me?"

"I didn't want to trouble you. Didn't want you to feel guilty."

"It's trouble for him, if I ever see him again."

"I handled it. Most men move along with a shotgun in their face."

"Well, I know you can handle yourself, but you cannot handle this child, this farm, a new calf, buying and selling, all on your own. You need help."

"I'll find someone I can trust."

Jakob took hold of his cup. Annalise turned and squared to him. He'd theorized long ago the gateway to one's defining moral element shone in the depth of their eyes. Annalise's eyes exposed a soul certain to drive her to aspire for everything good and right.

The best Jakob could do now, all he could offer the man who delivered him from the grave, was himself and his service, as long as Annalise required.

He set his cup on the table and clasped his hands. "Mrs. Denny, you need not search for anyone. I would be more than pleased to help you look after the place."

Chapter 62

Annalise withdrew from the kitchen to her bedroom to retrieve a blanket.

The coffee worked its way through Lucian's aged renal system, requiring a trip to the outhouse. He passed the boy into Jakob's arms, assuring his return within the shake of a lamb's tail. Jakob balanced the child on his knee. He had little experience with such matters.

The room fell silent with the final slap of the screen door. The boy sat still, looking at Jakob as if a colorful toy emitting intermittent bells and whistles. Jakob found difficulty reveling in his adorable facial expressions and large copper-colored cow eyes. He stroked the boy's hair and brought a hand soft against his cheek. He held tight to his torso and searched his eyes.

"Your father is a hero," he whispered. "Many a man returned home because he saw to it. Many children will be born, and many will know their fathers because of him. One day, you will know the truth of his legacy."

The boy smiled.

"I promise, you will not face this world alone."

Jakob closed his eyes and kissed the boy's forehead. He held steady, absorbing his scent, committing it to memory.

"Oh, my," Annalise said, surprised.

Jakob snapped back and displayed his best smile. "Lucian ran to the outhouse," he said, with hurried cadence.

"I'm so sorry, let me take him."

Jakob passed the boy into her waiting arms. Annalise inspected the child as if searching for damage. Jakob recoiled against his seatback. How long had she stood in the doorway?

"Thank you for keeping him."

"What a delightful young man. I have not held a little one in many years."

Annalise smiled. "I fear he'll soon be getting into all sorts of things."

She laid the boy on a small mattress near the stove, then draped him with a blanket. She filled Jakob's coffee cup before settling in the chair vacated by Lucian. "I appreciate your offer to help around here, though I'm curious as to why, since you already have a job."

"I have no family or home. I enjoy keeping busy and can work out a routine to meet both needs."

"I'm guessing you know something about farm life?"

"I grew up on a farm. My family had cattle and horses, hayed our own fields. I know enough, at least Lucian believes so."

"Well, I trust Lucian without reserve. Did you grow up in these parts?"

"No, born in New York."

"How did you find your way here?"

"Needed a new start and I love this part of the country."

"I'm not able to pay much but can offer room and board."

"I require neither," Jakob said.

Annalise froze in mid-motion of bringing her coffee cup to her lips. "What?"

Jakob smiled. "Lucian had the same reaction."

"You mean you're not drawing wages from him either?"

"Room and board."

"I don't understand."

"I have no need of money at the moment."

"It's not right for a man to work without earning a wage."

"It depends upon one's perspective. I desire peace and an opportunity to help where needed. I find peace in horses and livestock and felt a tremendous peace the moment I stepped on this property. I know no wage worth more than that."

"If you have room and board, you'd be working for me for free."

The brilliant, deep sea green of her eyes sparkled despite suppressed sunlight, setting in motion a childish flush and a crippling guilt and regret weighing in tons upon Jakob rather than pounds. "As Lucian says, you live to serve, not to be served. Mr. Lucian and Mrs. Margie provide a comfortable room and delicious meals. What more would I require?"

"Well, I could use the help and can provide meals whenever you need. There's a bunk room in the barn. You may do with it as you see fit."

"A perfect spot for an occasional nap."

The screen door squealed. Heavy stomps from the mudroom vibrated across the hardwood. Lucian entered with hands cupped to his mouth.

"You have a bright, healthy new addition, Anna," he said, swelling with pride. "She's as big as a donkey and feisty as a coon but will serve this farm well for years to come."

"How wonderful." Annalise's smile widened, sending delicate wrinkles extending from the corners of her eyes. Jakob could not get enough.

"I heard Momma grunting and checked her progress. I grabbed the calf's forelimbs to pull when she contracted and pushed. As clean a birth as I've seen in some time."

Annalise conducted a quick check of her son. He lay fast asleep. She offered Lucian an exuberant hug on her way to the mudroom. Jakob followed on Lucian's heels.

"I need to empty the coffee," Jakob said.

"You'll find the outhouse around the corner."

***

Annalise settled on her knees in the hay as nature took its course.

The mother sniffed and explored her calf from head to tail, her eyes growing wide and attentive as interest increased. Upon licking clean the birth fluids, she expelled a hearty bellow. Within minutes, the calf achieved an upright position.

"She's beautiful," Annalise said.

Lucian leaned against a support beam and brought his pipe to life. "I remember a time pulling a dead calf from its mother's womb one piece at a time. I'm always fearful of the worst, but feel much appreciation when things turn out as they should."

"What do you think about Mr. Tucker's offer to help out around here?"

Lucian pushed a hefty cloud of smoke into the rafters. "I admire a man who wants to work."

"But for nothing?"

"You too, huh? I'll admit, he threw me for a loop with that one. Claims he doesn't need money. I think he's a nice, honest young man, and suspect he's trying to find his way. So many of our boys coming home struggle to re-adjust to civilian life."

Annalise patted the calf's hind quarters. "There's a way about him. He seems a genuine, compassionate sort, content in his own skin. He reminds me a great deal of —" Her voice cracked.

"I'd agree," Lucian interrupted. "You give people a chance to prove they're something other than what they claim. The trick? You don't let them take you twice."

"Can he work both jobs?"

"I don't think he realizes the number of calls we receive in the middle of the night, and again when the locals check their stock between six and seven. It's not a consistent schedule."

"I could use help most in the late afternoon and evenings."

"It'll be a full day, but I'm betting he'd not want it any other way."

"I find him harmless and charming." Annalise blushed. "I returned to the kitchen and saw him kissing the baby's forehead. He held steady as if trying to recapture a lost memory. I thought it quite sweet."

"With us both keeping watch, I doubt he'd catch us off guard."

Annalise suggested it best to give mother and calf time alone. Lucian followed Annalise out of the barn, eventually passing her without notice. She'd stopped dead in her tracks, gawking at Jakob standing nose to nose with Bella.

"My goodness," she whispered, bringing a hand to her chest.

Lucian sidled up next to her. "Well, I'm not surprised after what I saw this morning."

Annalise drew a strand of hair to around her ear. "I don't understand. No male has gotten within ten feet of her unsecured since O'Dell left."

"It's a gift. He bought a horse this morning. Walked to the center of Joe's arena and stood still as a statue. Within a few minutes, a beautiful English horse broke from the pack and connected with him unlike anything I've ever seen. The horse picked him."

Bella brushed her muzzle across Jakob's face. Jakob responded by blowing puffs of breath into her nostrils.

"I don't understand. She damn near killed Leroy last week. She bit a sliver of Uncle Bill's shoulder at Thanksgiving, and I have to halter and post her before you can examine her."

"Some people have a special way about them. I can't explain it."

Jakob ran a hand along Bella's withers and patted her a final time. He skipped across the creek. "What a fine animal."

"Thank you. She belongs to my husband."

"An Arabian, correct?"

"Yes. We call her Bella. Did she give you any trouble?"

"No. I did not rush her. Is she not partial to strangers?"

"All but you, apparently."

"I tend to do well with horses and livestock."

"I'd say so." Annalise turned to Lucian and shrugged. "We discussed your situation. Lucian could use you in the mornings and afternoon. I could use you late afternoons and evenings."

"Sounds perfect."

"It's a long, full day, son," Lucian said.

"I spent the past five years fighting every second of every day for my life. This, I can handle."

Annalise smiled and extended her hand. "You're hired."

Jakob accepted, holding on much too long.

"Is something wrong?" she asked.

He hesitated, attempted to speak, but could offer only a shake of his head.

"Okay, then," Annalise said, releasing from his grip, fighting a strange sensation something lingered about his mind of greater significance than his desire to help.

Chapter 63

Jakob managed forty minutes' shut eye before waking to the sensation of feeling Annalise's hand in his. He entered the kitchen to the smell of bacon and homemade biscuits, and Margie hard at work.

"Good morning, Mrs. Margie."

She stood in front of the stove, draped in a yellow-checkered apron, flipping bacon and stirring eggs.

"Good morning, Ep."

Jakob eased into his chair. "Is Lucian about?"

"Oh no, he couldn't stand it. Wanted to check on Simpson's mare."

"Why did he not wake me?"

"He wanted you to enjoy a little extra sleep."

"He needs it more than I."

"He prefers short nights. After breakfast, he wants you to run out to Annalise's and check on the calf. Said he'd meet you out there."

"Sure, happy to."

"Are you hungry?"

"Yes, ma'am."

As always, Margie's breakfast filled Jakob to the brim. Her coffee surpassed any he'd consumed, and those biscuits—wow.

Jakob delivered his plates to the sink. Margie passed him a paper sack as he exited. She smiled and patted his shoulder, as if sending him off to school.

Jakob squinted at the bright, high sky as he wandered down a single dirt path carved by cattle years ago. Dew splattered on the tips of his boots. The sun swept across the back of his neck to equalize a gentle nip, though a hint of spring hung in the air. Apple and cherry trees pushed forth buds, promising Margie fruit enough to add to her collection of cellared goods.

He entered the main barn through an attached surgery where Lucian kept hours one day a week. He filled Liesel's feeder with bales of hay mixed with alfalfa and brushed her as she munched away. It pleased him he'd found such a delightful beast with the personality of a newborn lamb.

She'd never replace Sascha but responded to commands as Sascha did. When he was on her back, she felt like one of his limbs. She proved a quick study of his ways and responded to directions and commands without hesitation.

Jakob led her to the pasture and waited until she found interest in other grasses near a small spring-fed pond. He returned to the surgery, retrieved his medical bag, and tossed it into his truck.

At Lucian's urging, he'd rescued a 1937 half-ton flatbed Ford and a small two-horse trailer from a cobweb and dust-caked stall in an outbuilding. Twenty dollars repaired the engine, added a new set of brakes, used tires for both truck and trailer, and a new front windshield. Margie stitched a fashionable seat cover made of potato sacks. Jakob had added bins against the cab to store supplies.

He arrived to find Annalise working a painted mare in a round pen.

"Good morning," he said, climbing to straddle the top rail.

"Morning," Annalise shouted. She kept the mare at a graceful trot, working the horse one way then another without benefit of a lead rope. Simple hand signals and arm gestures spurred the mare's precise response. Annalise moved like a ballerina. Jakob settled his chin into a palm. *Poetry in motion.*

Jakob felt their relationship had ebbed slightly beyond employee-employer two nights prior, when she caught him off guard admiring him as he mucked a stall.

"You weren't kidding when you said you enjoyed work," she had said, catching him in a moment of deep contemplation.

Jakob jumped. A playful smile ebbed across her face. He dropped his rake and approached the stall gate, draped his arms over the top rail, then removed his hat. "I do not consider it work. I enjoy it too much."

She pushed off the timber and stepped onto the bottom rail to pull herself up. "My husband says the same thing. He loves this place, from cobwebs sticking to his face, to the smell of manure."

Jakob's heart skipped, as if shocked by a bucket of cold water dumped on his head. It set his soul aflame when she spoke of O'Dell in present tense. His mind erupted in a frenzy of incoherent contrivances, honing on how he could surrender information that felt as heavy as a ship's anchor around his neck. He could deliver O'Dell's dog tags and letters home, which she would accept as fact, including how the two came to meet on the battlefield. But would she believe her husband dead? He doubted she'd accept his account, his military allegiance, or motivation for seeking her out now. He felt the time not right.

He spat out the first vanilla response he could think of. "Many things to appreciate here."

"You enjoy it, huh?"

"I expect the same of heaven."

His perception sent her face to glowing. Jakob turned away but for a moment, as he could not free himself from the spell of her eyes. They drew him in as would a fantastic whirlpool. When fixated, his mind went blank. He looked to her and smiled. For a brief instant, all fell silent around him.

Annalise brought the painted mare to a halt. Lucian approached. The slap of his pipe against his palm echoed across the pasture.

"How's our new addition today?" he called out.

"Fine," Jakob replied. "Sturdy as an oak and hungry."

"Good to hear. And how are you this fine morning, my dear?"

"Fine, Lucian."

"We must split up today, Ep. Jake Godfrey has a mare in choke. Take my tubes and go clear her."

"I have not performed a choke procedure on my own."

"You can do this. Make sure the tube is in the esophagus. Nothing to it."

Jakob hopped from the fence. "Are you sure about this?"

"I trust you, son. If you have any trouble, pull the tube, and call me at Branson's. He has a Hereford ready to pop."

Jakob bid Annalise a good day. He pulled the required implements from Lucian's truck, backed out of the driveway, and turned west. He kept his eyes glued to the road as he ran through the stomach pump procedures, paying little attention to an olive-green sedan with a large white star stamped on the driver's side door, passing in the opposite direction.

Chapter 64

"So, what do you think?" Lucian asked, placing his arm around Annalise's shoulder.

"He's a hard worker, disciplined, eager to please. It wouldn't take a smart person to suspect he spent time in the military."

"And personally?"

She pulled her gloves and stuffed them in a back pocket. "He's as gentle a spirit as I've met." She turned to Lucian, squinting against the sun. "He's unique in ways I'm used to and comfortable with. He's carrying a heavy burden, though I don't know what, but I enjoy his company. At times, I feel I wish he'd never come. It's difficult because I feel he's a carbon copy. It caught me off guard."

Lucian agreed. "He reminds me of him, too. I'd hate for my life to depend on the difference between their characters."

Annalise sighed.

"You need him to go?"

She looked to the ground and kicked at the dirt. "He loves it here. Told me so himself. I don't have the heart to destroy what little peace this place offers him. It's not his fault he reminds me of O'Dell."

Annalise moved the mare from the pen with a pat on the rump. She looked beyond Lucian, noticing two soldiers standing at attention near the back corner of the house. She gasped. Lucian turned on a dime.

Annalise exited the round pen in a sprint, racing across the pasture and over the creek, skipping over steppingstones O'Dell placed and spaced for her gait. She stopped dead on the other side. Lucian pursued as fast as his old bones could carry him. Annalise dropped her head and cupped her hands to her mouth. Her body slumped at the sight of two strangers. Lucian caught up but said nothing.

Annalise moved forward, her chest heaving, though not in response to her sprint across the pasture.

"Mrs. Denny?" the tallest and most decorated of the two asked. They removed their caps.

"Yes."

"I'm Captain Christopher Brock. I'm afraid we have some bad news."

***

"I understand any apology at this point does little to comfort," Brock said, "but for the record, please know, we're doing all in our power to account for those missing."

Annalise sat in her chair, rocking away, lost in a daze. Lucian stood behind with arms folded. O'Dell was not on a hospital ship, or on his way home. They'd not yet accounted for him. The letter? A military mistake, or as the captain described, "An unfortunate rush to inform."

"How can this be?" she asked in a whisper.

"I don't have an answer," Brock said.

"How did it all play out?" Lucian asked.

"His dog tags identified him as Sergeant O'Dell Denny, and he corroborated in perfect English. A field medic claimed he identified himself as John Jones in a brief exchange before the soldier lost consciousness. An Army Intelligence representative confronted the soldier about the name Jones, but he claimed it a nickname. AI requested your husband's file. Of course, the picture did not match the patient. Authorities detained him, but he escaped onto a transport vessel posing as a corpsman. From there, he blended in, assisting with the injured, I'm told, then made his way onto the St. Francis and disappeared until the ship made port in New York Harbor. He escaped in a body bag."

Lucian dropped his arms. "What?"

"Yes, sir. He gained access to the ship's morgue and stuffed himself into a body bag. A witness claimed the soldier fled the shore morgue in a jeep. He swiped a second jeep and ditched it in the city. He's duped a lot of people, but I believe he had help."

"Amazing," Lucian said. "An escape for the ages."

The soldiers looked to each other, their embarrassment clear. "We're dealing with a smart man and doing all in our powers to find him and get you some answers, Mrs. Denny."

Lucian shook his head. "Does he pose a threat?"

"We have no way of knowing, of course, but, as I mentioned, we have sound intelligence, and many examples of American-born Germans forced into the conflict who want no part of it. They're desperate for a way out. He's too smart and resourceful to show up here. I can't say he's responsible for Sergeant Denny's plight. He may have stumbled upon his dog tags and saw an opportunity to flee. I'm told we have a photo on the way."

"My husband's dead," Annalise said, "and the Army let his killer escape."

"Not necessarily, ma'am."

"Then prove it."

"I'll do my best and not rest until I've accounted for him."

"It's easy to claim the Army's competence and concern. If you can't stop one German from escaping three American vessels and entering the country illegally, how can you find one missing man in all of Europe?"

"I understand your frustration, Mrs. Denny."

"Frustration?"

"I have twelve visits in this region today, delivering to eleven other families news of their kin missing in action. It's not a duty I enjoy in the least or take for granted."

The captain took to his feet. He handed Lucian a card. "If you have any questions, or stumble upon any information, please call. Do you have a number I can reach you?"

Lucian scratched his number on a separate card.

"Again, I'm sorry, Mrs. Denny. I'll not rest until I can provide you with answers."

Annalise wiped tears from her cheeks. "You mean his corpse, don't you?"

The captain and his counterpart withdrew.

Lucian struck a match against the fireplace. "What can I do for you, my dear?"

She shook her head. With the soldiers gone, she let her emotions release. Lucian took hold of her hand. "This doesn't mean he's dead. It takes months for the Army to inform civilians of soldiers taken prisoner. You must keep the faith."

Lucian eased Annalise from her rocker and collected her into his arms. A sliver of late-morning sun splashing through pines scattered in the front yard forced his eyes closed. He struggled to rationalize his own words and figured it unlikely O'Dell would lose his dog tags. He suspected Annalise knew better, as he proved an assiduous caretaker of his possessions.

Annalise trembled. "He's dead. I know it, I can feel it."

"You don't know for sure. We mustn't rush to judgment."

"I loved him so." She buried the crown of her head into his sternum. "I know he's gone. He would not lose his dog tags. The soldier killed him and took them."

"I'd believe he's a prisoner of war long before I'd believe he's dead."

Annalise pushed from him. Her eyes appeared dull and bloodshot. "I let him go without telling him. I hurt him so much."

"Do not beat yourself up. You made the right decision. Can you imagine the mental burden and distraction? He would've refused to go. And, believe me, thousands of men learned of their first child overseas. I know this may sting, but he needed to go. He would've crucified himself for the rest of his life had he sat on the sidelines."

He tightened his arms around her as her sobs intensified. He kissed her forehead. The two swayed to the rhythm of her shaking.

Lucian's eyes wandered from the view outdoors to the oil painting hanging on the far wall. He chewed on their first meeting, an eerily similar encounter with Ep. O'Dell, too, came to town in search of a fresh start.

Concern for O'Dell's welfare seeped to the forefront of Lucian's reverie. For the first time, he considered his new assistant more than a lost soul seeking a new beginning.

Chapter 65

The second Sunday of each month proved the most sedate of all Sundays. Save a dire medical emergency, Lucian reserved this time for a small animal clinic on a first-come, first-served basis.

He provided his time free of charge, though few families paid nothing. Most donated a small pittance or offered vegetable, beef, pork, or chicken products as appreciation. Margie kept the children occupied with baked treats and homemade lemon ices and ice cream.

"Our warmest day yet, despite the rain," Margie said, looking out the kitchen window to a thermometer nailed to a tree trunk. "It's already fifty-eight."

She turned when her husband did not respond. Lucian sat puffing his pipe, staring into his coffee.

"You've had something on your mind for days. Please tell me what it is."

He released a cloud of smoke and watched it slither through an open window. Margie joined him at the table. She delivered a toasted egg sandwich with bacon and tomato.

"I have a feeling I cannot shake. It keeps me up at night."

"The captain told you they'd contact Anna as soon as information became available."

"It's not that. It's Ep."

"Ep? What does he have to do with anything?"

"Nothing, but I have this feeling he didn't wander here by accident."

"I don't understand."

"I don't either." Lucian took a bite of sandwich. A streak of yolk dripped down his chin. "Ep and O'Dell seem like carbon copies. Their mannerisms, work ethic, respect for others, love of animals and people."

"I've noticed, too," Margie said. "I feel it more of a comfort than distraction."

"It's as if O'Dell went away and came back in another's skin, with a slightly different accent."

"What does it mean?"

Lucian returned the sandwich to his plate. "This sounds awful, I know, but it feels like Ep showed up to replace O'Dell. I don't believe it's a coincidence, but something of purpose. I don't know why, but my gut keeps telling me O'Dell died a tragic death."

Margie took a quick sip of coffee as she mulled over his words.

"I don't want to feel this way. It makes me sick to my stomach."

"You told Anna we must not rush to judgment."

"I know, but I'm losing confidence by the day."

"You cannot let on you've lost hope, not until we know for sure."

"I don't think what I think matters. She's convinced he's dead."

Margie moved next to Lucian and delivered a kiss on his cheek. "We need to give it more time. We need patience. Life happens in God's good time, not ours."

A knock on the back porch beat by a second Jakob entering the kitchen. Sheriff Perry plodded in from the mudroom. Margie flipped on the radio and started another round of coffee and egg sandwiches.

"Morning, gents," Lucian said.

"Good morning," Jakob said, taking his seat.

William stashed his rubber cape on a corner coat tree and kissed Margie's cheek as he passed into the kitchen. "Morning, sweetheart," he said. William pulled a chair from the middle of the table and his pipe from an inside coat pocket. He shook Lucian's hand.

"How come you always kiss my wife and shake my hand?"

"Would you rather it be the other way around?"

"You need to find your own wife."

"Why? Margie does for me what I'd ask of any woman, without the expense."

Lucian inserted his pipe into his mouth and shrugged. Jakob chuckled at the typical banter between them.

"Anything pressing today?" Jakob asked.

"I expect a slow surgery with the rain. We'll need to run out to Bickford's and perform a post-mortem on those sheep he lost. He's concerned of epidemic. I told him, if so, he'd have lost more, but, what the heck do I know, I've only been a vet forty years."

Margie delivered two more sandwiches and a stack of potato pancakes.

"Have you seen Anna?" Lucian asked.

"Yes."

"What do you think?"

William took a bite. "She's convinced he's gone, told me she's certain he's dead. I told her she needs to let the Army do its job, but she's adamant."

"I don't know what else to say to her," Lucian said.

"I know less about women than any man alive but have a ton of experience with women's intuition. They know when I've arrested their husbands before I tell them. I'd trust Annalise's internal sense before my best guess. It's a shame. I can't imagine how she'll go on without him."

"You think he's dead, don't you?" Margie said.

"I don't know," William said. "I do know he wouldn't have lost them dog tags without a fight. I think it'd be a billion to one that the same Nazi who found his tags made his way here. A billion to one."

Lucian tapped his pipe against his palm. "I can't imagine O'Dell gone. I considered him invincible."

"Ain't none of us invincible to what's going on," William countered.

Margie sniffled and brought the edge of her apron to her eyes.

A series of chimes from the radio interrupted a local farm update.

***

"Ladies and gentlemen, the Voice of America interrupts this broadcast to bring you a special news report from the National Broadcasting Company. We join the President of the United States of America, Harry S. Truman, live from the radio room in the White House in Washington, D.C."

The radio snapped and cracked. The men moved to the edge of their seats.

"This is a solemn but a glorious hour," Truman began. "I only wish that Franklin D. Roosevelt had lived to witness this day. General Eisenhower informs me that the forces of Germany have surrendered to the United Nations. The flags of freedom fly over all Europe."

"For this victory," Truman continued, "we join in offering our thanks to the Providence, which has guided and sustained us through the dark days of adversity. Our rejoicing is sobered and subdued by a supreme consciousness of the terrible price we have paid to rid the world of Hitler and his evil band."

Jakob kept his emotions controlled, despite finding it excruciating bearing witness, via radio broadcast, to the finality of a country he so loved.

"Let us not forget, my fellow Americans, the sorrow and the heartache which today abide in the homes of so many of our neighbors — neighbors whose most priceless possession has been rendered as a sacrifice to redeem our liberty.

"We can repay the debt which we owe to our God, to our dead, and to our children only by work—by ceaseless devotion to the responsibilities which lie ahead of us. If I could give you a single watchword for the coming months, that word is—work, work, and more work."

"I'll have my celebration when them sons-of-bit...." William paused, knowing Margie did not allow cursing in her home. "Sons-of-guns Japs surrender."

"I expect their end soon," Lucian said. "Truman won't mess around now."

Margie's voiced choked. "So many lost, so many lives and families shattered. We must have faith O'Dell survived."

Jakob stood. "If you do not mind, Lucian, I think I will check on Mrs. Annalise."

"By all means."

"Now, therefore, I, Harry S. Truman, President of the United States of America, do hereby appoint Sunday, May 13, 1945, to be a day of prayer. I call upon the people of the United States, whatever their faith...."

Jakob exited. He could stand no more.

***

A low, distant rumble sent Annalise's livestock scurrying, despite conditions not suitable for thunder bursts. Bella recognized the sound of Jakob's truck and galloped to meet him at the pasture gate. Jakob turned the corner of the house and paused upon seeing Annalise sitting on a hay bale, with head in hands. A light drizzle fell from clouds more ominous than what dumped heavier rain earlier.

To this point, he'd held steadfast in his respect for their professional relationship but could no longer maintain the facade. She'd stirred his heart the moment they met, and he'd finally admitted days ago his feelings swelled beyond that of employee-employer. She'd never have to love him, but he desired her company the rest of his days.

He entered the pasture and drew upon her with Bella pushing from behind. Annalise released her head from her hands and turned.

Jakob placed a hand on her shoulder and rubbed. She reacted with equal uncertainty. Her hand shook as she placed it on his and squeezed. Mere seconds passed before she pushed off the bale and turned to face him. Tears, mixed with drizzle, spilled down her cheeks. Jakob kept hold of her hand and eased her into his arms.

Chapter 66

"Ep puzzles me," William said, polishing off the last potato cake.

"You too, huh?" Lucian replied.

"What, in particular, caught your attention?"

"Dead-on similarities in personality to O'Dell. I told Margie earlier this morning, it's as if O'Dell left and returned in another's body."

"I agree, though I've not spent near the time with him as you. I'm curious about the way he talks."

"I see nothing odd with his speech," Lucian said.

Margie joined them at the table. "I think he's a polite young man. He's respectful in the same ways as O'Dell."

"Well, keep in mind, I'm no expert on the spoken word, so says my eighth-grade education, but I find his speech rather formal, beyond what I'd expect from a New Yorker."

Lucian rubbed his chin. "Come to think of it, he doesn't have a New York accent at all."

"Not the first. I doubt he grew up there. But that's not what caught my attention."

"Why do you consider his not growing up in New York, strange?" Margie asked.

"It's not the city or lack of an accent, it's how he doesn't shorten his words—not one. I don't know the proper name for it, but where we say 'it's,' he says it is. Where we say 'I'm,' he says I am. It reminds me of the English fella who lived here. I'm not suggesting he's of bad character, just noticed it when we met. Most people shorten words in conversation."

I hadn't noticed before," Lucian said, "but now that you mention it."

"He's a genuine, educated, compassionate sort, content with whom he is," Margie said, interrupted by the ring of the kitchen phone. She pushed from the table to answer. "Hello? Yes, Jessie, he's here, hold please... Bill, it's for you."

William pushed from the table with a grunt. "Yeah, Jess. No fooling? Is that right? Okay, on my way."

Williams planted the phone on the cradle. "Gotta go, friends."

"Trouble?" Lucian asked.

"Yeah, accident at the Tioga train station."

Margie helped William with his cape.

"Have a good day, Loosh."

"You, too. Be careful out there."

William kissed Margie's cheek and exited.

The radio spewed multiple reactions to the news of the day. Margie returned to the table to finish her coffee. Lucian looked out the window into a sea of rolling gray skies enveloped in mist.

"I never thought this day would come," Margie said.

Lucian didn't budge. Her comment vaporized into the atmosphere like pipe smoke.

"Lucian?" she said, placing a hand on his forearm.

He turned at the sensation of her touch. Forty-five years of marriage laid waste to all possibilities he could hide his burdens, as the telltale signs proved as consistent as a sunrise. It started with a nervous chewing of his bottom lip. His face flushed, the tips of his ears turned crimson, and eyes darted about as if tracking a pesky fly.

"Tell me, dear," she said.

Lucian puzzled a moment. "The captain said the German spoke fluent English."

Margie set her coffee cup on the table. "You mean to sit there and tell me you think —"

"I'm not thinking anything," he interrupted, "or suggesting a thing."

"Not Ep," she said. "Why, that's the most ridiculous thing I've ever heard. He's a sweet young man and a Godsend to you. He's no Nazi."

"I'm not implying anything, yet, but I sure as fire want to know if he's from New York like he claims. If so, case closed. You can bet I'll have Billum investigate. He'll know who to call."

**

Holding Annalise's hand exceeded all expectations Jakob had built up in his mind. Pulling her into his arms proved a delicate sensation, despite her rough and tumble profession.

For a moment, he felt like a benevolent emissary of no particular nationality, free of guilt by association, and stripped clean of the burdens of knowledge. He felt able to express desires without reserve.

Annalise remained tucked in his arms until the last tear drained. She released, despite Jakob's hesitation to let go. He wished it to last a lifetime.

She stepped away. Jakob lost himself in her eyes.

"I'm sorry," she said, unable to find a proper position for her hands. "It's a bad day and I'm not handling it well. I'm sorry to dump my emotions on you."

Her words floated by uncollected. Jakob's imagination played out a fantastic scenario in which he would spill the truth, she'd believe him and accept him for his real self.

She noticed him drifting. "Ep?"

Jakob twitched. "Forgive me."

"I said, my reaction was a mistake."

Jakob worked through the disappointment of her words. He'd forever regard the encounter as the opposite. "I understand. I only stopped to check on you. I figured it a difficult day for you."

She wiped her eyes. "It's sweet of you, and I appreciate it, but I need to get back to work. Their war is over, mine has only begun." She brushed past him toward the barn.

"Annalise?"

She paused and turned.

"I need to tell you something."

She moved in close. Jakob stammered, attempting to continue. The voice inside his head warned she'd never forgive him, never believe his account, blame him for O'Dell's death. His heart pined to fulfill the promise made to his friend. His soul loved a woman he had no business loving. He feared delivering the gruesome details of O'Dell's final moments would push her off the edge of a cerebral cliff.

"Yes?"

"You can trust me," he said.

"Yes, I know. You'd not be here if I felt any different." Annalise turned. Bella followed.

"I do not wish for you to go through this alone."

Annalise stopped. Drizzle exchanged for a soupy mist. "I've experienced alone before. I have my husband's son and this farm to think of."

"I understand." Jakob approached and ran his hand across Bella's rump to her withers, up under her mane to her ears. Annalise stood ahead, holding tight to Bella's halter, rubbing her nose. "I can help you fulfill the dreams you and your husband had for this farm. I can help ensure it provides for you and your son for years to come."

"Why? Why would you want to spend the rest of your days here?"

Jakob placed a final pat against Bella's neck and withdrew. Lucian would expect him to help open the surgery.

As he stepped across the creek, Annalise called out, "I didn't mean it the way it sounded. I... I didn't mean to...."

Jakob turned. "I know alone. I also know I cannot think of any place I would rather be, any other person I would rather be with, or any other worry or trouble I would rather have."

***

"What in the hell happened here?" William asked.

"I don't know, Sheriff," the engineer said, pointing to a row of cars on the track to the left. "He jumped from a boxcar, sat on his knees, and waited. He had plenty of time to move. I pulled the brake, but way too late."

What remained of the man's body lay in mangled parts and pieces scattered about, his battered head unrecognizable, resting in a ditch between the north and southbound tracks. Passengers gathered on a veranda, unable to turn from the carnage, each relaying in whispers what they witnessed.

"Suicide by train. Any idea of his identity?"

"No, sir," the engineer replied.

"It's hard to tell now," the conductor said.

The lower half of the man's body, though gouged and fractured, lay intact. William searched the pants pockets for identification, discovering a few coins and a blood-soaked handkerchief.

A siren wound down as an ambulance pulled up to the station. Two men hustled across the tracks with a stretcher.

"Won't need a stretcher, boys," William said. "Trash bags and a rake will suffice."

Railroad personnel helped collect the remains. William chose two witnesses to collect their statements.

"Take the body to the morgue in Wellsboro," William instructed. "Tell 'em I said to put these remains on ice. I need time to figure this out."

Chapter 67

Jakob enjoyed extended jaunts on Liesel on days when the schedule proved light. Lucian fiddled about the property and surgery, often finding time for a nap on a hammock strung between two cherry trees near a corner where his herd of cattle congregated.

Jakob requested a special pardon this day, as he and Liesel intended to blaze a new trail to Annalise's property.

Margie packed his saddlebag with ham sandwiches and apples, and filled two canteens: one with water, one with lemonade.

Following ancient trails, Jakob found his way to the farm in less than two hours. The stream running through the middle of Annalise's pasture branched from a stream formed two miles north of Lucian's property. They followed the vein northwest, passing a gristmill and decrepit trestle bridge beset with ivy creeping up and over its wooden spans. A brick grain elevator near a fence line separated Annalise's property from a neighbor. From there, a piece of cake.

Jakob guided Liesel out of the creek bed to a dirt road. At spring's persuasion, the surface laid well hidden from the sun under a canopy of branches stretching from ditch to ditch. The *thud* of Liesel's hoofs stirred birds into flight and squirrels scrambling for higher branches.

They slowed to a lazy trot upon nearing the home. Jakob spotted Annalise's babysitter, Mrs. Perriwinkle, rocking the boy on the porch. Jakob waved. She returned a smile. A widow, who made it known she was better off for it, thought Jakob a handsome man, telling him so each time they met.

Jakob steadied Liesel short of the porch. "Good afternoon, Mrs. Perriwinkle."

"Hello, handsome," she said, working Jakob over from hat to stirrup.

"You enjoying the day?" Jakob asked.

"Soaking in some peace and quiet."

"Is Annalise running errands?"

"No, saddled up and went off for a ride. Poking about today, are we?"

"No, ma'am. Need to clean stalls and fix a few fence posts."

"It's Sunday, you know."

"Yes, ma'am. I do not plan on staying long."

She blew a kiss and readjusted the boy in her arms.

Jakob touched the brim of his hat. He guided Liesel around through the pasture gate and across the stream to the round pen.

He entered the barn, expecting to muck stalls first. He caught Annalise by surprise as she completed the final adjustments to her saddle.

"My goodness, you scared me," she said, grabbing at her chest.

"Mrs. Perriwinkle said you were off on a ride. I wanted to muck the stalls and fix those fence posts."

"I didn't hear your truck."

"I did not drive," he said, hitching a thumb over his shoulder. "Liesel and I made our own trail today."

"You rode all this way?"

"In less than two hours."

"You realize the return trip will take as long?"

Jakob smiled. "Maybe not. We know our way, now."

"It's also Sunday."

"I wanted a reason to take a ride."

"I'd do the same if this animal would take in a breath." Annalise held onto the girth strap, waiting. Her horse drew in. She pulled tight and slipped the strap to the next hole in line. She led her Bonny from the barn.

Jakob located his pitchfork and a wheelbarrow. He dug the fork into the soiled hay of the first stall.

Annalise poked her head through a side window. "Would you care to join me?"

Jakob felt his jaw unhitch. She hadn't sought his company at any point.

"I figured you would enjoy *alone* today," he replied.

"Not today. Anyway, Bella could use a good stretch of the legs."

Jakob tossed a saddle on Bella's back. He figured no other man had ridden her alongside Annalise.

He slipped his boot into the stirrup and pulled at the saddle horn. Bella accepted him without fuss and responded without hesitation. Annalise led them through a gate at the farthest point of the property, before bearing northwest along another tributary.

Dense pines and other flora lined the banks. Birds raced from tree to tree, chirping, gathering, watching. Water rushed along a bed strewn with rocks of all sizes and shades of gray, serving as a mental massage. Small, turf-covered islands scattered about the stream rearranged the flow of water to an inconsistent perfection. A light breeze delivered a mix of unique scents reminiscent of Jakob's beloved Rohr Valley.

The two crossed at a low spot in the creek where a large pine had toppled, and a bar of sand stretched to a couple feet below the waterline. The trail continued up a steep incline, weaving in and around massive boulders and downed rotting timber, glistening silver from pockets of sun splash. Bella's slip on a rock provided a moment of intrigue but recovered smartly.

The trail led to a summit before opening to an expanse ascending at a slight grade. A herd of whitetail deer perked, then pushed off into an adjacent forest as Bonny eclipsed the lip.

Bella took advantage of the wide-open vista to sidle up next to her friend. The horses slowed their pace, taking in the sun melting against their withers. Grasses not yet ripened for bailing waved in the breeze, teasing their appetites. Annalise crooked her leg in her saddle, allowing Bonny to choose their course. A group of clouds passed on the horizon.

Jakob held Bella short to cloak watching Annalise as her body swayed to Bonny's tempered gait. Captured by the pendulum motion of her ponytail brushing across the middle of her back, his mind drifted to the moment he felt her body press against his. If only he could kiss her.

"Tell me about your family," Annalise requested.

Bella's ears perked as Jakob turned. They reached a plateau exposing a group of trees protecting a large pond.

"My father died in the war and my mother and sister in a tragic accident."

"No aunts, uncles, or cousins?"

"None familiar to me. Mother had two sisters, but they died young. Father had no family."

"Were you close?"

"With my mother and sister. Father, not so much."

"I enjoyed a closer bond with my mother, though shared a fabulous relationship with my father. Not a day goes by I don't think of them. They died in an automobile accident before my eighth birthday."

Annalise let go a deep sigh, absorbing the surrounding beauty. Bonny led Bella to a shallow spot along the pond's bank. They dipped their noses in the cool water. Both riders stepped off.

Jakob dug through the contents of his saddlebag. "Care for a sandwich?"

Annalise shook her head.

"How about a lemonade?"

She smiled and accepted.

Jakob settled on a large, downed trunk running parallel to the water. Annalise joined him, albeit from a distance. He fed an apple to each horse.

They sat with not a word spoken. Miniscule insects skipped across the water, dodging bubbles of surfacing fish. Frogs hopped along the bank, sending slight ripples outward. Birds flittered above, chastising the strangers with angry chirps. A hawk suspended high above, gliding against the breeze.

Jakob took a bite of sandwich built with thick-cut slices of sugar-cured ham. Annalise sipped her canteen of lemonade.

Upon securing the cap, she turned, and as casual as the breeze brushing against them, asked, "Ep, are you in love with me?"

Jakob thrust forward. The sandwich slipped from his fingers to the ants and insects below. He hadn't prepared for such brazenness.

"I ask, because I want you to know, I'll never love another man, not the way I loved O'Dell."

Jakob sat still, unable to work through the shock.

"You're a charming man. I trust you and find your company most pleasant. You make me feel safe. I cannot say the same for any other man I've met, other than my husband. Another time and place, perhaps, things might be different."

Jakob wiped again at his chin.

"I believe love can strike twice in a lifetime. I'm sure it happens all the time. But I believe the love O'Dell and I shared does not happen twice in a lifetime. An all-consuming love, whole and complete to the core. Most of me has died, never to return. No man should have to accept so little in a companion."

Jakob looked away. The breeze stiffened, as if winter, not summer, neared.

"I believe in my heart you didn't expect to have such feelings. Have I misjudged you or the situation?"

Jakob sighed and shook his head.

"You carry a tremendous burden," Annalise said. "I didn't want to cause additional pain. My husband's dead. He's gone. Inside, I feel as if his death happened long ago. I must make sure my son grows up to be the man my husband expected."

Several minutes passed with the breeze and push of water against the bank accounting for all conversation.

Jakob picked through their previous interactions, recounting those moments he'd overplayed his hand. Other than offering comfort the day Germany surrendered, he didn't believe he'd crossed the first line. William's assessment of her intuition convinced Jakob that whatever cells accelerated the trait, she'd received an overdose at birth.

You wanted the right moment to tell her, Jakob whispered inside his head. He gritted his teeth, knowing he'd crammed the evidence in an envelope between the mattresses of his bed.

"I apologize for my directness," Annalise said, "and, if you feel you can no longer stay on at the farm, I'll understand. I don't wish for you to leave, not by a long shot. I enjoy your company, but would understand, nonetheless."

A frog struggled to climb onto a branch poking from the depths, catching Jakob's attention.

"We should head back," she said.

Reeling from the gut-punch, Jakob steadied Bella a few horse lengths behind, contemplating how and when he'd surrender the truth.

Upon their return, he rushed to re-saddle Liesel. Annalise suggested he stay in the bunkroom for the night, knowing the sun would set well before he made it back home. He declined.

He led Liesel from the round pen to across the brook. Annalise sat on the back porch in a rocker, holding her son to her chest.

"Ep," she said, "are you okay?"

"I am."

"Please forgive me."

"You need not apologize. I never intended to add to your burdens."

"I am fond of you and am flattered beyond words. I don't want to hurt you. I think you've experienced enough hurt. Why does this farm mean so much? You hardly know me."

"With some things, you know, it does not take weeks, months or years. You feel it and are as sure of it as anything you have encountered before."

Annalise lifted from the rocker, moving to the edge of the porch. "And you? What's important to you?"

"I do not think you will care for my answer."

"Please, tell me."

Jakob stepped into his stirrup and pulled himself onto Liesel's back. He questioned his ability to match her boldness. The sun displayed its first hint of blood-orange as it started its lazy descent. Shadows stretched across the ground twice as high as the trees projecting them.

Liesel spun, expecting the *click-click* of her master's lips. "I desire peace and a place I can put this war behind me. I have nothing left and want out of life only what will make me whole again. Serving others provides me peace. My greatest childhood influence believed in placing yourself second. I found my way to this community for a reason. I found my way here to find you."

Annalise rearranged her son in her arms as a swell of emotion pushed into her throat.

"I found something here in you and this farm, the kind of something most men spend their entire lives chasing and failing to acquire. I would never expect you to love me as you did your husband, or at all, nor would I expect you to forget him. You should celebrate his life for all time. I mean to replace no one. I mean only to serve and provide."

Jakob eased his heels into Liesel's flanks. She set off in a rush, hooves thumping against the earth like mallets on a kettledrum.

***

Annalise held steady against a porch timber, watching as Jakob and Liesel melded into shadows introducing the arrival of dusk. In a moment of pure bliss, she rubbed the back of her neck to suppress that familiar tingle of hair follicles forced into a tizzy. She'd experienced the sensation only once before and swore it could never happen again.

"I can't love you, Ep," she whispered, pushing from off the post, "but how I wish I could."

Chapter 68

Sheriff Perry covered his phone in response to a knock against the frosted glass of his office door.

"Sorry to interrupt, Bill," a part-time deputy said, poking in. "A couple government men out here want to speak with you."

"Tell 'em to wait. I'm on hold with New York."

William brought the handset to his ear. He leaned back in his chair and dropped his feet on the corner of a small, dusty wooden desk bought at his own expense when county officials said it was an unnecessary burden upon taxpayers.

"Yes, William Perry, here." He returned his feet to the floor. "I see. Okay. And what years did you search? Got it. Okay, I appreciate your efforts. Thank you."

William recorded the information on a scratchpad and returned the phone to its cradle. He tapped the end of his pencil on the pad, debating whether it worth the effort to check additional sources. He pressed an intercom button. "Send them in."

The deputy escorted the visitors toward two chairs aligned to the far side of his boss's desk. The nearest agent moved in cadence with the *tick-tock* of a simple clock mounted on the wall behind the desk.

William conducted an immediate evaluation. They wore near identical outfits — fedora, black wool suit, white shirt, conservative tie.

The first man, a gangly looking sort of medium build, approached with an exaggerated, overconfident stride. His skin was a muted olive-green, his eyes beady and set deep, a knife scar traced along his left cheek, despite his attempt to disguise it with makeup.

The second agent shuffled along rather than stepped. He seemed nervous and out of place, and, too, of average height, but thinner, with splotchy brown spots dotted about his face and neck.

William bore the scars of naivety plenty at the start of his career, not so much these days. Men made simple mistakes when attempting deception. He'd learned all the signs, tricks, and triggers. Before the agents settled in their seats, he pegged them for rats. They'd have to prove him wrong. He jiggled his coffee cup toward his deputy. "Coffee, boys?"

"Thank you, no," the first agent responded.

"One, Jed," William said.

"I'm Captain McInnis, Army Intelligence," the man said, then pointed to his partner. "Staff Sergeant Thomas." He flashed a badge and returned the leather piece to an inside coat pocket.

William outstretched an arm and snapped his fingers. "May I see your credentials? Eyes aren't as good as they used to be."

The agent's effort to cloak surprise proved as pathetic an attempt as William had seen. His hesitation, though less than the flutter of a hummingbird's wings, convinced William of his intent to deceive. *Gotcha.*

The agent laid the wallet on his desk. William flipped through it. Name and picture matched. "What can I do for you, McInnis?" he said, tossing the wallet back.

The agent removed his coat and placed it on his lap. The other kept his buttoned. One sleeve hung limp.

The deputy returned with a cup. He remained behind his boss's chair.

"I would appreciate a moment to discuss a confidential matter," McInnis said.

"Go ahead on, Jed."

The deputy exited. McInnis moved to the edge of his chair. "In case you've not seen the news, we suffered a serious breach of our national security. A German soldier posing as an American GI entered the United States illegally at New York Harbor."

"We? Who's we?"

"We, us, the military," McInnis said.

"Okay, what does that have to do with Tioga County?"

"He used the alias O'Dell Denny. We tracked the name to this community. Do you know Sergeant O'Dell Denny?"

"I do."

"Are you aware of Sergeant Denny's missing-in-action status?"

"Are you asking or stating?"

McInnis's eyes narrowed. He extended an arm toward his partner. Thomas delivered a business-sized envelope from an inside coat pocket.

McInnis extracted a black-and-white photo and flipped it onto the desk. "Our man. He's also used the alias John Jones."

William's experience during tense situations among despicable characters prepared him for the shock. He'd owe Lucian an apology as he underestimated the chances, by a wide margin, of Ep Tucker having anything to do with O'Dell's demise. He spent a quick moment reviewing the headshot of the same Ep Tucker dressed in full German military gear. William kept his poker face intact. "Not seen this man in these parts."

He shifted the photo to the center of the desk.

"We'd appreciate it if you'd keep the picture handy and let us know if you come into contact with him. He's considered armed and dangerous. Here's my number." The man pushed a white card forward.

"We've contacted the state police and other county authorities. It's important we apprehend him. We want to avoid publicity on this one. I'd prefer you speak to me before proceeding with any other agency."

"I'll do my best. If I see him, I'll let you know."

McInnis stood and replaced his coat. "We'll check in again."

"You do that. Good day, gentlemen."

***

Lucian had dispatched Jakob at first light to a small hobby farm past Stony Fork. Settled on his knees in a crusty old barn, he held a ewe in his lap, stroking her head. The poor beast wandered too close to the south end of a mule and suffered a devastating blow. Seeing no options for recovery, Jakob put the poor beast out of her misery.

He sat with the animal well beyond her owner's interest, stroking her head. Whether the final kick of the ewe's legs, or the sum of recent losses, Jakob broke. He no longer wanted to carry the weight of his burden. Regardless of the consequences, he needed to clear his soul. Whether Annalise accepted his version of events, the time had come.

Interaction with her had turned unbearable, not due to actions on her part—though she kept dialogue to a minimum—but for his allowing her to wallow in anguish and uncertainty this long.

He had trouble sleeping, finding a couple hours a night, if lucky. His appetite diminished to less than what would keep a sparrow alive. Headaches proved a mainstay, as did an occasional lightning strike on the left side of his chest.

He'd forgo his next call on the docket and return to the farm to retrieve the evidence.

Upon arrival at the McKenna ranch, he parked near the surgery. Liesel held steady at the gate, having recognized the sound of his engine long prior. Jakob kissed her nose. She tickled his neck with her whiskers.

He entered the mudroom and removed boots caked in blood and muck. He walked down the short hallway, pausing at the kitchen, where Margie sat at the far end of the family's table, her hands in her lap and face drained of its usual pleasant peach tint. She looked as if she'd seen a ghost.

Jakob approached with a tentative gait. "Mrs. Margie?" he called out, cocking his head. "Are you okay?"

Margie's body trembled. Jakob pulled a chair and sat down. She deposited on top of the table O'Dell's dog tag, a wedding ring, and two letters — one stained with blood. "Who are you? What have you done to our O'Dell?"

Jakob dropped his elbows on the table and brought his hands against his face. When he released, he settled against the seatback, facing a large caliber pistol pointed at his chest.

Chapter 69

Upon the agents' exit, with privacy restored, William placed a call to the state police. As expected, they knew nothing of the AI agents. He offered a description of the two and detailed the conversation between them.

He left his deputies with clear instructions, as he would not return until nightfall, if at all. William pulled away from the courthouse, intent on finding Lucian, steering with one hand, and sipping a cup of coffee in the other.

With livestock recovering from the effects of the long Pennsylvania winter, farmers summoned Lucian to all corners of the county to deal with everything from pneumonia, fits of coughing, limb injury, and pathology disorders.

Following a couple stops and several phone calls, William located Lucian settled on a knee in Jerol Johnson's barn, tending to an ailing calf. He stepped beyond the threshold of a large sliding barn door as Lucian instructed Mr. Johnson to hold the calf steady.

Lucian worked his hand down the calf's leg. A quick diagnosis determined a clean fracture of the radius with no displacement.

"She'll heal well if we plaster cast her," Lucian said. Mr. Johnson agreed. Lucian turned to collect the supplies necessary.

"Billum, what are you doing out all this way?"

"Sorry to have caught you at such a time. We need to talk."

"New York?"

"Among other things."

"I need to cast this young lady first."

"I'll wait."

With casting completed, Mr. Johnson led the calf from the barn. Lucian turned as he rinsed away encrusted material attached to his fingers and forearms. "So?"

"It's not good," William said. "There's no record of an Ep Tucker born at any of the hospitals local to Astoria. My contact checked plus or minus five years to his stated age... nothing. He also couldn't locate a birth certificate."

"I have to admit, I'm not surprised."

"It doesn't get any better." William pulled the photo from his shirt pocket.

"Two men dropped this off at my office this morning. They claimed to be representatives of Army Intelligence, but they aren't. I caught 'em dead to rights. I've dealt with representatives from AI since the war started, and ain't none of them looked like those two baboons. Don't know what their game is, but it's fishy."

"You couldn't hold 'em?"

"On what charges?"

"I don't know. You've been pretty creative in the past."

"I'm willing to let them play out their little game a bit longer. They'll slip up. Besides, they corroborated what those two real AI men told you. They said it's the fella who used O'Dell's name to gain access into the country."

Lucian brought the photo closer. "It's him, all right."

William observed with interest Lucian's examination of the picture. His curiosity piqued as his expression softened. "What?"

"Forty years I've tended to beasts unable to communicate how they came to injure themselves, yet I know what troubles them. For me, it's similar to knowing the difference between color and odor. I understand their pain and can pinpoint their afflictions through observation. How they move, stand, lie down, or respond to touch. Over time, I've honed those same skills with my own kind. A man has to say little or nothing at all for me to square right versus wrong, steady versus uneven. And I'll tell you, this ain't adding up in my head. I don't see this man killing O'Dell and stealing his identity. He's the most selfless individual I've met, other than O'Dell. Does he remind you of a killer?"

William worked through his most recent interactions with their guest. "Other than his not wanting to discuss his past, I'd say he's earned my optimism over pessimism. Anna formed my opinion for me. She's fond of him, and I ain't met any woman as particular. Any display of distrust or folderol on his part, she'd have escorted his ass off the property with a scattergun aimed at his back. Now, she ain't said anything, but I've seen enough for myself when they're together. She trusts and cares for him, more than somewhat, I think."

"Margie senses the same. I trust her instincts more than mine. She'll struggle with this. So, what do we do?"

"We show him this picture. I suspect he'll do the rest for us."

William removed his cap to wipe sweat from his brow. "I find it amazing. He speaks better English than all of us."

"The AI officers mentioned documented cases of American-born Germans forced into action who surrendered without firing a shot, all desperate to flee the Nazis and return to the States."

"I guess it's possible he was just looking for a way out."

"I think our boy landed between a rock and a hard place. I'll tell you, though, he's gotta prove from here to hell and back he didn't kill O'Dell."

"I agree. You know his whereabouts?"

"I sent him out to the Hickert farm this morning."

"Think he's still there?"

"No. Probably on his way to Jimmy Wynn's by now."

"Quite a drive from here."

"Yes, but I say the sooner we sort this out, the better."

"I'm right behind you."

***

By the time Shimmel rejoined his men, the German push had disintegrated, as elements of Patton's Third Army pushed through Bastogne from the southwest. By February, the Allies had cut the head off the insurgency, pushing Hitler's last main fighting force well within German borders.

Before month's end, the Red Army crossed the Oder River to a position fifty miles from Berlin. Having accumulated the necessary points, and satisfied Germany's hold on Europe over, Shimmel, a career man, exchanged his combat status for an instructorship in Washington, D.C.

"They sure as hell didn't give you much time," Polak said. He passed a cigarette to Sperro.

"The Army can move fast when it wants to," Sperro said.

Hansel took a swig from a bottle of French wine retrieved in the ashes of a blown-out café. The men huddled under the eve of a makeshift supply hut amid the chaos of soldiers coming and going, yelling and directing. A misty drizzle added to the gloom of the moment. A jeep purred mere feet away, ready to whisk Shimmel to HQ.

The bottle and cigarette passed around the small circle a half dozen times.

"How do you think the kid's doing?" Hansel asked.

"Spring's a tough little shit," Polak said. "I hope they sent his ass home."

"I'm sure they grew tired of his bitching to return to the fight," Shimmel said.

Hansel pulled in a final draw of the cigarette.

Shimmel finished the last drop of wine at the others' insistence. He looked them over. "I'm sure we all agree what happened here stays here, right?"

"No one would believe it anyway," Polak said.

"I don't believe it myself," Hansel added.

"It's Jakob's lone chance at a decent life," Shimmel reminded them.

"You think he made it?" Sperro asked.

Shimmel shrugged. "We put him in the best position possible for a fighting chance. If he found his way off the ship in New York, I'd bet anything he made it. He's a smart, smart man."

The drizzle changed to rain. Explosions of heavy droplets against the canvas brought a pause to their dialogue. Shimmel extended a hand to each man. He would have no hugs.

"I'll see you boys on the other side. In a few weeks, this shit'll end. No heroes, right? Stay sharp." He tossed his duffle bag into the back of the waiting jeep.

"So, what's next?" Sperro asked. The men moved from under cover and surrounded his position.

"Once settled in D.C., I'll see if our boy found his way to the Pennsylvania countryside." He paused a moment to reconcile the oddity of his feelings for Jakob. "I can't explain it, but I need to know he made it, need to know he's okay."

"Give him our regards," Hansel said.

Shimmel smiled and saluted. His men reciprocated as their brother and safety net disappeared down a mud-rutted road, leaving a void greater than any imagined.

Chapter 70

Jakob did not figure Margie the type to allow a gun in her home, let alone know how to operate one.

"Margie, there is no need for a weapon. I am not running away as much as I am running to something."

"You murdered him. You killed our O'Dell to escape Germany."

"No, ma'am, I did not."

"I don't believe you."

"No one will believe my story."

"Who are you?"

"Jakob von Rüdel."

"You're a Nazi. The Nazi who killed O'Dell and stole his things."

"No, ma'am. I am an American-born citizen from Astoria, New York, born January 2, 1921. My father taught English literature at Columbia University, my mother worked as a dressmaker. We returned to Germany in 1925 after my father accepted an instructorship in Berlin. We settled in Düren."

"What do you want with us?"

"I owe O'Dell a debt. I escaped to the States to tell Annalise what happened. O'Dell saved my life, twice."

"He's dead?"

"Yes, ma'am. He died in my arms."

Margie brought her free hand to against her mouth. A patch of sun spilling across the center of the table highlighted specks of floating dust. Jakob wanted to comfort her but kept his place.

"O'Dell was as good a man as I have ever known." Jakob pushed from the table and turned. He walked toward the kitchen, wondering if Margie would pull the trigger. He poured a cup of coffee.

With his back turned, he said, "I want to tell you everything, Mrs. Margie. I cannot carry this burden any longer."

He returned to the table, and for the next two-plus hours, shared his entire life story, leaving no detail untold. When he recounted the events of his last day as a civilian, the horrors he witnessed at his father's delight, and at Shanna's expense, Margie placed the gun on the table and drew a chair next to his.

He shared his experiences on the battlefield and the moral dilemma earning his traitorous label, how O'Dell risked his life seeking him out in the middle of the night, how he nursed him back to health, and protected him from his own men who wanted him dead. At one point, Jakob paused, unbuttoned his shirt, and exposed his wounds.

He held Margie's hand when he spoke of O'Dell's final moments. She kept hold as he detailed their mission to save Shimmel, their capture, escape, his father's death, Sascha's demise, and his having to bury his family. He detailed his escape from Europe and the Gestapo, and rescue by an old country veterinarian on a dirt road.

"It's like a novel written by Hemingway or London," Margie said. "Every detail begs for a turn to the next page."

"I took O'Dell's tags and letters home to offer proof to Annalise what it meant to O'Dell that he had a son and that he did not blame her for not telling him before he left. I did not intend to use the tags or letters for any other purpose. I owe O'Dell my life and now I owe his family. I intended to stay in this community and work the farm until she needs me no more."

"You're willing to give up the rest of your life for her?"

"For O'Dell, yes."

"I can't imagine the burden you've carried."

"I fear most those hunting me."

"Hunting?"

"Your military, my military, others."

"I can understand why our government seeks you."

"Your government knows less than my government. Hitler's network runs deep. Nazi intelligence officers and secret police live and work here, similar to United States intelligence agencies working abroad."

"Oh, my," Margie said. "And you suspect they've followed you here?"

"I fear they will hunt me the rest of my days. They may know my whereabouts."

"We must talk to William. He'll know what to do."

"I have little confidence Sheriff Perry or your husband will believe me. If you call Germany home in these times, the world assumes your allegiance to the Nazi party. I will live with the label the rest of my life unless I can disappear. I desire nothing more than to live my life in peace on the back of a horse."

"I would agree with your assessment regarding William. But my Lucian knows me, and he'll believe if I believe."

"And Annalise? How do I tell her?"

Margie brought a hand against her cheeks and sighed.

"I have another matter to discuss." Jakob leaned forward, placed his forearms on the table, and slumped. He could not look Margie in the eye. "I have fallen in love with her."

Margie froze. A bull near the barn released a tremendous bellow, timing the moment with precision. A cuckoo clock ticked away the seconds, a product hand-manufactured by artisans native to Germany's Black Forest region.

"And you're the only one who can tell her of O'Dell's demise," Margie said.

"I did not mean to fall in love with her."

Margie smiled. "Love... you don't know when it'll strike or under what circumstances. I wouldn't blame any man falling in love with Anna. She's a fine, upstanding woman. But, I'd say in your case, I cannot fathom her reaction."

"I no longer have any internal dilemma," Jakob said. "She deserves to know the truth, regardless of the circumstances or what comes of me. I promised O'Dell. I suspect she will blame me, but I can live with her reaction knowing I fulfilled my promise and debt owed."

"That *would* be the right thing to do," she said. "I don't know if she'll accept your personal history. I'd find this difficult for anyone to accept without struggle, especially a woman who's not seen her husband in four years. She loved O'Dell. Loved him more than anything."

"I know, and he, her. Her love kept him going. She has already accepted O'Dell's death, but she will not believe I had nothing to do with it, and may turn me in." Jakob leaned against the seatback and crossed his arms with a heavy sigh. "I do not know. It does not remove the point. She must know the truth."

"And if it goes as you fear?"

"Disappear, if I can, if I have time to do so. I have always held a fascination for the American West. I assume ranchers in Montana or Wyoming could use a good hand, despite a lack of personal documentation."

"What do *you* want?"

Jakob turned to the window. Liesel hopped and skipped about as if playing with an imaginary friend. He shook his head and said, "I want to spend the rest of my life with her."

Another pause kept the two in deep contemplation.

"It's possible I can help," Margie said. "I have a first cousin, Jack, who owns and operates a dairy farm in the northeast corner of Ohio, in Kunkle. It's the biggest farm in the state. We exchange regular letters, Christmas, and birthday cards. He's always looking for good men. It's at least a starting point. I'll call him this afternoon."

Jakob straightened. "You would call on my behalf?"

Margie smiled a mother's smile.

"It's okay, Jakob," she said, patting his hand. "I'll do whatever I can to help. I believe in you."

Jakob's eyes welled at the sound of his name. It felt as if the locks of a mighty dam cracked, setting free millions of gallons of the liquid it meant to contain. Jakob brought Margie's hand to against his forehead and sobbed. Margie moved to him and placed her arms around his shoulders.

She held on until his body slackened and sobs dispersed. She slipped into the kitchen and returned with a damp rag.

Jakob worked it about his face. The cool of the water brought relief to the spike in body temperature.

"Have you decided how to tell her?"

"No, but I shall not wait any longer. I will saddle Liesel and ride out to her."

"Would you like for me to go with you?"

"No, I do not want her influenced. I am prepared for whatever reaction may come."

"You sure you want to ride and not drive?"

"A ride will do me good. Give me time to think this out."

"I must speak to Lucian."

"Please, let me talk with Annalise first."

"I understand," Margie said.

"Thank you."

She touched his cheek. "You *are* in love with her, aren't you?"

Jakob nodded.

"I know, because you're willing to let her go."

Chapter 71

Liesel's ears perked at the sight of Jakob toting his saddle, blanket, and her bridle looped over his shoulder. She flared her nostrils and completed a jubilant buck, showing off muscles in her fore and hindquarters before bolting to meet him.

Jakob kissed the crown of her head. Liesel shifted parallel to him and rooted her hooves. She expected a quick dressing and escape from this field full of dissimilar creatures.

Jakob secured O'Dell's dog tags and letters in a shirt pocket. Liesel meandered forward. The journey proved a curse and blessing. With no need to deploy his navigational prowess, and under the influence of Liesel's pleasant amble, he succumbed to memories of those intimate moments shared with Annalise.

With eyes set on the trail ahead, he pictured her in the lead, her body swaying to Bonny's gait, her posture perfect, soft shoulders merging toward a thin waist, hair reflecting sunlight, gleaming, like strands of glass.

"I love her, Liesel. I do not know why this happened, but I love her," he said, speaking in collective reverence to both mother and horse. Liesel's hooves crunched with steady tempo on the macadam, yielding Jakob's favorite sound.

"Why did love strike with all hope lost? Why has it cast its spell twice in times of circumstance I cannot control? How could I fall for the woman of a man who saved me?"

He directed Liesel from the riverbed to the road. Her gait struck up clouds of dust, powdering low-hanging leaves as they passed. The grain silo appeared, then the gable end of Annalise's house through leaves of a large hickory. The home's board-and-batten siding appeared silver one second, dark gray the next, as clouds bobbed about the sun.

Jakob tugged on Liesel's reins as they exited a soft curve. Mrs. Perriwinkle slouched in the rocker with the boy fast asleep on her lap.

He eased Liesel to the porch. "Mrs. Perriwinkle?"

Liesel snorted. Mrs. Perriwinkle snapped to attention and realigned her hair to behind her ears.

"Good day, Mr. Tucker."

"Hello. A beautiful day for a nap."

"No napping with this child."

Jakob smiled. The boy hadn't moved the first muscle. "Is Annalise about?"

"No, drove to town to exchange some eggs."

"Do you expect her soon?"

"No, she left only a few minutes ago."

"I guess I will have to wait. I can watch the boy for you if you need to go."

"Well, thank you, Mr. Tucker. I have a few errands of my own to run."

"No problem. Glad to help."

Jakob dismounted. Mrs. Perriwinkle passed the child over the porch railing. Upon settling in Jakob's arms, the boy opened his eyes but for a moment before collapsing against his shoulder. Jakob placed a kiss upon his check.

Liesel followed in Jakob's wake to the barn before peeling off to graze. Jakob kept the bunkroom neat and clean, and several weeks ago, exchanged the hardboard bunk for a rope hammock.

A wood crate sat near where he placed a copy of his favorite book: Betty Smith's *A Tree Grows in Brooklyn*. He eased into the hammock, setting the child on his knee. The boy opened his eyes and smiled. Jakob returned his smile and brought him against his chest. "I hope I can see you to a ripe old age," he whispered.

He eased into the hammock. Within minutes, and with the boy spread out tummy down, both fell asleep to a gentle sway and the sweet aroma of fresh hay.

***

Along their route from the Wynn farm, William claimed the lead from Lucian, and after engaging his lights and siren, cut their travel time in half. They entered the town square in a rush, sending dust pushing into Annalise as she traded a crate of eggs for several loaves of fresh bread with the town's bakery. William slid into his private parking spot with Lucian nearly kissing his back bumper. Both exited their passenger-side doors in haste and hurried toward the courthouse.

"Uncle Bill," Annalise called out from across the street, "what's the trouble?"

William looked to Lucian and gritted his jaw. He retraced his steps down the sidewalk.

"Hello, sweetheart. No trouble. All's well."

Lucian followed, appearing a little less certain of William's description of the moment.

"Something's wrong, I can tell."

"No, everything's fine," William said.

"Then why does it appear as if you've robbed a bank?"

"Just stopped to make a phone call."

"Takes both of you to dial a phone?"

"We had a little trouble this morning, but all's well."

"What trouble?"

"You know I never discuss police matters with family."

Annalise shook her head. "You two look like you're up to no good."

"Don't you worry. Everything's under control."

"I'll just bet." She flashed her uncle a questioning grin. "I'll see you both later."

"Have you seen Ep?" Lucian asked.

"No. Why?"

"No reason. I have another run for him is all."

Annalise returned to complete the swap. She hopped in her truck, waved, then entered the one-way traffic pattern out of town.

"Damn women's intuition," William mumbled.

The men turned back toward the courthouse. Lucian stalled William's progress with a tap on his shoulder. "Billum, don't turn immediately, but there's a green sedan with white stars on the door parked down the street. I noticed it when I got out of my truck."

William bent down low as if to tie his bootlaces. As he turned for a peek, the sedan pulled from its parked position and sped off out of town.

"What do you think that's all about?" Lucian asked.

"I don't know, but those two counterfeit AI monkeys are up to something."

***

"Well, thank you, Mrs. Wynn," Lucian said. He glanced to the clock above William's head. "I'm sure your horse can wait until first light. Yes, ma'am... yes, ma'am... no, ma'am... no, he'll be fine, I promise. Okay... okay... thank you."

Lucian rolled his eyes. "I'm surprised the sound of her voice hasn't killed that poor beast." He tapped at the hook. "Ep called her and said he had to take care of another, more urgent matter."

"Has he skipped a case before?"

"Never. He always goes where he's told or informs me first of any changes to the schedule."

"Hello, Sarah, it's Lucian. Yes, ma'am. Well, Sarah, I've told you many times you cannot train a cat to stop chasing and killing mice... yes, ma'am... yes, ma'am, I understand. Well, I'd suggest you check his mouth before letting him in the house... yes, ma'am. Can you please ring my home?"

The line rang well beyond normal for Margie to answer. Lucian's chest tightened. "Sarah, let it ring a bit longer, if you please."

Lucian waited. No answer. He dropped the phone to its cradle. "I've gotta check on her. I'll meet you at Anna's, say, around two?"

"Fine. But if he's at the house, you call me. Don't confront him on your own. We don't have the first idea how he'll react. We need him alone."

"It's not in the boy, I'm sure of it."

"Yeah, raccoons are cute and furry, too, until you back them in a corner or try to give 'em a hug."

Lucian grabbed his hat and turned for the door.

"You still carry that old cavalry pistol in your truck?" William asked.

"I do."

"Keep it handy. Use it if you must."

Chapter 72

Annalise brought her truck to a sliding stop upon noticing the absence of Mrs. Periwinkle's rusted green Packard.

"Mrs. Periwinkle?" she called out, rushing through the front door.

"Mrs. Periwinkle?"

She hustled up the parlor stairs, rousing balusters to a quiver, all the while calling her sitter's name. She searched the attic rooms. Her son's bed remained as she left it. She returned to the first floor to search the kitchen and mudroom. A peek out the back door revealed Liesel and Bella milling about the round pen. Jakob's saddle, tack, and blanket set draped over the gate. A slight relief settled, but maternal instincts still urged panic.

She blew through the back door and skipped across the creek toward the barn. Bella cut off her path, assuming it was play time. A dozen geese fluttered overhead at low altitude, honking in high decibels, catching the horses' attention.

The barn doors were wide open. "Ep?" she called out.

A mute cast of yellow leaked under the bunkroom door onto the cobblestone floor. Annalise entered, then stiffened, as her breath escaped in a rush. The sight before her had played out in dreams she'd dreamed a thousand times. She brought a hand to her mouth. A torrent of tears erupted.

Her son had burrowed his head under Jakob's chin, his small, round face turned toward her. His skin gleamed a brilliant peach. His arms draped over Jakob's shoulders, Jakob's hands resting on her son's back and bottom. She felt her husband's moment stolen, lost forever. *It's the world's fault, it's your fault,* she said inside her head.

"You have no right," she whispered. Annalise buried her head in her palms as she fell against the doorjamb. All fell silent, other than a faint whistle emanating from her son's nose as he breathed slowly, peacefully. When she released, somehow the view altered, as if props switched between acts in a play. The look on her son's face depicted that of security and trust, and upon Jakob's, that of a mentor and protector, as it should be between father and son.

Annalise pushed off the jamb and moved toward the hammock. She traced the soft lines of Jakob's face. A three-day growth appeared soft as goose down. A peaceful breath sprung from his lungs, elevating her son to a cadence nothing else on earth could emulate. The scene filled her with idyllic charm.

She returned to the moment when the two shared their embrace. Years had passed since she last pressed her body against a man not of kin or close friendship. She felt the beat of Jakob's heart accelerate the longer their bodies fused. Though she broke from the embrace first, she did so with incertitude.

Annalise traced along Jakob's cheek with a finger. She marveled at his interaction with the stock, how they trusted him, how he spoke to them through a loving and compassionate touch. She often caught glances of him sitting on the edge of the back porch or walking through the pasture. She'd spied him dreaming dreams while he napped in the bunkhouse.

"I could never love as I loved O'Dell," she whispered, "but I can love again. I could love you."

What flowed forth from her lips tasted as sweet and decadent as the finest honey but laced in a guilt and anguish striking the root of her convictions.

She ran her fingers through his hair. Her touch brought his eyes fluttering and dancing with confusion. A smile erupted across her face.

The instant Jakob met her eyes, the bunkroom door slammed shut. Annalise spun on her heels. A man in a dark suit pressed forward, pointing a pistol.

"We meet again, Herr von Rüdel," he announced.

Annalise froze. Jakob grabbed tight of the boy and slipped his legs over the hammock.

The stranger waved his gun. "That's right. Keep coming."

Jakob strained in the half light. His eyes honed, then he muttered, "It is you."

"We warned you. There's no escape. You have no friends or places to hide." He noticed Jakob inspecting his right arm. "Do not worry, it's as good as new."

"Ep, who is this man?" Annalise demanded.

The agent let slip a sarcastic laugh. "Ep? I will add it to your long list of aliases."

Annalise's eyes widened. "What's he talking about?"

The agent moved on Annalise, grabbed her shirt collar, then pushed her against the barn wall between studs laced in cobwebs. "You keep your goddamn mouth shut and don't move."

He turned the gun on Jakob and worked a half circle toward the middle of the room. "You will come with me now."

"No, I will not," Jakob replied.

The mathematician rushed him and pressed the barrel of the gun against his forehead. He grabbed the boy by the scruff of his sweater and retreated. Annalise screamed; the child let go a blood-curdling yelp.

The agent backed toward the door, trading his aim between them both, holding on to the boy by the scruff of his neck as a cat her kitten. The boy dangled, his arms flailed, and feet kicked about.

"Please, let him go," Annalise begged.

The agent settled the barrel of the gun against the boy's head. Annalise screamed.

"Shut up! Shut up!"

"Okay, okay," Jakob said. "I will go with you. Please, put the boy down."

With the suddenness of an advancing storm, the agent's demeanor turned eerily calm. "You do not give the orders and will address me as sir. Say it."

"Yes, sir."

The agent allowed a moment's terror as he settled a cold gaze upon Annalise. He turned the boy for a view. "A handsome young lad. I would think a smart woman such as yourself would consider in whose company she leaves her child."

Annalise turned to Jakob. He'd bowed his head and closed his eyes.

"I must apologize, Mrs. Annalise Denny, but this man's name is not Ep."

"How do you know my name?" she said over her boy's whimpering.

"We know all."

"Who's we?"

"The Gestapo," Jakob said.

"You shall pay for that," the agent said, pointing his pistol at Jakob's head.

"Gestapo? What do you want with us?" Annalise asked.

"Only to witness your friend here deliver the terrible news he's been keeping from you these many months."

"Please, no," Jakob pleaded.

The mathematician smiled. "Oh, I'll not tell her... you will." He placed the barrel of the pistol into the boy's ear. Annalise screamed.

"Okay," Jakob said. "Please, don't hurt him."

"I find your sentiment for the enemy touching." He waved his gun. "Tell her now, or the boy dies."

Jakob took a deep swallow. "I am Jakob von Rüdel, a soldier of the German Wehrmacht, forced into the war by my father."

"He forced you to do your duty," the agent corrected.

"I was born in Astoria, New York. My father moved our family to Germany when I was but a child. I made my way to America to tell you the truth regarding O'Dell. I knew him. He saved my life on the battlefield. I came here to tell you the truth about his death."

Annalise stumbled backward into the wall and fell to her knees.

"He found me in a pile of dead soldiers. The SS led me and many others into a forest for execution as traitors. He attended my wounds and nursed me back to health."

"That is a lie," the agent said. "You were shot and left for dead by an American patrol."

"No, that is not true," Jakob said.

"What did you do to my husband?" Annalise asked.

"He killed him," the agent shouted.

"No," Jakob yelled. "I did not, but I was with him when he died. An officer of the SS executed him as a spy as we attempted to extract Corporal Eli Shimmel and others from a POW camp. Your husband died in my arms. Corporal Shimmel assisted in my escape from Europe. Please seek him out. He will corroborate my story."

"He is lying," the agent said, enjoying Jakob's struggle. "He murdered your husband and led his men to the camp. They all hanged for their crimes."

"No, Annalise, you must believe me. Please, seek out Corporal Shimmel. They all survived."

"You're a Nazi," she whispered. "You lied to me. You killed my husband."

"I am not a Nazi. I did not fire a single shot during the war. You must believe me."

Jakob pulled O'Dell's letters, dog chain, and wedding ring from his shirt pocket and tossed them at her feet. Annalise recoiled as if protecting against a coming blow.

Jakob stepped forward. Annalise scooted farther from him, wiping tears from her face.

"Oh, Herr von Rüdel, the lies... the lies," the agent said, smiling. "Mrs. Denny, this man killed your husband in an attempt to flee justice."

"Annalise, I love you."

She did not respond.

"Annalise, I love you... you must believe me. I tried to save your husband and his men. Ask Margie. Please."

Having had enough of the squirming child, the agent tossed the boy at his mother's feet. Annalise reacted as if punch drunk, despite his screams. She knelt to gather her son and O'Dell's items. The agent rushed to place the gun against the back of Jakob's head.

"Move it," he said.

Jakob stepped toward the door. Annalise pulled the boy tight against her body and backed away.

"Annalise, please, believe me. I love you. I did not kill your husband."

"Open the door," the agent demanded.

Jakob lifted the latch. Annalise resurfaced from the depths of her confusion.

"Wait," she said. "Where are you taking him?"

"To Germany to hang for his crimes against the Reich."

The agent buried the sole of his boot into the middle of Jakob's back, sending him crashing through the doorway and onto the cobblestone at the feet of a second agent. The agent dragged him toward the barn's entrance.

Annalise made a break for the door. The mathematician slipped through and slammed it, sending dust billowing into her face. Annalise attempted to push through, but the agent secured the latch. She rammed her shoulder against the solid plank.

"Please, wait," she yelled, pounding at the door with a balled fist.

"Good day, Mrs. Denny. We shall avenge your husband's murder."

Chapter 73

"You know, I've never beat around the bush, so I'm just gonna say it," Lucian started.

Margie sat at the kitchen table, apron tucked about her legs, positioned erect, as if awaiting Sunday sermon.

"This may unsettle you, but Billum and I have this under control. There's no reason for concern."

"I'll let you know if I'm worried once I hear the news," she said.

Uh, well, yes." Lucian cleared his throat. "It appears our houseguest lied about his identity." Lucian passed the military photo.

Margie brought the picture to the end of her nose. The gravity of Jakob's circumstance came full circle as she matched this man, feature for feature. In uniform, he looked identical to the Nazis depicted in Saturday matinee newsreels. But she knew better. "The boy in this picture is not the man we know."

Lucian dipped his pipe into a packet of tobacco. "Of course, he is. Look at his face. It's the same man."

"That's not what I mean. Our Ep is not a Nazi."

"That may be, but we still don't know his name."

With a calm cadence, Margie said, "Jakob von Rüdel."

Lucian froze. His eyes drew over his bifocals. "What did you say?"

She returned the picture to the table. "Jakob von Rüdel. Born in Astoria, New York, but returned to Germany with his family at a young age. His father forced him into the war."

Lucian's pipe bounced off the hardwood. His eyes narrowed. "How in the he... heck do you know that?"

"He told me."

"He told you? When?"

"A few hours ago. He stopped by before going to see Annalise, to tell her...." Margie paused. She so disliked betrayal.

"Tell her what?" Lucian inched toward the edge of his seat.

Margie looked about the room, her nerves preventing a focus on any one object. She'd not yet reconciled her emotions regarding O'Dell's death.

"Sweetheart, tell her what?"

Margie brought the apron to her face and dabbed at the corners of her eyes. "O'Dell died in his arms."

Lucian's brow crinkled. A fly buzzed by his face, prompting a swat. "Then, it was him." He fell against the seatback.

"He made his way back to the States to tell Annalise what happened. O'Dell saved his life and Jakob promised to pay back the debt owed. He used O'Dell's name to escape Europe but didn't do it for his own sake or by himself. Men in O'Dell's unit helped him."

Lucian crossed his arms. She'd entered unfathomable territory. "I don't believe it."

"It's true. It's as true as I'm sitting here."

"I don't believe it. Our boys wouldn't help a Nazi escape."

"He's not a Nazi."

"He's German, ain't he? He's a soldier in the German Army, right? If it waddles and quacks—"

"It doesn't make him a Nazi any more than it makes you a Democrat or Republican. It's a choice based on beliefs."

Lucian shook his head. He shot upright as if an electrical current made its way into his britches. His speech turned animated. "You don't mean to sit there and tell me you believe him?"

Margie fidgeted with her wedding ring, thinking how crazy her husband must think her, and how Jakob needed her support. She drew her eyes forward.

Lucian's mouth fell open, a look not unfamiliar. He stood and paced, returned to his seat, stammered and stuttered a moment, and said, "How can you accept his account?"

"Because what he told me, the way he told me, no man could make up."

It didn't take two hours, but Margie relayed Jakob's story in full. Lucian sat stiff as a plank, consuming every detail.

"You're right," Lucian conceded, "no one could make up such a story."

"What will happen to him?"

"If those Army boys catch up to him, I suspect they'll arrest him and hang him for impersonating or killing an American medic. No one can prove he didn't kill O'Dell."

"Hang him?" Margie pushed from her chair.

"I don't think you can steal the name of an American soldier to gain access to the wrong country."

"But he's an American citizen."

"I don't think it's gonna matter."

"We must help him," Margie said, resolute. "We have to help him."

"Help him? What would you propose?"

"I don't know, but we can't sit back and do nothing."

"Margie, we're talking about the United States military, not the county government... Oh, no."

"What? What's the matter?"

"I'm supposed to meet Billum at Annalise's. He means to confront Ep... I mean Jakob."

"Bill knows?"

"Not all of it. I need to go." He neared the mudroom, stopped, and turned. "You stay here and stay in this house. Lock all the doors."

"For heaven's sake, Lucian, the boy wouldn't hurt a slug."

"I worry what he might do if cornered. It's also possible there are others looking for him."

"I can take care of myself."

"I know, but you lock these doors."

Margie joined him at the door. "Please, Lucian, you must help him. I want you to help him."

He grabbed her shoulders, pulled her close, and kissed her forehead. "Are you sure? I mean, are you absolutely sure you believe this?"

"As sure as I am of my love for you."

***

William set out for Annalise's via a back route. He followed along the same water artery feeding her stream before crossing a series of covered bridges.

He approached a slight veer foretelling his niece's property line but slowed and moved onto the shoulder to allow the same green sedan he'd noticed in town to pass.

William brought the squad car to a screeching halt near Annalise's truck. He rushed up the steps and through a wide-open front door.

"Annalise?" He worked through the sitting room, stopped at the staircase, and shouted her name before moving through the kitchen and onto the back porch.

Bella and Liesel bucked and snorted near the barn. Between their whinnies, Annalise screamed for help, prompting a hurried rush across the pasture at a pace his body would later remember.

"Annalise? Annalise?"

"In here, Uncle Bill, in the bunkroom."

William slit a rope that had tied the latch shut. Annalise rushed into his arms.

"They took him." The boy started screaming. She raced out of the barn with William trailing.

He grabbed her by the shoulder. "Who took who?"

"Gestapo agents took Ep at gunpoint. They left a few minutes ago." Annalise pulled away.

William set off in pursuit. He grabbed her as she reached the back door, spinning her, forcing her to pause.

"Stop," he said, his speech in tatters, his breath frenzied. "You must stop and tell me what happened."

Annalise rushed through the affair. The account confirmed to William his correct assessment of the two bogus agents, but left wide open the mystery surrounding the man named Ep.

"You stay here," he demanded.

"No, I'm going with you."

"No, you're not. You stay here with the boy. I'm not your uncle right now, I'm the sheriff and that's an order. You stay in this house, keep the doors locked, and your shotgun by your side. And, by God, if anyone tries to force their way in, you shoot them. Do you understand me?"

William pulled out of the driveway, sending dust, rocks, and other debris into the front yard. He gunned the engine and sped off.

***

Jakob sat in the back seat of the sedan, looking out the window at the creek bed passing at an ever-increasing rate.

Despite the mathematician snuggled next to him, spouting insults while pressing the gun against his ribs, Jakob's mind drifted, consumed with the moment of his embrace of Annalise—how her body felt so perfect against his, her breasts pressed against his chest, her hands settled against his waist, the perfect swale of her lower back.

He crushed his eyes closed, regretting having acted the proper gentleman instead of stealing from her a desire which he'd forfeit forever: her lips against his.

"Once we pass off Herr von Rüdel," the mathematician directed to his accomplice, "I suggest we pay a visit to his young friend. It would serve her well to be filled with the semen of the Reich... from both ends."

The driver let go a cackle and pounded the dashboard with his fist while thrusting his hips forward in vulgar fashion. Jakob's throat tightened and the flesh of his cheeks burned hot, knowing the danger he'd brought upon them all. His heart rate spiked at the slimy smile on the mathematician's face.

"You will die before you have a chance to send me back to Germany," Jakob charged.

The agent laughed. "Threaten if you like. You have no idea what's in store for you. And, long after you have choked on your last breath, we'll be fucking your dead friend's wife."

The driver slowed as a single lane covered bridge neared. Jakob and the mathematician lurched forward against the front seat as he pressed the brakes. The motion spurred a plan.

Jakob and Liesel had traveled this route twice. A second, more narrow bridge lay ahead another mile at a spot where the creek expanded to ten times as wide, twenty times as deep, with a large hickory five hundred feet from the bridge's entrance.

Another hundred feet beyond lay an abandoned mill, its wheel still tumbling with the current. Jakob glanced between the landscape and the rope binding his hands. In their haste, the agents used a length too short for thorough constriction and bound his hands in front, instead of behind. The mathematician did not think to sit on his dominant-hand side.

Jakob knew he needed to free Annalise and the McKennas of his burden. He'd not hang as a traitor, but die, right here, right now, with intent on taking with him the worst scum his country produced. He needed but to wait. The landscape would provide his prompt to strike.

Slack in the rope allowed Jakob to ball his right hand into a fist. He kept his thumb extended beyond the second knuckle of his index finger. He spotted the tree just ahead.

As the vehicle reached the mill and slowed, Jakob thrust his fist into the mathematician's face, driving his thumb deep into the man's eye. The eye turned to mush against his nail. The man screamed. The driver hit the brakes, providing Jakob the momentum to thrust forward and over the bench seat.

With a grunt, he grabbed the steering wheel and yanked it hard right.

Chapter 74

The car shot right and careened off stone piers supporting wood trusses attached to the superstructure. The momentum of the plunge sent Jakob onto the front passenger floorboard.

Grunts and gasps echoed against the shatter of glass and grating metal as the vehicle entered the first of a half-dozen rolls down a steep, boulder-encrusted embankment.

Bodies flung about as each man endured the other's boot heel, elbow, or knee against soft tissue areas of his own body. The driver slammed into Jakob on the first revolution; by the second, he disappeared.

In a blink, undiluted symphonic bedlam traded for the peace and tranquility of rushing water as the vehicle hit upside down. The impact drove Jakob against the dashboard. The car bobbed and groaned as sand and grit-mixed water poured in through the shattered windows.

The initial onrush stole Jakob's breath, chilling him to the bone. Before the car submerged, he filled his lungs with the last bit of oxygen concentrated in the uppermost corner of the floorboard.

He stabbed for the steering wheel. As he tried to clear the window frame, a hand grabbed his ankle. With a tremendous burst, he launched his free leg and connected with something fleshy, freeing him of the clutch. As spasms hit, he broke through to the surface, gasping for air. He spotted a downed trunk extending from a sandy patch on the opposite bank.

With chest heaving and arms and legs feeling the weight of anchors, he pulled himself out of the water and onto his back. His relief lasted but a blink.

Bubbles exploded upon the surface near the center of the creek. Jakob staggered to his feet as the mathematician surfaced, securing a hand to his blinded eye, begging for help. Jakob worked across the downed trunk to the waterline. "Over here," he yelled.

The agent splashed about in a panic, gasping and spitting like a child tossed into the water for the first time.

"This way," Jakob said. "Keep coming."

"Help me," the agent begged, "Please, help me."

"You can make it."

The agent struggled on, submerging and resurfacing, pleading for assistance. Jakob moved to the edge of the log. The agent kicked himself to within a few feet. Jakob jumped in. He grabbed the agent by the neck and pulled him toward the tree. With a clump of the man's hair secured, he repeatedly slammed the agent's head against the log until his skull split. Jakob pushed the agent below the surface, holding steady until the last bubbles popped. He released. The body surfaced, floated downstream, and snagged on a mishmash of logs and limbs clogged against a beaver hut.

Jakob crawled ashore and stretched out on a patch of ground to soak in the sunlight. The sound of a car sliding to a stop above sent him pushing from the sand and fleeing into the woods.

He worked his way through brush and branch. *This will never end until I disappear for good.*

***

William flipped on his lights at the sight of splintered wood and clumps of stone scattered across the road. Tire marks revealed a vehicle completed a right turn where one did not exist. He worked his way down the embankment, following the path of destruction.

Lucian happened by within minutes, "Billum?"

"Down here."

Lucian worked down the slope. William stood on the bank with fists buried against his hips.

"What happened?" Lucian asked.

William pointed toward a tree branch bearing strange fruit. "McInnis, one of the goons who stopped by my office. Appears he was thrown from the vehicle."

"Who are these people?"

"I came from Anna's. She said the Gestapo took Ep. They...."

"You mean Jakob?" Lucian interrupted.

"So, you know?"

"He told Margie his entire story. You won't believe it. I mean, it's remarkable, and Margie believes him. What's this about Gestapo?"

"Anna said these two identified themselves as Gestapo and led Ep, I mean Jakob, by gunpoint out of the barn to return him to Germany to hang as a traitor."

"Any other bodies?"

"Over there." William pointed to the beaver hut. "It's not our boy. I think it's the skinny shit with McInnis. If Jakob's with them, he's dead, because the car is at the bottom of the creek, and I don't see three bodies or footprints."

"We have to find him," Lucian said.

"I'll call Charlie to pull the car. Our guest might be inside."

Lucian shook his head. "Margie's downright adamant on helping this boy."

"How the hell does she intend to help?"

"I don't know. What does Anna think?"

"She's worried for his safety, which surprises me."

"I suppose one of us should run out there and tell her what's happened," Lucian suggested.

"Good idea. I'd do it, but I've a crime scene to process. Might take some time."

"Yeah, just what I thought you'd say. You always find your way to the best teat, don't you?"

***

Jakob exited the woods and worked up a steep incline to an unfamiliar dirt road. He moved toward the afternoon sun.

Waterlogged boots challenged each step. He'd plodded along nearly two miles when the ground rumbled beneath his feet. He turned to see a dump truck approaching.

The driver throttled down. Gears ground the truck to a pause several yards past. Jakob chased along, swatting dust from his face. He stepped onto the passenger side-rail.

"Wellsboro?"

"Hop in," the driver replied, "going right through it." He gave Jakob a once-over. "I didn't realize it rained today."

"Had a little mishap fishing," Jakob replied.

Jakob insisted the town square close enough to his eventual destination, but the driver insisted a few more miles to the McKenna farm made him no never mind. He dropped Jakob off at the end of the dirt road leading to the farm.

Jakob suppressed the squeal of the back-screen door, then peeked into the kitchen. Disinfectant hung heavy. The house sounded empty.

He worked down the hallway to his bedroom, where his clothing laid folded on the bed next to an open suitcase. A piece of paper on the pile revealed hand-handwritten directions to Kunkle, Ohio. Jakob collected his belongings and made quick work of condensing and packing.

He settled at the small desk and pulled out two envelopes, addressing one to the McKennas, the other to Annalise. From his wad of cash, he removed three one-hundred-dollar bills and placed them in his pocket. What remained, he divvied between the two envelopes. He located a pencil and a piece of paper.

***

> *Dear Mr. Lucian and Mrs. Margie,*
> *Please forgive me for leaving in a manner which you may question. I can no longer, in good conscience, remain, as my presence places you all in grave danger. I pray my leaving affords you an opportunity to resume your lives in peace, as you once knew. I beg your forgiveness, from the bottom of my heart, for the lies and deceit I have brought upon your doorstep. I should have known better, but felt Annalise deserved to know the truth. Please know, my intentions were honorable. To offer my sincere thanks is neither sufficient nor equal in return for what you provided me. I am forever in your debt and will have you in my heart all the rest of my days.*
> *Your faithful servant,*
> *Jakob*

***

Jakob inserted the note and sealed the envelope. With suitcase in hand, he crept down the hallway and laid both envelopes on the table. The cuckoo clock coincided with the time Margie set out to collect eggs most days.

He hitched his trailer and collected from the barn a few items purchased for Liesel's care. With possessions stowed, he eased the truck out of the driveway, battling tremendous guilt for sneaking off like a thief in the night. He hoped the McKennas could forgive him.

Jakob brought his truck to a stop alongside the road within view of the grain silo marking Annalise's property line. He crossed the stream and moved into the woods before settling behind a post along the fence. Lucian's truck sat in her driveway. Jakob surveyed the property, seeing no signs of them near the barn. Liesel stood erect at the gate, ears perking at each sound.

As the last bit of sunlight dipped behind the bluffs, Jakob rushed into the pasture. Liesel spotted him and broke. He grabbed his saddle, tack, and blanket, and headed for the far corner of the property. Liesel followed on his heels, cloaking his stride.

He led her through the woods and over the creek. Jakob secured the trailer, maneuvered a U-turn, then set out toward the setting sun in search of Ohio.

***

Cody, Wyoming, November 2009

Paul turned to a rap on the den door. Monica poked through, flashing that smile he so loved. He adjusted in the chair. "You still up?" he asked.

She entered adjusting the sash of her robe. "I managed a couple hours. Can't seem to find sleep in that room without you. How are you?"

"Almost done. Just a few more chapters to go."

"Any earth-shattering developments?"

"Not really. Absolutely love the story."

Monica settled on the armrest, then placed a kiss atop his head. "You know, after you left the kitchen this morning, Rachel remembered an offhanded remark your mother made about the colonel. She said she overheard Abigail ask your father where they were to meet the colonel just before they took that long trip that one summer. It's not much, but at least it connects him a bit more to your parents."

"I guess."

"Well, just thought I'd share that with you. Guess I'll try to get a bit more sleep." She kissed him again. "Try and get some sleep yourself, once you finish."

Paul patted her hand. "Won't be long now."

Chapter 75

"Come up with anything?" Lucian asked.

William shook his head. He moved from behind the ambulance to Lucian's truck and placed his hat on the roof. "Nope. My men searched in both directions but found no sign of a third body. We'll search again at first light. How's Anna?"

"Devastated, I'd say," Lucian said, "especially after I told her what happened here, and all Jakob told Margie. She stared right through me, tears spilling, holding onto the boy. I told her you'd call on her."

"If those two fellas didn't survive, I doubt Jakob did. I'll bet he's snagged on the bottom or stuck near the dam."

"I dare say it's gonna be an unpleasant evening," Lucian said.

"I'll follow soon. We'll drag the creek in the morning. I sent the other bodies to the morgue, and Charlie left with the car. I need to wait for the county crew to set a temporary barrier."

***

Lucian entered the kitchen to the smell of fried chicken and fresh bread. Margie stood at the stove stirring a boiling pot of green beans. She always wore a simple skirt and apron when she cooked. Lucian paused at the doorway, gawking.

Margie bent low to check the contents of the stove. She popped up, startled. The oven door slammed against its frame. "My goodness," she said, "you're a sneaky one tonight."

"Sorry, just enjoying the view," he said, smiling.

"I'll have your dinner soon." She rechecked the oven.

Her demeanor appeared opposite to what he expected. He could tell in the way she moved about, the way she tried to stay busy. "Are you okay?"

"Yes, fine. Go on ahead and clean up."

"Are you not curious about Jakob?"

"Oh, yes. Did you speak with him?"

"No, afraid not. I have some bad news, though."

Margie whipped her potatoes. "Bad news?"

"German military police found Jakob before we could. They took him at gunpoint from Anna's barn. Billum found their car in the creek by Buckley Bridge. Both agents died. He could not find Jakob."

Margie did not budge.

"Did you hear what I said?"

"Yes, dear. I'm sure he'll turn up."

Lucian cocked his head. "That's all you have to say? You're the one pleading we help him."

"Accidents do happen."

Lucian approached. He placed his hands on her shoulders. She turned.

"Okay, what is it? What's going on?"

Margie rolled her hands in her apron.

"Tell me."

Margie swallowed. "Did you see his truck outside?"

Lucian shook his head. "No, I suspect he drove it to Anna...." He stopped short. "Wait. His truck wasn't there. I saw Liesel. Where's his truck?"

"He took it."

"Took it? When?"

"Three hours ago. He packed all his things and left."

"Did he appear hurt?"

"No."

Lucian rushed through the kitchen and down the hallway. He opened the bedroom door. The room appeared as pristine as the day Jakob arrived.

"Where'd he go?" he yelled from the hallway.

Margie turned to cover her green beans.

"Margie, where did he go?"

"He left." She approached the dining area and retrieved the two envelopes from the cabinet where she kept her Sunday-best china.

"What's this?"

"See for yourself."

Lucian inspected the envelopes. He opened the one addressed to "the McKennas." The stack of hundreds surprised him into a chair.

"I don't understand. Why would he leave all his money?"

"The man he is, I guess. He doesn't care about himself, only about doing right by others."

"You know where he's gone, don't you?"

"I have a good idea."

"And you'll not tell me?"

"I'll tell no one. I'll be damned if I let anyone hang that boy."

Lucian perked. He'd not heard Margie utter the first profanity in all the years of their union. He planted his elbows on the kitchen table and cupped his hands to his forehead. "You realize what you're doing? The magnitude?"

"I alone know his whereabouts. If I keep it a secret, I implicate no one."

"Be reasonable, Margie. At least sensible."

"I don't care. He deserves to live out his days in peace. God knows he's experienced more hell on earth than any human deserves."

"Did you speak to him before he left?"

"No. I was collecting eggs at the time and did not want to interfere. I did not want him knowing someone observed his escape."

The screen door slapped. William stepped in from the mudroom. "Sorry, I can come back," he said.

"No, come on in," Lucian said, "but you can cancel those divers, and you better call your niece."

***

"You know, I could arrest you for aiding a wanted fugitive," William said, picking the last bit of meat from a chicken leg.

"Fine," Margie replied. "Arrest me."

"I'll never understand you."

"Thank goodness I married Lucian."

"Why put your neck on the chopping block for this boy? I'll give ya, his story is one for the ages, if true."

"Because he has no one and everyone deserves someone. Can you image losing family, home, and country all before the age of twenty-six?"

William shook his head. "How do you know he's telling the truth?"

"I know. If, for any reason, I didn't believe him, we'd not be discussing this now. For God sakes, I had a loaded pistol in my hand pointed at his chest. You weren't present when he emptied his soul to me. You didn't see the look in his eyes or feel the emotion spill from his soul when I called him by his real name. I mean, the weight of the world lifted off him in an instant. I witnessed it all, and believe him, without reserve. It's called having faith."

"Faith can be a slippery slope," Lucian said.

"You attend church on Sunday, Lucian. Why?"

"Well, I... I...."

"Did you see Jesus die on that cross? No, you didn't, but you believe he died for us. You believe he died for our sins. You've told me so yourself. That's called faith."

"Okay, Margie, point taken," William said, "but the intelligence community will keep after him. Word's already spreading. Twenty-five people witnessed us pull the sedan with big white stars out of the creek, including Syd and his photographer. He'll have it in the morning paper."

"I'm sorry, but I'll not tell a soul," Margie insisted.

"You'd lie to the military if they discovered you had information as to his whereabouts?"

"I'll do whatever necessary to protect him."

"You'd lie under oath?"

Margie let go an exaggerated huff. "Take me to jail, because I'm not telling you, Lucian, a court of my peers, or Uncle Sam... period." Margie slapped her palm on the table and excused herself.

Lucian shrugged.

William tossed the spent chicken drum onto his plate. "Oh, Margie, no one's going to jail. I just need some time to figure this out."

"I don't see this as your burden."

"Your burden is my burden. You've cooked my meals, washed my clothes, stitched my cuts, and tended to all my aches and pains. If you feel so strongly about the boy, I'll figure a way so both of you can live without fear of having to look over your shoulder. I know one thing—Annalise feels something for him. She acted mighty relieved when I told her there's a chance he survived the wreck. I think she's in love with him."

"She's not alone in her feelings," Margie said. "And it's not puppy love."

"I know. She told me he professed his love for her." William leaned back in his chair and stretched his legs. "I can outsmart the county government. Been doing it for years. Outsmarting the U.S. Government, well...."

"Only a handful of people knew Jakob and fewer still who had words with him," Lucian offered.

William pushed from his chair. "More coffee, anyone?" Halfway up, he paused. "Wait a minute... wait a minute." He retook his seat. "I have three bodies."

"Three? You said you found two," Lucian reminded.

"No, I have three, well, two and some parts of a third. I have the two Gestapo clowns and a drifter torn to pieces by a freighter. Little left of him, but that's to our advantage. No way to identify and contact next of kin."

"How does a mangled body help Jakob?" Margie asked.

"Loosh, you have the number of the AI man who visited Anna?"

Lucian dug his wallet from a back pocket and pulled the card.

"I think I figured a way our boy can disappear forever," William said.

He picked up the phone and tapped the set. "Hello, Sarah, long-distance operator, please. No, ma'am. I already told you, I cannot arrest your sister for parking in front of your house. It's a public street." William rolled his eyes. "Please, Sarah, the operator."

Margie offered William her seat. She poured another round of coffee.

"Yes, Langley, nine-nine-seven-nine-six."

"Good evening, Captain Brock, please."

William moved to the edge of his seat. "Captain Brock, William Tobias Perry here, Sheriff of Tioga County. Lucian McKenna passed along your number. I believe I have your man. If you meet me at the Wellsboro courthouse, I think we can wrap this thing up. No, sir, I've not mentioned this to anyone yet. Fine, fine. I'll meet you in an hour."

William cradled the phone. A split second later, it rang.

"Yes, Sarah? He is, uh-huh, okay. On my way."

"What?" Lucian asked.

"Syd and his photographer are poking around the jailhouse. I gotta go."

***

Captain Brock, accompanied by a small entourage, entered the courthouse. After shooing away the town's newspaper man, William placed a call to the county coroner and requested his presence.

The men took several minutes to introduce themselves.

"Sheriff Perry, may we speak in private?" Brock asked.

"Of course," William said. "Gentlemen, if you'll excuse us for a moment."

William settled in his chair and lit a half-smoked cigar. He held open a box of La Fendrich brand given by his staff for his last birthday. "Cigar?"

"No, thank you," the captain said. "Cigarette man."

"Well, smoke 'em if you got 'em."

"Thank you, no. My men caught wind of an accident involving a military vehicle."

"News sure travels fast 'round here." William plopped his feet on his desk and sucked a lengthy draw. "I had a visit a few days ago by two bogus characters claiming association with Army Intelligence. They're after the same man. They left this."

William pulled the picture of Jakob from his pocket and passed it across his desk. The captain brought it close for inspection. "He's our man, all right."

"I received a call from Mrs. Denny this morning. She said those same two caught her by surprise in the barn and identified themselves as Gestapo agents."

"We have intelligence corroborating active Gestapo cells in the States. This incident surprises me, though, as I've not seen or heard of such bold and public confrontations. They mostly stick to the shadows."

"A few days back, witnesses reported a suspicious character hanging around the train depot in Tioga. No one had ever seen him before. He jumped out of a boxcar in front of a freighter. Engineer said the man slipped and fell running across the track and he didn't have time to stop. Ran right over him. Witnesses said the man acted nervous, suspicious, running from something. A deputy of mine was on site waiting for his wife and witnessed the entire event. I showed him this picture. He identified this man. I instructed him to never speak of it again.

"This afternoon, I happened on an accident near Buckley Bridge. I recovered two bodies and identified them as the two men who visited myself and Mrs. Denny. We pulled the car from the creek. It's a green sedan with white stars."

"You've had a busy couple of days. I commend you on ensuring we have no loose ends. Where's the vehicle now?"

"At the county garage."

"Easy enough to trace where they stole it. And the bodies?"

"In the morgue, listed under John, Joe, and Jeff Doe."

The captain pulled a notepad from his coat pocket. "Who's privy to the Gestapo agents, other than yourself and Mrs. Denny?"

"No one," William replied. "If word of this finds its way into the community, I'd have mass hysteria on my hands. I'm not interested in bringing a circus to town. It's why I called you."

"I assure you, the government agrees with your assessment. We must keep this under wraps. Can you trust Mrs. Denny to remain quiet?"

"A safe bet, I'm sure. She's my niece. Our local newspaperman snapped a picture when we pulled the car. I've asked him to sit on the story until I can contact next of kin. He understood and agreed. By the time he hears from me, the story's dead."

"I'm sorry. I didn't realize Mrs. Denny was kin. I still don't have information on the whereabouts of her husband."

"I think she's come to grips with his death," William said.

"We'll take the vehicle and bodies off your hands. May I see the remains?"

"You may. Fair warning, though, your boy is nothing more than freshly ground beef."

"Understood, but I need to confirm I saw him."

Chapter 76

Annalise spent the night in a rocking chair with her son, though she could not find sleep, thanks to a phone call in which Margie shared that the two Gestapo monsters had met their rightful deaths, and Jakob fled town without seeking her out.

Annalise's heart ached for all Jakob had endured. If Lucian believed Margie, which Margie swore he did, she'd not deny Jakob's claim of his intentions to return to the States. She wished to put her arms around him.

Annalise entered the barn before daybreak. She stood alone against a wall of the bunkroom, looking at the hammock and the lone possession Jakob left behind.

She picked up his copy of *A Tree Grows in Brooklyn*. He'd underlined a passage within the first fifty words.

> *This is the forest primeval. The murmuring pines and the hemlocks,*
> *Bearded with moss, and in garments green, indistinct in the twilight,*
> *Stand like Druids of eld.*

She traced her fingers over the page, contemplating what passed through his awareness, producing a desire to underscore. She'd someday read the book to attempt deciphering why it meant so much.

She layered the first stall with straw, leveling the spread with her pitchfork. Tires crunching gravel caught her attention. She leaned the pitchfork against the stall gate, grabbed her son off a mattress in the bunkroom, and moved across the pasture.

By the time she entered the kitchen, the visitor dropped the doorknocker against its steel plate. She placed her son on the mattress near the stove. "Coming," she called. She wiped dust from her jeans and opened the door. Her heart sank.

"Mrs. Denny?"

Another man in uniform. *Will it never end?* "I know my husband's dead. You need not bother coming back."

"Yes, ma'am, I know. He died trying to save my life. I'm Shimmel, Corporal Eli Shimmel."

Annalise's fingers slipped from the doorknob. "Oh, my God, it's you... you're alive," she whispered, bringing a hand to her mouth.

Eli Shimmel, the man her husband described in multiple letters; the man Jakob claimed had aided his escape. She stood like a statue, stunned.

"I'm sorry for dropping in unannounced, but I needed to see you." He passed his credentials. She inspected the badge and picture. "I've dealt with plenty of suspicious people in recent days. Can you prove your identity?"

"I suspect your husband wrote to you more than any soldier ever wrote to his wife. I'm sure he mentioned a German soldier we found in a valley east of Bastogne. O'Dell carried him out and saved his life. I guess you've heard by now."

"Yes, I have. You know the soldier's name?"

"Jakob von Rüdel."

"Yes. He brought me O'Dell's unsent letters and a few personal items. I've read the letters a thousand times in the past few days. My husband described you as a pain in his rear end."

Shimmel grinned. "Yes, ma'am. I also have this." He passed the picture of her holding the baby above her head in their kitchen. "Jakob secured this, along with O'Dell's letters and dog tags, the day he died. He gave the picture to another man in our unit, Joe Polak, in case he never made it back to the States."

She returned his identification. "Please, come in."

Shimmel entered with hat in hand. They endured a moment of awkward silence before she offered a cup of coffee.

"Yes, thank you."

She led Shimmel into the kitchen. He stopped at the mattress and settled to his haunches. "Well, hello there, young man," he said, taking hold of the boy's hand.

Annalise turned.

Shimmel put his other hand on the boy's head and ran fingers through his hair. "Your father was so proud of you," he whispered.

Annalise began to cry.

Shimmel returned upright. "I'm so sorry," he said. "I didn't mean to upset you. I can't imagine what you're going through."

Annalise shook her head and wiped her eyes. "It's not your fault. You must excuse me. I'll have a difficult time meeting anyone who knew my husband. Please, sit down."

Shimmel rested his cap on the frame of the chair next. He settled and crossed his legs. Annalise placed a kettle on the stove and lit the burner. She turned and leaned against the countertop. Shimmel met her eyes.

"So, it's all true," she said.

He brought his hands together on his knee and interlocked his fingers. "I don't know all Jakob told you, as he's a humble fella. I know throughout our ordeal he never lied to us. It's a story most folks would never fathom could happen during such hostilities. It's remarkable when one accounts for the sum of all its parts. But it happened, and it's changed the lives of several men I know."

"Did O'Dell suffer?"

Shimmel shook his head. "I don't know, I wasn't there. O'Dell banded the men together to rescue me. He refused to leave any man behind. You need to know your husband was a hero. Hundreds of wives and children had their husbands and fathers returned home because of his actions. He saved countless generations, both friend and foe. He knew no uniform. I served with a great many men, but none more courageous or dedicated than your husband. He taught me a great deal about life."

"And Jakob?"

"After O'Dell died, Jakob led the men on. He did it because he felt he owed O'Dell a debt for saving his life, and because it's what O'Dell set out to do. Jakob and a few collaborators rescued five of us from the POW camp. He's unlike any man I've ever met, other than your husband. Their convictions carbon copied each other."

Annalise let his words soak in. She opened a cupboard and collected two coffee cups, then turned at a knock at the front door.

"I'm sorry, please excuse me."

"Of course," Shimmel said, coming to attention as she exited.

Seeing Margie without Lucian surprised her. Annalise reached out. The two embraced in a deep and lengthy hug

"My dear, are you okay?"

"Yes, you won't believe who's here."

"I can come back another time."

"No, please come in. There's a man here who served with O'Dell."

"Oh, my," Margie said.

"It's okay, please come in." Annalise escorted Margie by the arm.

"Corporal Shimmel, please meet Mrs. Margie McKenna. Margie, Corporal Eli Shimmel."

Shimmel extended his hand. "My great pleasure, ma'am."

"Pleasure's all mine, Corporal," she replied.

"Please, call me Eli."

Shimmel gave up his seat and moved to the end of the table. Annalise fetched another coffee cup.

"I'm so sorry to interrupt. I don't mind coming back."

"It's no interruption at all, Margie," Annalise insisted.

"Not at all," Shimmel agreed. "I'm not here on official business. I had a week's pass and wanted to meet the wife of the man who saved my life."

"O'Dell seems to have made a habit of that," Margie said.

"By the hundreds."

The three settled in, each taking a sip of coffee.

"I know the story," Margie said. "I dare say it's the most fascinating and remarkable chain of events I've ever heard."

"You met Jakob?"

"Yes. He stayed with us. Worked for my husband, Lucian, the county vet."

"Makes perfect sense. He and O'Dell talked horses non-stop. He told O'Dell his father took him to Western movies as a boy."

"Yes, he told me the same," Margie said.

"The men overheard Jakob say one day he wanted to ride a horse clear across Colorado to the Pacific Ocean."

"I've never met anyone who has such a way with animals," Annalise said. "It's like he can speak to them."

"There's a lot special about Jakob," Shimmel replied. "I take it he's not here?"

"No, he left us. We don't know where he went. I don't know if Annalise told you, but he escaped capture by his own people and ours. He left a note apologizing for putting us all at risk, said he had to disappear."

"I guess there's nothing else he can do. If he's caught, they'll hang him. It won't matter who comes to his defense. He was hell-bent on making sure you knew the truth, Mrs. Denny. You also need to know we talked Jakob into using O'Dell's name. We had to beg him. I'm sorry if you feel we disrespected your husband. As it turns out, even in death, O'Dell saved another man's life."

Annalise attempted to speak but choked on her words.

"Corporal, please don't think me rude, but would you mind if I had a private moment with Annalise?"

"Not at all, ma'am." He took a last sip of coffee. "You have a lovely spread here, Annalise. May I take a walk about?"

"Of course, make yourself at home."

"Thank you, Corporal," Margie said. "I won't be long."

"Take all the time you need, ma'am. It was a pleasure meeting you." Shimmel shook her hand. "I hope our paths cross again."

Chapter 77

After the screen door slapped shut, Margie passed an envelope to Annalise.

"What's this?"

"Open it."

"I don't understand. Why would Jakob do such a thing?"

"He left a great sum to us as well."

Annalise pulled the wad of cash from the envelope and fanned it out on the table. Margie sipped her coffee and removed her hat. She snapped her purse closed and took Annalise's hand.

"My dear, you know Lucian and I love you, and there's nothing in this world we wouldn't do for you. So, please know, we're here for you. You *will* struggle with O'Dell's death. His memory will never leave, nor should it. It's nothing to feel guilt over or attempt to corral. It's part and parcel of falling in love with the right man. You should also not stop yourself from moving on with your life. I know O'Dell. I know what he'd tell you. He'd want you to find a man who'd take as good of care of you as he would. He wouldn't want you alone or unhappy, and he'd want his son looked after.

"Jakob left you money, but his more significant and selfless gesture was leaving *you*. He understands the danger. He left because he loves you. He told me so, though I could see it in his eyes and hear it in his voice when he spoke of you."

Annalise shook her head. Her chest heaved. She wanted to say it but couldn't.

"If the good Lord intended to carbon-copy O'Dell, Jakob is the result. He's a fine young man who's welcome in my home anytime, regardless of the lies he told and what he had to do to stay alive. He, too, will face a lifetime of guilt, but he also deserves someone who'll stand behind *him*, stand with *him*, believe in *him*, and afford *him* peace. As I told Lucian, he's made enough trips to hell and back. He deserves the love and support you'd offer."

Annalise let go of Margie's grasp. She brought her hands to her face and sobbed. When her emotions eased, Margie placed her hand under Annalise's chin and guided her eyes toward her.

"Are you in love with him?"

"Yes."

"Do you feel guilty?"

"Yes."

"O'Dell died knowing how much you loved him. You must honor his memory by living your life to the fullest and allow your son the same. He needs a man who'll teach him the ways of the world. I couldn't pick a finer man for you. Jakob's character shines so above and beyond most."

"I didn't want him to leave." Annalise turned from Margie, biting at her lip. "I wanted him to stay. I wanted him to stay so badly."

Rain ticked against the metal roof. A rush of wind found its way down the stove's exhaust pipe. Cattle bawled in the background, either cussing or praising the precipitation.

"I do love him, Margie, but feel so guilty. I feel ashamed of myself. I didn't expect it to happen and never meant for it to happen. When I felt myself slip, I wanted to stop it."

"Did you expect to fall in love with O'Dell the way you did? Did you expect you'd see a man at a livestock auction and end up marrying him? Of course not. But that's what love does. It slithers along in the grass, and when you're not paying attention, it rears up and bites you. Bites you right in the... well, it bites you. O'Dell did what he felt he had to do. He saved so many men and kept intact so many families. Think of the many new births in this world men will credit to him. I know you're so proud of him. Honor him by living your life as he'd want you to live it."

Annalise swallowed. "I suppose it doesn't matter. I'll never find Jakob now, unless he finds me, someday."

"What would you do if you knew his whereabouts?"

Annalise turned toward the window. A moth plunked against it from the outside, expecting a better life within. *What would you do?*

She turned slowly. Her eyes drifted from the kitchen floor. "I'd go to him. I'd go to him and tell him I'm ready to start my life over... with him."

Margie smiled. She unsnapped her purse and passed a small white card. Annalise inspected the printed address in bright blue ink. "Kunkle, Ohio? I've never heard of it."

"I grew up around those parts. Met Lucian there by chance one summer. I came out of a corner drugstore as he came in. We smacked into each other. He said hello and smiled. I knew in an instant I'd marry him one day. Had I left ten seconds earlier, our paths may have never crossed. My shoelace had come undone, and I used those ten seconds to stop and tie it. You never know how the most innocent of events can change your life forever."

It did not take long for Annalise to figure the significance. Her body quivered with a tempered excitement. Goose bumps covered her arms. "How do you know this?"

"Does it matter? Listen, his whereabouts must remain our secret. It's his one chance. I've not shared this with Lucian or your uncle, but they know I know. What you do with it, well, that's up to you. Please, whatever you decide, follow your heart, not your head, and don't tell a living soul. His life depends on it."

Annalise saw Margie to the front door. "Remember," Margie said, "not a word to anyone." The women hugged. A knock upon the back door broke their embrace.

"Take care, my dear, and call upon us anytime," Margie said, blowing a kiss as she exited the front porch.

"I'm so sorry," Annalise said, letting Shimmel in out of the rain. "Our conversation went beyond what I expected. I forgot you were here."

"No problem. I enjoyed the walk. You have a beautiful place. I know why O'Dell spoke so fondly of it."

"Would you care for another cup of coffee?"

"No, thank you. I should return to base."

"Corporal, may I ask you a personal question?"

"Of course."

"What made you want to help Jakob escape?"

He wiped away rain droplets from the bill of his cap. "I wanted nothing more than to put a bullet in his head. I wanted to kill him because Nazis murdered many of my family members. O'Dell stopped me, and I'm thankful he did.

"O'Dell and Jakob did not subscribe to the first rule of war, which is, you stick your neck out for no one. No way, under any circumstance, do those two not forge a friendship beyond the war. O'Dell saved Jakob, despite me. I tried to talk him out of going into the dark, chasing after a ghostly whimper. But he would not hear of it."

"Why did you go with him?"

"Because I knew we'd not survive without him."

"So, you saved him?"

"I don't know. O'Dell saved Jakob, Jakob saved me and the rest of our squad, and we did what we felt necessary to help Jakob escape a certain death. We refer to it as a debt of war."

"Would you do it again, if given a chance?"

"For Jakob, yes. Mankind has seen enough evil. Jakob is the type of man we need to rebuild and heal."

"Corporal, I haven't seen my husband in nearly four years. At times, it feels our life together was but a dream. Jakob arrives and it feels like O'Dell returned, but in another man's body."

"They're as close as two men can be without popping from the same womb."

"Yes, I agree. And what if I told you I'd fallen in love with Jakob? Would you think less of me?"

"I'd say four years is long enough for anyone, and knowing O'Dell as I did, he'd agree. I'd also say, aside from O'Dell, you'll not find a better man. I have a relationship with Jakob because of Jakob, not me."

"I'll get him," she said.

"So, you know where he is?"

"Yes."

Annalise expected Shimmel to ask, but he let it ride. He replaced his cap and straightened his uniform. "Your husband would want you to move on."

For reasons she could not explain, Shimmel's words carried the heaviest weight of all. She moved into him and wrapped her arms around him.

"I'm so sorry," he whispered. "I'll regret forever I was not there to protect O'Dell. I hope someday we can all meet again."

"I hope so." Annalise walked him to the door. He passed her his card.

"Just so you know, the boys vowed never to speak of this. If the story shows up as a paperback at the five and dime, it won't have come from us. You need anything, anything at all, I know five guys who'll be here before you can blink. I dare say, anyone who knew O'Dell would feel the same."

"Thank you so much. You don't know how much your words mean to me."

Chapter 78

By the time Annalise cared for her stock, fed the boy, packed a bag for him and a trunk for herself, the afternoon sky lost its grip to the stampede of dusk. She waited for any impulse to suggest she'd made a mistake. One did not manifest. A schoolgirl-type tingle settled in its place, a sensation not experienced since first spotting O'Dell. Guilt remained and pecked at her conscience, but she could not deny Margie's and Shimmel's advice to live her life to the fullest.

She pulled up to the McKenna farmhouse, disappointed in not seeing her uncle's squad car or Lucian's truck. She collected her son, walked up the front stairs, and entered. The McKennas insisted long ago she need not knock. Family never knocked.

"Well, hello, dear," Margie said from her position at the stove. The boy let go his mother's hand and raced like a drunkard into Margie's waiting arms. She picked him up and planted a long kiss upon his cheek.

"Would you mind watching him a few days?"

"Leaving town, are we?"

Annalise smiled.

"I'm so pleased," Margie said. She patted his behind.

"I hoped Uncle Bill and Lucian might be here."

"Both running late this evening."

"I wanted to speak with them together."

The familiar crusty clatter of Lucian's truck trampled over the calls of toads and crickets settling in for their evening concert. He'd had a long day but seemed to catch a second wind upon seeing Annalise's boy in the kitchen. Lucian picked him up and tossed him toward the ceiling, instigating a happy squeal.

"Don't waste all your energy, my dear," Margie said. "He's staying with us a few days."

Lucian pressed his nose against the boy's. "Fine and dandy with me." The boy threw his arms around Lucian's neck. He carried him to the kitchen table and sat down.

"You off on a trip?"

"Yes," Annalise said, "a few days, maybe longer." She joined Lucian at the table.

Lucian blew quick puffs of air into the boy's face. His giggle aped a bleating baby lamb. Lucian looked to Annalise. "What is it, sweetheart?"

His insight never ceased to amaze her. She could cut a quarter inch off her hair, and he'd notice. She sat quiet a moment. Lucian helped the boy to the floor. He ran to Margie and buried his face in her apron.

"Anna?"

"Well, I'm not sure where to begin."

Margie grabbed the boy by the hand. "How about let's go see if we can find some eggs," she said. She lit a lantern and led her favorite little man through the mudroom.

Lucian's pipe came to life. Annalise loved the aroma.

She clasped her hands together. "I've fallen in love," she said, unable to look him in the eye.

Lucian dragged a few puffs. He leaned back and crossed his arms. "You should not feel ashamed, my dear. Jakob's a fine man."

Annalise looked up slowly; her eyes widened.

"I wasn't valedictorian of my class, but I'm not stupid."

"I guess you're not surprised I'm going after him."

"My lone surprise is, after a hundred years of marriage, my wife excludes me from certain details."

"Do you think less of me?"

"My dear, you could never disappoint me or Margie. You're a daughter to us. It takes great courage to move on. Your decision does not diminish in the least the relationship you had with O'Dell, his memory, or what you'll feel for him the rest of your life. It takes great character to pick one's self up. Many won't, and their lives will waste away to nothing. O'Dell would roll in his grave if he knew you gave up. I'd also bet Jakob will never let you forget O'Dell, nor expect to replace him. I suspect he loves you that much."

"It means a great deal to hear you say those things."

"I assume Margie told you of his whereabouts."

"Yes."

"And you'll keep it to yourself?"

"I have to."

"I know. It's for the best. It's his one chance until he melds back into the fabric of society. Thanks to Billum, he has a decent head start. Nobody chases a dead man."

They shared a cup of coffee. Lucian retold the story of the first time he met O'Dell. Annalise shared the first time she saw him. Margie returned with her apron in a bunch with no less than a dozen brown and spotted eggs.

Annalise bent low and kissed her son. He scrambled over to the cuckoo clock to wait for the next show. She hugged Lucian and thanked them both for their help and support.

"Good luck, sweetheart," Lucian said.

"Take all the time you need," Margie added.

***

William sat in his chair, a cigar dangling from his lips, feet propped on his desk, sifting through a stack of paperwork. Annalise knocked.

"Yeah?" he growled, not bothering to look up.

"Uncle Bill?"

His back straightened, sending the stack of papers to the floor. He pulled his cigar and placed it in an ashtray carved from obsidian. Annalise approached. Darkness shrouded the office, save a single, low-wattage bulb lamp on the corner of his desk.

"Hello, sweetheart."

"Hello. Do you have a few minutes?"

"For you, of course. Have a seat. Coffee?"

"No, thank you," she said, taking the first chair nearest his position. "I have a thermos-full in the truck."

William swiveled toward her. An amused look spread across his face. "Heading out, huh?"

"Yes."

"You understand what you're getting yourself into?"

"I do."

"You believe he's worth it?"

"I've lost one good man. I cannot lose another."

"You know he can't stay here. The Army's off his scent, but too many people saw him, interacted with him, and may figure this out one day. We need to keep him dead."

"I understand." Annalise mulled over the property and plans O'Dell had. This had been her home for more than half her life. She recognized the difficulties of starting over.

"What are your plans for the farm?"

"I'd prefer to keep it in the family. Maybe you could retire there."

"Might work." William pushed from his chair and took a chair next to her. He placed his arm around her shoulders. "There's plenty of time to decide. I'll keep an eye on the place while you're gone. As a matter a fact, I might spend a few nights out there."

"Chester's son will take care of the stock."

"Fine."

Annalise laid her head against his shoulder. "What would Papa say to all this?"

"He'd have loved O'Dell. Hell, everybody loves O'Dell. And I believe he'd recognize you'd spent enough time alone. I can't guess his reaction to Jakob. I mean, you'd have to have taken part in something of this magnitude to form an opinion. But your father loved you more than anything and would want you to be happy. I suspect he'd feel as I do."

"And how's that?"

"Jakob's a good man caught in a most unusual circumstance not of his own doing. I think he's earned the right to enjoy peace in his life and deserves a great woman. And you, my dear, are a great woman."

"A soldier in O'Dell's group called on me, a man named Eli Shimmel."

William recognized the name from a letter Annalise once passed to him. She detailed her conversation and how it helped her decision.

"I'd agree with his opinion. You've spent enough time alone." William moved his chair in front of her. He grabbed her hands. "Listen," he said, squaring up to green eyes so resembling those of his sister-in-law. "It doesn't matter what I say, what Lucian or Margie think, or what anyone in this town thinks. You do what's best for you and your son, and the people who love you will rise to the top. It's up to each of us to find and make happiness for ourselves. If this man brings you the joy you deserve, I don't give a shit where he came from. As long as you don't settle... I love you."

Annalise wiped her eyes. William pulled her close and planted a kiss on her forehead.

"I suppose you're privy to his whereabouts?" he asked.

"Yes."

"And won't tell me?"

She shook her head.

"Does Loosh know?"

"No."

"Good. I'll tell him you told me. It'll drive him nuts."

Annalise wiped her face through a laugh.

"You need money?"

"No, thanks to Jakob."

"And junior?"

"He's staying with Margie and Lucian."

"Fantastic. I'll see him twice a day. Guess it's time he has a real name, huh?"

"Yes, though I hope we both have a new name soon. Uncle Bill, do you have a map?"

William rummaged through his desk drawers and a wooden file cabinet to produce a recent printing.

"Whatever comes of this, we'll work through it," he said.

He escorted her to the top steps of the courthouse. Two large, porcelain-clad lamps atop stone pedestals cast a silver radiance on their faces, like moonglow on a snow-covered night. They embraced a final time.

Annalise set out in hopes Jakob would accept her for who and what she was, the love she would always have for O'Dell, and concede to her desires to spend the rest of her life with neither knowing for sure what lay in wait beyond the next daybreak.

Chapter 79

A woman driving 180 miles alone can change her mind, and with little reason. Annalise fought her way through storms, a flat tire, and running the gas tank to near dry, but adrenaline kept her wide awake and in constant thought of Jakob's reaction to their eyes connecting.

One small town after another dotted the way until she passed the banks of Lake Erie, where the road turned south. Silos stretching into the sky exchanged for mammoth smokestacks belching varying shades of industrial waste. Soot covered homes and businesses told a disparaging tale of the rough and tumble struggles associated with a life dedicated to coal and steel production.

She passed through Cleveland and the railroad hub of Toledo. The chaos of industry reverted to rural simplicity and charm in a snap. The unincorporated hamlet of Kunkle lay sixty miles down the road.

Margie insisted her cousin's farm would be easy to find. She described two massive brick silos striped with blue paint near their caps, and a long, tree-lined driveway marked by a tree trunk carved in the shape of an eagle's head.

Annalise noticed the silos soon after the sun made its debut. A near half-hour drive, and several dirt and gravel-mixed roads later, she spotted the eagle's head, like a feared sentry protecting its kingdom.

She guided the truck along a series of winding turns until a final, sweeping curve spilled out to an open, treeless vista, exposing a grand two-story stone house and several outbuildings constructed of the same material. She spotted Jakob's truck and trailer tucked under a grove of elms near a large barn.

She brought the truck to a stop near the home's front porch and exited with map in hand. She looked a mess and felt near exhaustion, but Jakob had seen her in this condition before, and what better time to bring all expectations into full spectrum. She took a quick moment to inspect all within view, concluding O'Dell had wished this for their future.

The home looked like an advertisement. The porch, a masterpiece in its own rights, combined simple country charm with splashes of elegant accessories, including chandeliers constructed of elk horn. She peeked through a large floor to ceiling window. A large brass lion's-head knocker centered on a massive door. She dropped the latch against it several times.

Annalise breathed deep as footsteps approached. A woman opened the door, her smile warm and inviting. She was of slim build, but fit, with a hard jaw line and bulk at the biceps.

"I'm so sorry to interrupt you," Annalise began, "but I'm looking for the man who owns that truck," she said, pointing toward the barn.

The woman's expression changed. "Is there a problem?"

"I'm sorry. I'm Annalise Denny."

"You're Annalise?"

"Yes, ma'am."

"My dear child," she said. She stepped over the threshold and hugged her. "I've heard so much about you in Margie's letters. What are you doing in these parts?"

"I've come to see your guest."

"Stephen?"

"Uh... yes."

"My goodness, where are my manners. I'm Katherine. Please, do come in."

She placed her arm around Annalise and led her into the kitchen to a long farmer's table with bench-style seating flanking either side.

"He arrived and went straight to work. They're in the north pasture. It's branding day. I understand you have a farm yourself?"

"Yes, but nothing near this scale."

"Well, Jack's family has owned this spread since 1803. It started out at two thousand acres and has since grown to over six thousand. We're lucky to have Stephen. I've never seen stock draw to anyone as they do him."

"Yes. He has a special way with animals."

"So, what was so important for you to drive all this way, if you don't mind my asking?"

"I'm here because I need to tell him I love him."

Katherine's eyes widened and her head jutted forward. "My goodness. A mighty long journey to express one's love."

"It's necessary."

"Well, I dare say he'd not stay a bachelor long around these parts. One of our girls will grab him."

"The very reason for my trip," Annalise said, smiling.

Katherine traded a smile with her. "So, how do you want to do this? Would you care to wait until they come in for lunch, or do you want to go out there?"

"A walk would do me good. If you'd point me in the right direction, I'd prefer to see him right away."

"Well, okay. I usually take the truck, but how about we saddle a couple horses and ride out?"

Annalise smiled. "Suits me right down to the boots."

Katherine led her down a path to the pasture where more horses grazed than she could count. Liesel spotted her the moment she stepped through the gate. She galloped up to her, kicking and snorting.

"She knows you, doesn't she?" Katherine said.

"Yes, she spent time on my farm. She's a wonderful animal."

"Imagine Stephen's surprise if you ride up on his horse."

"What a perfectly romantic idea," Annalise said.

Katherine led the way toward the north pasture. The trail snaked through land bound by neither fence nor other definitive marker. A lazy brook trickled alongside in no particular hurry.

It was all Annalise could do to keep Liesel at the same pace as Katherine's Tennessee Walker. She considered the many reactions Jakob could have. A nervous edge settled. Her skin turned hot, and her stomach developed a tickle.

The landscape pitched forward at a steep angle, forcing the horses to dig into the earth to work toward a plateau several hundred yards ahead. Liesel's hoofs pounded against the ground like a great steam pile driver.

Katherine's horse led Liesel up and over the rim. A sea of wildflowers spread before them. Ahead, Annalise spotted a weathervane suspended against the crystal blue of the sky. The landscape flattened with each yard traveled, revealing a magnificent red and white painted barn.

A flurry of action played out in a corral attached to the barn's west side, where no less than twenty men worked in tandem. Annalise searched for Jakob. The men dressed identical: jeans, boots, t-shirts, and cowboy hats.

She focused her attention on a group wrestling cows to the ground as Jakob preferred hard labor. She let go a playful laugh when she spotted him. He held a young Hereford against the ground as another man pressed the brand against its hindquarters.

Jakob glanced their way but for a moment, as did the rest of the men, before continuing with his work. He prepared to secure the next calf before stopping to look again.

Katherine pulled back on her reins. "Go on," she said. "Enjoy the moment."

Annalise leaned forward and whispered in Liesel's ear. "Let's go, girl." She popped the reins. Liesel flattened her ears, dug hard into the ground, and bolted.

Jakob moved through the gate to a secondary fenced area. He brought both hands above his brow, shielding the sun.

Annalise pulled hard on the reins as she approached the fence. Liesel hit the brakes, sending a dust cloud high into the air. Annalise dismounted and wedged herself between the rails.

***

Jakob took off his hat. "It cannot be." He started forward.

Annalise raced across the sand surface. Jakob's eyes grew wide, reflecting the brilliance of the high blue sky. Annalise did not bother to slow her pace or utter a word. She leapt into his arms and planted her lips against his. Jakob's hat slipped from his fingers as she slammed against his chest, her momentum sending him spinning in circles.

Cowboys whistled and slapped ropes against their thighs.

Jakob held her tight. Annalise worked her hands over his jaw and through hair drenched with sweat. She kissed his cheek and neck, then returned to his lips, wanting more, releasing a passion that had lain dormant for years.

The other farmhands soon lost interest and returned to the business at hand. Katherine tied up her horse and settled into her own duties. By the time the two pulled from one another, both saw stars.

"My God, I cannot believe it is you," he whispered. She ran her arms around his waist. Jakob pulled her tight.

"I love you, Jakob," she said. She absorbed the delightful thump in his chest, knowing the fury she set aflame. "I love you and want to spend my life with you."

***

Jakob brought his hands to her face. Her cheeks felt soft as silk. He pushed strands of her hair behind her ears. Her eyes sparkled, more lambent than emeralds. He kissed her again, this time much softer. The shape and taste of her lips ignited a desire he'd never known. When he

- 330 -

opened his eyes and pulled away, her eyes remained closed. "Do you realize I will be on the run the rest of my life?"

"No," she said, "my uncle convinced the army you died in a railway accident and has evidence to prove it."

"What?"

"It's a long story, and I'll explain it all later. Right now, I want to discuss us. We can change who we are, change our names. We'll go somewhere where nobody knows us or can find us ever again."

"But your farm? Your uncle? The McKennas?"

"We can move all the animals. My family and friends want this for you. They want this for me. I'm ready to start over and I want to start over with you."

Jakob shook his head. "What kind of life can you expect for you and your son?"

"The best life because it's the life I want. Come with me."

Annalise grabbed him by the hand and led him to the barn. She pulled the map from her back pocket, unfolded it, and slapped it against a shutter.

"I want you to close your eyes."

"What? Why?"

"We decide where we'll make our life together, right now."

"You are giving up a steady and comfortable life for the unknown."

"You are my life now. Go on, close your eyes. We'll make our home wherever your finger lands."

A light breeze brushed past, delivering a faint scent of alfalfa. In Jakob's mind, what he saw most clearly now were those things yet to come, a wife, a son, and a new beginning.

He pulled in a deep breath and released. With a contentment he'd never known, he directed his arm forward and pierced the map with the tip of his finger.

***

The End or the Beginning?

PART THREE

Chapter 80

Cody, Wyoming, November 2009

Paul turned the final page and added it to the stack on the floor. He removed his bifocals and rubbed the bridge of his nose. The landscape through the mutton-framed windows of his father's den glowed a soft peach as dawn broke behind the mountains. He pulled the chain to the lamp.

He extended the recliner to its full horizontal position. His eyes settled on the picture of his parents above the fireplace as he digested with intrigue the story from the mind of Jacqueline Astell. He felt it a worthy piece and one that could flourish with such a well-known author attached and prologue by a famous decorated war veteran.

Why did she hand-write 'The End or the Beginning' in pencil? he wondered.

His mother read mostly non-fiction and magazines on the art of riding and general horse care. She owned one novel: Margaret Mitchell's *Gone with the Wind*.

Paul sifted through the story and its characters until the sleepless night caught up with him. He drifted off to a rustling in the kitchen.

***

As the dining room erupted in a whitecap of conversation and laughter, Paul stumbled from the hallway, glassy-eyed, hair a mess, yawning in multiples, to find his siblings and their children enjoying brunch.

"Hello, sweetheart," his wife Monica said.

"Good morning, everyone," he replied.

"Morning's long gone," his brother Kim said, laughing.

Monica rushed him a cup of coffee. Paul's nephew, ever the polite gentleman, vacated his seat at the head of the table.

"Yeah, I guess it is," Paul said, taking a seat, rubbing his hand over his face.

Monica settled next to him. "I take it you enjoyed it."

"It's interesting, well written," he said, breathing in the sweet aroma of hazelnut with a splash of Baileys.

"Can you give a quick synopsis?" his sister Heather asked.

"Tells the story of an American medic who befriends an American-born German soldier on the battlefield in World War Two. The medic ends up getting executed and the German soldier escapes the war using the medic's name to find his wife to let her know what happened to him. They fall in love."

"Sounds quick," Monica said, laughing.

"It's deep and detailed," Paul said, "and makes you realize how improbable events can come together to produce reality."

"So, it's a love story?" Heather asked.

"Not per se, but it ends up revealing an improbable love scenario, which surprised me, considering the wartime episodes. It's a great story. If I didn't know any better, I'd say it's a true-life account. I don't understand why Astell didn't seek publication."

"Maybe she didn't think it was good enough," his sister Rachel said.

"It's odd," Paul said. "She concluded the story by handwriting in pencil, *The End or the Beginning?*"

The table fell silent as all attempted to conjure an explanation.

"What time do you have?" Paul asked.

Kim looked at his watch. "Near ten."

Paul took another sip of coffee then excused himself. He dodged children running to and from the dining room to a small kitchen desk where his mother kept a cordless phone.

"Colonel Jekel, Paul Bacca. Good morning."

"Good morning, Paul," the colonel replied.

"I hope I didn't wake you."

"You don't wake at four your entire life and all of a sudden sleep until ten."

Paul laughed. "No, sir, I guess you don't."

"I take it you finished the manuscript?"

"Yes, sir, plowed straight through last night. It's always hard to put down a good book."

"So, you enjoyed it?"

"It grabbed my attention. I didn't expect such a story from the mind of a poet."

"May I drive out to see you this morning?"

"Certainly. Eleven?"

"Fine, eleven it is. See you then."

Paul returned to the dining room and informed his siblings of the colonel's pending visit.

Allan arrived at eleven on the dot. Unlike his previous visit, he dressed in street clothes: black shirt, eggshell-colored pants, brown cowboy boots, and dark sports coat. He exited the Bentley with the help of his driver. A second man popped out to lead him by the arm toward the front porch. Paul met them at the top step.

"Good morning again," Paul said.

"Good morning, Paul. Please meet a dear friend of mine, Major Gordy Brotten."

"Please to meet you, Major."

Paul invited them in. He introduced his wife and siblings. Monica offered coffee. Several minutes passed with small talk until she returned with two steaming cups.

"Here you are, Colonel, Major," she said.

"My dear, please, call me Allan."

"Yes, sir," Monica said, saluting.

Allan took a sip of coffee, then said, "Please don't think me rude, but may we talk in private?"

"Of course," Paul said. "We can use my father's den."

"Thank you." Allan followed Paul down the hallway, with Brotten bringing up the rear.

Paul arranged two chairs near the fireplace. He stoked the fire, added a few more logs, and invited the men to sit. Monica entered with another cup of coffee for her husband. She smiled before turning to exit.

"Mrs. Bacca, please pull up a chair and join us," Allan requested.

"I'm sure you don't need me in here."

"Please, sit with us," he insisted.

She looked to Paul. He shrugged. "Okay," she said, settling on the armrest of the recliner.

"How long are you in town?" Allan asked.

"Most of the family is leaving in the morning," Paul said. "Monica and my daughter will head back to Colorado later this afternoon. My brother and I plan to stay on a few more days to sort things out. Then, it's back to work and life."

"Yes, it's unfortunate, the sun and moon don't stop for those who pass on." Allan took another sip of coffee. "So, tell me, what did you think of the story?"

"An intriguing tale with interesting characters, captivating plots and subplots. I'm surprised it came from Ms. Astell. I would liken it to Edgar Allan Poe writing comedies."

Allan scooted forward in his chair. "I thought a visit important because I want to tell you the truth about the manuscript."

"The truth?" Paul shot a quick, nervous glance to his wife.

"Yes. The fact is, Paul, the manuscript is not a work of fiction. It's a true story. The greatest untold story to come out of that war."

"You're kidding?"

Allan's expression turned serious. Paul straightened in his chair.

"No, I'm not. It's as true as the Bible."

"I wondered that, but have a hard time believing it," Paul said.

"There are many things I'm set to reveal to you that you won't believe, but they're as true as I'm sitting here."

"How do you know this?"

"Because, Paul, I'm Corporal Eli Shimmel, and this man to my right, is Private Dan Hansel."

Chapter 81

Paul pushed from his chair. He needed a moment to pace off the shock, working back and forth in front of the fireplace as Monica watched helplessly.

"You're Corporal Shimmel?" he repeated, through bursts of mocking laughs.

"No, but I lived Corporal Shimmel's experience. Alexander Shimmel and Eli Scandella, both friends of mine, died on the beach at Normandy. I assumed their names for the story."

"Your story?" Paul asked.

"Not mine. I just happened to be in the right place at the right time."

"I don't understand."

"You read it. Have you heard such a tale in all your years of publishing?"

Paul shook his head.

"As I said, it's a great story, and in my opinion, *the* greatest ever to come out of the war." Allan gestured for Paul to come forward. Paul drew near and grabbed hold to help him from his chair. Allan kept hold of the grip and moved in close.

"It's your story, Paul... your family's story."

Paul stared deep into his eyes and smiled. "What are you talking about?"

"Son, there's no easy way to say this and I'm way too old to beat around the bush, so I'm gonna tell you straight up. O'Dell Denny was your biological father."

Paul's knees buckled, as he made an errant stab at the oak mantel affixed to the fireplace. His breath grew labored and face flushed.

Monica rushed to his side and wrapped her arms around his waist for support. "Paul, what's he talking about?"

"You're lying," Paul mumbled. "Why would you do this?"

Allan moved in on the couple and placed his hands on Paul's shoulders. "Paul, look at me. Look at me."

Paul shook his head. "You're lying."

"Paul, your mother is Annalise. Her real name was Eleanor McEuen. Your stepfather is Jakob. His real name was Erich Wetzell. Your mother changed her entire life to protect him and your siblings."

Paul continued to deny the claim. "How could you do something so despicable mere days after we buried our mother?"

"Paul, you need to take a deep breath. Your mother provided all the proof you'll ever need. You must believe me."

Paul's eyes darted around the room, unable to focus on any one thing. He worked backward through the book, matching names to situations, searching for anything connecting his life to the events.

"Do you remember the physical condition Hansel and Jakob found Shimmel in the prison camp?" Allan asked. "Do you remember the wounds described?"

Paul nodded. He closed his eyes and described the broken nose, lash marks, and swastika carved into Shimmel's back.

Allan turned to Monica. "I'll beg your pardon, Mrs. Bacca," he said.

Brotten helped remove his jacket and assisted in unbuttoning his shirt. He dropped the sleeves to below the elbows. A scar in the shape of a swastika glowed bright red against skin riddled with lash marks.

Paul's eyes watered over. Monica gasped.

"I don't have to tell you the story. You read it. You must trust it and accept the people involved."

Brotten helped Allan re-button his shirt. "You own sole rights because your mother wrote the book under her pen name, Jacqueline Astell."

"What?"

"It's true."

"My mother is Jacqueline Astell."

"No, it was her pen name. I'm surprised you did not connect the dots yourself, though I realize it was a long shot under the circumstances."

"How could I conclude any of this? Do you know what you're asking of me?"

"Yes, I do. Would you recognize your mother's handwriting?"

Paul paused. "Yes... well... I think so."

"Did you see the handwritten question at the end of the manuscript?"

Paul pushed off the hearth to gather the manuscript from the corner of his father's desk. He turned over the final page.

"There's a letter in the safe from your mother explaining everything. You'll find the handwriting identical."

Paul ambled across the room, mumbling the words *The End or the Beginning?* He plopped down in the recliner, feeling as if beaten with a crowbar.

"Do you remember William and your mother's trip to Europe the summer you graduated junior high?"

"Yes. They did not return until the start of school in the fall."

"Correct. I, Dan, and the men whose character names were John Spring, Angelo Sperro, and Joe Polak, met them at Bastogne to recount the events, and to visit William's mother's and sister's graves. Your mother decided then to write the story. She mixed and matched first and last names of friends of ours who didn't make it home. Made up others. No other way to tell the story and protect the identities of all involved, especially William. She wrote poetry as a hobby and did not expect or want the success achieved."

"This can't be happening," Paul said. "I don't understand. Why did she lie to us all these years?"

Allan passed Paul an envelope. Paul extracted a small black-and-white photo.

"Recognize her?"

"Of course," Paul said. He released a heavy sigh.

"She's holding you above her head. Please understand, Paul, your mother was hell-bent on making sure William lived out the rest of his days in peace. You read the story. You know how this all went down. She believed he earned the right after all he endured. He deserved your mother, this family, and this life. She had to protect him at all costs, which meant telling no one. They became Abigail and William Bacca, a maiden name belonging to the great grandmother of the woman characterized as Margie. Don't accept for one moment she didn't live with guilt. She did. But she also believed William deserved an opportunity to live free and at peace. For my money, she made the right decision."

Paul traded the recliner for a view of Hart Mountain. He glared from one end of the horizon to the other and settled on a cloud edging over the peak. In a whisper, he said, "I remember."

"You remember what?"

"The cuckoo clock. I see it in my mind. I remember it, remember wanting to touch it. When I read about it in the manuscript, it didn't register. It's clear in my mind, now. I also recall the scent of pipe tobacco and a speck of a memory of my mother screaming once."

Monica's voice rose an octave. "Honey, please, for God's sake, tell me what's going on.

"It seems my real father died in the war, but...." Paul could go no further, as a sluice gate opened. Questions poured into his already crammed conscience.

Monica rushed to the desk, grabbed the manuscript, and settled in the recliner.

"The God's honest truth spreads throughout this story on how it all went down," Brotten said. "For years, your mother sifted through facts and historical documents. She wanted it dead-to-rights. Your father was the finest, bravest man any of us ever knew. He's an American hero. He saved so many lives and returned so many young boys to their homes, including the enemy. All your father was, was pure and right, and all about doing for others first."

"I'm living proof," Allan interjected. "I'm alive because of your father and stepfather. And as far as William goes, he's a carbon copy of your father. Had you known them both, you'd not bet your life on the differences between them. They risked their lives for us. It's why we agreed long ago to bury this story in the sands of time. No one dared risk William's or your mother's life."

"I have no words, at least nothing of sense at the moment," Paul said. "I haven't read a more remarkable, unbelievable account. How could all those men, all those years, keep this quiet?" Paul cupped his hands to his face and returned to the view of Hart Mountain.

"A brotherhood, my boy, bound for eternity by your father and stepfather."

"Why did my mother not mention her writing? Why keep it a secret?"

"I told you earlier, she did not want to influence your career or place you in obligation. She had a talent and wrote poetry for the peace and joy of writing. She didn't do it for fame or fortune. I talked her into sending a couple poems to my publisher, somewhat as a joke. The agency loved them and published them. It surprised her when it caught on so. All royalties received went straight to charity. Look it up in William's paperwork. Plain and simple, she wrote this manuscript so her children would know the truth."

"Why did she end the story the way she did?"

"In your mother's eyes, you're the head of this family. She signed it with a question mark because she wanted you to decide what to do with it."

"You mean to publish?"

"Whether gifted to the masses as a non-fiction or fictional account, or keep it buried in the annals of your family's history."

"I can't keep this from my siblings."

"I don't see how you could, but you must reconcile the pros and cons of it all. Your mother trusted your judgement."

"I have a million questions," Paul said.

"As anyone would expect. Your mother answered many in her letter, and I'll help until my dying day, as will the other surviving members. You can call us anytime."

Allan passed a folded half-sheet of paper with names and numbers of the men involved. He identified each by their character names. "Charlie, the character Joe Polak, died some years ago, but the others live on."

Paul let go a deep, cleansing breath.

"I know you find this staggering, Paul, but you have in your possession the greatest untold story ever. Your father, stepfather, and mother are three of the finest people to grace this planet. I wish you'd met your father. You'll find his letters to your mother, photos, and other items in a safe deposit box at the First National Bank downtown. It's all in your mother's letter."

"I can't fathom this. How can I ever come to grips with this?"

"Time and tide, son. Both men loved you more than you could ever know. And your mother, well, a saint among mortals. Keep in mind the character of a person to keep such a secret, with the sole purpose of protecting the one you love. I find it simply remarkable."

Allan grabbed Paul around the neck and pulled him close. "You call me, anytime, day or night, if I can help."

"I appreciate the truth, but I hope you understand my reaction."

"Of course. No one would ever begrudge you confusion, shock, even feeling a bit betrayed. But I believe you'll reconcile this one fine day and come to terms with it all. I'm also certain you'll want to read the story again, and soon."

"I don't really know what to say. I don't know how to respond to you bringing this all to light," Paul said.

"I understand. You need not concern yourself with my feelings. You need time to absorb this. I made a promise to your mother and kept it."

The room fell silent. Paul turned to Monica with his eyes glistening. She shook her head.

"Well," Allan said, "I must be off."

"Must you go, now?"

"Yes, afraid so."

Monica suggested she show their visitors out. Allan paused before exiting the den and turned. "Just remember, if you ever feel the need to question this, ask yourself what lengths you'd go to protect your wife and children. Your mother did the right thing for a great, great man."

***

After bidding the Bacca siblings farewell, Allan grabbed Monica's hand as they walked through the foyer.

"I'm not sure whether to thank you or cuss you," Monica said.

Allan winked. "Life throws many parties. All we can do is revel in the good ones, work through the bad ones, and do the best we can to understand the difference. Paul's a smart man. He'll come to terms with this, and it'll change his life, and the life of his siblings, for the better."

Allan offered a hug, then slipped into the back of his Bentley. Monica offered a final wave as they disappeared down the gravel road.

***

Monica returned to the den to find Paul at his father's desk, looking out the window with his mother's letter in one hand and the picture of her in the other. She pulled a chair next to him. They sat, each absorbing the improbability of this moment.

She grabbed his hand. He squeezed. The sun had pushed above the highest peak, its presence doing little to melt snow lingering from the last storm. They held hands as shadows of clouds passed across the mountainside.

Both lost track of time.

"You want to discuss the letter?" she asked.

Paul handed it to her. "It explains everything. Mother had a reason for all she did. She did not waste a single action or moment. Her love was strong for William, yet she managed the same for my father. And William made sure to preserve my father's memory. It's remarkable. It's remarkable a man would marry a woman knowing there was always another, yet not let it affect the relationship in the slightest. I agree with Allan. What remarkable character."

"Have you decided what to do?"

"It's in these moments a fella could use the advice of his father, and from what I read, my father was all about good and right. My siblings deserve to know the truth about our father."

"This will blow their world to pieces," Monica said.

"It'll take time, but they'll work through it and reconcile, knowing Mother's determination when she set her mind to something. They adored the man William was. When they hear his story, it'll only add to the admiration."

"And you?"

"I'll do whatever to find out all I can about my biological father, but feel a tremendous sense of pride, based on what I read. We need to start a pot of coffee because I'm going to sit down with them and share what I know."

"Have you considered how you'll break it to them?"

"No, and it may take a while for it to sink in, but I'll share mother's letter first, then discuss the manuscript."

"What then?"

"Jacqueline K. Astell was an American poet. One of the finest of the twentieth century. As far as I'm concerned, and as far as the world knows, she never attempted a work of any other genre."

"So, that's the end?"

"No. I also believe, more than ever, the world needs a story such as this. Needs to know goodness can rise from the ashes of the worst of what men create. With Colonel Jekel's help, I have no doubt we can conjure a fictional author to attribute this fictional story and offer the world a most special experience."

THE END

Summer Song
Though deep and dense the forest tall,
What songs of summer do befall?
A whispering breeze, birds in call,
And shadows rustling, despite it all.
The light of morn is but a guest,
Strewn in patches among the rest.
A pathway forms by beast and era,
Which beckons lovers, but alone am I.
To tarry and capture a rhyme or reason,
With sodden heart that disrupts the season.
~ Jacqueline K. Astell

Your Eyes
Within your heart, I found my soul,
Within your mind, a haven for my fears.
But, within your eyes, I found my life,
And in your stare, love beyond compare.
Your eyes draw my emotion, with but a simple glance,
Revealing many wonders and a love to chance.
Your eyes are a sunrise, bringing hope to the day,
Making impossible, any desire, to turn and stray away.
~ Jacqueline K. Astell

ACKNOWLEDGEMENTS

No book is produced and published without the support and help of many. I offer my sincere thanks and heartfelt appreciation to those who assisted in bringing *A Debt of War* to life, specifically my publisher, Dave Lane (aka Lane Diamond, Evolved Publishing); editors Robb Grindstaff and Anne Storer; cover designer Alena (L1-Graphics); cover model, Paul Hickert; author headshot, Juliana Barnerd; beta readers John A. Barnerd, Sam DeRusha, Mae Kasten, Christie Kleinmann, Sandy Koch, Michael Logan, John Morgando, Diane Perry, Sharon Reller, Allan Ringering, Clint Ringering, Jerry Ringering, Rob Schwartz, Terry Sitze, John Spring, Patty K. Tomerlin, and Sissy Ward; military consultants Lt. Col. Casey Grider, United States Air Force, and Michael E. Haskew, editor, World War II History Magazine; translation consultant Torston Schulz; veterinary consultant Dr. Edmar Schreiber; and reference consultant Amanda Fontenova, Luzerne County Historical Society, Wilkes-Barre, Pennsylvania.

I'd also like to thank my family members and the many wonderful friends who've supported my writing efforts over the years.

~~~

About the Cover

When I first conceptualized the cover for this story, I knew immediately whose image I wanted depicting my protagonist. I'm honored and thrilled to have secured the likeness of one of my dear friends and former Murray State University roommate, and current actor, Paul Hickert, whom you may have seen appearing as a guest star in such network television hits as The Blacklist, Law and Order: Special Victims Unit, Manifest, FBI, and Bull.

Thank you for your friendship, continued support and collaborating spirit. To learn more about Paul's acting career and credits, please visit his IMDb page at: **www.imdb.com/name/nm3288472/**.

ABOUT THE AUTHOR

When he was in the third grade at East Alton Elementary School, East Alton, Illinois, Michael Ringering selected Miriam E. Mason's Broomtail for a class-assigned book report, and from that moment on, set his sights on writing short stories and other works of fiction.

He published his first novel, *Six Bits*, in December 2011, earning finalist designation in the 2012 USA Best Book Awards for Fiction. He's also published four short stories: "Willy the Whale" (2017), "A Face on a Train" (2017), "A Calico Tale" (2018), and "The 9:15 to Grand Central" (2019).

In December 2017, he started his third novel, a trilogy concept based on a childhood memory, and continues to work on several shorts. All these older works are being revised and will re-release with Evolved Publishing in the second half of 2021.

Michael was born in Alton, Illinois, and raised in nearby East Alton, where he graduated from East Alton-Wood River High School in 1984. He is a 1989 graduate of Murray State University, earning a bachelor's degree in business administration. Following a 14-year career working in media relations and communications in Major League Baseball, he entered the healthcare industry where he serves as a practice administrator.

Michael resides in Southern Illinois with his fiancée, Jackie; two dogs, Big Dog and Victoria; three goats, Macey, Abby, and Annie; two horses, Lilly and Sophie; and a slew of chickens.

For more, please visit Michael Ringering online at:
Website: www.MichaelRingering.com
Goodreads: Michael Ringering
Facebook: @mcrevolvedpublishing

WHAT'S NEXT?

Micheal Ringering always has at least one book in the works, including the upcoming re-release of the newly revised and edited *Six Bits*, as well as his third novel, *John's Donuts*. Please stay tuned to developments and plans by subscribing to our newsletter at the link below.

www.EvolvedPub.com/Newsletter

MORE FROM EVOLVED PUBLISHING

We offer great books across multiple genres, featuring high-quality editing (which we believe is second-to-none) and fantastic covers.

As a hybrid small press, your support as loyal readers is so important to us, and we have strived, with tireless dedication and sheer determination, to deliver on the promise of our motto:
QUALITY IS PRIORITY #1!

Please check out all of our great books,
which you can find at this link:
www.EvolvedPub.com/Catalog/

Thank you!